GW00703014

Crisis in a Surrey Harem

Lucy Abelson

A LONE HARE PRESS BOOK

First published in Britain by the Lone Hare Press

Copyright Lucy Abelson
First Edition 2012

The right of Lucy Abelson to be identified as the
author of this work has been asserted by her in accordance
with the Copyright, Designs and Patents Act 1988.

All rights reserved. No part of this publication may
be reproduced, stored in a retrieval system, or transmitted
in any form or by any means, electronic, mechanical,
photocopying, recording or otherwise, without the prior
permission of the copyright owner.

All the characters in this book are products of the
author's imagination or are used fictitiously. Incidents that
take place in real places are imaginary. Any likeness to a
living person is entirely co-incidental.

ISBN 978-0-9557631-4-4

Printed and Bound in the UK by MPG Books Group
Bodmin and Kings Lynn

This book is dedicated to my beloved husband
Rupert with gratitude he's stuck to wife Number One

There is a tide in the affairs of men,
Which taken at the flood, leads on to fortune

Julius Caesar by Shakespeare

There is a tide in the affairs of women,
Which, taken at the flood, leads – God knows where.

Don Juan by Byron

Jules's Harem

Wife number One
Flick, champion lady golfer at Bisley Heath

Wife number Two
Roxanne, animal lover and wild child

Wife number Three
Tessa, psychologist and counsellor

Wife number Four
Mandy, former model who runs a fashion
boutique

Grace's Godchildren

Steve is the son of Frankie, Grace's former domestic help and closest friend; he works for Jules.

Jules is a multi-millionaire debt-collector and wild-life enthusiast; he's had four wives. His parents are jewellers and pawn-brokers Faye and Jeremy Challenger.

Tarquin is a famous sculptor encouraged by Grace. He is the son of farmer and golfer Giles and Mary Hobbs.

Ned the vet is the son of the late Monty and Deborah Cordrey, former Lady Captain and prominent member of Bisley Heath.

Adam is an accountant and former employee of Jules's Griffon Trust; he is on the Bisley Heath committee. His mother is Patsy who worked for Grace as her personal assistant.

Bisley Heath Golf Club

Club Champion	Roger Melbourne (Dodger)
Captain	Matthew Lomax
Lady Captain	Camilla Wilmot
Treasurer 1	Jack Metcalfe
Treasurer 2	Adam Scrivenor
Ex Lady Captain	Flick Challenger
Ex Lady Captain	Deborah Cordrey
Chef	Dan Needler
Ground staff	Ross Cameron
Secretary	Miles Thorogood
Committee Members	Mark, Andy, Horace, Giles

CHAPTERS

If you have tears, prepare to shed them now.

Act 3, Scene 2 Julius Caesar by Shakespeare

Prologue

A girl slips from her perch astride the bough of a tree. She grabs a branch as she tumbles. There she hangs by her outstretched arms. Above her dangles a chainsaw. Its blades are buzzing. Whilst she gasps for breath, she sees it drop. She tries to swing out of range, but the blades catch the tops of her arms.

She falls to the ground. Half-stunned she lies on back looking upwards at her detached arms which still hang from the tree's branch, but they can not be her arms because she can feel her arms hurt. They must be the wrong arms.

"Mummy mummy," she cries instinctively for the wrong mother, who can not hear her anyway.

She struggles to move, but can not heave herself up. There are other people around the garden. She must call someone else. The man she loves is there, even if he is the wrong man. She shouts for him and she sees him appear from a nearby field. He starts to run towards her, but before he reaches her, she feels her mind begin to glaze. Her ideas blur. The word "wrong" reverberates in her brain. Wrong mother; wrong man. Is this the story of her life or her epitaph?

1. At the Inn on the Beach

Today was not turning out as she hoped. The charm of a day by the sea had dwindled, despite the sun glistening on the waves. Here she was, invited by a man she liked, actually more than liked, but he suffered from attention deficit as far she was concerned.

Dodger gazed out over the water; he seemed far more intrigued by something he saw on the horizon than anything Impey might say. With the elbows of his muscular arms planted firmly on the round wooden table, binoculars held to his eyes, he stared through the vast window of the Inn on the Beach at a distant yacht.

Bored by boats, Impey scanned the water for wildlife. A circle of foam with birds circling above suggested a ring of dolphins fishing to her. She always enjoyed watching one black snout after another break through the water's surface whilst they tossed their catch. She dropped her hand down to the brown leather pouch clipped to her belt, where she kept her own binoculars. It was empty. They must be her glasses Dodger had trained to his eyes.

How annoying was that? He must have taken them when he was nibbling her ear, pretending to whisper something important. Despite his bulky shape, soldiers in his regiment had not nicknamed Roger Melbourne after Dickens' Artful Dodger for nothing. Since he sat alongside her, she should have spotted his arm duck underneath the small table, but she had been as blind as any would-be terrorist whose gun Dodger might take from an inside pocket. Perhaps realising she was about to protest, he took the glasses away from his eyes and held them out to her. "So it's true," he murmured, "take a look."

"What?" asked Impey irritated. Presumably Dodger spent so much time moving other people's possessions around these days, when he did his conjuring act, that he'd taken her glasses without a qualm. She didn't like other people using them because they invariably altered her settings. Animals and birds moved so quickly she never had time to readjust the glasses to spot a creature she wanted to see. Already the dolphins' circle of foam was dispersing. She seized the glasses from Dodger's fingers which looked far too stubby to be nimble enough to pinch anything unobserved, but then his large brown eyes looked too soft for a soldier.

Damn it. There were no dolphins now. Impey moved the glasses so she could train them on to the spot in the distance where Dodger still stared. As she anticipated, the lens were distorted but she could just make out a body stuck on the end of a boat. "Omigod; there's a corpse hanging on that yacht."

The words sounded ridiculous when they dropped from her lips, but Dodger seemed to take them seriously. "Not yet," he muttered, "but she's lost her arms."

Impey swivelled the lenses round so she could see more clearly, then gave a chuckle. "How stupid of me; it's only a figurehead." She screwed up her eyes as she twiddled again with the black plastic adjustment ring. Now, with their magnificent clarity, she saw a torso of a naked armless woman. Stuck on the prow of the ship, the icon gazed out to sea with an enigmatic expression on her face.

Impey frowned as she turned back to the table. That face was familiar. Was it the slant of the one eye she could see, or the droop of the full lower lip? "She reminds me of someone I know."

"Of course she does; it's Flick."

Impey wrinkled her nose in disbelief. She laid the binoculars beside her on the table. "Flick Challenger? Last year's Lady Captain of the club?" She tried to soften a sharp note which crept into her voice. The sleek and beautiful Flick was Dodger's regular playing partner on the course at the Bisley Heath golf club, where they were all members. "How come she's stuck on the front of a boat?"

A horrid suspicion Dodger had not been straight about his reason to bring her here flashed through her. He'd stressed how much she'd like this Inn because it stood on the beach where she could look out over the water at the marine wildlife. They could get up a good appetite for lunch by having a swim in the bay first.

In spite of her wretched finances she'd bought a new swimsuit by opening an account at another shop, something she'd sworn she'd never do for she'd written enough articles on credit for newspapers to understand its traps. The multi-coloured costume was meant to be a bait, or at least a signal she had changed. She wanted him to notice her body. With strategic holes in the sides, it showed her broad figure to advantage, as slim without being skinny.

The allure of the colourful sexy stripes which snaked up and down the costume were lost on Dodger, who remained miserably un-enticed by any exposed flesh; he simply remarked she looked like a "rainbow fish". Their time in the water had been hardly a frolic either – he'd pounded through the waves as though on a military training exercise. When Impey had managed to intercept him, he'd admitted in a splutter, between sturdy splashing strokes, that he was upping his fitness for some new job he'd taken.

Now he smiled at her as though on automatic pilot since the lines on his forehead were furrowed. "She was once married to Jules. It's his yacht."

"Jules who?"

"Challenger of course. He's in quite a state about it; I'd have thought you might have heard."

"I haven't the faintest idea what you're talking about." Impey smiled at the tousle-headed young man dressed in black, who bent over to place carefully a vast plate of hot fish and chips in front of her. "Thank you," she spoke with emphatic politeness whilst she smiled at him.

Her manners were lost on Dodger. He still stared at the dot on the horizon whilst his plate was deposited in front of him. "I can't think why it's there when Jules wants to play it down. Perhaps I oughtn't to have mentioned it."

Impey seized the plastic squeezy tomato sauce bottle in front of her. "If you don't want this squirted straight at you, you'd better explain exactly why you wanted to come here."

Dodger laughed, "To be with you of course."

Impey rolled her eyes as she shook her head, "Aha, but it just so happened..." She hoped she wasn't blushing. The same tenderness she'd heard in his voice, when he'd asked her to spend the day with him, rang in her ears.

"You're right." Dodger raised his broad hands palms forward in a sign of surrender. "I needed to see the yacht's figurehead as well, especially after what Jules told me had happened to one of his wives."

Hardly my business. Impey stuck her fork into a large fat chip and held it in the air as she spoke with irritation. "Didn't he split up from Flick years ago?" She stuffed the big chip into her mouth. Now she thought about it, she remembered

15

someone mention the name Jules Challenger, saying something about the "wanderer returns" and adding pointedly that his name was still listed under "O" for overseas in the club diary.

"Why hasn't he moved on?" Impey doubted her own husband, from whom she'd been divorced exactly a year, today being the anniversary, even kept a photograph of her. If he had, her successor would surely have cleared them out.

Dodger sliced a neat square in his golden battered fish. "Jules is very attached to that statue. She's very important to him."

So the bally thing's a 'statue' now is it? Impey chewed a piece of fish before she cleared her throat to say, "Why the great interest in it anyway?"

"You saw; it's been mutilated." Dodger spoke through gritted teeth.

Impey's bluey grey eyes widened as she looked at him. "Looks okay to me."

"You are joking. That statue used to be so lovely, the way her arms stretched out in front and behind. It wasn't a vulgar thing until someone chopped her arms off. Anyone would think she was meant to look like the efffing Venus de Milo."

Impey speared another piece of fish whilst she suppressed a chuckle. The figurehead did look rather like the famous sculpture, only now she considered it, Flick herself resembled Venus. "But the Venus de Milo is very beautiful."

Dodger put his knife and fork down. He fingered his misshapen right ear, the result of one brawl too many on the rugby pitch. "You don't understand: it's a bloody insult; you obviously don't know the Venus rhyme."

"It's a rugby song?" She guessed.

He nodded. Head forward, he leant over the table to recite in a low voice;

'Twas on the good ship Venus

By God you should have seen us

The figurehead was a whore in bed

And the mast the captain's penis."

Impey chuckled. "It's just a vulgar ditty. You can't take it seriously."

"Whoever chopped off the statue's arms is making a point; Jules sees it as a serious threat."

"Isn't that a bit melodramatic?"

"Not to Jules; he calls it 'a warning shot across my bows'".

Impey stared sceptically at Dodger. She knew a little about the legendary Jules Challenger; he'd been a junior champion at the club. One of her friends had been crazy about the handsome blonde youth. He seemed to have cast a similar spell over the normally cynical Dodger. His praises for luxury yacht owner covered a vast swathe of talents. Jules Challenger was apparently fantastic at any sport he might play. On top of that he was musical too; he played the guitar.

"A real renaissance man like Henry the Eighth?" teased Impey. She'd heard people comment on a number of women in Dodger's hero's life.

"Well he has been married four times," admitted Dodger, "but..." he hesitated.

"You're about to say four women in a man's lifetime isn't much." Impey wished Dodger would pick up his fork and eat his food. It made her feel greedy to be half way through her huge plateful when he'd barely started his. What on earth did it matter if someone had altered the boat's figurehead, even if it was an effigy of Jules's first wife? She drummed her fingers on the side of her water glass. "Why he's so interested in Flick now, even if she is a top favourite at Bisley Heath?"

Ironic to think of someone as bold and fit as Flick being threatened. She even has her own support group which could be called a gang. Impey glanced back at the water where she'd seen the ring of foam. *Same as a dolphins' pod really. The best players at the club are in the same team. Trouble is they include Dodger.*

Dodger grinned at her. "Miaow. Miaow." He mewed.

"For goodness sake. You know exactly what I mean. Whoever cut up that figurehead probably hadn't a clue it was modelled on Flick."

Dodger picked up his knife and fork. He stabbed a chip which he lifted up to thrust forwards at Impey in time with his words. "Jules thinks he or she did."

Impey shrugged whilst she shovelled more food into her mouth. The Flick she knew who partied late into the night before a day's work, which might include a cross country dash to a golf tournament did not seem to have a fearful fibre in her body. "It seems a bit random to threaten Flick. Why not Jules himself?"

"That's just it." Dodger shook his knife at Impey. "She's the emblem of his company. That's what he thinks might upset someone."

"Why should his work upset people?"

"He's a debt collector."

"So what? People don't look at credit like that these days. It's hardly like the Victorian era. You don't go to prison for debt this century. If Jules Challenger's so unpopular, he must be a pretty foul loan shark."

"No he isn't. He's a hell of a nice guy. Honestly, you'd really like him Imps; he's into animal conservation in a big

18

way. And he doesn't just throw money at it; he really goes for it himself. He's got the most amazing pet vulture."

"Sounds suitable. Takes one to own one. Birds of a feather and all that." The sight of pain rather than amusement in Dodger's eyes stopped her flow.

"Actually he's helped loads of people back on their feet besides..." Dodger's voice trailed off.

"You?" Impey asked incredulously before she could stop herself.

"Of course," Dodger's voice was nonchalant, "he's given me work."

Impey swallowed the words *in lieu. You mean you owe him?* So Dodger had racked up debts which had to be paid off somehow. She took a gulp of wine. In the dearth of parties in these days of recession, she'd guessed his work as a magician was sparse. Invitations to meals had been few and far between, which was why today's outing had been a nice surprise. "What sort of work? Is he giving lots of office parties then?"

Dodger reddened. "No, sadly not. He's asked for a bit of personal protection, that's all."

That's all? So that's why the need for fitness. "You mean you're acting as his bodyguard?" Dodger had never spelt out what he did in the army, which made her wonder whether he had been in the SAS.

"Now who's being melodramatic? I simply hang around a bit to give him reassurance."

Though it was a warm day a cool sea breeze blew through an open window near them. Goose pimples rose on Impey's bare arms. What on earth had Dodger got himself into? *What sort of Mafiosi style businessman needs a personal bodyguard?*

Of course in a recession people had to branch out, try alternative work. She herself had taken on a different type of writing over the last three months, but it was very respectable. She'd edited the memoirs of a prominent former diplomat, also an eminent Greek scholar, who'd risen from an impoverished childhood in war torn Greece where he'd had to scavenge for food from dustbins. Since his bereaved family were anxious everything should be correct, there was a lot of tedious time-consuming fact checking. More worrying, she had yet to be paid. She had however taken the precaution of going to see her building society manager because she was a couple of months in arrears with her mortgage payments. The memory of his words, accompanied with a sympathetic hand gesture, reassured her. "Don't fret; we've no plans to foreclose."

She forced herself to smile across the table at Dodger, only to see him turn his head away. He glanced towards the open entrance at the top of the stairs which led up to this first floor where they sat. A slightly built man of medium height wearing a beige cotton zip-up jacket over mole-brown chino trousers stood there.

He was on the prowl. She recognised the signs of an animal sniffing the air. His body was unnaturally taut for someone entering a bar. Whilst he hardly moved his head, she noted his large brown eyes swivel about the room. The set of his head, the pointed nose and backward sloping jaw reminded her of an otter or a ferret.

Dodger lifted his knife in the air in a way that might constitute a wave to the fellow, but Impey dismissed the idea: Dodger had invited her here to be with her. Why should he greet some strange man who, from the way he twisted round his face to peer at everyone present, was evidently here to meet someone else?

Whilst Dodger looked down, suddenly intent on eating his fish and chips, the man made his way towards their table. "Hi Melbourne", he said on reaching them.

"Hello." Dodger looked up casually. He raised his eyebrows as though surprised to see the incomer, "what brings you here?"

"I just slipped off the yacht to come over here."

Aren't you going to introduce me? Impey wondered whether she should ask the old-fashioned question when the stranger turned to her and said, "And you must be Impey Dalrymple."

"That's right." She frowned as she glanced quickly at Dodger. He'd admitted he'd done undercover work in the army, but this acting experience did not stop a red tinge creep up his neck.

"I am," she replied coolly, "and who might you be?"

"Steve Hemmings," he smiled. "I'm glad I've bumped into you both. Mind if I join you?"

"Sure," said Dodger nonchalantly, ignoring Impey's glower whilst she gave a slight shake of her head.

"And I thought you wanted me all to yourself," she murmured to Dodger.

"I'll take that as an invitation for later," he retorted with a crooked grin, "in the meantime why don't we let Steve entertain us."

"Just tell me what you've cooked up together," said Impey. "I don't seem to be in the loop here."

Steve sat down next her on the wooden bench. "We certainly want to include you. – Jules Challenger, I expect you've heard of him," he paused whilst Impey nodded, "has heard a lot about you and is very keen to meet you."

"I don't think so," said Impey, embarrassed by the prim squeaky note in her voice. She smiled and softened her voice. "His activities aren't really quite my scene."

"Are you sure about that?" asked Steve in a slightly odd tone.

"Definitely." Impey forced herself smile regretfully. "I'm afraid there'd have to be a compelling reason for me to see Jules Challenger."

"Well you do owe him a lot of money."

"Rubbish," exploded Impey rolling her fingers into her fist, but she restrained herself from thumping the table.

"I'm afraid it's not," said Steve with an apologetic shake of his head. "You see he's bought the mortgage on your house."

"But my building society manager said he'd no plans to foreclose," said Impey in puzzlement.

"Quite," said Steve, "he's sold your debt instead."

2. A statue comes home

Grace hobbled into the room. The parcel she carried was heavy, heavier than she'd expected, but she couldn't ask anyone to help. They would naturally offer to place the object inside somewhere for her. Far better for no one to know she'd recovered it.

She could scarcely believe how lucky she'd been to track down the bronze, then manage to buy it. The sculptor's works were collectors' items these days. She was surprised anyone would part with an early one, especially a bronze as beautiful as this, even at the hefty price she'd paid.

For the same sum she could have bought a top of the range Volvo, which her orthopaedic consultant suggested might be more suitable for her than the low-slung Jaguar she drove. She smiled at the memory of her riposte, "I may be old, but I don't have to act it, even if I do have gammy loins." Anyway, forty thousand pounds was petty cash to her, even if she didn't want to advertise the fact.

How fortunate the dealer agreed to deliver it to her house today, before her hip replacement tomorrow. Painful though it was to take a step carrying this weight, she'd be more immobile for weeks after her operation. She must hide the bronze now. Once she was back from hospital in a week's time, she'd have loads of visitors, professional people to help her dress and cook her meals, as well as friends calling to see how she was. Not a single one of them must see the sculpture. A secret is not secret if one person knows it.

The bronze was so striking that anyone who saw it must be curious about the girl who modelled for it. You wouldn't have to recognise Roxanne to be fascinated by her looks, those long curling locks that framed her narrow face with alert darting eyes and perfectly shaped slim nose. The young sculptor had captured her magnetism, as Grace knew he would, when she commissioned him years ago.

There was no obvious place to hide a three foot high statue in her open plan sitting room. Grace sighed as she looked round at the various pieces of antique furniture she'd bought over the years. She would love to display Roxanne on the circular mahogany pedestal table in the corner of the room, but how fatal would that be? The reappearance of Roxanne in any form would rake up all the awkward questions the real girl had raised fifteen years ago. Her death did not make the answers any less painful.

Grace staggered to her chintz covered sofa where she dropped the parcel.

"My child; my child" she cried, "why did I give you away?" It was the same question Roxanne had asked her repeatedly. "You knew what it was like to be looked after by unrelated strangers. Why did you do the same to me?"

"I wanted you to have a family, people to belong to, to be part of a culture. I found parents who loved you, respectable people." She could have added that she made sure they had the funds to give her daughter everything she could have needed, but that wasn't what Roxanne wanted to hear.

She wanted recognition, to know who she was. "Why on earth did you call me Roxanne?" she would cry impatiently, "a nothing name, not from your family."

"So you could make your own life," Grace had told her. "You can be free to be yourself, not fettered by the past." She hadn't wanted her child to know about the dark side of life, the evil that her forebears had endured. Innocent people were happy people not haunted with nightmares over the anguish of loved ones.

A tear ran down her cheek as she thought of her own parents. She blinked, then, with her little thumb and forefinger, pulled a white linen handkerchief edged with lace from the sleeve of her pink cotton waterfall cardigan to dab her cheek.

Roxanne didn't realise how fortunate she'd been, a girl who doted on animals, to be brought up on a farm in the wilds of Wales, instead of here in suburban Surrey. Her adoptive parents had adored her and they were still alive. If Roxanne were worried or upset she could have picked up the phone to talk to someone who'd known and cherished her all her life, not simply felt charitable towards a lonely refugee child.

As a bewildered kinder transport child, seven year old Grace had been met at Guildford station by a kindly but undemonstrative childless couple, who could not speak a word of her language. She had not understood until after the war exactly why she'd been sent away or that she was the only one of her family to survive. All she had left of her family were memories. They were so precious they must not be lost. In her mind she cherished pictures of her mother, father, brother and sister. They were her family. She did not want to have it replaced, to belong to another family.

It was too late now to change her mind. Too much damage would be done. In nineteen seventy-four she'd made the right decision. It was what the biblical Solomon would have advised: she'd sacrificed her baby to give the child a better life with a mother and father who could love her.

Provided no one knew, all should have been well – but then Roxanne turned up at the door of her office. Grace smiled when she thought of the stir Roxanne had made in her office. Papa always told her she was a trouble-maker, in his teasing jovial way. What would he have thought if he could have met his grand-daughter? The wide mouth on his plump face would slice into a smile before he gave his wonderful deep masculine chuckle that she could still hear in her mind.

Only Roxanne's arrival out of the blue hadn't been funny, but disastrous, ending with her terrible death. For years Grace had tried to block out of her mind the vision of that mass of blood and gore which was her daughter lying armless on the ground in her garden with her severed limbs alongside her.

Grace fumbled with the strong string which bound the box. It was too tight to pull over the corner of the cardboard. She looked down at her knobbly arthritic fingers with irritation.

She hadn't been so helpless the day Roxanne died. Fifteen years ago she'd been fit enough to run down her garden when she heard the commotion. She'd also had the wit to rush back to the kitchen to bring back as much ice as she could to pack Roxanne's arms into a box to be taken to hospital in the forlorn hope that they might be re-attached, whilst everyone else had stood around helplessly, except the man who was giving Roxanne the kiss of life. She swallowed a sick feeling which rose in her throat. An unwelcome picture of the bloody severed limbs darted into her mind. She wrinkled her forehead, frowning to blot out the image. She'd done everything she possibly could to save her child, but her efforts were in vain. Her beloved daughter, who'd never known her mother adored her, had died on the way to hospital.

People tried to comfort her that it was simply a terrible accident. There was nothing Grace could have done to prevent it. Yet for some reason Grace found it less upsetting to think it was needless, to feel she or someone else might have saved her child. It was a relief when Tessa the psychologist the police drafted in to help everyone said she believed there was "no such thing as an accident". Someone was always culpable by negligence if not intent.

I can't go on thinking like this; I must get on, do something. Frustrated by the tight binding round the box, Grace heaved herself on to her feet. It was less painful to limp over to the antique rosewood bureau where she pulled open the flap of the desk. Inside it lay an antique silver pen knife which she picked up to slice through the tape.

Moments later she had the box open, with the lid labelled DVD cast to one side on the sofa. Lying in front of her was her daughter, or rather the bronze version of her. The likeness was as remarkable as ever.

Grace leant over the box to stroke the sculpture's slender arms. They were hard, like Roxanne's muscular limbs, but beautifully shaped. Her fingers slipped over the curves, stopping at the hands which clasped the wolf cub. Why on earth the sculptor had to include that wild creature she couldn't fathom. She'd refused to have it in her house, another decision she regretted. It meant that Roxanne's sittings including the wolf cub had to take place in the sculptor's home which made her wonder...

Had the sculptor had been in love with Roxanne? The conclusion was obvious when she looked at his work. Depicted in the dungarees she always wore, their very utility seemed to emphasise her femininity. Her beauty sparkled in the narrow vixenish features of her face.

Tears pricked Grace's eyelids. With her brown spotted gnarled hands, she stroked the sculpture's face. "You were beautiful my girl".

In her mind she heard Roxanne's reproachful answer, "You could have told me."

That was Roxanne all over, always wanting to be told things and not satisfied with the answer. She was too young to know there were some things you may be better off not knowing.

She argued with herself over and over again as to whether she was glad Roxanne had found her. Wonderful though it was to see her, the girl brought problems, problems Grace refused to inflict on anyone else. She gritted her teeth. Her own adoptive parents used to say "What can't be cured must be endured". She'd hated that. At least it wasn't true of her painful hip; she was getting that sorted.

Her musing was interrupted by the sound of her front door opening. One of the key-holders, women who helped her out, must be entering the house. Any of them might remember Roxanne or certainly heard about her. She must hide the sculpture now. Panic-stricken Grace tried to lift the box up as she stood up, but an intense pain in her hip made her cry out.

She dropped the box on the floor. Unable to bend down easily she thought maybe she could push it under the sofa with her foot before whoever it was arrived, but Frankie rushed into the room.

"Are you all right?" she asked. "I heard you cry out."

"Yes, yes," mumbled Grace vaguely as she tried to shovel the box sideways with her foot encased in its neat grey lace-up court shoe.

"What's that?" asked Frankie, noticing immediately. "Can I help you with it?"

"Nothing, nothing," replied Grace swiftly, cursing for once Frankie's willingness to help her. Usually her former cleaner's enthusiasm was a blessing.

Despite her embarrassment Grace smiled at her old friend. Her presence as always was reassuring. She proved Grace was not a bad person; she'd helped Frankie, a single mother, in more ways than simply supplying her with a job. She'd given her a livelihood, helped her make something of her son. Maybe it wouldn't matter so much Frankie seeing the sculpture. Steve her son was the one man who had not been in love with Roxanne, or at least Grace did not think he had.

"Are you sure I can't do something with that box for you?" persisted Frankie. "It looks far to big and heavy for you to lift."

"I'll sort it out later." Grace tried to keep urgency out of her voice, "There's no need for you to bother with it." She regretted a moment later that she had not been more commanding.

"But that's why I'm here, to do any last minute stuff you might need." Frankie's dark, almost black, chignon passed in front of Grace's face as, with a supple dive, her slender figure bent down to lift up the box. "Now where do you want it put?" she asked with the box resting on the flat palms of her hands and outstretched arms.

"I don't know," mumbled Grace. In an awkward movement she bent down to picked up the lid labelled DVD which she thrust over the box. With luck Frankie had not registered whom the sculpture inside represented nor even noticed it. "I just want to stow it away somewhere." She added in a casual tone.

Frankie might not recognise Roxanne after fifteen years. She had not spent much time with her. Nor had she seen much of the sculpture which had been in the Challenger's home because Grace had given it to her daughter as a wedding present when she married Jules. Her tiny figure fidgeted uncomfortably on her slim legs. Maybe she should confide in Frankie?

No, she must not; she must continue the pretence that the sculpture was unimportant. "Stuff it in there if you would dear." Grace limped over to the cabinet on which her huge wide screen television stood.

Staggering a little with the weight of the box, Frankie followed her across the room. "Now what else can I do for you before you go into hospital?" she asked in a reproachful tone, as though Grace had intentionally denied her the opportunity to be of use, whilst Grace bent down awkwardly to open the cabinet's glass door.

All Grace wanted to command was that Frankie mention the sculpture to no one, especially not her son Steve, but she restrained herself. She might trust her friend with her life, but a son comes before any former employer. However much Frankie might owe her, she had a husband to confide in now too.

Let her think the bronze was an insignificant if rather big trinket, sufficiently unimportant for its cardboard box to be viewable through a glass door. It was safer that way. Everyone would be happier not knowing the truth about Roxanne.

3. Impey meets a wolf

Impey's foot stabbed the accelerator of her new second-hand Honda Jazz. She whizzed past a large lorry bumbling along the road. She'd dallied over dressing this morning, wondering whether she should cancel this meeting with Jules Challenger, which meant she'd probably be late. *It doesn't matter,* she told herself. Jules wanted to see her, so even if she was not at his house at ten o'clock sharp, he would wait. A man as fearfully rich as Jules was reputed to be, should have time at his disposal; he could rearrange his appointments. Other people would fit in with him, as she had, she thought rather stupidly, done.

So he'd bought her mortgage? That did not mean she owed him anything other than money, which she should be able to pay off soon, once her payment came through from the wretched Nikos family. Her fingers tightened on the steering wheel. She wished they'd stop whinging about funds stuck in poverty-stricken Greece.

Jules hadn't mentioned money over the phone when she'd rung to arrange the meeting. She was the one who'd brought up the subject of her mortgage, but he'd sounded completely uninterested in that. Perhaps that shouldn't have surprised her, bearing in mind the deep voice which answered the phone was Jules himself, since Steve had given her his direct personal line. He was cagey about why he wanted to see her, said he'd tell her when they met. Presumably he hoped she'd write something good about him for the business press.

She did do interviews with businessmen, but usually at the request of a newspaper, or by arrangement with the magazine or newspaper first. Editing the Nikos memoirs had been a departure from her normal practice, but he was a professional person, not a businessman. She did not do whitewash articles, especially if the businessman concerned was engaged in some dubious practice. Her articles were always impartial. She'd have to make sure Jules realised that. The knowledge he had her mortgage made her feel slightly sick, but she would make damn sure he realised he couldn't blackmail her into writing some smarmy article about him.

Thank goodness Jules lived only a couple of miles from her cottage. His place was next door to the club. High fences either side of the building, blocking all view of the garden were the only suggestion of Jules's fabled vast wealth. His home looked modest, a two storey dwelling in an unmade-up road where none of his neighbours' houses she had passed to reach the end of this cul-de-sac looked particularly grand either. With its ornamental rusty brickwork, Impey reckoned The Lair was built some time in the early twentieth century.

She parked the Jazz on the yellow gravelled drive outside a double garage, which looked as though it was converted from former stables. A strange high-pitched whine greeted her ears as she stepped out of her car. She shivered. It sounded like an animal's warning cry, but she supposed it might be some sort of sophisticated alarm system. No – that eerie howl could only come from a wild animal, although it came from inside the house. She was relieved when a couple of raps on the brass knocker on the panelled oak door blotted out the noise.

A small plump woman with short straight dark hair opened the door. *Was this wife number four or five?* Her lips parted in a welcoming smile. "Come in. Jules is expecting you." She led the way to a room at the back of the house and knocked at the door. "She's here," she called.

32

Alongside the sound of an animal's whine came the shuffling noise of furniture moving. "Tell her to come in," said a low human voice.

Whilst the woman backed away hurriedly, Impey opened the door to see a large grey creature bound towards her. *I must be loopy; I knew that call; it's a wolf.*

A thickset man leapt, as though he had springs in the ancient trainers on his feet, to grab a collar round the wolf's neck. He wrestled him on to his side. After a momentary gurgle, the wolf's vast jaw opened for his long pink tongue to emerge; he started to lick his master.

"I gather you don't mind animals," gasped Jules, as he staggered to his feet, "or I'd have put Caesar outside, but now he's such an old man I do like to have him by me when I'm working here in my study." He pointed at a spot on the floor by the fireplace to which the wolf slunk before he held out a broad hand with stubby fingers. "I'm Jules by the way."

"Yes," Impey shook his hand, "and I gather your friend's called Caesar." She glanced at the wolf who gazed directly back at her with his slanted amber eyes as though assessing her suitability to be there. Now she was only a few feet away from him, Impey could see his thick grey fur was speckled with tawny and cream; he was a very handsome creature.

Although the place was remarkably clean for a shared study, it was obviously Caesar's den as much as Jules's. The corner of the room was strewn with objects like stuffed toy animals, rubber rings and balls, presumably Caesar's toys. Fixed to the cream painted walls were stilts to hold shelves full of books, files and other office equipment. Apart from a couple of moulded white plastic chairs on single steel poles, which looked as though they belonged in an up-market kitchen or hairdressers, the only furniture on the bare wooden floor was a vast ancient desk in the corner of the room. A brass metal rim ran round the top of the desk, on which stood a huge computer, a screen and other peripherals.

Jules hesitated, then balled his hand into a fist, "Before you sit down, could you hold out your hand to him like this so he gets your scent? Or you could let him smell your nose if you prefer?"

You are joking. Impey held out her arm gingerly with her fingers folded into her palm, towards Caesar's face.

The wolf took a couple of steps towards her, which made her want to shrink back towards the door, but she stood firm; she knew she mustn't show fear. Caesar sniffed her hand before his muzzle moved to her body and snuffed around her crotch.

Jules's face reddened. "I apologise if he's a bit intimate. Sometimes he's like that with women. Pat his tummy if you like, but avoid his head."

Impey nervously patted the wolf's side. To her surprise Caesar responded by rubbing his head against her side.

"He obviously likes you," Jules laughed, "but then he has excellent taste. Now do sit down. No don't let it down," he added hastily as Impey grasped a handle beneath the seat of one of the chairs, to lower it. "You must be higher than Caesar, so he looks up to you."

Impey scrambled up on to the chair which was set sufficiently high for her feet only just to touch the floor, although she was above average height. She crossed her legs behind the stalk holding up the seat as she eased herself into a comfortable position. "Of course," she nodded. She understood the principle. Pack animals like wolves had to appreciate another creature's place. "So why did you want to see me?"

Jules perched on the edge of an antique leather topped filing cabinet. One of his battered trainer shod feet was on the floor, whilst his other leg hung over the corner. In this pose Impey could see how muscular his chunky figure was. He looked at her full in the face, gripping her vision in a manner disconcertingly like Caesar's, although Jules's startling cornflower blue eyes were hardly wolfish; nor was his golden streaked hair or his wide smooth face, about which there was a youthful chubbiness. His jeans and open-neck shirt also gave him a look of a superannuated student, which made the appealing tone in his voice sound more like a request to join in some fun game than a serious commission. "I thought you might be able to help me."

"Do you want some media coverage then?" It was hard to fathom what other use she could be to him. "I'm afraid public relations is not my forte. I don't do presentation; I'm more of an investigative journalist." *This should put you off.* "My strong point is ferreting things..." Her voice tailed off as Jules interrupted her.

"Ferreting!" He rubbed his broad hands before clapping them together. He shook his joined hands backwards and forwards at her. "That's exactly what I want you to do, but it's personal, not business." He leant forwards. "I need someone trustworthy and discreet to find out something for me."

"Oh? What would that be?" Impey had a horrid suspicion she could guess.

"I've got a sculpture," said Jules, his head nodded slightly as he spoke, "which I'm very attached to. It's been desecrated by someone and I want to know who."

"You mean the figurehead on your boat?" Impey saw instantly she was right from the glint in his blue eyes. "That might be rather a tall order for me. I'm an absolute land lubber. I wouldn't know where to start research on the high seas." She slipped off the stool.

There was no point in staying. She should have guessed what Jules wanted before. Through the French windows she glanced out at his garden, if you could call the rough area of land with a few messy flower beds and lawn "a garden". A large square, surrounded by high wire, had a muddy pond and various hillocks as well as bits of climbing equipment inside it. This was presumably a play place for Caesar. She hesitated. No. Jules's care for his pet was not necessarily a recommendation for him as an employer. She bent over to pick up her handbag, and then jumped back smartly.

Caesar had leapt forward to snatch up her bag in his teeth.

"Oh, I'm so sorry," apologised Jules, "I should have warned you it's better not to bring a leather handbag when you come to see me. Is your hand all right?"

There was a little blood oozing out of a scratch on her hand, but Impey was more worried about her best good quality leather handbag, which Caesar had deposited between his front paws. "Yes fine, but I would like my bag back."

"Of course, of course." Jules hopped off the filing cabinet, pulled open a drawer of his desk and took out a harness. He stepped forward, then with a dextrous flip, he slid it over Caesar's nose whilst he scooped up the small handbag. He tossed it to Impey. "Keep it on your lap whilst you're here." He slipped the harness back off the wolf's nose.

I wasn't planning on staying. Impey wanted to say as she caught the squashy brown bag, but before she could take a step towards the door, Jules leapt towards her and caught her arm. Then he turned towards Caesar. "Bad boy," he scolded the animal. "Shame on you," he growled in a deep tone. "She's a friend. Friend," he repeated, drawing out the word.

The wolf sunk down from its haunches into a supine position on the floor. He stared up at Impey with a look in his amber eyes suggestive of remorse.

"Now say you're sorry," growled Jules in a deep voice.

The wolf raised himself back into a sitting position. With his ears cocked up, he raised his right front leg and let the paw drop whilst he bowed his head.

"It's really not his fault" said Jules, "the trouble is my mother used to give him her old leather handbags to play with when he was a pup which enhanced his instinctive sense of leather as prey."

Impey's fear, tinged with the fury over her handbag, subsided, although she could see the wolf's slight tooth marks in its soft leather. Clutching it, she hopped back on to the chair. "I'm afraid it's no use; I wouldn't know where to begin. I've done the odd bit of detective work, when animals are involved, but it's always been on land. I haven't tackled anything out at sea. You'll need some sort of specialist marine detective agency, if not the coast guard."

Jules shook his head. "I don't want to get involved in anything big time or official. Anyway this didn't happen at sea." He rolled his eyes as he spoke. "Someone broke into my property here."

"Heavens! What with Caesar around?"

"No unfortunately I left her in the garage."

For a moment Impey wondered why he had called Caesar a 'her', before she realised Jules referred to the figurehead. She wrinkled her forehead, about to ask why it was there, but Jules anticipated her question. "I'd brought her on shore to be touched up and varnished; she gets a bit battered on the boat."

"I suppose she would," Impey nodded. "Listen, I'm not trying to make light of anything that's happened, and I know I haven't seen your statue properly, but it's awfully strange that whoever did it made such a good job of it. I mean," she gasped as she stopped speaking. There was a look of suppressed fury on Jules's face. "I'm terribly sorry, I didn't meant to upset you." She glanced nervously at Caesar, who gave a slight whine in sympathy. "Listen, I'm obviously not the right person for..."

"Oh you are, you are," Jules's expression softened into a smile. "It's not you, it's the cock-up, sorry, I shouldn't have said that; I mean it's the stupidity of my staff that upsets me. After the break-in, they found my figurehead in the garage with her arms ripped about. She was such a mess that they sent her straight off to the sculptor for repair and that bastard turned her into a hack version of Venus de Milo."

"So why don't you go back to him and ask him to repair it how you want it?"

Jules shifted himself off the filing cabinet. He rubbed his forehead with a stubby hand. "He won't, or rather he says he can't."

Impey wrinkled her retroussé nose. "How odd. Why's he being so bolshie?"

Jules's shoulders lifted; his mouth turned down at the corners. "I don't know; he doesn't like me. That's all. He

38

didn't like me buying his sculpture so I don't suppose he'd want to do me any favours."

"Surely if it was all a long time ago, he might feel differently now, especially if you were prepared to pay him handsomely in a recession."

Jules rocked from one foot to the other as he shook his tousled fair head. "I doubt it. He felt tarnished by accepting my money for her in the first place."

"That's very odd. There must have been some other issue for him to feel so strongly. He must have been in love with the model." She didn't like to name Flick.

"Oh yes, yes, of course he was; he was eaten up with jealousy when I married her, but that's not my fault. I didn't know she was his girlfriend when I met her."

"So how did you meet?"

"My godmother asked me to go with her to an exhibition at the Wimbledon College of Art, where another of her godchildren was exhibiting. I didn't particularly want to go because I'd never rated the guy, always thought he was a bit of a brute,, but when I got there, I found it all really interesting. There were lots of huge sculptures, but what caught my eye was the wooden carving of this girl. It was so beautiful, the most wonderful work of art I'd ever seen; it hit me straight away that I had to buy it."

"A must-have. Are you always so instinctive with your business?"

Jules laughed. "No, I analyse everything, but this was different. I was much younger then, only nineteen, the same age as Tarquin the sculptor." He stopped talking abruptly to take a couple of steps towards her and pull up a chair next hers. "But that's all irrelevant. All I want to know is who messed up my girl."

"Wouldn't you be better to ask the police?"

"It's a bit late for that, if indeed they'd be remotely interested over what to them would be a small item. — Another reason I'm so angry with my staff for whisking the girl back to Tarquin. They've destroyed any evidence of the original crime, but anyway that's not the point. I'm not after a prosecution. All I need to know is what happened and why, whether my instinct about this is right: I feel it's not an isolated piece of vandalism, but a personal message for me and I want to find out what. That's why you'd be such a good person to help. I can tell you're sensitive and intuitive too." He fixed his sapphire blue eyes on hers with an intense stare.

Don't be flattered into something you might regret. Impey gave a nervous giggle. "How on earth do you think you can deduce that?"

"It's written all over your face, but anyway, your reputation at the golf club precedes you. No one can hide what they're like at a golf club."

"If I'm going to work on this for you, you'll have to be frank with me." Impey pushed a strand of brown hair away from her eyes. *I've been here before; people giving me half the picture so I'm landed in some embarrassing situation.*

Jules rubbed his chin. "I'll make it as easy for you as I can. You'll be completely free to act as you like. I'll only ask you to promise me one thing." His voice deepened and Caesar gave a low growl. "No publicity." Jules's head went on one side as his eyes scrutinised her face as though searching for a key to her integrity. "I'll pay you well; I'll make it worth your while, but I don't want to find myself splashed all over the newspapers or tweeted about on the internet."

"Or you'll set Caesar on me?" Impey glanced at the wolf, whose ears pricked up at the mention of his name. His eyes fixed hers again with such a wistful look she felt as though he was reproaching her.

Jules gave a mournful laugh. "I wouldn't risk that. Tough though he looks, he's a very old boy with a heart defect. Attacking someone could be the death of him." He shrugged his broad shoulders. "Anyway I like to trust people."

Impey glanced at the wolf's grey muzzle, streaked with white. He obviously was old, but well-cared for. "You can rely on me," she heard herself say. "I wouldn't sell your story; it's hardly in the public interest."

"The public interest themselves in all sorts of things which shouldn't concern them," said Jules wryly. "But don't let's get bogged down with that. It can't possibly be necessary for anyone other than me to know what happened to my girl."

"Except for the real girl your figurehead represents?" commented Impey.

"Take that as read; that's one reason I must know who did it. I wouldn't want anything to happen to her; you've met Flick, my first wife, I suppose?"

"Of course; she's been Lady Captain at the club. I don't know her well, but she sometimes plays with a sort of boyfriend of mine." Impey studied Jules's face to see if he showed any inkling of jealousy, but he smiled amiably.

"Dodger's a great guy; he does a bit of work for me occasionally, but what I need you to do is essentially women's work. I want someone who'll chat to people so nicely you extract information from them which they might not want to give."

Like I need to do with you. "Can you just tell me a bit more about the origin of the sculpture before I start. Did you know it was Flick when you bought it?"

"No. She was simply Tarquin's model. I heard later she'd been at the exhibition and I was mortified I hadn't spotted her. So I made being given her name part of the purchase deal. Naturally I asked her out and we went from there. I had no idea she was Tarquin's girlfriend." He softened his voice as though to emphasise his innocence of the relationship.

Impey wrinkled her face. "You think he still nurtures resentment? That he wants some sort of belated revenge?"

"Could be. He was nuts about her."

"Surely he'd have grown out of that now he's a successful adult, which I presume he is. He must have moved on."

"Like a normal person would?" Jules shook his head. "Not necessarily. His sort of lifestyle doesn't bode well for normality. The guy spends hours alone carving stone, metal and any other stuff he can get his hands on, not exactly a life which encourages rational behaviour."

And I'm talking to a man who's been married four times and keeps a wolf.

"He's made threats against me in the past, sold a hideous effigy of me once which wasn't very pleasant, but I ignored it." He hesitated. "I suppose I could have sued him but I didn't."

"What other enemies?" asked Impey. "Might there be other people who might want to hurt you." *Blimey you've obviously passed through a number of women too.*

"I suppose so," Jules nodded; his mouth turned down at the corners gloomily. "Plenty of people resent money." He

42

rested one hand on his knee whilst he massaged his drooping forehead with the other.

"You don't think this has been done by someone with a misplaced sense of humour, rather than someone bearing a grudge, do you? An ex girlfriend perhaps?"

Jules's voice lowered. "Of course there are my girls." He cast a sideways glance at Impey as if daring her to mention "wives". Then he said the word himself. "Doesn't matter that I'm separated from my ex-wives. I still care for them all; I make sure they're okay." His broad mouth twisted into a rueful grin. "Some of the guys call them my harem."

Impey opened her mouth and ran her tongue over her top lip, then restrained herself from speaking. Her instinct told her Jules would not respond to questions; he would tell only what he wanted her to know, not what fascinated her, which was why someone who appeared to be so kind and loyal couldn't make a relationship with a woman stick. *Still maybe if he doesn't allow them to have leather handbags that explains something.* No that was a frivolous thought.

"The girls, the ones I've married I mean," he fixed his radiant blue eyes on Impey's smoky blue ones, "you'll have to talk to them of course. You can get their details from Steve. He looks after them for me."

"You think one of them might be responsible."

"Either of them," he sighed.

"Erm, aren't there four?"

Jules's breath came out in a gasp. "Yes, but no way would Flick damage her sculpture; she loved it." He said passionately before pausing. "And obviously you can't talk to Roxanne."

"Why's that?"

43

Jules looked at Caesar whose head had dropped mournfully. "Because she's dead," he muttered.

"Oh dear. I am sorry. Was she ill or something?"

Jules face darkened. He shook his head as he stood up before reaching out to caress the wolf, as though for reassurance. "No. She lost her arms."

Impey stared at him in horror.

"They got chopped off," he added curtly.

4. Jack takes some money

Jack heard a growl above his head. Startled, he looked up, half-expecting to see a dog in the dark starlit sky. The guttural noise drew his eyes to a huge bird whose outstretched wings, as wide as Jack's six foot height, gleamed white in the moonlight. Open-mouthed Jack stared up at the monstrous creature as it swooped down to where he knelt. The bird headed for his arm, as if it intended to seize the money out of his hand with its hooked beak. Jack's knuckles on his fist tightened as he grasped the rolled bank notes, but he hardly felt his fingernails pressed into the palms of his hand. He ducked his head down to curl himself into a ball, his arms tucked underneath his chest.

A whooshing noise accompanied by a gust of air told him the bird had passed narrowly over his body. When the sound tailed off, Jack raised his head cautiously to see the bird soar away in the sky. Fury that a mere bird could have turned him to a quivering bundle replaced fear. If he had his gun here with him, he'd shoot it.

His chest pounded down to a level he guessed the company medic he was due to see next week would find satisfactory. He wouldn't want to describe this incident to any doctor or he'd probably be referred to the new company psychologist, taken on to stroke the guys suffering from stress. Ridiculous to worry; the twenty-two paper notes he clutched didn't count as *real money,* unlike the multi-digit figures which flashed around his computer screen at work. He transferred the money from his right into his left hand so he could scrabble around on the ground for the car key he had dropped. Ah! There it was beneath his car door. He noticed the red stone on the key ring glint. The heart-shaped jewel

Rosie had given him embarrassed him when other blokes saw it, but now the sparkle of its facets was useful.

Jack bent one long leg to plant his foot firmly on the ground. With his fist on his knee he pushed himself back up to stand on his feet. He stuffed the money he'd taken from the club's safe into the back pocket of his now filthy cream trousers, before he clicked the key he'd retrieved to unlock the door of his Mercedes. To make a quick getaway he'd parked in the President's empty space nearest the closed clubhouse, which was shrouded in darkness.

He tugged the driver's door open, but before he could step into his car, he heard the unmistakeable patter of paws on the tarmac coming from another creature, this time with four legs. Head over his shoulder, he saw a grey thin-legged animal with a long pointed nose, bound towards him. He blinked. Surely it couldn't be? Yes it was a wolf, a sodding wolf. Mesmerised by the glare of its amber eyes, Jack hesitated, but only for an instant as the creature tensed on his haunches, ready to spring.

Jack dived into his car and slammed the door shut behind him. Once he let go of the handle, his hand trembled so much he took a few moments to slot the key into the ignition to start it. With his left hand Jack smacked the black leather covered steering wheel. *Damn it.* He refused to be frightened.

His relief at the welcome purr of the engine was disturbed by two piercing whistles. In the mirror he saw the animal crouch down behind the car. His left hand, clenched on the gear lever, pushed it into reverse. He was tempted to back the car over the animal, but his foot stuck down on the brake. That would be unsporting, cowardly even.

46

A man ran up to the creature; he slipped something silver, presumably a collar over its head. With a jerk of a short chain he pulled the creature out of Jack's way. The man waved whilst Jack drove away, but Jack did not return the salute. Surely this guy had no right to be in the club's grounds. No one told him the club was now employing security. Could that creature be some demonic Alsatian guard dog? No; the guy in his jeans and a tatty sweater was not wearing a guard's uniform.

Maybe he shouldn't mention it. The less notice of tonight's activity the better. There'd be a hell of a row if the men in blazers with significant striped ties found out he'd taken the money, but they wouldn't. He pressed his foot down on the accelerator. The quicker he got back home the sooner he could sort out the business.

Through the mirror, as he drove away, he looked back at the solid old red brick clubhouse. Money was just cement; it held the organisation together but it could be replaced. And Rosie would wash away the stains on his trousers. As the guys said, "A happy wife is a happy life." He'd got her the money she wanted.

****

Archie was curled in a little ball in the back of the car.

"I don't want to get out," came the muffled squeak when Rosie drew the car to a halt in the school car park.

Rosie sighed. He'd been saying he didn't want to go to school ever since he'd woken up early yesterday morning with a tummy ache. Yet he was perfectly well. Or at least the doctor said he was yesterday when she'd taken him to the surgery. After he'd thoroughly examined him, pressing his tummy in different places and looking at his tongue, he'd said in an undertone to Rosie that he was ninety-nine per cent certain the pain was psychological.

Rosie was now embarrassed she'd said fiercely to the doctor, "My child's not a nut case", to which he'd replied, "Your words, not mine. All I'm saying is his pain may be masking some underlying distress."

There was nothing hidden about Archie's unhappiness now as Rosie opened the car door beside him. "Come on. Time to get out."

"I don't like it here."

"Yes, you do." Rosie looked down the lane where all the cars bringing children to the school were parked. A couple of mothers were walking two children along the side of the road. "There's Damian and Noah, your friends."

"They're not my friends; they hate me."

"Nonsense. You've had loads of play dates with them."

Archie's small gold topped head popped out of his cocoon. "I won't any more. I don't like the way they play."

Rosie patted her son. "Oh? Why's that?"

"They're nasty to me. They won't let me be a policeman."

Rosie smiled indulgently. "But that doesn't matter. You could be something else important and useful like a fireman."

"No. They say I've got to be a robber like Dad."

Rosie froze. She glanced across the car park to where Nancy and Mel were hurrying Damian and Noah into the playground in front of the grey stone Victorian school building. "Your father is not a thief."

"They say he is. That's why I've always got to be the robber now, like him."

"That's ridiculous," said Rosie in fury. "It's plain bullying and lies. It'll have to stop. I'm going to see Annette, Miss Barker I mean, and she'll put a stop to it. She leant over and undid the strap holding her son.

He pushed her back. "No," he shouted, "no" as he scrambled out of the Mercedes. "You can't speak to her. She mustn't know Daddy's a robber."

"But he's not," protested Rosie, trying to stay calm. "He wouldn't have job in London to go to if he was a thief." She picked Archie's flat school bag off the back seat and handed it to him. There wasn't much in the bag because he'd been too preoccupied last night to do his homework.

Archie's blue eyes met hers. "How do you know he hasn't got a secret den in London? That's what the boys think."

"Well they think wrong," said Rosie firmly, "and you must tell them so or I will."

She bent down to kiss him but he broke away from her before she could embrace him. "No. No. No. You mustn't," squealed Archie. With his brief case bobbing up and down beside him, he scampered away down the lane towards the school buildings. He'd turned into the playground outside the school and reached the school door before Rosie could catch up with him.

Where on earth did he get that idea from? No way would Jack steal anything.. Rosie's hands tightened on the wheel as she drove away from the school. Someone must have put the children up to it. Horrible to think it might be envious parents. Jack's accountancy firm was doing well, even in this recession, but she hadn't boasted about it. She'd been sympathetic, well

49

she felt sympathetic, to the girls whose husbands had lost their jobs.

It was a relief she wasn't one of them. She didn't want to go back to work as an accountant. Meeting Jack had been the one perk in that dreary job. She had much more fun at home with her children, or as Jack would say, with that ironic grin on his oval face, "working in a different way with money."

Well that's what she'd do now. She must have some light relief after driving an eight mile round trip to take children to different schools.

Mandy Park was having an Open day. Rosie had thought she'd give it a miss. She had enough casual clothes, certainly more than she needed for golf, but it was always a light relief to go to Mandy's clothes shows. Everything was set out so nicely. Mandy let her guests try on anything they liked, which was a treat in itself because she never badgered you to buy, although she might emphasise how great you looked in whatever she produced for you to wear.

Jack might say it was a soft sell, but at least Rosie felt better after visiting Mandy. Even if she bought nothing, the outing was therapeutic. She regarded Mandy as a friend; she always provided coffee or some other drink with the nibbles she laid out for her guests, making it a social occasion. Rosie usually found she knew one or two of them.

There were often other members of Bisley Heath at the house, though Mandy herself belonged to some other club. She'd once confided in Rosie that her former husband, as well as her erstwhile boyfriend, were both long-term members of Bisley Heath, which she'd implied was why she certainly would not want to belong to it, though she remained on good terms with her ex. It had been his idea for her to go into selling clothes from home. He was so keen on it that he had set her up in the business himself. "But he's like that," said Mandy.

Mandy's scruples about a presence at the club because of her ex-husband Jules Challenger and her erstwhile boyfriend Adam Scrivenor meant little to Rosie. She'd never bumped into either of them, although she had heard Adam's name mentioned because he was on the committee with Jack. The probable disapproval, even hostility of Sandy the club's popular professional was, Rosie suspected, more likely to have deterred Mandy from trying to sell fashionable clothes at the club. All the same, she could appreciate what Mandy meant when she'd said Bisley Heath lived in a commercial dark age. Jack often said much the same, only he thought it added to the club's charm, a refreshing change from the City.

Rosie guessed there would be other people at the open morning the moment she arrived outside Mandy's little terraced house in Camberley. She thought she recognised at least two of the cars standing in the road near number nine. They didn't look the sort of four by fours, or vast people carriers, parked outside her older children's private school or even Archie's village school; they were much more like the small hatchbacks driven by older women, which filled the golf club car park on ladies mornings.

Escape time. With a breath of relief, Rosie drew her large Mercedes estate to a halt three houses away from number nine. If other girls from the club were at Mandy's open morning she could banish her worries about Archie from her mind for a few hours; they would chat about other things than children. As she walked up the garden path between Mandy's neat flowerbeds full of purple and pink pansies, she relished the thought of being able to pick her way through Mandy's clever selection of garments. Though an elegant beanpole herself, Mandy was adept at finding the right outfit for any of her customers. She understood about clothes, but then she was once a model. Through the front room window Rosie could already see a couple of rails of tempting trousers and shirts. Beside them on a long trestle table were stacked woollen jerseys and colourful fleeces.

Rosie reminded herself she must not buy anything. Last week she'd cleaned out her bank account buying a carpet from a Turkish man who'd turned up on her doorstep. Not that she regretted it, since it was a bargain, but she felt she'd better draw in her horns with regard to spending money at the moment. There was no harm in looking though. If she really liked something, Mandy would probably let her have it on credit. She'd done that before. Anyway she could now buy something with her credit card. Mandy's generous ex-husband had recently equipped her with a card machine in her home, Rosie recollected, as she pushed open the front door of number nine, which Mandy left on its latch on her show days.

It would be good to be greeted by Mandy's smile. Her wide mouth always stretched across her face with a welcome beam whenever Rosie arrived. And it wasn't just because she was such a good customer, as Jack would say. They were mates; or so she thought.

When she walked through the open door of the living room Rosie could not see Mandy's expression. Her head was lowered as she was evidently involved in an earnest conversation with the two ladies in jeans who flanked her, both of whose hair styles from the back were familiar. The short brown curls of one and the chin length blonde streaked grey of the other belonged to a couple of prominent ladies from the golf club. As they were not people Rosie would choose to interrupt, she decided to lurk behind the nearby clothes rail looking at the garments until Mandy was free to attend to her.

She did not mean to eavesdrop, but as the voices rose in conversation, she could not avoid hearing what they were saying.

"I heard that's who it was who took money from your club's safe," said Mandy.

"Quite disgusting," said the grey-haired lady, "and very surprising. We don't usually have people like that at Bisley heath. Actually people like that don't normally play golf."

"I would understand it," said the short brown curls, "if he'd taken the money for a sick child, but it was nothing of the sort."

"How do you know?" asked Mandy.

"Because they'd have said wouldn't they," said the short brown curls. "Anyway they'd have probably rung a friend, not pinched the money from the club on a Saturday night."

Rosie crouched behind the clothes rail. Nausea suffused her. Surely Mandy would say something to defend her but she didn't. Instead her head nodded whilst the grey-haired lady continued in a crisp tone, "I'm very surprised he's lasted so long as the club's treasurer."

Rosie couldn't bear to wait to hear any more. She must get out immediately, without being seen. The door was still ajar. A couple of steps and she would be back through it.

How on earth did anyone know about Jack's visit to the club? There was only one possible person who could have told them, but she was one of Rosie's closest friends. Indiscreet though she was, surely she'd have the sense not to repeat something so damaging about Jack? Only one way to find out; Rosie would ring Impey instantly.

5. Coffee at the Metcalfes

Impey was about to lift her phone off the hook on her kitchen wall to ring Jules's sculptor when it rang. She'd delayed making the call all day, wondering whether to go or back out of the investigation. Now she had an excuse to let it slide for another day. Rosie was on the other end of the line in distress, begging her to come round and see her.

The moment she walked through Rosie's door, the sight of the new carpet now on the floor hit her. Rich red, deep indigo blue and gold stood out amongst the maze of colours depicting the ancient symbolic tree with fruits and animals entwined in its branches. Impey bent down to touch it. A slightly dusky scent reminiscent of an oriental bazaar wafted up into her nostrils. She stifled a sneeze whilst head down she ran her fingers over the luxurious dense pile. Here on the plain stripped wooden floor of the huge living room, for better or possibly worse, was magic.

How she wished she had not said how much she'd liked the wretched thing when the Turkish salesman had spread it out on the gravel in front of the house. *I would if I were you.* The words felt like bile in her throat. *Go for it.* She would never have encouraged Rosie to buy it if she'd guessed Jack would raid the golf club safe for part of the money.

As she straightened up, she noticed Jack's ugly metal gun cupboard hung high on the wall. His firearms were always locked away out of reach so that no unwary person or child could hurt themselves. How could someone as scrupulous as he was about his guns, be so casual over money? He was a partner in a top firm of accountants in the City, as well as honorary treasurer of the golf club, where his professional skills were valued. Members used to say how lucky the club was to have Jack on the committee. He was talked about as a future captain. *Well that's unlikely now.*

"You didn't tell anyone did you?" Rosie's voice was tearful as she bustled about the room carrying a tray with a stainless steel teapot, a jug of milk, mugs and a matching tin with a funny picture about shopping on it. Her strong angular face, usually so cheery, was blotchy. When she'd put the tray down on the table, she pulled a white tissue with a cartoon on it from under the sleeve of her red and pink striped sweatshirt to wipe her eyes.

Impey held up her hands palms forward. "Honestly, I promise." *I wouldn't want to admit I knew anything about it.* But she could hardly say that. She'd kept quiet when she'd heard people at the club talking about "Jack's hand in the till."

"Of course I haven't." *Though I wish I'd told you what I thought at the time.* No she didn't. She wished she could have turned the clock back and not have been there, watching television with Rosie that evening when the salesman arrived in his white van to deliver the rug the Metcalfe's had bought on their holiday in Turkey.

"Come out here," Rosie had called from the doorway, "and look at these."

Spread out in the drive were a couple of other rugs and this magnificent carpet. Though slightly damaged by water which had penetrated their warehouse in England, they were in near perfect condition. "They're quite usable," said the Turkish salesman. He wondered whether the Metcalfes might be interested in buying one.

Jack had been so busy working upstairs that at first when he arrived at the front door to look at the carpet spread out in front of his house, he thought it was the one they'd already bought. "Okay, let's have it," he said when Rosie told him this other one was such a bargain.

"And Impey thinks so too." She said those weasel words.

That was the moment the Turk mentioned he would only accept cash.

Inevitably they did not have enough in the house, so leaving Rosie and Impey with the children, Jack took off in his car with their debit cards to raid their different bank accounts using cash points, but he finished three hundred pounds short. Although by this time the clubhouse was closed, Jack used his treasurer's key to get into the office, where he borrowed the three hundred pounds from the safe.

"However it got out, those dreadful old ladies have exaggerated everything and made it far worse," said Rosie. "Some of them ought to get a life and find something better to do than gossip."

"They care about the club," said Impey defensively. Most of the older lady members had been her mother's friends. She liked them too. After her mother's death they'd welcomed her into the club. From dolphins to chimpanzees, every mammal she'd studied needed to belong to some group and hers was Bisley Heath. It was a warm friendly place where she felt at home; she didn't want her safe haven spoilt.

I'll be tarnished by association. In London, as a journalist, it hadn't mattered who she was friends with; her contacts gave her titbits of information. That was what life was about, but here in the country it was a different game. People were more earthy. They saw you like apples laid on a tray. Mushy brown rot staining a shiny healthy green skin would infect any fruit in contact with it.

Hey, she mustn't feel like that. Rosie was her friend. Impey herself was embarrassingly indebted to her, since Rosie and Jack had, in a small way, subsidised her recent holiday to Turkey with their party, a trip which had included the fateful visit to a carpet factory.

What a wise choice she'd made not to go that carpet factory, although it seemed a duff one at the time. She'd stayed behind to spend the day with Ned, the unattached man, whom Rosie had invited Impey on the holiday to meet. "Such a super guy" she'd said, "and nuts about animals like you." If doctors were the most desirable of people, Rosie reckoned vets, such as Ned, could not be far behind.

Tall handsome Ned with his wavy black hair was indeed what Impey's grand-mother would have called 'eligible', although she might have criticised his diction, whereas Impey found his lisp rather endearing. Unfortunately their time together never materialised because he flew home that day after an early morning telephone call saying his mother was ill, a summons Impey found a little disturbing for a man in his late thirties.

"I wouldn't care so much if it were only women at the golf club who're being so beastly." Rosie began to sob. "But this morning I had a terrible problem getting Archie to school because some of the other boys are taunting him about his father being a thief. They said he would always have to be the robber when they played "cops and robbers" because his father was one."

"They're just little boys," said Impey, for lack of anything more comforting coming to mind. "They'll forget about it."

"Then, when I popped in at Mandy Park's open morning to look at her new range of clothes, there were a couple of women in the room talking about us as though Jack was thief too. It's so unfair when he's given the money back; there was never any question of his *not* doing so."

"I thought he was going to do that first thing on Monday."

"Of course he was," said Rosie passionately, "but he got a five A M call from the States asking him to get to the office early, so he had to go to London. He was in meetings all day, but when he came home he was sick and he was still throwing up all Tuesday so the earliest he could get the money back into the safe was Wednesday, by which time Miles that gormless secretary was having kittens."

Rosie opened the tin with a cartoon on it and tipped some biscuits out of it on to a plate that matched her mugs. "Like a shortbread biscuit?" she managed a smile, "they're actually home-made. I picked them up at a charity fair I had to go to."

"Thanks." Impey picked up a thick crescent shaped biscuit. *Fattening.* "Though I shouldn't." Ever since she'd left London a couple of years ago when her marriage broke up, her weight had risen. Slowly she nibbled the biscuit which she would have refused in her more weight-conscious days.

Trouble was here in the country it seemed rude not to accept someone's home cooking, or as with Rosie now, un-sharing. An unholy wish Rosie was not her friend stole over Impey. She nibbled the rich buttery biscuit. Was this what treachery felt like, a kind of sea-sickness that swilled around in your stomach? No she mustn't let herself feel guilty; this was not her fault. She did not suggest Jack could take the money from the clubhouse.

"Mind you," said Rosie as she poured out tea for both of them. "Some people aren't so censorious. Ned, the vet, you remember him from the holiday?"

Impey nodded. "The one who had to fly home to look after his mother."

Rosie obviously hadn't taken in that unsatisfactory situation. "I rang him earlier and he says it's just the sort of thing that gets exaggerated in golf clubs, and he should know; his mother's been the Lady Captain."

"I suppose so." Impey smiled to disguise her duplicitous feeling. Both her parents had been club captains too. There was even a bench inscribed in their memory at the halfway hut. They would have been appalled at the thought of Jack's hand in the club's till, even if for only a short-term loan.

"It's given me an idea that I think could help rehabilitate us in the club. The Ladies Invitation to men's competition is coming up. If I asked Ned to play with me, you could invite Jack."

Impey tried not to grimace. Normally she wouldn't have minded playing with Jack, who was a very good player, especially with Ned as the other unattached person in the four, but in present circumstances? In her mind she could hear her late mother's voice asking why on earth she mixed with such people. Golf was a game of trust; a club should be a refuge from unsavoury people. She would have to find some excuse. No, she couldn't be that mean. She must stick by Rosie. *What are friends for?*

"It's all so mad" moaned Rosie, "Everyone's gone berserk about a silly little bit of cash which Jack's returned."

Impey fingered her tawny shoulder-length hair. In the city she'd seen men, at lunch with a couple of chums, hand over half a dozen pink fifty pounds notes to pay for platefuls of food and goblets of wine. She wondered how to point out kindly to Rosie that three hundred pounds might be petty expenses to Jack, but for most of the ladies at the golf club, it was probably more than a week's housekeeping money.

She opened her mouth to try to say something, but shut it again.

Tears were now coursing down Rosie's face. "It's so awful because it's all my fault. Jack only borrowed the money because I loved the carpet. If I hadn't been so smitten with it, he would never have bothered."

"Sounds a right Adam and Eve job," joked Impey. If she couldn't cry with Rosie, she might as well try to make her smile to cheer her up. She eyed the symbolic tree of life on the carpet. "The serpent tempted you. Then you enticed your man to ..."

"Right," said a deep male voice, "only you've got the wrong snake. The Turkish salesman was an inoffensive little trader. Someone else is far more venomous."

Both women started. They turned round in unison to see Jack's large frame filling the doorway.

"Jack, what on earth are you doing here?" Rosie leapt up to cross the room to her husband; she wrapped her arms round him.

Impey glanced at her large round white watch. It was four o'clock in the afternoon, time Jack would normally be at work.

Jack gently unwound his wife's arms. He strode across the room to the table where he picked up a couple of shortbread biscuits. "Didn't have time for any lunch. The Captain called an emergency committee meeting at the club." He stuffed both biscuits into his mouth and chewed them, his chin moving aggressively whilst he paced around the room.

"Why didn't you ring?" asked Rosie.

"Didn't have time. I only just caught the train and I had to cancel things and sort out some other work whilst I was travelling."

Impey stood up. "I'd better be going; you'll obviously have lots to discuss."

"Yes, but it would be good for you to hear it." Jack thumped the table with his large clenched fist. "People like you should know what's going on at the club."

Impey bit her lip. She could guess what Jack would say next.

"I've been pushed out of course. – That's what the emergency meeting was about. I've got to resign from being treasurer giving some spurious reason about pressure of work."

That sounds merciful. "But wouldn't you prefer that?" asked Impey before she could stop herself.

Jack's brown eyes blazed. "Certainly not. I want club members to know why I'm going. In no way have I harmed the club like Jules Challenger will."

"Jules Challenger?" exclaimed Rosie. "I think he was married to Mandy Park."

"And Flick of course. I gather he's had quite a few wives." Jack eyed Impey. "A zoologist like you could probably say if that's typical of snakes."

"Well they do have two hemipenes," said Impey, "that's er... penises."

Jack gave a dry chuckle, "Only two? That's a surprise considering the speed he spreads the seeds of trouble; he got everyone worked up into a frenzy before I had a chance to return the money. It's absolutely absurd when you think of the things that are going on in the kitchen with that crooked cook, which I've been trying to put a stop to, but no one seems to mind his scams because he's won some award."

"What things?"

"Oh never mind. The point is Jules decided to finger me; he told everyone he'd seen me that Saturday night." Jack paced about the room. "He saw his chance to dispatch me."

"But why should he want to get rid of you?" asked Impey.

"To put his own stooge in as treasurer. He's bought a huge stake in the club, or rather he's bought the club's debt which gives him a big stake, but he needs someone on the committee to use it. Says he wants the course more organic."

"That's not a bad thing is it?" asked Impey.

"It's ridiculous. We're already conforming to all the standards set by Natural England and co-operating with the Surrey Wildlife Trust. Last thing our ground staff need is another person burbling on about Natterjack toads."

Impey wanted to protest that the small reptile population benefitted the ground, but before she could speak, Jack continued, "Anyway, according to Ned, who's a friend of his, his real aim is to use our land to make a ruddy wildlife park."

"Not at the expense of the golf course," said Impey. "He's keen on the game. I understand..."

"You mean you know him?" growled Jack as he strode across the room to her.

"Not as such. But I have met him." *Better not say I'm thinking of doing a bit of work for him.*

"Well take my advice, and keep out of his way. Flick and Mandy may have escaped all right, but one of his wives wasn't so lucky; she was cut up with a chain saw, I hear."

"I think that was quite a long time ago," said Impey.

"Doesn't make it any better. Challenger's a dangerous man, but there are club members who've got his number. They'll sort him out; they don't want someone prowling round the club at night with wild animals." He glanced across the room, up at his gun cupboard, "Somehow or other we'll stop the bastard."

Impey realised she must still be looking sceptical because, though she shrunk back in her chair, Jack's hand gripped her shoulder. "Watch out for him Impey. He's a loan shark who's stacked up God knows how many wives, and now he wants to loot and rape the whole damn club."

6. Grace has a visitor

"Griselda", he taunted the woman in the wheel chair.

"I'm Grace," she cackled.

"You were born Griselda." He hissed, his sibilous voice making the name sound sinister.

"You call me Grace," she repeated. "Grace Deer's my name." The old lady's gnarled knuckles griped the arms of her wheelchair. She had a right to the name. Graciella, a form of Griselda, was the name her parents gave her.

"Begged, borrowed or stolen," sneered the man. "Hardly appropriate for someone who's main joy in life is shooting defenceless animals."

"I've helped humans," retorted the old lady in her cut glass voice. "People are more important to me." She hadn't known what a deer was when, as a panic-stricken refugee child she'd arrived in England; she'd chosen the name Deer because so many kindly people called her "dear". It seemed a better name for a child with an unpronounceable foreign name which the nice people mangled so horribly.

She swallowed, making a slight noise in her throat as she tried to push down the memory of that craving she'd had for people to speak to her with affection since all the people she'd loved had left her life. There was no point in trying to explain that to the angry man who'd burst into her tiny bungalow in the cosy Surrey village where she'd always felt so safe. "You were grateful enough for my help in the past."

"That's because I didn't understand the strings attached," said the man. He looked down to stroke the wolf alongside him, "did I?"

The wolf's hackles rose at the hostility in the man's voice.

64

When he was a boy he was afraid of her, she'd sensed that. Though her other four boys were in awe of her, she'd believed they loved her as well. That was what made her efforts worthwhile. *I'm a giver. What I've given my boys, their parents never could.* It wasn't only money. She'd expanded their horizons, made them view the big picture; she'd shown them they could come from nothing, or like her, less than nothing, and succeed. What you needed was courage.

Grace crushed the flutter in her stomach that threatened to spread through her body and make her limbs tremble. She knew she must not show fear. Predators sensed it. Fear made them lust for power. She'd learnt that as a child herself flying birds of prey to hunt with her family in Romania.

Though she was a tiny woman, from her high chair she could stare down at the wolf. She knew this was what she had to do because she'd done it before, seventy years ago standing on a high rock in the Carpathian Mountains. Then she had her little brother with her, a boy killed later by a human enemy far more ferocious than any wolf, especially this wolf. This thickset creature with his glossy grey coat threaded with gold hairs was not starving like the hungry wolf she'd faced down aged nine years old.

She'd been exhausted then too, after climbing for a couple of hours up the mountain to the hidden underground church of the Archangel Myhayil, but she'd been determined to find this special place. The memory of her indignation at the aged crone who looked after the church allowing her small brother to enter, but refusing to let her into the inner sanctum because she was female, made her mouth twitch with a faint smile.

Her ebony brown eyes whose laser beams had splattered the illusions of so many of the men who'd worked for her, fixed on the wolf's slanting amber ones. With a whimper he sunk down on his haunches.

"You coward," the man laughed. He looked round the sunlit open plan living room. "So where is she then?"

"Where is what?" The old lady asked calmly. "My jewellery and other valuables are all in the bank; I only take them out when I need them."

"I hardly need jewellery," snorted the man, "and I'd look pretty silly trying to sell your stuff that's labelled and insured on the internet, no it's..."

"If it's money you want," she interrupted in a contemptuous tone, the burglar box is by the front door. You may take all the money you want, but please leave the box. It's not valuable, but it's quite pretty and I like it."

"Don't be ridiculous," the man laughed scornfully, "do you really think I want to go away with your petty cash?"

"A couple of thousand actually," interrupted the old lady "and there's a couple of hundred in the kitchen in a tin in the kitchen for paying the cleaner and so forth." She didn't like the glint in the man's eyes, but maybe he could be bought off. Most people could. As a boy he'd always been susceptible to the presents she gave him, as grateful as the other children. How odd it was that now he'd become so resentful.

"Well I might as well take it anyway," he nodded at a door the other side of the room, "that way I presume."

She nodded. There was a panic button in her kitchen as well as one next the front door. If she could only direct him to a biscuit tin before he reached her money box maybe she'd have time to raise the alarm. Her neighbours had no idea of her wealth, but they were kindly people. They would probably come round immediately fearing she had had a fall.

"You'd better come with me," he said, "don't want you scarpering yet."

"Okay, Okay."   Fear made her voice croak. She swallowed, noticing the wolf begin to rise on his haunches. *He knows; he's scented my fear; he's guessed I'm going to lose, but he also knows something's wrong.* She had the strange feeling the wolf was trying to choose between them, to fathom out who was the true leader. "What about him?"   She tossed her small narrow head towards the wolf.

"He'll stay." The man picked up Grace's tan leather handbag from an occasional table and flung it at the wolf. "Have fun," he smiled.

Now he was taunting her. He knew her love of handbags. All the boys did. It was one of their jokes. They thought she did not hear them laughing about it, saying that her one bag cost more than all their five mums' bags put together. She let them cheek her. Why should she explain that one small bag was all she had when she, the one and only child of her family who'd escaped the holocaust, came to England?

She tried not to wince. The wolf would have her scent now. He was chewing at something that belonged to her. She handled her bag every day, feeling inside for her purse or her car keys. There was a linen handkerchief inside it too.

"Thought I'd give him a taste of you first," said the man as he loped across the room with an easy stride. "Come along."

Grace loosened the brake of her wheelchair to follow him to the other side of her sitting room where he opened the door and stood back to let her go through first. She swivelled round to park her chair by the stove. Somewhere on the white units was a gas light which she might be able to use as a weapon.

"That's the tin." She pointed across the kitchen at a blue tin on a shelf with some brightly coloured pink flowers on it.

He picked it up to empty it on the units work surface, from where he swept the notes and coins off into his hand, before he stuffed them in his pocket. Then he picked a cloth off the sink to wipe the tin. "Better not leave any fingerprints."

Desperately she looked around for something she could hurl at him. Though her eyesight was not what it used to be, and she was enfeebled with arthritis, she'd been a good shot in her past sporting days. If she hit him in the face she might have time to reach that panic button. The flare to light the stove was not in sight, but the pepper pot might do as well.

She seized the Perspex pot and flung it at his head. If she caught the right place on his forehead she might even concuss him.

It was a futile gesture.

With one hand he caught the pepper pot. "Good try," his sneering laugh made his nose run. He picked a grubby white handkerchief out of the pocket of his jeans to wipe it.

"For God's sake," she cried impatiently, "tell me what you want, take it and leave."

"You can't give me anything. What you've taken is irreplaceable. You know that, but I need the sculpture. It ought to belong to me. You should never have had it."

"It's not here." She shrugged her shoulders, playing for time. Now she had a bargaining counter. The way he'd wiped that tin told her he wouldn't want to ransack her house because that would leave evidence he'd be wary of giving.

"So where is it then?"

She widened her lips in an apologetic grimace that she meant to be a smile. "I don't know where it's being shown."

"You're lying," he shouted, "the sculpture must be here. Frankie said you'd got it back." He strode across the room, seized her thin dyed blonde hair making tears start into her eyes as he yanked her head back. His fleshy face seemed huge so near to hers. "Where's the sodding statue?" The s sounds slithered together as the hiss in his voice increased with his rage.

"Not here; it's far too valuable." She looked at him appealingly. "Once a sculptor's known, his early work commands a terrific premium." – She should know; she'd been vice-chancellor of a university with a magnificent art faculty.

He let go of her hair to give her face a stinging slap. "Do you think I don't know that? Just tell me where it is."

And then? He wasn't saying he'd let her go. "I really don't know."

He gave the side of her head another blow which made her head reel. She wanted to cry but she couldn't. Throughout her childhood she'd held back tears so often that they wouldn't come now to help relieve the pain. Anyway she didn't want to give this brute the satisfaction of seeing her anguish. She steeled herself for more. Whatever it cost her, she would not tell him where it was, but he'd never find it because it was so obvious, still wrapped in tissue paper in a box labelled DVD beneath the television. She could look at it whenever she liked, which was what she wanted, but she didn't want to display it. Why should she who'd achieved so much need to show anything to anybody?

If she could hold out for ten minutes, her Bridge four would be here. A couple of them would have to ring the bell, because she'd shut the door after she'd made the terrible mistake of letting this man into her house. Only Sally her young girlfriend could let herself into the house. She had a key. Then she would use the alarm by the front door. She was a sensible girl.

In spite of her throbbing head, Grace gave a weak involuntary chuckle. *When she sees that wolf Sally will think she's strayed into a real life Cinderella story.*

"What's so fucking funny?"

"My Bridge four – they'll be here any minute."

He put his powerful hands round her thin sinewy neck making her gasp to breathe. "Then you've got any minute to give me that sculpture."

"Never," she said, feeling the breath drain from her body. If she had to die this way, she would leave the earth knowing she refused to be bullied.

"I mean it," hissed the man, "I'm not afraid to kill you." He loosened his grip round her neck.

"I know," she whispered with the little remaining strength she had left. She gulped and tried to clear her throat. Maybe she should tell the brute where the sculpture was? She did not need it.

Early in life she'd lost the people most important to her. She'd tried to make others take their place, but now it hit her with harsh reality that in this one part of her life she'd failed. Gratitude was temporary but resentment was permanent. Whatever she gave this man it would not assuage him. She shook her head feebly. "Never" she gurgled, "you'll never get it".

A quote from Shakespeare's "Julius Caesar", the first Shakespeare play she'd learnt at school, about the good people did being "oft interred with their bones" and "evil living after

70

them", echoed in her mind. She recalled how the other children in her class had not understood why this thought upset her so much. As large hands curled round her neck again, squeezing the breath out of her, she fought the pain with the remembrance of how she'd made those children understand about the survival of good things. Everything she'd achieved, she done for her lost family.

The man who was killing her would never have that satisfaction.

7. Impey meets Tarquin

The couple of empty buildings in Curtain Road made Impey wonder whether the outskirts of Shoreditch were still the fashionable edge of the art scene. She'd heard it was referred to as "London's new Bohemia" because so many artists had turned spaces in local disused warehouses into work places. Even if now there were not hosts of art galleries around, Impey felt a definite buzz of energy when she stepped off the red 243 bus from Waterloo station to Old Street.

A surge of regret had run through her as she made her way here. Londoners seemed so much livelier and more sociable than country people. She'd enjoyed a chat about the unseasonal coldness of the summer weather with a cheerful elderly Indian man on the bus which made her glad Jules's investigation had brought her here. The Metcalfes were over-reacting to him, which was not surprising, but she would not help them by joining in their vendetta, although, by the sound of it, the man she was about to meet had similar feelings.

Tarquin's studio was in a three storey terraced house, which, judging from its grey brick flat front, might once have been a warehouse, although the upper two floors had attractive dome-shaped windows. Impey peered through the large square ground floor window at some vast edifices which stood on a cheap grey linoleum floor, a brand she recognised since she'd considered using it for her own bathroom.

He was lucky to have such a large space, but he certainly needed it for his huge creations of silvery metal tubes. Most of them were at least shoulder high; many would tower above her. Surely he couldn't expect ordinary people to buy them? *Where on earth would you put one?*

She shook herself. That showed how suburban she'd become. Individuals wouldn't buy the huge objects most of which seemed to be composed of different shaped and sized metal tubes. Any buyer would need a large display area like a vast office forecourt. This was stuff that banks or other corporations bought in their balmier days to enhance their prestige.

Glad she'd had a few moments to get an impression of Tarquin's work, Impey rapped on the grey painted door. Research on the internet had given her some idea of it; nonetheless she was unprepared for the hugeness of these metal pieces.

An attractive blonde receptionist led her into a recess. Behind a plain Formica topped table on tubular legs, sat a tall dishevelled man. This must be Tarquin. He was exactly as Jules described. His mass of black hair and the stubble on his face did give him the look of a tame gorilla.

Impey's incredulity that the strange objects in the room could be much vaunted works of art must have shown on her face. She had scarcely introduced herself as arts journalist wanting to hear about his work in progress before he snapped at her. "I don't do this for a fashion statement. I'm interested in the interaction of shape and substance which together make form."

"Of course," agreed Impey as she wrestled with the concept. The ease with which she'd walked into his studio had not prepared her for any difficulty in conversation with Tarquin; she had not expected a sculptor dealing with solids to talk about abstractions. "I simply wondered how you marketed your work."

Tarquin's large forehead knitted. "I don't know what you mean. Sculpture isn't like frozen peas; you don't market it." He walked over to the biggest object in the gallery. With a large rough-skinned hand he gestured at it. "What do you think this represents?"

Impey looked at the array of glinting tubes. *Aggression* was the first thought that struck her. "Is it to do with warfare."

Behind closed lips a laugh sounded from Tarquin's throat. "If that's the way you see it, so be it."

Impey frowned. She shifted from one flat shoed foot to the other. "But what did you have in mind when you created it?"

"A shape."

"But you must have had some feeling," she persisted. Standing there in his smart dark blue designer type jeans topped with a lilac shirt whose rolled-up sleeves and open neck revealed a plethora of curly black hairs, his appearance suggested a much softer character than his work. He did not look like the creator of such a vast warlike construction. Yet there it was. " An ugly monstrosity" was how she'd have described it in private to a close friend, though Tarquin's obvious pride in it would have made her hesitate before denigrating it to anyone else, let alone in print.

"From a writer's point of view," she hesitated seeing his large nostrils reveal a few dark hairs as they twitched in derision at her appellation of herself, "I mean someone who writes my sort of stuff, it would help if you could give me a bit more background colour."

"Like what?"

"What motivates you; the thoughts that go through your head before you begin to sculpt."

This interview was hard work. The way Tarquin stood with one large hairy-backed hand on his hip and the other dangling was so self-assured she felt anything she might ask would accentuate her ignorance. She cursed herself for knowing so little about modern art, let alone understanding it. There was a group of smaller tubes which looked so like a lot of erect penises, that she assumed its origin must lie in some sort of frightful phallic dream, but Tarquin was so sensitive about the abstract nature his work that she felt to mention the similarity would antagonise him.

To upset him would undermine the purpose of her visit. Her plan to take an admiring interest in his work to lull him into a relaxed enough mood to talk unguardedly about himself, had failed. Her progress towards the topic of his early life was minimal. Worst of all, a bored expression crept across his large hairy face.

He pulled at a large earlobe reflectively. "Are you really interested in sculpture?"

"Yes and no," she replied. She didn't know why she didn't protest that his work fascinated her, but felt that, like an unwelcome natural lie-detector, her face would betray her. "Of course you're right," she admitted, "I do have another reason for coming to see you."

Tarquin smiled. "I thought as much. You're not quite like your average art journalist, too home counties. Something tells me..."

"Okay; you're right. Jules Challenger wanted me to come and see you." There, she'd blurted it out. *How ridiculous. I'm never normally so loose-tongued.*

It did not seem to matter. Tarquin laughed. "I could have guessed; you're the type he likes."

"What's that like?"

"Kind of natural – or at least you will be until he does you over."

"I'm only working for him; I'm not his girlfriend."

The big man beside her rocked his head sideways back and forth. "And what sort of work would that be?"

Impey looked at her watch. It was a few minutes past twelve o'clock. "Tell you what, why don't we talk about this over a drink and some food." Anything to get the man away from the testosterone-charged atmosphere she felt here in the gallery. *What woman could possibly want to play around with steel tubes all day?*

She was surprised and relieved at the speed with which Tarquin agreed, once he'd ascertained Jules would be paying. "He owes me," he said gruffly.

"Don't you think you've got your own back on Jules?" Impey asked when they sat opposite one another in the Rivington Grill at Tarquin's favourite table.

It was big enough for four, but a waiter, dressed all in black from tee-shirt top to sleek black trousers, swiftly removed the surplus couple of chairs. From the speedy way the waiters reacted to him she guessed Tarquin was a regular, though such a mainstream place wasn't what she'd have expected a man like him to choose. On the white damask tablecloths were matching napkins. The chunky dark wood salt cellars and pepper pots were homely.

Nonetheless, Tarquin informed her plenty of foremost modern artists, including the renowned Tracey Emin, were patrons. Was the picture hanging on the wall above his head opposite her by someone similarly famous? After being surrounded by Tarquin's work, the painting of the scantily dressed fair-haired girl lying on her stomach with her legs in the air, a couple of balloons, one red and the other green, tied to the soles of her feet, seemed reassuringly normal.

Tarquin had ignored the regular menu to study the most expensive à la carte main course. When he'd slapped the menu folder shut, he'd asked, "What makes you think I've done anything to Jules?"

"The figurehead of Flick, his wife is what I'm here about; Jules is terribly upset about the way you repaired it." There was no point in fudging the issue.

"Oh come on," Tarquin gave a short dry chuckle, "I did what was needed."

Impey smothered a smile. "Not as far at Jules is concerned. He wanted her arms restored, not have her altered to make her look like the Venus de Milo."

"Hmm. She was changed." Tarquin leant to one side for the waiter to put down the twenty-eight pounds seventy-five pence Aberdeen sirloin steak he'd ordered, in front of him. "Jules made her different. I didn't."

Did he mean Flick or the effigy of her, or maybe both? Impey hoped she'd get enough information out of him for Jules not to renege on his offer to pay for lunch. She'd asked for fish despite Tarquin's suggestion, backed up by the waiter that she "really should try the rabbit pie". She ate enough of that at the golf club.

"He didn't change your sculpture; he doesn't know who did it and he's terribly upset about it – he loved your work."

"No, he loved Flick, I'll give him that, but he changed her and he shouldn't have expected me to remember what she was like twenty years ago."

Impey picked the pink flesh off the bone in her fish. "Surely it was Flick herself who changed. She's a strong character. Jules couldn't have altered her."

"Yeah well he did."

"In what way?"

Tarquin dug his knife into a piece of steak he held with his fork. "Verbally, her voice. Before he got hold of her she talked in an ordinary way. Meeting the Challengers changed that. Once she started going to their cocktail parties, they turned her into one of them. She started calling everyone 'Daaa-ling'" he drew out the word in an affected treble tone, "her voice turned to treacle; she went madly posh."

"I don't suppose that did her art career much good."

"Her art no, but her job prospects yes. Jules stopped her doing anything original and creative, which he thought was a waste of time. He got her going on interior decoration instead." Again Tarquin drew out the words, this time with a scornful tone, more resonant, to Impey's ears, of the upper classes in the nineteen fifties, if not the nineteen twenties, than the present day.

"Perhaps she was simply fitting in with the golf club. I'm afraid there are one or two, or there certainly used to be a few people at Bisley Heath who talk like that."

"And who do you think introduced Flick to that damned game?" Tarquin stabbed three large chips together. "Jules did. She wasn't that keen on him until he took her off to the golf course."

"Really?"

"Sure, it was the most bizarre thing. One moment she was laughing about Jules being so all over her, and the next she was fawning over him because his mother, Faye gave her some of her old golf clubs." He sawed a piece of steak delicately with his knife before adding in ruminative way. "My mum had loads of old clubs she could have given her."

"Does your mother play golf then?"

"Yeah, a bit, but not as much as my father, Giles Hobbs. I expect you've heard of him? He's on the Bisley Heath committee."

Impey frowned. She thought she might have done. Or rather, she could picture the name "Giles Hobbs" written somewhere.

From the way Tarquin spoke, it seemed Giles, his father, felt a similar enmity towards the Challengers. He launched into a diatribe against the Challenger family's' way of life, which was a highly-charged, wealthier version of Impey's own late parents' life style. She winced. *He really is belligerent.* Perhaps it was true that hairy men were more fuelled by testosterone than the hairless. – Hairier chimpanzees were meant to be more powerful. Across the table, the black hairs on Tarquin's chest seemed to bristle as he spoke. "So you see, she became like them."

"Was Jules's mother really so awful?"

"Not if you like that type of person I suppose," Tarquin shrugged. His large nose crinkled in a sniff. "It was their effect on Flick I hated."

"Because she was your girlfriend?"

"Yeah, you could say that." Tarquin's full lips tightened. The unsaid words, *she was my life,* hung in the air. There was a hint of moisture in his eyes.

"But you must have had other girl friends since," Impey persisted.

Tarquin dropped his knife. "For fuck's sake, what's all this to you? Why's Jules so keen to know about me that he sends you trotting along to ask me about my life? No don't answer, he's scared of me."

Now we're getting somewhere. "Why should that be?"

"I bashed him up once as a child; I'd think I'd have finished him off, if our Godmother hadn't stopped me."

She'd screamed at her gardener to pull him off Jules. A rich woman with a large garden, she'd liked it to be played in by her godchildren, or at least children she termed her "godchildren" since religion was not involved. Amongst them was Steve Hemmings, the man who found Impey at the Inn on the beach.

There was also Ned the vet. "You've met him, I suppose," asked Tarquin casually.

Impey nodded.

"And Adam Scrivenor?"

"No." It was another familiar name though.

"You will. He's the other one caught up in Jules's games. That's what happens to people involved with Jules. They end up working for him one way or another. He manipulates them, flies them like he did with his pet owls."

His own pet owl. Impey imagined the golden-haired boy Jules holding out the bird for her to take a turn having the owl nestle in her hands. She could almost feel a fluffy bird rubbing his soft downy face against her cheek as she held him to her face. "That's rather sweet."

"Oh yeah, sadistic I'd call it." His mouth twitched into a smile at her puzzled expression, "sweet to kill things, innocent little voles and mice running around minding their own business."

"Oh you mean he flew the owl," gasped Impey. She tried to control the admiration that she felt rise in her voice. She pictured the owl swirling around the sky between green leafed trees before he swooped down into a flowerbed to catch a small unwary creature. "In your godmother's garden?"

"Sure we had a lot of flipping displays of that bird."

80

"It must have been beautiful to watch."

"What, seeing that bird's talons tear some tiny mouse apart right in front of one's eyes? It was bloody gory I can tell you." He speared a bit of steak on to his fork, stuffed it into his mouth and chomped on it. "I tell you, the man's a bloody sadist. We never got on so I can't think why he wants to know anything about me now, unless he still hates me."

"Oh I shouldn't think so; he doesn't seem the hating type."

Tarquin made a sound in his throat between a snort and a laugh. "You didn't see him that day we fought. There really were daggers in his sweet little blue eyes. I know what he said even though I could hardly hear it because his lips were bleeding and swollen and I'd knocked one of his teeth out; he lisped 'I'll get you back'."

So he did. He took your girlfriend. That was not going to be a helpful thing to say. "I got the impression," Impey said gently, "that he wants to know if you're still interested in Flick. He saw the way you adapted your sculpture of her as a statement."

Tarquin laughed drily. "And his sending it back to me wasn't? Why can't the man leave me alone? He got Flick and he lost her. That's what he does with women."

"I think he still cares for her, well I know he does. He's worried about her. I mean I know it sounds strange, but he thinks someone mutilated the statue as a warning and I suppose he thought if you still cared about Flick you might have some idea if someone wanted to hurt her."

"He wants to know whether I'm still seeing Flick?" Tarquin shook his large head. "Well frankly it's none of his business or yours. Listen to me: if you're really a journalist, you can write about my work, but I'm not interested in talking about the women in my life. As you seem like a nice, if misguided girl, let me give you a bit of advice. Keep away from Jules Challenger. Do you know how many goddam times that man's been married?"

"Four."

"Doesn't that tell you something? I don't suppose he told you about the weird hobbit who took Flick's place?"

"He said her arms got chopped off in a dreadful accident."

"Doesn't that tell you something? She was messing about with a chainsaw. I mean who in Godsname lets a nineteen year old muck around with a chainsaw?"

Impey wrinkled her face. "I suppose it was her choice to use it, though I don't quite understand how she sliced her own arms off. Wasn't anyone else around?"

"Yeah that's a goddamn mystery. We were all there at Grace's place. Adam, Steven, Ned, Jules and me. I told you, she had this habit of getting her so-called godchildren together although actually we were merely kids she happened to want to be involved with because she didn't have any of her own. Anyway, she was closeted in the house with Jules talking money and the rest of them were doing stuff in the garden."

"What were you doing?"

"Finishing touches to a bronze of Roxanne which the old girl had already given to Jules and Roxanne as a wedding present. Apparently she screamed but I scarcely heard her. Grace had huge grounds with that old house. Poor old Ned found her covered in blood with her sliced-off arms lying beside her."

"Ned, the vet?"

"Yeah. Poor bloke. He was nuts about Roxy, called her his soul mate; he was devastated when she dumped him for Jules." He paused. "Nice guy, great with animals. Can't think why he still hangs in with Jules though I suppose he wants to look after Caesar."

"How do the other godchildren feel about Jules?"

"God knows. Steve still works for him, but I think he had a falling out with Adam over some woman. There was a time though when they were great buddies. Adam worked for him at one time." Tarquin's great hairy chest shook as he laughed. "He's a kind of measly little guy, but Jules got him taking Caesar out debt collecting. He was a hell of a success door-stepping people with a wolf on a chain."

"That doesn't sound very nice." *And I'm an animal lover.*

"Course it wasn't, but then Jules isn't quite the Mr Nice guy you take him for.
Told you," Tarquin nodded grimly. "Keep away from Jules Challenger; he's trouble. I wouldn't want to take his money."

"He must have paid you for the repair you did."

"No. Steve rang and told me he was going to send her back for a proper," he pulled a face as he as he enunciated the word 'proper' in his version of the Challenger tone, "refit. Like I said, I wouldn't take his money."

"Bit late for that," laughed Impey looking at their empty plates. She picked up the wine bottle to pour the dregs into Tarquin's glass. "Let's toast to this being the last lunch at his expense."

Tarquin gave another sardonic throaty laugh; he held up his glass, "to money the great corrupter. If you're really a journalist you'll get a good story looking at Jules's own murky life."

8. The Ladies Invitation

"For God's sake!" Dodger thrust his driver back into his golf bag, having socked his ball what looked like a couple miles down the fairway, "I didn't *set you up* with Jules: he simply asked if I knew anyone who could do a discreet investigation for him, preferably a woman, so naturally I thought of you. You should take it as a compliment." He punched her lightly on her arm.

"Oh I do." Impey wished she'd never mentioned Jules. They were meant to be having fun. The Ladies Invitation to men was one of the club's best social occasions.

Jack, Rosie's husband, was being charming to her, despite her lacklustre performance. He managed to hit the ball as though he didn't have a care in the world.

Rosie's play wasn't much better than hers. Maybe that was what was irritating Dodger, who was Rosie's partner for the competition. His round face creased into a smile. "If you didn't analyse so much you'd play much better golf too."

"I normally do." Impey longed for Dodger to see her at her best, especially since she felt in competition with Flick.

She tried to brush away all thoughts of her rival twirling herself into a beautiful arc before she swept her ball into the distance to the admiration of all in view. It was a glorious day. Sunshine made the grass and foliage of the trees shimmer different shades of green whilst pink buds peeped out from the luxuriant thick heather.

She loved this course where she'd played as a child. Her parents might have died five years ago, but in Impey's mind, they still walked here chatting to one another. How glad they would be she was back playing golf at Bisley Heath, living a healthy life, though they might not be so happy about her move into private detection.

The crack of Jack's drive interrupted her musing. "Damn it, I'm sorry," he said, "that went right into the middle of the trees, but I know exactly where it is; it's absolutely in line with the tall oak, probably about three or four feet in front of it."

"Been there before?" Dodger teased.

"All too often," Jack responded amiably, striding up the fairway with Impey trailing along after him. He stopped suddenly about sixty yards short of the tree. "I don't believe it." He barked sharply. "That socking great bird's taken my ball."

Impey gazed at the spot where Jack pointed.

A large white bird with wings outstretched rose gracefully into the air. A lump of something was indeed inside her curved beak.

Impey watched the bird. "She looks like a vulture."

"It's an 'outside agency' as far as golf's concerned," grumbled Jack, when they reached the bit of ground where the bird had settled, "which means we can put down another ball without a penalty." He hoisted his bag of clubs off his shoulders, unzipped a pocket full of balls to pluck one out and drop it beneath the oak tree. "Goddam it, that bird's taken my new ball."

"But any bird of prey might have picked up a mouse or a vole."

"I saw him," said Jack in a high-pitched strangulated voice. He swerved round to point through the trees at another part of the course, "he went off in that direction and what's more I can still see him over there above the fifth fairway."

Impey stared along the line of Jack's arm, more intrigued by the sight of a vulture in Surrey than a golf ball. "I can't see him," she said sadly, "I wish I had my binoculars."

Jack delved into a leather pouch hanging on his golf bag. "My golf range finder will do. I use one like this for shooting bloody birds." He took out an object that looked like a one eyed binocular which he put to his eye. "He's there on the fifth all right; what's more he's bloody well swooping down again. Oh my God, I don't believe it."

"What?"

"Take a look at this!" Jack handed Impey the rangefinder which she put to her right eye.

Impey swirled the range finder around but could not see the bird. She took it from her eyes to hand it back, but Jack would not let her. He put his left arm round her shoulders and with his right hand he held her right arm up to her right eye before twisting her round and pointing her view in the right direction shoulder height.

Ahead of her, in the centre of her sight, was the bird. She was definitely a vulture, but more astonishing was where she perched, on the handle of a golf trolley. Beside was a little net bag into which she dropped a golf ball. Then a hand came into view to stroke the bird's feathers. Before she swivelled the rangefinder left, an odd instinct told Impey what she would see; the bird perched on Jules Challenger's trolley.

"What were you doing in the woods together?" Dodger asked jovially when, having hacked Jack's replacement ball out of the woods, Impey and Jack rejoined the other pair on the fairway.

"Bird watching," explained Impey, embarrassed that Rosie was giving her a very odd look, obviously having seen Jack put his arm round her.

"Oh yeah," said Rosie.

"Some guy," said Jack, "had this socking great bird pick up my ball then take it back to him – had the bloody thing perched on his trolley."

"It was Jules Challenger," said Impey, "I suppose he thought that if Ladies invitation allows people to bring their dogs along, why shouldn't he bring his bird." She laughed, "It would be a bit much to bring his wolf."

Jack slapped his forehead with his right hand. "Hell. I knew I'd seen him before. – Now I've got another score to settle with him."

Dodger glanced over his shoulder behind them. "Come on, come on," he urged, "we must make a move. The chaps behind are waiting for their next shot."

They hurried forward, but the incident obviously rankled so much with Jack that he began to hit the ball wildly. The sight of Jules in the vicinity wrecked his game. He would have been even more annoyed had he heard the conversation in the ladies cloakroom whilst the players were changing for dinner.

"I was playing with the most amazing man," brayed a large lady whilst they queued for a shower, "Jules has got this bird which goes and picks up golf balls, most amazing creature, found half a dozen really good balls, black Srixons and Pro vs."

Jules's partner was Camilla Wilmot, nicknamed the "Merry Widow". Apparently her late husband, an army officer, often told her that if anything happened to him, she should live life to the full for both of them.

Tonight her cheerful presence in the dining room lived up to his orders. She towered above the other women at her table and, judging from her girth and vast bosoms, pining for her husband had not taken away her appetite. Happily her gaiety was infectious. Though her voice was not loud, it had a carrying bell-like quality. This was useful at times when, as Lady Captain, she compèred events, most of which took place in this room.

Probably because she remembered so many happy family lunches here as a child, Impey loved this room with its high moulded ceiling and Delphic columns built into the walls. Numerous engraved dark wooden shields pinned on a wall were a testament to friendships which flourished here. They represented the societies of professional people or schools' old boys and other groups who enjoyed playing at Bisley Heath. On the other walls were the embossed gold framed pictures, landscapes of a rural Edwardian, Arcadian-looking England.

No doubt about it: Flick had done a brilliant job with her refurbishment, using different shades of paint to highlight columns and alcoves. The pieces of reproduction antique furniture might have strained the club's budget, but they looked good.

The elegant dining room made Impey nostalgic for the days her mother ran the Ladies section, but women like her were a dying breed. Girls like Flick did not want to be confined to the Ladies section. She sought a position on the general committee; she would stand for election at the annual general meeting this coming October. If she got in, she would be the first woman ever to sit on to the Bisley Heath board in any capacity, other than in an honorary position as Lady Captain.

Tonight for food, Camilla had chosen smoked salmon on a bed of leaves with a dressing, followed by Rabbit pie. This seemed to have become standard fare for the club's festive meals. Really, it was about time they asked the chef to produce something different, even if he did do the pie remarkably well. It was rather stodgy for midsummer.

Thankfully the men enjoyed it. Dodger laughed when Impey apologised for the choice of meal, especially when she had to admit she'd never cooked a rabbit pie in her life. His teasing her about her culinary prowess gave her a chance to suggest he cooked for her, if he wished to compete in the kitchen. Perhaps he could pluck food out of hat as easily as he could a rabbit.

The tinkling of a spoon against a wine glass at the next table made her swallow the question. All round the room voices dropped to a murmur as conversations died mid sentence. The captain was about to announce the results for today's competition.

Matthew Lawson pushed back his chair to rise to his feet. A tall handsome man any club would be proud to have as a leader. His face was broad with wide apart brown eyes. With the shoulders in his crested navy blazer over his blue shirt thrust back, he began to speak.

He welcomed all the members. How lucky the men of Bisley Heath were to have such a splendid bunch of ladies to invite them to this lovely dinner. He knew in some clubs legislation on equality had caused problems, but not at Bisley Heath as this wonderful occasion showed.

After the "Here here's" had died down, Matthew continued that men at Bisley Heath didn't have the difficulties a chum of his related happening at a nearby club. Jerry and Max, a couple of golfer playing an important match, caught up two women on their course chatting away as they played.

"'Mind if we hang back,' said Jerry to Max, 'don't want to spoil their fun; wouldn't want to drive into them or hit them.'

"'Absolutely old boy', said Max. 'We can pace ourselves so they don't get upset, seeing us behind them'.

"Since Max was being so agreeable, Jerry thought he'd better explain, 'You see my wife's playing with my mistress.'

"'What a coincidence,' said Max.

When the uproarious laughter died down, Matthew, renowned for his own capacity to scatter the people playing in front to the four winds, continued to praise the excellent relationships between the girls and boys of Bisley Heath.

Rosie rolled her eyes at Impey, who glanced at Dodger to see his reaction, but he seemed preoccupied with something else. Her eyes dropped to his hands. As she expected, he was involved in his own joke, slipping an ornate jewelled bracelet off Rosie's wrist, a complicated manoeuvre because any minute now she'd be putting her hands together to clap the winners. He must have sensed she was looking in his direction because he turned to grin at her, whilst he distracted Rosie by pretending to knock the wine bottle over.

Impey was surprised Rosie did not see him slip the bracelet over the neck of the wine bottle, but obviously she was unaware of Dodger's tricks. She was engrossed in the announcements of the prize winners which Camilla, as Lady Captain, was now announcing. Maybe Rosie hoped to be amongst them, but it was not to be; she and Dodger were pipped to third place.

Impey's mouth turned down at the corners in a smile of consolation as Camilla moved on to the second prize. *Excitement over.* Not yet, as Camilla revved up to apologise that she was "Today's winner with the splendid assistance of Jules Challenger."

It seemed a popular win. The room resounded with applause as people clapped. Everyone smiled until Jules started to speak.

"Thank you." He beamed round the room when he accepted the vast red and black golf bag, which was the man's first prize. "I have so many thank yous. Firstly to Flick for fixing me up with the Lady Captain no less, who's been such a great partner." He turned graciously to her and gave her a peck on the cheek. "Her feminine intuition made everything possible."

"Then I must say what wonderful condition the course is in." He lowered his voice. "But without wishing to be churlish, I should say that in some ways, it is perhaps a little too wonderful."

Behind her Impey heard an indignant cough. She turned round to see a couple of men on the table there frowning.

"I expect you all know," Jules continued, "this could be the last one of these great competitions which have been going for thirty years. The club's financial situation puts its future in peril. The harsh fact is that we're over-borrowed and some of our creditors want their money back."

As Jules drew breath, Impey could hear irritated murmurings. *Not surprising; this is hardly the right time or place for all this.* She wondered why Matthew did not shut Jules up but he stood rooted to his place beside the glowing winner.

"I apologise for introducing a note of gloom on this happy occasion, but I want you all to know we can do something to boost Bisley Heath; we can make it a premier golf club again, listed once more in the top hundred, but to survive in the harsh commercial world, we will have to leave our genteel cocoon."

Impey winced at the sound of rumbling growls amongst whispered protests.

"We should not compete to make our course the most manicured place in the south." Jules voice rose. "Prizes for grooming land are not what we should be chasing. We should look another way. Our survival must be for us to be different. We should be a more natural course like the great St. Andrews." He paused to look round the room for a reaction but there was not a murmur to be hear.

"It would profit us to go further. An organic course is where the investment money will go now, but we can do better than that. Now I know many of you who've seen my vulture Cally on the course today may be saying quietly to yourselves, 'What is this mad fellow suggesting?' Let me put your minds at rest. I'm not suggesting filling the course with birds which are not native to Britain. I rescued Cally as a chick from a zoo which was going bust and reared her myself. She could not have been released into the wild because she would not have been accepted there, but she is an ambassadress for her species, the Asian vulture, which is endangered as are many British birds. My plans are to make the course a welcoming place for all our indigenous wild life."

"What does that mean exactly?" asked the loud gruff voice of an older man.

"To start with we have to encourage the right local plant life for heath land, like heather. That vast bush of useless rhododendrons at the ninth should go. What we need is more heather for the sand lizards which are being restored to our native heathland."

Jules swept round to pick up a glass off the table behind him. He seemed unaware that the stunned silence that greeted him was not entirely favourable. The large colourful bush of red rhododendrons had been planted to commemorate the life of that eminent diplomat and scholar, of Greek extraction, Andrew Nikos, whose memoirs Impey had edited. The rebuilt refreshments hut beside the bush, which screened the new lavatory alongside it, were both bequeathed by the same keen golfer.

"And of course there are other animals we should be encouraging like the dormouse."

"Mice," yelped an older lady amongst a guffaw of laughter from the men at her table.

"Naturally," said Jules good-naturedly, "there are also hedgehogs, pine martens and stoats which we should have here before they become almost extinct like the red squirrel.

A murmur of approval at the mention of the red squirrel obviously spurred Jules on to continue. "So many wonderful animals have been lost to our country. Think how great it would be if we could have the wild cat, the lynx back here at Bisley Heath. Then there's the bison." Jules paused to look round the room where his words were greeted with a stunned silence. "How wonderful it would be if these creatures roamed our heath." He waved his glass in the air. "I ask you all to toast the future of Bisley Heath as a wild course: the first and greatest wild golf course in the country."

To Impey's amazement, Matthew started waving his hands to encourage everyone to stand up.

As people gradually staggered to their feet, some frowning and others grimacing, Impey turned to Dodger and mouthed, "What do you think of Jules's ideas?"

"Nuts, but harmless," whispered Dodger. Then as he rose he thumped the table. "Oh hell!"

"What's the matter?" asked Impey.

"Nothing." Dodger shrugged, but his eyes pointed towards the middle of the table. Instead of empty wine bottles, there stood a tray with a coffee pot and cups. The bottle, over whose neck Dodger had placed Rosie's chunky bracelet, had vanished.

"Help," Impey spluttered, but the rest of her words were drowned in the scrape of Jack's chair which he pushed back to stand up.

"We're going." Jack's face was flushed. "Come on Rosie, we're not listening to any more rubbish from that rat."

9. The contentious watch-bracelet

I sure do pick the wrong friends.

Impey stared at the text from Rosie. "Did U C my ruby bracelet last night?"

She winced; she had taken the coward's way out the previous evening and said nothing at the time. *Not my business if Dodger's party trick went wrong.* However impoverished he might be at this moment, he would never steal Rosie's bracelet. He'd done this trick before at parties – he'd remove a bit of jewellery from someone's body, a necklace usually, and, especially if the victim was a girl he was interested in, return it with a charming smile. He'd probably only wanted to divert the focus from Jules.

Rosie knew Dodger was a magician, but was she aware that taking and returning jewellery was one of his games?

Impey crunched on her toast whilst she eyed her mobile glinting on the work surface beside her chipped Bunnikins breakfast plate. Using the cream plate with its pretty design with rabbits dressed like people leading innocent old-fashioned lives like having picnics in woodland glades, was a comforting reminder of her childhood. No one in the cosy Bunnikins world of crockery played stupid tricks on each other which were likely to end in tears. She stared at her silver mobile. The question was whether to ring Rosie or Dodger.

"What bracelet?" replied Dodger when she asked him in the least accusatory tone she could manage, whether he had seen Rosie's bracelet.

"The one she was wearing; I thought it ended up hanging over the neck of the wine bottle which the waiter took away."

"Did it? Well I suppose you'd better ask the kitchen then." His distracted sounding voice floated into her ear. "Our staff is very honest. Someone will put it into lost property."

"It shouldn't be my problem," said Impey, infuriated, "you took the bally thing off her wrist."

"Are you going to tell her that?"

"I might well." Impey pursed her lips angrily as she pressed the red finish button on her machine.

Of course she wouldn't. Angry though she was with Dodger, she understood the *blame the messenger* syndrome well enough to know that were she to incriminate Dodger in the loss of the bracelet, Rosie would be cross with her – she'd be bound to say *if only you'd agreed to play with Ned Cordrey, it wouldn't have happened.* .

Easy for Rosie to suggest that a golf playing vet would be Impey's ideal mate, but like all too many married people, she'd forgotten that important instinct which pulls you to someone in the first place, that chemistry when the animal inside you draws you toward or warns you off a person. Ned was fun and he did share Impey's passion for animals, but to spend four hours in the same four as him with the other two being married, at a Ladies' Invitation event, even if he was playing with Rosie, meant they'd be paired in a sense, which was not what she wanted.

After a few moments thought over what to text, she tapped into her mobile back to Rosie, "Yes, I'm sure you were wearing a bracelet."

She mustn't get involved; she had work to do. Her interview with Tarquin had moved her, not forward but laterally. She'd acquired more background, but she had nothing to pin the figurehead's desecration on someone, which was what Jules wanted. To progress she needed to do more groundwork. Before she visited Jules' third wife she must know more about Roxanne, the woman who'd taken Flick's place.

She reached for her tooth-marked handbag which sat on the kitchen work surface. *I should have asked Jules to buy me another one.* Inside was the club's leather-covered diary with all the members' telephone numbers on the back pages. Maybe she should ring Flick. Her hand faltered before she dipped into the bag as she caught a nail on the silver clasp. *Damn.* Her nails kept splitting. She put her finger up to her mouth to bite off the loose bit then managed to restrain herself. No. However frustrating this investigation was, she must not let it get to her. It was only work. And Flick would not be a good person to see or Jules would have suggested it. A much better person to see would be that Godmother woman Tarquin had mentioned. She should be a mine of information.

****

Deborah Cordrey gazed at the watch bracelet in delight. She twisted her bony wrist round to watch the colours on the two beautifully painted ceramic oblong panels either side of the centre square. There were the same birds painted on each of the five oblong enamel panels. It had to be hers. Every Chaika watch was unique because the pictures were hand painted.

She flicked her wrist around to see that the gold chain holding the panels was slightly darker than she remembered, but age could account for that difference. Whoever wore it last night couldn't have realised it was ten carat Russian gold or she'd have taken greater care of her jewellery. It was ten years since the bracelet had disappeared. Deborah pressed the tiny knob on the side of the middle picture of two large birds. The lid flew open to reveal the watch. Since it had stopped at a quarter past four presumably whoever had pinched it had been using it only as a bracelet, or maybe they had no idea there even was a hidden watch. More likely they'd be too lazy to wind it up daily.

She could hardly believe she'd got it back after all these years. Yet there it was hanging over the neck of a wine bottle when she'd walked into the kitchen after the meal of the Ladies Invitation to men. Dan the head chef had no idea how it had arrived amongst the empties standing on a side table. One of the waiters must have picked it up off a tables when they cleared up the bottles, probably along with the odd surplus paper napkin used to carry a warm plate away from the serving table. He'd pulled a face when Deborah had said she would like to know on which table the bottle had stood, though he did suggest that, if he looked through his records he might possibly, at another time when he was not so busy, be able to tell her which members had bought that particular claret, but he knew more than one person in the dining room had chosen it. Since neither he nor any other staff evinced the slightest interest in the jewellery, Deborah had scooped it over the top of the bottle and dropped it into her own handbag.

Her only upset over this retrieval was Ned's reaction. She supposed that was the prerogative of grown-up children, the right to criticise their parents, but she wished he wouldn't be so critical. He was horrified she'd picked up the bracelet. Her protest that she could see nothing wrong in taking back what was rightfully hers, led to his question as to how she could possibly know or prove it had once belonged to her.

Not that easily, she'd admitted; she had no receipt for the bracelet, but she was sure this was hers. She'd been so thrilled when she'd found it unpacking Monty's suitcase after a business trip he'd made to Uglich in Russia where the famous Chaika watch factory was. He'd said he'd chosen it *specially* for her.

Maybe the thief had not even realised the ornate little painting of elegant white birds on the red background covered a watch. She was sure the bracelet must have been stolen from her. The only snag in this reasoning was that she could not remember ever wearing it to the club. Much as she hated the idea, after searching high and low for the bracelet all over the kitchen and in both bathrooms, she'd come to the reluctant conclusion it must have been purloined by a cleaner or even a visitor to her own house.

Ned said that was no excuse for her to steal the bracelet back. It would only cause trouble, he insisted, for Dan if for no one else.

That did worry her. Since she persuaded the club to take on Dan as a junior chef during her stint as Lady Captain twelve years ago, she would hate to cause problems for him. No one ever talked about it now, but at the time plenty of members had been appalled when it leaked out that he'd been in the juvenile courts and once received an antisocial behaviour order. Some said ominously that if he'd applied to become a member the club would have turned him down because the constitution forbade offenders joining, and what was different about his being a member of the staff?

She'd explained that Dan had the best references from a friend of hers who was a prison visitor. It had helped that her friend was, like Deborah herself, a magistrate, but she had still met with tough opposition from the men's committee. It was only when they'd agreed to Dan's cooking a trial meal that stomachs overcame prejudice and Dan was given a trial period as a junior chef at the club. Since then his promotion to chief of catering meant his tall lanky figure clothed in traditional chef's white attire with a striped apron flapping around his long legs was a welcome sight. Now he'd become an award winning chef, and was known all over the county for his delicious meals, there shouldn't be problems over anything he did, but Ned's words made her uncomfortable. – Some people had long memories.

"What on earth were you doing in the kitchen?" Her son demanded.

"I had to go and congratulate Dan on the meal," Deborah replied.

"Wasn't that the job of the Captain?"

"Yes, but Matthew Lawson is so gauche. He made some dreadful joke and completely ignored the tradition of thanking the catering staff for their efforts."

"Maybe he reckons if they're paid they shouldn't need thanks," said Ned caustically.

"That's not the point darling. Staff need to be appreciated, especially when they've stayed late on a Saturday night. You might not realise it dear, but there are plenty of golf clubs in Surrey that would like to poach Dan. He's done miracles for the club's food."

Yet Deborah knew she was on to a loser.

She feared Ned was a trifle jealous. After his father's death he'd been furious when she'd given some of Monty's possessions to Dan, but they were only things Ned would never use, like one of his old guns. She was glad to show her trust in the young man, who promised faithfully he would only shoot clay pigeons or the odd rabbit.

Whatever Ned said, the club was lucky to have Dan's services. Last night's pie, which Dan managed to do it at a very reasonable cost to the ladies, was delicious. Pity Matthew didn't appreciate that, but Deborah wasn't surprised. He'd laughed cynically once when she had said how clever Dan was to find free-range organic rabbits with such a good flavour. When she'd pointed out the Bisley Heath rabbit pie was known all over Surrey, Matthew had pursed his lips and said, "I'll bet."

She hadn't mentioned the dish last night to Ned because he was nearly a vegetarian, though he would eat poultry. Maybe he was cross because she'd rung him late at night, not that ten o'clock was late for a night person like him. Perhaps he was with a girl friend and didn't want to be disturbed.

She sighed as she dropped the bracelet into a cut glass dish on her kidney-shaped dressing table. Probably she confided in him too much, but as the only child he was the closest person to her since Monty's death a couple of years ago. Ned hadn't liked her playing in the Ladies Invitation with Chiz Batten whom Ned insisted was a womaniser, but at least he was fun to play with and his wife didn't mind. "Gets him out of my hair" she said.

Maybe if Ned would get married he'd be less difficult. She didn't want to lose him or for him to prefer another woman, but she yearned for grandchildren. In the past she hadn't worried that he was an only child; she hadn't particularly wanted more children. With her golf and her voluntary work as well as being the wife of a high maintenance husband like Monty, her life was full to over-flowing.

Only now Ned had left home and she'd had to retire from the bench did she feel the chill air of loneliness creeping around her at Vermont House. Being without grandchildren left a social gap too. In between the hands of afternoon Bridge with the girls, they chatted about their grandchildren; it was galling to have nothing to say.

In her younger days people were always turning to her for help. Her sharp mind and legal degree meant she was useful. She pursed her lips as she caught sight of her well-contoured face in the mirror on her dressing table; she knew she was admired although she made a point of being modest about her appearance.

That was why Ned's condemnation was so painful. Although she had great sympathy for society's have-nots, stealing was anathema to her. She recognised she'd been lucky that the small legacy her grandparents left her meant she'd never had to go out to work, but that did not mean life had been easy for her.

Monty was never able to hold down a job. She was forever having to give dinner parties and subtly organise gatherings to effect introductions or to cajole his various employers or work associates into continuing to do business with him; she'd had to put up with being patronised by his one long term boss, the ghastly Grace Deer for years. Grace called Monty her chief executive, although she used him as a glorified personal assistant. Deborah banished the word 'escort' which buzzed in her mind's ear.

Thank goodness Ned finished his veterinary training. At least he had a profession even if he was tarred with his father's brush of intolerance. She used to defend Monty to her friends by saying it was his *high standards*, which was what she now said of Ned, when she had to admit to friends that he'd changed his veterinary practice again. Sometimes she did wonder if he wasn't a little too critical of others.

She was relieved they'd been in agreement at the weekend over the Captain's decision to take the treasurer's job away from Jack Metcalfe, which they both thought rather harsh. Jack was such a nice man who'd done a huge amount of voluntary work for the club, doing the accounts and sitting on the committee. Borrowing three hundred pounds for a couple of days hardly amounted to serious embezzlement. A couple of hours of Jack's work would cost more than that and he'd done hundreds of hours of unpaid work for the club.

From what she could gather, that was typical of Jack's generosity. – Or so Ned suggested when he returned from his holiday in Turkey with the Metcalfes a couple of months ago. She'd had high hopes then, that he might have linked up with the Dalrymple girl, whom that nice young Rosie Metcalfe had invited to join the holiday party too, but it hadn't worked out. As soon as she'd mentioned her attack of shingles, he'd said he must come home to look after her. She was pleased and sorry at the same time.

Even if he'd been able to stay on she doubted Ned would pair up with the girl. "Oh her". Her son had puffed out the words and made some vulgar vet type quip about Impey being the sort of dog which never came into season, but that was Ned. Lovely available girls never aroused his interest.

A picture of a skinny red-headed girl came into her mind. Strange how a funny little tomboy like Roxanne had bewitched Ned, but to be fair, she told herself, the girl did share Ned's passion for animals. Lots of people had told her Impey liked animals too. So maybe there was still a chance he might fall for her. After all miracles did happen. She'd got her Chaika watch back.

10. Angst with Rosie

When someone presses your doorbell for five seconds presumably he or she wants you urgently. The sound of the bell drilled through Impey's head. At seven o'clock in the evening it could not be the postman. Nor was it likely to be someone delivering a parcel, especially as she was not aware she had ordered anything recently. She leapt out of the bath and flung on a towelling dressing gown. Maybe she had ordered something on line which she'd forgotten.

She wondered vaguely as she tore downstairs, whether she should install a peephole in the front door for times like this. Her cottage, the end of a row of small Victorian terraced houses, was not isolated but she was not over-looked. The walls were thick too. If someone forced his way into her place to molest her, she might not be heard however hard she screamed. Before her foray into detective work such an alarming thought would not have crossed her mind, but this evening, as a precaution, she looked through her sitting room window to see who was at the front door.

To her relief she saw Dodger. His fist was clenched as though he was about to bang on her front door with it. Probably he assumed the door bell had not worked. He must have sensed her presence in the adjacent room because he jumped over the flowerbed to rap on the picture window. "Let me in," he mouthed.

Embarrassed by her attire, or rather lack of it, Impey made her way to the front door. "Okay I'm coming," she said as she opened the door, "as you can probably see I was in the bath."

Head poked forward, Dodger strode into the hall. With his left hand he rubbed his forehead, "We've got problems."

"What do you mean?" Impey asked, not sure whether to be relieved or slightly offended he appeared not to notice she was so scantily dressed.

"The bracelet," he said, "it's got form."

"What on earth do you mean?" Impey gestured at the sitting room door. "Listen, why don't you go in there and pour yourself a drink, whilst I go and get some clothes on."

Without waiting for his reply, she dashed out of the room and upstairs to her bedroom where she grabbed a pair of jeans and an ancient pink tee shirt which she pulled on. When she arrived back in her sitting room she found Dodger pacing across it.

"It's damned awkward," he said.

Impey walked over to an oak corner cupboard which hung on her walls. She picked out a couple of glasses, a bottle of red wine and a corkscrew which she handed to him. "For goodness sake open this, pour us both a drink so we can sit down and discuss things calmly." She put the wine goblets down on a mahogany butler's table she'd recently picked up in a junk shop.

Dodger frowned as he pulled the cork out of the bottle. "You're not going to be very happy when you hear my news, however good this vintage." He looked at the bottle. "Two thousand and six Merlot is far too classy for what I have to tell you."

"Spill it out."

Dodger poured some wine into one of the glasses which he handed to her before he served himself. "Cheers." He clinked his glass against hers. "We might as well celebrate you being so pleased to see me before what I have to say wrecks everything."

"For goodness sake get on with it. I don't what you're on about: how can a bracelet have form?"

"Rosie was wearing a stolen bracelet."

"You mean you pinched it." Impey laughed.

"No. I mean Deborah Cordrey. Do you know her?"

Impey nodded. "Yes Ned, the vet's mother."

"She says the bracelet belongs to her."

"No way," Impey shook her head. "Rosie's had it for ages, well ever since I've known her and that's over five years."

"Yes, but Deborah says her bracelet's been gone for ages. She's absolutely certain it's hers."

"How on earth did she get hold of it?"

Dodger's head shook as he blew out of his mouth like a horse about to stamp its hoof. "The wretched woman went into the kitchen. I don't know whether you realised that one of the waiters came and took the bottle away with the bracelet over it. Obviously I simply wanted to help make the party go. You must admit things were a bit sticky. I thought I'd provide a bit of light entertainment."

Impey took a gulp of wine. "It's turned out to be rather heavy entertainment if you ask me. Rosie's terribly upset about the loss of her bracelet. It's one of her favourite bits of jewellery."

"Yeah, like it was one of Deborah's."

"Deborah Cordrey must be making a mistake. What on earth was she doing in the kitchen anyway?"

"Well, as you know, Matthew Lomax made a bit of a hash of his Captain's speech, forgetting to show his appreciation for the kitchen staff, so Deborah decided she

106

would put things right by going into the kitchen to thank Dan. When she was there she saw the bracelet, which I gather is actually a watch, hanging over the neck of a bottle."

"She had no right to take it," said Impey. "That's theft surely."

"Not if it was hers in the first place," said Dodger. The wine in his glass swirled dangerously near the top as he still paced up and down the room.

"For goodness sake sit down." Impey flopped down on to the sofa and patted it. She put her glass down on an occasional table in front of her, dropped her elbows on to the table and sunk her head down on to the palm of her hand, whilst she rubbed her forehead with her fingers for a couple of seconds before she looked up. "This is a ridiculous situation. We know the bracelet belongs to Rosie. Deborah Cordrey is making a frightful mistake."

"Not according to her son."

"Ned?" Impey wrinkled her nose. "Do you really think he'd know one bit of his mother's jewellery from another?"

"Certainly seemed to, I understand from Dan. I don't know Ned, except by sight, so I didn't speak to him myself. I simply asked Dan what had happened to the bracelet and he told me that Deborah Cordrey snatched it off the bottle before he could stop her. She told him it was hers. Obviously I asked Dan to get it back which he thought would be bloody awkward, but he said he'd ask Ned."

Impey wrinkled her nose. "And Ned asked why he should give back something that belonged to his mother?"

"No apparently he was very reasonable and said he'd talk to her, but Deborah is adamant that the bracelet's hers and is insisting that whoever was wearing it must have stolen it." He gave a deep sigh as he sunk down on the sofa next her. "So what do we do?" he asked helplessly.

"Buy her a new one?"

Dodger shook his head. "That's the point. Even if I could afford to, I couldn't without going to Russia. According to Ned, or rather Ned via Dan, that watch bracelet is unique. It was made in the Chaika factory in Russia and brought home for Deborah by her late husband. It's irreplaceable." He put his arm round Impey's shoulders and looked pleadingly into her eyes. "I really don't know what to do."

For a moment Impey relaxed in his grasp. All she wanted to say was *Don't worry. I'm in this with you. I'll do anything to help*. But she pushed back the impulse and found herself saying in a small nervous voice she hardly recognised, "I suppose one of us will have to talk to Rosie."

"Would you do it?" Dodger hugged her. "I think it would come so much better from you, woman to woman."

Impey grimaced. How could she refuse? She wanted to be close to Dodger, be in his confidence, help him out in any way. "All right."

"Great." He gave her another hug and drained his glass before he glanced at his watch. "Got to be going; got a meeting. Let me know how you get on."

****

The following morning Impey called at Rosie's house. To be as casual as possible she went round to the back door to find Rosie washing up in her vast kitchen. Somehow, even in this mundane role, without makeup, wearing a baggy white tee shirt over her dark blue jeans which clung with a tight fit to her enviably long slim legs, she looked elegant.

Her wide mouth broke into its usual welcoming smile at the sight of Impey whom she pressed to come in for a cup of coffee.

Brushing away the desire to ask Rosie where she'd got her jeans and, hopefully, learn they came from some chain store Impey could afford to visit, she explained about the demise of the bracelet.

"You can't be serious," laughed Rosie. She ran her hand through her cropped spikey blonde hair which, even though she was growing out the style, still managed to look stylish. "You mean that old trout insists my bracelet-watch belongs to her."

"That's about it," sighed Impey.

"This is all Dodger's fault," complained Rosie. She flipped a white switch on the white tiled kitchen wall down with a jerk. "If only you hadn't brought him to the game and asked Ned Cordrey instead."

"Actually," Impey choked the word out with an ironic half laugh, "that could have been much worse. Imagine what would have happened if Deborah Cordrey had come over to our table and seen you wearing her bracelet."

"Oh come on," exclaimed Rosie angrily, "I'd have explained it was mine of course."

"Yes, and you think she'd have been too well bred to mention it looked remarkably like hers?"

"Probably not. She wasn't too well bred to pinch it off a bottle in the club kitchen where she had no place to be anyway."

"Well she thought it had been snitched from her," said Impey awkwardly, feeling they were going round in circles.

"She thought wrong." Rosie spooned coffee into a couple of mugs. She poured in some boiling water before adding milk. "And Dodger will simply have to get the bracelet back from her; it's his job."

It took Impey five minutes to convince Rosie that Deborah did not intend to return the watch-bracelet. On the contrary, she was on the war path to find out who had taken the watch-bracelet from her. It would help, Impey ventured to suggest, if Rosie could find the receipt she had when she bought it.

Rosie gazed blankly at her. "Do you keep receipts for things you bought ten years ago?" She asked aggressively. When Impey shook her head, Rosie added, "I thought not."

"You need proof you bought the watch." Impey, bit back the words *I'm only trying to help,* as Rosie's face reddened with fury. "You should have a box with the jeweller's name on it."

"I don't because we bought the bracelet second-hand. That doesn't mean it didn't come from a perfectly respectable shop, even if that shop doesn't exist any more."

Impey sat down on a pine chair beside Rosie's kitchen table. She twiddled her mug of coffee in her hands. "But it does mean the bracelet could have been stolen from Deborah Cordrey. After all it's not as though you would ever have been to her house."

"Yes, I have, a few times years ago. She gave a party for all the new girls the year I joined the club because she was Lady Captain that year – and then she discovered that I knew how to work a computer so she asked me to go round a few times to teach her how to work hers."

"Was she with you all the time?"

"Impey, how could you ask such a thing?" shouted Rosie. "Of course she bally well wasn't every second. I went to the loo on my own, but I didn't poke round her bedroom looking for something to nick, even though she took my services for granted and didn't pay me anything."

Impey sipped her coffee. She had no doubt Rosie would ever steal anything. The trouble was would others? With Rosie's husband's reputation sullied over the borrowed cash, or as some saw it, purloined, from the club, some people might imagine Rosie would pick up jewellery she fancied if she saw it lying about. She tried to smile comfortingly across the table at Rosie, but though she guessed Jack's misdemeanour would be forgotten in time, buried in old committee minutes, she could not deny its ghost still pranced around the club now. The event of three weeks ago hung in the air ready to be plucked down for conversation.

Unfair though it was, Rosie not Dodger would suffer from his silly prank. Deborah, an ex captain with many close friends, would doubtless already be telling her chums how lucky it was the bracelet had surfaced in the Bisley Heath kitchen. How, Impey wondered could she possibly persuade Rosie that she urgently needed to talk to Deborah before the former Lady Captain launched a full scale investigation into the re-appearance of her watch in the Bisley Heath clubhouse.

"This is all Dodger's fault. I wish you'd never asked him to play with us," said Rosie through gritted teeth. She glared at Impey, "he must sort this out."

"If Dodger could get the bracelet back for you he would," Impey assured her, "but short of breaking into the Cordrey's house, there's no way. Dodger's deliberately kept quiet about who was wearing the bracelet, but Deborah's determined to find out."

111

Rosie rolled her eyes, "She would – I'm beginning to wish the damn thing had been properly stolen so I could claim for it on insurance. God I'm furious with Dodger; he's really trouble Impey. You should give him up."

"There's nothing to give up." Impey tried to keep a wistful note out of her voice.

"I can't think why you like him, a thicket of a man with a cauliflower ear. He's messed everything up."

"He's really sorry about it and so am I."

"You're mad to have anything to do with him Impey. He's very in with that Jules guy who's bought the house next to the club, the one whose socking great bird picked up Jack's ball. You know he's been married four times."

"Well he's very charming."

"Sneaky people often are. He put the finger on Jack over that money." Rosie took a gulp of coffee before she banged her mug back down on the table.

"Why should he do that?"

"I don't know, but Jack's very suspicious of his motives. You know who's been co-opted on to the committee instead of Jack I suppose?"

Impey shook her head. She did not like to admit how totally uninterested she was in the club's administration.

"Flick Challenger, Jules's ex-wife."

"What as treasurer?"

"No, she's become the social events person instead of Adam Scrivenor, the guy who used to do social stuff. Now he's the treasurer. Jack's absolutely gutted."

Rosie pointed to three bulky folders full of foolscap paper which were stacked on the dark shiny granite work-surface of her kitchen units. They represented, she told Impey, a mere fraction of the work her husband had accomplished in his time as treasurer, when he'd shared responsibility for improvements to the course and the clubhouse.

"All he sees now is the work he's done going down the drain. He says Jules is a scheming manipulative bastard, after power in the club for his own ends."

Impey wriggled uncomfortably on her pine chair. Something about this accusation tallied with Jules's claim he was *going to save the club*. "Jules isn't on the committee. I don't see how he'd be able to wangle through anything much, even with Flick's support, that's if she wants anything to do with her very ancient ex."

Rosie sank down on to a pine chair beside her large square kitchen table. Elbows on the table, she sank her head into her hands; she was a picture of dejection. Then she raised her head to cry, "You just don't get it Impey, or maybe you just don't care if everything Jack's worked for to improve the course and its facilities is likely to go down the drain if Jules gets his way. After all, you're the one who's mad about animals, so probably you'll love it if Jules turns Bisley Heath golf club into a sodding wildlife park."

"So people keep saying, but Jules can't do that; he doesn't have the power."

"Oh but he does, Impey. He's picked up a huge stake in the club by buying our debt or mortgage or whatever you like to call it from the titchy building society we owed money to for all the repairs and improvements we made to the clubhouse."

"But Jules has still got to get the club's committee to agree to any changes he wants to make and Flick's only got a social position."

"Yes, but she'll be a Jules supporter. The key person is Adam Scrivenor, the new treasurer. He goes back a long way with Jules. Jack's discovered they were childhood friends and Adam used to work for Jules."

"That doesn't mean he's keen on wildlife."

"He likes that damn wolf. After a match the other day he told some dreadful story about how Jules used to bring the wolf into his office. Can you believe it? The guys who worked there were encouraged to take the wolf out with them when they went debt collecting. He, I mean Adam, actually laughed when he said people paid up pretty damn quick if he arrived on their doorstep with a wolf."

11. Impey breaks into Grace's house

Impey mulled over Rosie's feelings. *She's gone over the top because of Jack's dismissal and the problems with the bracelet. Jules talks about saving the club, not destroying it. He won't be planning to turn it into a zoo-type wild animal park; he probably only wants to secure our land for small native Surrey wildlife.* Since Jules had told her Caesar had a heart condition, and was not likely to live much longer, his plans would not be based on his elderly wolf. Jules would be concerned about the decrease of hedgehogs, newts and the rare Natterjack toads as well as birds.

Rosie was apoplectic when Impey suggested birds of prey would not cause too much trouble and that they might even be useful keeping down the rabbit population. *Did Impey not realise Jules sold balls his vulture picked up, including the one purloined from Jack, for charity?*

When Jack had complained to the club's secretary about this outrageous activity, apparently Miles, a neat slim dark-haired young man, who was new to the post, admitted apologetically that Jules had mentioned the bird to him before the Ladies Invitation competition. Jules had also pointed out that since the club allowed dogs to accompany players on the course, he assumed a well-behaved bird flying overhead would not cause a problem. In the circumstances, Jules now having a large stake in the club, the secretary assumed it was politic to agree.

Rosie fumed over the naivety of Miles. If only he'd had the position longer he would have realised that although Jules was a long-standing member with his name printed on more than one honours board, his parents had left the club under a cloud. Jack was digging amongst the older members' reminiscences to see what he could unearth.

Impey sighed over the bread and cheddar cheese ploughman's lunch she ate in her small sitting room whilst Robert Peston's nasal voice, reminding her of the way Ned Cordrey spoke, delivered a homily on the economy from the television opposite her. She'd been tempted to suggest Jack rang her uncle George who, now in his late seventies, was a long-standing club member, but resisted it. George, a former army Brigadier, would be bound to be so appalled by Jack's misadventure with the club's cash that he'd probably refuse to speak to him.

He might tell Impey, unless he considered it *hush hush*, as he would term it. More relevant to her, George might give her useful background before she visited Jules's godmother this afternoon. Impey liked to be well-prepared for interviews. Any information George gave her would help. Since Grace Deer had built up a huge computer software business from nothing, she was bound to be a shrewd cookie whom it would be difficult to joggle into any indiscretions.

Fortunately George, though his post prandial nap was disturbed, was happy to give Impey the low down on the Challengers. "Thought they were treated a bit shabbily actually," he honked down the phone, "lot of snobbery about in those days. Know what I mean?"

"No. What did they do?"

"Nothing really. – It's what they were; they were jewellers."

"That's awful. You're telling me they were drummed out of the club because they were in the wrong trade."

"No, it's not as simple as that. Out of their second-hand business they moved into pawn-broking. As times were tough in the seventies, various members used the Challenger shop to raise a bit of cash and that led to trouble, suggestions

Faye Challenger was touting for business in the ladies cloakroom"

"So the Challengers were asked to leave?"

"Not in so many words. There was just a bit of an atmosphere because they were seen to do well out of other people's misfortunes. And they were rather showy which in those days didn't go down terribly well – not like razzmatazz does today."

"Pawn-broking; now that is interesting. D'you know if they're still practising today?"

"Nah, haven't seen the Challengers for ages. Played with old Jeremy some years ago in some do. Forget where but possibly one of the posh W clubs nearby." This was George's own appellation for the smarter local clubs, Worplesdon, Woking and West Hill. "Now I come to think of it, maybe it was Foxhills."

"So someone or more than one person must have liked them enough to put them up for whatever club they joined."

"Yeah well Jeremy is a nice fellow. Bought a bit of stuff second-hand from him myself. Not quite so keen on Faye so..."

You wouldn't ask them to dinner. "That's wonderful, so helpful, thanks awfully," interrupted Impey quickly, not wanting to hear more,

"Watch it with young Jules," continued her uncle. "Some of the boys are say he's trotting around the course with that damn wolf, and my pal Giles, who farms, says he saw him at a country livestock market enquiring about wild boars. We certainly don't want them here making a damn mess all over the course."

"Giles," queried Impey, "you don't mean Giles Hobbs, Tarquin Hobbs the famous sculptor's father."

"Toby's the boy's name," snorted George. "Some stupid woman got influence over him and told him he'd never make it called Toby, so he changed it to some name he picked out of a comic. Frightfully upsetting for poor Giles and Mary."

"They must be pleased he's such a success as Tarquin though?"

"Hardly, the stuff he's making now I gather. Used to do some spectacular work. Saw a wonderful bronze he did years ago of a young girl with a wolf cub. Quite amazing."

"Was that the wolf Jules has now?"

"Heaven knows. As I said that mad boy seems to be moving on to wild pigs. He's..."

It had taken another ten minutes before Impey was able to extricate herself from George's telephonic grasp as he launched into a detailed description of the damage wild boars had made on the exceedingly smart Pevero course, in the best part of Sardinia, where the 'flaming creatures' had dug holes. "Caused no end of rows over whether you can pick your ball out of a hole or not," George grumbled. "Golf rules only cover holes dug by a 'burrowing animal' but what the hell's a boar? Anyway we've done without them in this country for three hundred years so I can't see what use they'd be now."

I wonder if Jules knows what he's getting into, mused Impey as she drove towards the exclusive Gong Hill Drive in Frensham where Grace Deer lived. She had tried to persuade her uncle that any grazing animal's dung was likely to be rich in nutrients which would benefit the earth, but the notion had not appealed to George. He'd shuddered at the thought of excrement on the golf course. Jules might not think it mattered, but the members certainly would.

Some members were already furious Jules felt he was in a position to say how the club should be run. He hadn't been diplomatic when he gave his thank you speech after the invitation dinner. Impey decided to ask Grace whether he'd always had the capacity to antagonise people? She'd known him since he was a child; she must have witnessed other people's reactions to him over many years.

Her one storey dwelling, too grand to be termed a 'bungalow', stood at the end of a shingle gravelled drive which opened out into a semi-circle outside her house. A single garage was part of the long low red brick structure.

Impey parked the Jazz and walked up to the front porch where a large letter wrapped round some others, kept in place with an elastic band, was stuck in the letter box. She frowned. *How odd. Looks as though no one's in.* She pressed a bell by the side of the door. When no one arrived to open it, she tried again to no avail. Five minutes later after a couple more rings on the bell there was still no answer.

Damn. She's forgotten I'm coming. Impey had arranged this meeting three weeks ago, the day after she'd seen Tarquin. Though Grace had not been excited about seeing her, she was perfunctory rather than unwilling. She did not sound at all like the sort of person to forget an appointment. The possibility she'd wasted petrol in driving here, as well as paying extra to get her linen charcoal suit cleaned in a day to wear to come here, irritated Impey so much she felt like kicking the door.

Perhaps she's deaf. No, she'd sounded far too alert not to have some hearing system installed in home if hearing was a problem, but Grace was elderly. *Perhaps I'm being unfair – she might have fallen and hurt herself.*

Impey made her way round the side of the house to the back. In the middle of a smooth velvety lawn lay a neat circular arrangement of flower beds with an array of beautiful pink and white roses in the centre. She walked on to a paved terrace where she rattled the brass handle of a long transparent glass door, through which she saw a tidy living room furnished with polished antiques. In frustration she rapped on the window before she made her way round the other side of the building.

Here, behind the garage, was obviously the utility room, with an unfastened casement window wide open, though a door to the side garden was locked. Impey poked her head through the space to see a washing machine which looked as though it was full of clothes. She glanced round the room. On the white door of the tumble drier was a dark reddish brown smear which looked like blood.

Do I go in? Before the impulse could go cold, Impey dropped her handbag through the window, wincing as she realised her mobile and her tape-recorder might be damaged as the bag hit the stone floor. Then, with her hands on the window-frame, she pulled herself up and climbed over into the small room.

On closer inspection she thought the stain on the tumble drier was definitely blood, but that did not mean anything. Grace or someone else could have pricked her finger on the clasp of a skirt or some other sharp edge.

It was more likely, if some accident had befallen Grace, that she would be lying unconscious in some upstairs room. Feeling rather embarrassed, more like an intruder than someone with help in mind, Impey left the utility room to find herself in a large square kitchen. Everything looked clean and tidy. Nothing was amiss here, except there was a glow from a button on the built-in electric oven which suggested it was switched on. Presumably Grace had left something cooking for her return, surmised Impey, until she opened the oven door to find nothing inside the oven.

She must be suffering from some kind of memory lapse to go out leaving the oven on. Impey strolled round the large tidy kitchen. Everything else seemed to be as she would expect, except that the black lid on the stainless steel dustbin was slightly raised, obviously not shut properly. Poking out of it was a tiny bit of leather.

Impey tapped the dustbin lid open. Lying on top of the rubbish was a battered leather handbag. Or was it just an old one? Impey picked up the taupe coloured bag. Now she held it in her hand she could see it was tattered in places, though strangely it did not look old. It was definitely a fashionable design.

There was a strange smell about the bag too. Impey put it to her nose to sniff. *Animal?* How odd. This close to her eyes, she could see huge teeth marks all over it, as though some large dog had chewed it. Yet other bits of the bag looked too new for Grace to be ready to dispose of it, unless she had been disappointed with the purchase, despite the bag being such an expensive brand. Obviously for a millionairess the decision to abandon a thousand pound plus bag came more lightly than to someone like Impey, but it was odd nonetheless.

She unclipped the bag's gold clasp. There was no purse inside and the pocket for a mobile was empty, but there was some makeup. Impey drew out an old-fashioned gold compact case with ornate markings on the lid which she flipped open. It was full of loose powder. Delving further inside the bag Impey found an expensive brand of dark pink lipstick. She pulled off the lid to find the stick was still so shaped at the tip that the owner could have used it only once or twice. *No this bag was not destined for the bin.*

On impulse she decided to take it with her. It might be significant. Plastic supermarket bags hung from a hook on the wall. Impey plucked a Waitrose bag off and dropped the handbag into it, as a precaution in case anyone who saw her leaving the house thought she was a thief.

It had been warm in the kitchen with the oven on but it was warmer outside in the hall. Impey undid her linen jacket and was about to go upstairs when there was a peal on the door bell. In a moment of excitement, she hoped perhaps Grace had returned, having forgotten something, including her front door keys. However, as Impey stepped towards the front door, it opened and a young woman entered the house.

"Hi! Who are you?" asked a stocky woman who wore a calf-length mauve cotton skirt, a violet check shirt and a toning headband over her straight chin length brownish blonde hair. She was, Impey reckoned, probably in her mid-forties, about ten years older than herself.

"Lorna Dalrymple." Impey thought she had better give her proper name, which sounded more dignified, since she was supposed to be here on business, when the other woman clearly had a key to Grace's property.

"Oh yes, you're a journalist aren't you. I think I've seen the odd thing you've written. I'm Sally Markham, by the way; I live a couple of doors away."

Had Sally not had such a look of serious concern on her face, Impey might have made a joke about herself not writing 'odd' articles. Instead she said, "Yes, I'm here to see Grace Deer."

"But she's not here." Worry rang in the rising pitch of Sally's voice. "I don't think she's been here for a few days."

"How strange. She arranged to see me today."

"Yes, it's most peculiar. We were meant to be playing bridge here three days ago and she wasn't in when we turned up. Obviously we thought she'd gone to someone else's house by mistake, but we couldn't get any answer from her mobile."

"Have you tried her since?"

"Yes repeatedly, but I only get the message service. That's why when your car turned up and stayed outside the door, I thought maybe you might know what had happened, whether she'd had a car accident or been admitted to hospital for some reason."

Impey looked at Sally blankly. Everything the other woman said made her feel more and more uneasy. A picture of the armless figurehead flashed into her mind. Jules had thought it was a warning about his relationship with Flick, that something bad would happen to her, but maybe it was about another woman in his life, his godmother.

Mentally she shook herself. *No. There's probably a good reason why Grace isn't here like a sudden medical thing which made her forget about the bridge game.* "Have you rung the hospital to ask if she's been admitted there?"

"No. I didn't really feel that was my place; I'm not a relative, not that Grace has ever spoken about any. She came here as refugee when she was a child you know."

"I didn't; I hoped to learn more about her today. I'm really interested in her godchildren, the boys she helped?"

"Them." Sally gave a scornful laugh. "What a bunch of takers. You know she had a hip replacement recently and none of them have been near her to help."

"I suppose they're all busy with their work," Impey said lamely. Something about the situation made her want to explore the house further. "Maybe we should ring the police to report Grace is missing."

"No, don't you worry," said Sally dismissively, "I'll do that after I've rung the hospital to make sure she isn't there."

"Will you let me know how she is please?" asked Impey. "I'd like to meet her when she's up to it." She hesitated, wanting to ask if she could look round in the meantime but Sally had obviously galvanised herself to take control.

"Now if you don't mind, I'd better get on with things." Sally opened the front door again.

"Thanks." *Better go before she asks me how I got into the house.* Impey gave a last glance round the hall before she left. *I wonder if she's right that Jules hasn't been here.* She could have sworn there were some golden brownish grey hairs on the carpet which looked as though they belonged to a wolf. *Maybe it's my imagination. Perhaps they're only dog's hairs.*

12. Flick's first committee meeting

Flick looked round the room. Let people complain it cost an arm and a leg to rebuild the clubhouse, part of which was creating a place upstairs the right size for committee meetings. It was worth it. The magnificent matt oak shelves she'd had fitted, filled with the great golf classic literature and leather-bound sheaths of club documents, showed the dignity of Bisley Heath. She was proud of her role in the planning group who'd created this room, but even prouder to be here as a committee member; now she was part of the club's history, the first woman to be on the committee in her own right.

They had the vast oak table, at which they sat on the matching dining chairs, when she'd attended the golf club committee meetings as Lady Captain a couple of years ago. Then she was a mere representative of the ladies section, expected by the Bisley Heath men to be more an observer than a participant.

Today her position was different, much stronger. The overall Captain, Matthew Lomax, had rung to ask whether she would agree to being co-opted on to the main committee. They'd chosen her to fill the space left by Jack Metcalfe's forced resignation. Well if they thought she was going to be as docile as she'd been a couple of years ago, they were mistaken.

Now she had this year's Lady Captain as back-up, not that the vast Camilla Wilmot would necessarily see it that way. She glanced at her friend sitting next her. Presumably Camilla thought her navy blue gabardine trouser suit looked official, but it was a terrible sartorial error. No large busted woman should ever wear a tailored jacket, let alone in regulation officer blue, unless she wanted to look comic.

Flick herself wore a figure-hugging dress in her favourite fuchsia pink, lightened by areas of cream, to celebrate her appearance as a truly independent female committee member. She refused to feel uncomfortable because the brightest colour amongst the men's sober suits and blazers was Malcolm's dull green sports jacket. She could rejoice; she had planned to stand for election at the next annual general meeting, but they had selected her in advance instead of either of the male candidates.

The passed-over guys had given her snide congratulations, which she reckoned she'd accepted gracefully. She wasn't going to be upset by their hints she owed her success to her relationship with Jules.

She glanced at her vivid pink nails which she'd varnished the previous night whilst she planned what she might say tonight. It was lucky Adam Scrivenor was already on the committee. He could slot into Jack's position as treasurer, leaving her to become the member responsible for social affairs, much more her scene.

Adam was droning on about last year's expenditure at this moment. Boring. She'd guessed he'd become an accountant. He was always the parsimonious one of Jules's old friends. He'd squint through the little round metal framed glasses he used to wear, to analyse the restaurant bill, to work out what everyone should pay, whilst the rest would have been happy to divide it equally between them. Anyway, all too often in her view, Jules picked up Adam's tab.

She wondered whether Adam would admit to his former friendship with Jules, when the time came to discuss Jules's involvement with the club, whatever that might be exactly. Jules hadn't come clean with her about all his plans at the ladies invitation. Typical Jules, he'd excited everyone around him with his ideas for an organic wildlife course without spelling out what this entailed.

Cally his new bird was a laugh though. How could Jules want such an ugly creature with a bald head and scraggy white feathers round her neck? The way he'd tamed her was a miracle. That adoring expression in the bird's huge dark eyes when she looked at Jules was weird too, so unbelievably reminiscent of the way real girls looked at him. Maybe Cally was the proof a big ugly bird could win a man's love by being subservient. One of her favourite authors said something like that recently in the Daily Mail.

Flick had been astounded at the way the vulture perched on Jules's trolley, her vast wings tucked into her side. You only realised how long her wingspan was when she soared into the air. Then she looked spectacular. Far from being any trouble she was useful. Jules said it was because a griffon vulture's eyesight was as powerful as any binoculars that she could find a ball anywhere.

"The Griffon Trust," said Adam coincidentally, jolting Flick into the present, although he had mumbled the word into the table in front of him, "have bought our debt from the Guild Bank, which bought the Cathedral Bank which was originally the National Cathedral Building Society, which bought the Surrey and Hants Building Society from whom we had our original re-mortgage to build the extension."

"Sounds absolutely mad to me," said Mark Sawyer, a large man in an old-fashioned check sports jacket, "like a demented nursery rhyme."

"That's what banking's become," growled Horace, his shock of white hair shaking as he banged the table with a gnarled fist. "There's no idea of service to people any more, it's all about pouncing on then and grabbing their money."

Adam raised his head. The corners of his mouth curled into a smile. Flick remembered the way his wide lips twisted into an ironic expression as his most attractive feature. His sense of humour was surprising in his circumstances, being the only child of a single mother, especially a mother like Patsy, whom Flick had confided in her friends was a "model of what not to become". The remark haunted her now Flick herself was the mother of a son with an absent father. She felt she should have been kinder about Patsy, who had an unfortunate facial tick, the result, rumour had it, of an abusive relationship. To support her son, Patsy, Flick remembered, worked for Grace Deer. According to Jules, she paid Adam's boarding school fees so she made the subservient Patsy work all the hours God sent.

"We have to be grateful to the Griffon Trust," said Adam, his tone suggesting the opposite. "We were dropping behind in our repayments to the bank."

"How come?" asked Mark. "I thought we were ring-fenced by the members."

"Well some have fallen off their perch," sighed Adam, his phraseology making Flick wonder if he'd got Cally on the brain, "whilst others simply can't afford to support us any longer. We've lost sixty-five members this year."

"And gained?" asked Horace.

"Fifteen," replied Adam.

"Does that include the five girls we've taken in?" asked Camilla. Normally so voluble, the large lady seemed strangely subdued in the presence of seven blokes. Her large blue eyes widened in apprehension as she glanced at Flick across the table with a silent plea to support her if there was any question of raising women's subscriptions to the same level as men's in the name of equality. Another rampant fear in the ladies section was that men might be allowed to play on Wednesdays, their hallowed ladies day. Since most younger men would be at work, the girls' worry was an invasion of older retired men.

Adam nodded, but to Flick's relief, did not raise these knotty issues as Horace barked suspiciously, "Does our debt changing hands make any difference to us?"

"It means whoever runs the Griffon Trust has a significant interest in our club," said Mark, the lean-faced lawyer, "and that man is Jules Challenger, but we should be all right because he's a long-term member of the club," he smiled at Flick, "and we now have a member of his extended family on the committee."

Flick gritted her teeth. *So that's why they wanted me on the committee, to parley with Jules. They must have thought my playing with him a couple of weeks ago meant something.* Her stomach fluttered. *Well maybe it did. After all Jules has grown up since we were married. He's mature as well as fun now.*

She wasn't sure how things stood between Jules and Adam, but felt instinctively from the way he leant backwards when Jules's name was mentioned, that his former hero-worship of her first husband was finished. Though what he said about Jules was measured, every time his name was mentioned, she thought Adam flinched.

"We split up a long time ago, though we're still good friends," she admitted, "but I don't see him that often." She smiled round the room at the assembled men. When none of them spoke, she added, "But, as you know, he has ideas for the club."

129

"Buying our debt can't give him carte blanche to dictate what happens here." Mark raised the sandy eyebrows on his clean-shaven face at the new treasurer.

Adam doodled some figures on the notepad in front of him. "We need to agree to re-negotiate the terms." Shaking his head slightly he continued, "The Griffon Trust has offered to extend our borrowing time so that we can implement some revenue raising projects at the club."

"And what might they be?" Horace raised his tufted white eyebrows as he pursed his lips suspiciously whilst he glanced round the room to ascertain who else was of like-mind.

"It's no secret that Jules is a wildlife enthusiast," replied Adam in a sardonic tone, "with somewhat unorthodox views on ecological course management."

"Ridiculous," barked Horace, his cheeks reddening at every word, "exactly what I knew you'd say. Last thing we want is wolves and wild boars rampaging all over Bisley Heath. I s'pose you know that idiot has been looking at wild boars, though what on earth ecological use they would be God only knows."

Despite his calmness, the edge to his tone gave Flick the impression Adam's words were not intended to pacify the other committee members. "I gather the way they rotate the earth with their trotters forms a natural method of tining the ground."

"Bloody absurd," said Horace, "there's no way we're going to have damn pigs rampaging on our fairways."

"I don't suppose Jules would want that darling," Flick found herself saying. "After all he has been a scratch golfer."

"Plays off twenty now though," said Andy, a craggy-faced Scot, who sat at the end of the table. He was the member responsible for the maintenance of the grounds.

"The problem is," said Mark, "that we could do with more time to repay the debt. We would have been in serious trouble if the original building society had foreclosed on us. We'd have lost the freehold title to our land."

"So the club might not have been able to keep going?" questioned Camilla.

"It could have come to that," explained Mark, "though like one or two other clubs, we might have been bought by someone, possibly a foreign national, Japanese or Malaysian," he hesitated. "There are scrap metal dealers who've bought up some clubs in the area."

"Nothing wrong with them," growled Horace, to the assenting nodded heads of the older men at the table. "They're likely to have some common gumption."

"They might have more respect for us," said Mark. "I was going to bring it up any other business, but I may as well mention it now. Jack Metcalfe's complained about the bird Jules brought round the course at the Ladies' invitation competition. He wants the committee to rule that dogs are the only pets allowed on the course."

There was an embarrassed silence.

"Bloody ridiculous. If I'd had a gun in my golf bag, I'd have shot it, said as much to Jack. He's a great shot himself." Horace nodded; he held one gnarled clenched fist in front of the other, almost as though he had a gun in his hands which he was about to raise to his shoulder.

"I suppose we should take care not to upset our major creditor," said Mark, "regrettable though his activities are."

"It's a bit difficult to stop birds flying," commented Flick. "We'll look ridiculous if we make a special local rule saying people mustn't have birds perched on their trolleys."

"Don't think we need worry about that," said Andy, "There are plenty of ridiculous golf rules and I think we should show some respect to Jack. No offence Adam, but Jack was a bloody fine treasurer. It's a pity he was silly enough to borrow money from the club. We over reacted chucking him off the committee, especially knowing what we now know about Jules Challenger. After all he was the one who fingered Jack in the first place, and he's been listed as an overseas member for years when he's been living in this country."

"To be fair," said Flick defensively, "he's hardly played here, he's been so busy, and anyway he's more than repaid the extra ten thousand or whatever it is he owes us in subscriptions by salvaging the club."

"For years he didn't pay a proper subscription; he's as much a crook as Jack."

"No, he's not. That's a bloody awful thing to say."

"Jules Challenger's a schemer. Weren't his parents chucked out of the club?"

"No, all they did was tout for business but they weren't very subtle about it."

"Pawnbroking's not exactly the type of thing we like touted at Bisley Heath."

The men's accusations and counter accusations rang in Flick's ears. She looked across at Camilla, whose rose pink lips were apart as though she wanted to suck in all the juicy gossip she could possibly digest.

Flick sank back in her chair. She did not want to hear all this. Her first in-laws had been generous to her. The garnet earrings that hung from her ears were amongst the jewellery

Faye had given her. The Challengers had not only introduced her to golf, but also put her up for the club at a time when it was difficult to join clubs, especially prestigious ones like Bisley Heath. Their second-hand jewellery business developed naturally into pawnbroking because that was what some of their customers wanted. People at Bisley Heath had approached Faye confidentially in the cloakroom about their problems, not the other way round.

Flick couldn't admit it here, but Jules's debt collecting had been her idea. When he was sent down from Cambridge, she suggested, as a joke, that if he'd got nothing better to do, he'd better go and see some of the people who owed his parents money to collect it.

He'd taken her seriously. From that first outing, Jules progressed from collecting money for his parents and their business acquaintances to buying debts. They were together when he started Owl Finance, which morphed into the Griffon Trust, but he'd kept her statue as his company's emblem because he loved it as the memory of her. He swore he'd always value her for giving him so much.

Flick focussed her eyes on to Adam. "How much do you know about his plans Adam?" *Come on, be honest,* she wanted to say. *Remember all those university vacations when Jules gave you work?* She was irritated by the ironic grin on Adam's wide mouth stretching across his round face. Damn it; he owed Jules. "I can't believe Jules has definitely said he'll put wild boars on the course?"

Adam gave his ironic little smile again, "He's talked more about birds; he wants to bring back sparrow-hawks to west Surrey because he thinks they would counteract the crow menace."

"Surely we'd have double trouble," said Mark.

"Apparently not. Sparrow-hawks kill and eat crows in their territory which would be a great help to our greens staff who have to spend a lot of time clearing up the mess crows make as well as trapping them."

"So some of his ideas could be useful," said Flick.

"I'd like to believe so," said Adam, his voice sounding all too reasonable, "but generally I feel we have a problem."

"Too bloody right," said Horace.

Matthew Lomax, held up the palm of his hand. "I think we've gone round the point long enough. Time for a vote whether we re-negotiate the loan, knowing what we do about Jules Challenger's terms. Hands up those in favour."

Flick raised her arm. "Listen, playing off two, I don't want our course ruined, but I can't believe Jules would either."

The temperature in the room could not have dropped ten degrees, but it certainly felt like it. Flick's lonely hand in the air felt cold. She wished she'd worn something close fitting because she felt a chill breeze through the open window swirl inside her loose linen smock top, but she ploughed on. "Jules has got a golf blue from Cambridge. He's still in touch with his team mates, who're up and coming people in the golf world. They're potentially people who'll be Captain of the Royal and Ancient. One of them plays regularly with Prince Andrew."

"So I understand," said Matthew, a smile on his genial face. He'd informed the committee that he would not show his hand unless his casting vote was needed.

Emboldened Flick continued, "This pig business is a red herring, sorry," she paused whilst everyone groaned jovially, "Jules often looks at all sorts of odd things, but he wouldn't have made the money he has if he was impractical; he's very canny."

"Stealing Jack's ball at the invitation was a really subtle touch," sneered Andy.

"That was unfortunate," replied Flick, "but Cally's an amazing bird. She knows not to pick up balls off fairways or greens, or from people he plays with."

"Glad to hear it, wouldn't want her pecking at my goolies." Mark laughed as he raised his hand.

Gradually four of the other members of the committee including Camilla, but not Adam, followed suit, leaving Matthew to give his casting vote in favour of renegotiating the loan with Jules. The club would accept some of his terms in exchange for a longer time to pay off the debt.

In the lounge after the meeting closed, Adam bought her a drink. "Well done!" He handed her a glass of red wine, "you were very brave, just as I would have expected, though I was surprised you defended your ex so strongly in the circumstances." He gave her his funny little smile.

"What do you mean?" Flick put the glass of wine down on a round occasional table. "I was surprised you weren't more loyal to your old buddy."

"I tried to be fair. My job is to put the club's interests first, whoever introduced me to the club in the first place, but your loyalty's truly commendable after what happened to Tarquin's model of you." He raised thin dark eyebrows. "You haven't heard?"

Flick shook her head.

Adam took a gulp of his own glass of white wine before he put it down next her glass. Then he massaged his neck with the pale fingers of his right hand. "Someone chopped the arms off it."

"My sculpture? Someone did a Roxy on it?"

Adam nodded, but whatever he mumbled next was lost on Flick.

Her mind was suffused with a terrible picture of her beautiful wooden self mutilated, turned from sculpture to scrap. She rolled back the sleeve of her loose blouse to see her real arms. Neither they nor her hands were as slender and smooth as they were when she was eighteen, when Tarquin had moulded them into a work of art which he wanted to keep for ever. *Tarquin would have kept it safe.* He used to be obsessive about his early work; he couldn't bear to part with it. At college she'd helped him make notes of every purchaser with contact details.

Fury engulfed her. Lucky she was a good actress. She could pick up her glass of wine and sip it whilst she smiled at Adam, rather than throw it at him, especially as she was aware some of the men in the lounge were looking in their direction. They must be able to feel the intensity of the exchange between Adam and herself, which was crazy when she'd never had a meaningful conversation with him before in her life.

Adam was just another of Grace's protégés whom Jules was kind to, employing him, and helping him get started in accountancy. How come he knew, but Jules couldn't be bothered to tell her, something so crucial to her identity? When they'd split up the one thing she'd wanted more than anything else was her effigy and so did Tarquin, but Jules refused to relinquish it to either of them, because it was the symbol of his company.

Forget about it being my naked body. His solicitors had argued the figurehead, as they called her effigy, stuck on the front of Jules's floating office, was a business asset, a work of art photographed for his website as well as his office stationery. She'd fought for it and lost, and now it was eff-ing well destroyed.

How could Jules have let her arms be cut off, like those of the dreadful tragic Roxanne who'd taken her place all too quickly in Jules's life? When she'd heard about the accident, Flick had not wanted to know any details, but people would tell her. Faye had rung her up in tears, as though Flick should comfort her, the ex-mother-in-law. Still that was hardly surprising since she'd wailed over the phone to Flick when Jules had married Roxanne. *Darling, she's not ready to be a wife; she's still a wild child.*

Flick could only sympathise with Faye, but she had found the only way to shut up other people was to tell them she was better off out of Jules's life; she should have stuck to that resolution. She certainly would now. *You can forget about any support from me now Jules.* Only probably, once again, she'd made a decision too late.

13. Head to head with Flick

Flick sat nursing a cup of coffee with both hands on one of the new sofas in the corner of the Bisley Heath lounge. With one elderly man sitting beside her and the other couple standing, almost as though in attendance, she did not look as distraught as Impey had imagined from Jules's early morning telephone call.

Calm her down any way you can was Jules's instruction half an hour ago. *I've told her to ring you.* Impey had scarcely switched off her mobile, which she'd then plugged in to charge on her bedside table, when it had rung again. This time Flick was asking, but it sounded more like a royal command, to meet immediately at the clubhouse. Even tucked away in an alcove, she still managed a regal aura, but maybe it was the presence of the three guys near her.

As she walked across the room, Impey recognised Adam Scrivenor, the new treasurer who'd taken Jack's place. All three men were dressed in golf gear, obviously about to play, but had, it appeared, delayed the start of the their game to talk to Flick.

"Hello darling," Flick greeted Impey, with a gracious nod at the men which seemed to suggest they could leave her now.

The older friendly-walrus type man hoisted himself off the sofa, saying, "We'll leave you two gals in peace."

Flick stood up to bid the three of them good-bye with a peck on each of their cheeks, reminding Impey of her days as Lady Captain when she'd dispensed prizes at the end of competitions, giving a light kiss to the winners. Somehow, even in her distress, she looked as gracious as she did in those days, dressed in beige chino slacks with a cream polo shirt, her long gold streaked hair hung in its usual sleek bob, clipped behind her ears to show her large pearl earrings.

She sat down again and folded her arms across her chest. *The barrier signal.* Well versed in Desmond Morris's lore, Impey instantly recognised her body language.

"I'm sorry, " said Impey standing awkwardly on one foot by the knee height walnut veneered occasional table in front of the sofa, "if my involvement in this business upsets you. I honestly think Jules brought me in because he wanted to sort things out giving you the minimum of pain or stress." In her shabby jeans type trousers teamed with an old blue collarless shirt she felt a mess beside Flick, but she had dressed in a hurry to come and see her, thinking that the club's respectable dress code would not matter too much at eight forty-five on a Tuesday morning.

"You are joking," said Flick sarcastically. Her bosom inside the close-fitting shirt heaved up and down. "Frankly my dear, this is nothing to do with you. We both know what all this is about, or at least I do, Jules's next big idea."

"The wildlife course?" Impey sat down opposite her on one of the club's new wooden-armed tub chairs. Flick must already have ordered coffee for her too, or the men who were with her, since a large cafetière beside some coffee cups stood on a tray there on the table, but to her chagrin there was nothing to eat. She clenched and unclenched her buttocks, half-inclined to rise to go to the bar to ask for some toast, but before she managed to move, Flick replied.

"Got it in one, but that's hardly any more surprising than finding you involved at all." Her greeny-blue eyes glared at Impey whilst she picked up the cafetière to wave it at her. "Coffee?"

Impey nodded. "Thanks."

As she poured the dark brew into one of the plain white cups, Flick continued in a gentler voice. "I suppose you are known for your love of animals, but what I don't understand is why I had to find out from someone like Adam that my sculpture had been massacred."

"Oh the basic body is still there," Impey tried to give her voice an emollient tone, "and Tarquin Hobbs has tried to sort out the arms, though of course without them it's less recognisable as you."

"Now you really are joking. You mean Tarquin knew about this and he didn't tell me either?" Flick put her coffee cup down on the table to rub her forehead with her pink manicured fingers. "And someone like you, no offence meant, who's not exactly Sherlock Holmes or the Silent Witness, is given the job of finding out how it happened, then explaining to me what is going on."

Impey sipped her coffee. "It's not exactly like that. Jules brought me in three weeks ago because he was so worried about what had happened to the... I mean your sculpture. He was very unhappy about the way Tarquin repaired it, though I don't think it looks too bad."

"You think I should be grateful for being turned into a...an efff... a simpering Venus de Milo?" Flick raised one eyebrow, but the way her mouth turned down at the corners suggested her smile was not of amusement, even if she had retrained herself from swearing.

Impey shook her head. "No, I simply think your face still looks lovely and so does your body, as far as I could see in the distance with binoculars."

Her tummy rumbled loudly and inelegantly. There had been no time for breakfast and last night's supper had been a mainly liquid meal with some old girlfriends she used to work with in town. Feeling it about to happen again, she cast a hopeful look at the bar, behind which Nellie, the plump barmaid with long blonde ringlets was standing.

It was a relief to see a friendly face since Flick was certainly not mollified by any compliments. "What I'd like to know is exactly what your involvement with Jules's business is? I can see why he's going for someone like you with regard to his plans for the club, because everyone knows you've some animal qualification degree, but I can't see why he's bothering you over my statue."

"He didn't want...," Impey began to say but stopped before she completed her sentence with *you to know*. That would obviously be unpopular. She continued, "As I understand it, Jules is devastated by the assault on his figurehead and is desperate not to upset you. So he asked me if I could find out subtly who desecrated it."

Flick's finely-shaped nostrils flared in derision. Her lips opened, as though she was about to say something but decided against it.

"Just a minute." Impey stood up and took a few steps towards the bar counter. "Is there anything I could have to eat?"

"Toast," offered Nellie, "or something more substantial?"

"Toast would be fine," Impey turned back to Flick, "would you like some too?"

"No thanks." Flick did not want to be diverted. She dropped her head to one side as she scrutinised Impey's face. "So why did Jules pick you?" she repeated.

"It must be because Dodger told him I'd done some detective work."

Dodger! Impey was not altogether glad to see his name made Flick's face light up. "Are you going out with him or something," she asked.

"Or something." Impey hoped she was not blushing.

Flick held out the white china coffee jug to Impey offering her another cup before she poured some for herself. "I s'pose he's a better bet than Jules." She narrowed her blue eyes whilst she scrutinised Impey's face. "I strongly advise you not to fall in love with him."

"I wasn't planning to." Impey sat down again opposite Flick; she hoped the hot tinge she felt creep up her neck was not flashing red like a traffic light. How had she let this conversation degenerate into man talk? "He's paying me well to try to discover whether someone in his inner circle has some sort of grudge against him because, according to his staff, there was no sign of an intruder when the sculpture was vandalised. I hoped you might come up with some ideas."

Flick blew a puff of air contemptuously out of her deep pink lips, a gesture that might have looked inelegant in anyone else. "It's ages since I've had any dealings with anyone to do with Jules. The only person I know who's still working for him is Steve Hemmings – you've met him I expect."

Impey nodded.

"Yeah well, all the others who hung around when I was married to him nearly twenty years ago now have gone their separate ways. Tarquin was the first," she hesitated as though about to confide that it was because of her, but added instead, "I gather the others followed suit, though for a while they were all nuts about Foxy Roxy, as they called Roxanne. There was a pub where they all used to drink."

"Caesar too?" asked Impey to lighten the tension.

"Sure. Roxanne insisted he went everywhere with the gang, so I've heard." Flick stopped talking as Nellie arrived at their table with the toast and marmalade that Impey had asked for.

"Thanks." Impey bent down to delve into her handbag for her purse to find her club card to pay for the breakfast. As she handed it over, she said, "I suppose it's natural for groups of close friends to break up."

"I don't think this was completely natural; from what I've heard there was a huge row when they bust up."

"What about?"

Flick shrugged her shoulders. "Don't ask me, ask Adam and Ned."

"I suppose Roxanne's death created quite scandal?" surmised Impey.

"You're telling me. People used to try to talk about it to me, but I didn't want to hear about it because I'd finished with Jules and his mates whom he couldn't be parted from. I made a new life for myself, or so I thought until last night. Roxanne was nothing to do with me." Flick picked up her cup and took a gulp of coffee.

"D'you think Roxanne was murdered?"

"As I understood it, that was never proved, although initially I heard someone was arrested, then let go. The final verdict was that she had a terrible accident messing around with a chainsaw and bled to death." Flick shuddered. "It was pretty horrible, but I'm afraid I can't talk about it because I blanked out everything people said at the time. It all happened too soon after I'd left and I didn't want anything to do with Jules and his problems." She grimaced at Impey. "In fact I don't know why I'm talking to you now. Jules is trouble, even if he is Surrey's answer to St. Francis of Assisi, able to charm the birds in the air and tame a wolf."

Impey grinned at her, encouraged by a lighter note in Flick's voice. "You don't think Grace Deer is involved do you?"

Flick's wide mouth twitched into a smile. "I wouldn't be at all surprised. Grace has a finger in every pie. It was partly 'cos of her my marriage bust up."

Impey frowned. *How bizarre.* She bit into her toast. "What do you mean?"

"She couldn't let go of her boys. It was easier dealing with my in-laws than it was with her, especially as she was funding Jules."

"I thought he was at Cambridge when you met him?"

"Yes, believe it or not now, he was reading medicine. I thought I was going to marry a doctor." She grinned ruefully at Impey.

"So why didn't he become a doctor?"

"He got sent down from Cambridge, too many birds in his bedroom probably," she grinned at Impey's startled expression, "Real feathered birds, owls and the like."

"Yes, I know he's an austringer." Impey ladled some marmalade out of a little glass bowl on to the side of her plate, took up her knife and spread some on to her hot buttered toast.

"What on earth's that?"

"A falconer basically, but someone who flies larger birds like hawks."

"He's that all right – you know he's got a vulture now. Actually she's quite sweet in a savage way." Flick laughed. "At least he didn't bring that damn wolf with him."

"Didn't you like Caesar?"

"Don't know him. He arrived with Roxanne after I'd left. She was nuts about animals too." *Like you,* was unsaid. Across the table, Flick raised one eyebrow again at Impey. "She was training to be a vet."

"What, like Ned?"

"Yeah, she was Ned's girlfriend first I believe, but she was crazy about wild animals. You'd have to be to have a wolf cub wouldn't you?"

"So you think her love of wild animals drew her and Jules together?"

"Who knows darling," drawled Flick, lapsing into the speech mode Tarquin had suggested she'd picked up from Jules's mother Faye. "Tell you what, she was quite different from me. Actually she was quite a wild girl herself, which probably appealed to Jules, that and her hair. It was a real red gold; she looked liked a girl out of a Botticelli painting, except that she was slight and skinny, always wore dungarees and her hair was usually tangled."

"She liked a bit of rough?" Impey suggested.

Flick shrugged her shoulders. "Wouldn't like to speculate about that."

She was clearly reluctant to say much more about Roxanne. Although the accident had happened nearly twenty years ago, Flick would not savage the girl who'd taken her place. One of Flick's qualities, which endeared her to the club's ladies, was that she did not *do* nasty remarks.

Little by little Impey pieced together a picture of a tomboy like woman, who even as an adult loved climbing trees. The day of her death she'd been up a Beech tree in the huge grounds of Grace's house. She'd tied a rope to a bough above her in preparation for lopping off another branch alongside. According to Flick, the story was that when she turned on the chainsaw, Roxanne lost her footing with the result the saw slipped out of her hands. It cut off her arms as she grasped another branch and tried to swing out of its way.

Or this was what the forensic people deduced from an examination of the tree.

No one saw what happened.

The chainsaw was still hanging buzzing noisily, stained with her blood, when Roxanne was found lying on the ground beneath the tree.

"But why does Jules blame Adam for her death."

"Adam and Ned; they were both in the garden at the time."

"Then they must have heard the noise of the tree's branch cracking and her screaming."

Flick raised both her long slim pale manicured hands in the air facing Impey. "I don't know; I don't want to know and I advise you not to go there either."

Impey took a few sips of the coffee in the hope some inspiration might strike. How could she cajole Flick into telling her what Jules wanted to know. Why should anyone stray into his garden, take the emblem of his company and desecrate it? "Do you think anyone might have mutilated the figurehead to try to upset your relationship with Jules, maybe not liked the idea of your getting back together."

Flick laughed. A teasing note entered her voice. "Are you worried some other woman is trying to get her claws into Jules?"

"I didn't exactly mean that."

Flick shook her head. "I've absolutely no idea what goes on in Jules's love life these days, except that a great big female vulture loves him."

14. Deborah finds the police

The cheek of it! Deborah Cordrey could hardly believe what she was hearing when Rosie rang.

After a lot of small talk asking how she was and saying they hadn't seen each other for ages, Rosie said, "I gather you've got my watch and I wondered if I could possibly have it back?"

"My dear," replied Deborah in the caustic tone she used when she reprimanded witnesses, or even legal personnel in the magistrate's court, "I have indeed recovered a Chaika watch, which belongs to me. I'm very surprised to hear that it was in your possession prior to turning up in the club's kitchen."

"That was Dodger, I mean Roger Melbourne's fault. He thought it would be an amusing conjuring trick to take it off my wrist and hang it over a bottle. Then the waiter whisked it away; that's how it ended up in the kitchen."

Deborah frowned as she looked at the phone in her hand. She prided herself she could hear honesty in a tone of voice. The sound of guilt did not resonate in Rosie's. Instead, her indignation rang loudly and clearly in Deborah's ears. "My dear," she said in a mollifying voice, "this watch is very precious to me. It was a present brought home for me from a business trip by Monty, my late husband."

"But my watch won't necessarily be the same one." Rosie's tone grew louder and even more indignant. "Anyway, mine, which we know was the one you found in the kitchen, is very precious to me too. Jack bought it for me after our son Archie was born. You can ask him."

The contentious bracelet lay on the dressing table in front of Deborah. As she looked at the beautiful white birds on the face of the panel, fury rose inside her. She gritted her teeth whilst she tried to control the anger making her heart thump. The pleasure that suffused her since she'd found the watch was dissipating into a strange emotion she hardly recognised; she felt as though she was gripping on to a brittle ledge which was breaking away from a cliff.

There was no way she could explain to Rosie why she must cling on to the watch, because it represented her husband's love for her. She had very little tangible evidence of their happy marriage. Monty had been so hard up when he'd asked her to marry him that her engagement ring had been crystal instead of a diamond. It was almost a relief when it came apart, saving her the embarrassment of wearing it.

Should I give it back? The question tormented her even after she had managed to ring off, having set Rosie the challenge that "One of us needs to have proof of ownership".

She tried to think logically, but all she could deduce was the fact that if Rosie had not stolen the bracelet, she had still been in receipt of a stolen good, however she had acquired it. Yet this righteous thought did not take away the knowledge that the club was full of people who might see things differently; they might perceive the one who took the bracelet from the kitchen as the thief.

Proof was essential, but how could she get it? There'd been no receipt when she'd found the watch unpacking Monty's suitcase. Probably he'd thought it didn't matter because she wouldn't have been able to change it anyway. *So no evidence.*

She rose slowly from the double bed where she'd been sitting and straightened out the lovely handmade quilt given to her and Monty for their pearl wedding anniversary. Grace, presumably advised by Monty, had commissioned a dear friend of hers, who did exquisite needlework, to make this double bedspread for them. Woven into it were images of their life together. Deborah's slim fingers traced over the embroidered depictions of her house, Ned surrounded by animals, and herself with Monty on the golf course. The quilt was so beautiful she sometimes wondered if she should hang it on a wall as a testament to her happy marriage, but that would be vulgar.

She made her way downstairs, temporarily distracted by the thought she would like to replace the threadbare stair carpet. The green twist pile had been so fashionable in the seventies when they bought the house, but now everyone seemed to go for cords which were much more serviceable. Then in the kitchen as she lifted the lid of the Aga stove to put the kettle, which still managed to stay bright blue despite the bits of enamel chipped off, on to the hob, the brainwave struck her. *No evidence maybe, but there is a witness.*

She spooned the instant coffee, her favourite rather expensive luxury brand into a cup. *Why didn't I think of it before? Because of her.* Usually she tried not to think about Grace, but on this occasion she could help. That had at least to be acknowledged as far as Grace was concerned; she was truthful, even if most of the time Deborah did not want to hear what Grace had to say.

Grace was on that trip with Monty. She'd arranged for him to accompany her, much to Deborah's chagrin. It had been particularly galling when Deborah's own sister had asked, on being shown the bracelet, whether it was so splendid because it was a *forgive m and have me back present.*

A sip of the velvety coffee took away the nasty taste that had arisen in her throat. Deborah hadn't seen much of Grace since Monty died, but when she had, Grace had been very pleasant. She'd continued to send the large hamper of goodies at Christmas which she'd done when Monty worked for her, and she'd invited Deborah to one or two of her larger parties, which Deborah had attended, though she sensed they were for the people she imagined to be Grace's second team friends, but it was possible Grace did not actually have a first team of close chums. Though she'd run a successful public company, she was in a way an outsider. *That's why she needed Monty.* He was always the centre of everything.

Deborah put down her coffee cup to reach out for the white phone which hung on the cream wall. Her hand stopped on the phone. Grace could be abrupt on the phone. It would be difficult to broach the subject in a way that would be sure to get her co-operation. Without seeing the bracelet itself, she might not, probably would not remember it. A much better strategy would be to go and see her. She had no plans for the day which she could not shelve, just a National Association of Decorative and Fine Arts Society meeting this afternoon about the history of the Grandfather clock, in which she was quite interested, but the main purpose was to meet her more cultured chums. Since it was only nine-thirty in the morning, she could easily return by three o'clock.

Whilst she backed the car out of her garage, it occurred to her that in her turmoil she'd omitted any plan B if Grace was not at home. She stopped the car in the drive and got out to go back into the house. In a flash it came to her that the purpose of her visit should be something ostensibly kind to Grace.

She knew the very thing. It was sitting in Monty's photograph album, nestling amongst the pictures of his golfing triumphs when he received prizes from dignitaries in that world. She'd been tempted to destroy the picture, which she hated, because there was something suggestive about the body language, although they were at a business reception taken on that very Russian trip. Since removing the nine by six photo would have made a gap in the book, she'd left it stuck there. Now she was glad she had. The photo gave an excuse to visit Grace.

No time like the present. She rifled through Monty's old desk to find it. Along with it, she also picked up one of Grace's business cards, headed with his name, which she scratched out, and a matching vellum envelope. She attached them firmly together with a large gold paper clip.

What Deborah had not expected to see was a police car parked in the drive outside Grace's house. She had been a little surprised but pleased, when she reached Grace's entrance, to find the electronic gates between the high dark green laurel hedges, already open. This she assumed must mean Grace was at home. Only when she turned the curve in the drive did she grasp that there were already visitors to the house.

Nonetheless she parked her Ford Focus on the yellow gravel. The police held no worries for her – she was so used to seeing them in court. Presumably they were here because Grace had been burgled or had some sort of accident, she mused as, having alighted from the car, she walked to the front door.

A bold rap brought a tall thin man in uniform to the entrance. He seemed pleased someone who'd known Grace had arrived. "Was she expecting you?" He asked eagerly.

"Not exactly," Deborah replied, feeling it would be a bit odd to say an outright 'no'. "I was popping in because I happened to be in the area." *Well that's true enough.*

"You didn't have a date or anything?" queried the police.

"No we didn't have that sort of relationship," replied Deborah, wondering what the man was getting at. "Our friendship was on a much more long-term casual basis."

"You know her well then?"

"Pretty well, though I haven't seen much of her recently."

"You don't think she would be the sort of woman to take herself off and go walk about without telling anyone?"

"Certainly not," Deborah shook her head, "unless she'd changed very much." She could have added that Grace was most punctilious when it came to checking Monty's expense account.

"Yes, that's what her cleaning lady said." The policeman nodded a long angular head. "She said it was most unlike Miss Deer to go away without leaving money for her in a box hidden in the kitchen units; she's terribly worried about her."

"There's probably a logical explanation," said Deborah. "Grace is always very organised, but she can be secretive too."

"Yes, but on this occasion she's changed a routine she's had going with her cleaning lady for years. There's no money in her box and she says there's no money in the box by the door that Miss Deer called her burglar box."

"Perhaps there was an intruder whilst she was away?" suggested Deborah. She was beginning to feel uncomfortable. Apart from being a great disappointment, the absence of Grace in the house coupled with the policemen's presence was spooky.

"Maybe," agreed the policeman, "but her cleaning lady says there's no sign of her having taken any clothes with her. She says it's as though Miss Deer has vanished into thin air. That's why she called us."

"Have you been to see the neighbours?" asked Deborah. "I'm pretty certain that in the past she used to leave her key with someone a couple of doors down." For a moment she could not think of the name of the woman Monty used to describe as "comely" with a wicked grin. She rubbed her forehead with her right hand, suddenly conscious how much more freckled it was with brown spots than her left. Monty used to tease her about the evidence of her golfing hands.

"Yes, there's a Sally Markham who's been most helpful. She's only worried that she didn't call us earlier when Grace let them down for a game of bridge, but she didn't want to cause an unnecessary fuss." The policeman grimaced.

"Well I'm sorry I can't help more," said Deborah. She looked through the doorway into Grace's large lounge where a man in white clothing was examining the contents. Aghast she asked, "Do you expect foul play?"

"We don't know," said the policeman, "and unfortunately the domestic help cleaned the place thoroughly before she went to look for her money. So although when Miss Deer was out and hadn't left a note with any particular instructions, which worried her, she still got on with her job all too well as far as we're concerned."

"Grace might have gone away for a few days," said Deborah hopefully although a sick chill feeling flooded through her. "Is her car here?"

"Oh yes; and it hasn't been touched for days."

There has to be a logical explanation. The words drummed through her mind, but the situation defied logic. Fear pierced with regret that the one chance she had to use Grace's goodwill, to kindle a relationship with someone who mattered to Monty almost as much as she did, was gone. Grace had disappeared. Her home had a desolate air of abandonment. *She's gone away somewhere to "shuffle off this mortal coil".* Ned said that about pets, especially cats, who often left the home to hide somewhere when they died, much to the distress of their owners.

Deborah turned away to leave.

"Before you go," said the policeman tapping her lightly on the shoulder, "I wonder if you would take a look at something for us, seeing as you've known Miss Deer for such a long time."

"Okay." Deborah agreed unemotionally, suddenly feeling in a trance-like state with the shock. She couldn't imagine any of Grace's possessions would mean much to her, but she followed the policeman into the lounge.

Across the room, beside the television, one of the boiler-suited men was holding a three foot high bronze sculpture of a long-haired urchin-like girl. "Do you recognise this?" He asked.

"Oh my God," gasped Deborah, before she could stop herself, "it's Roxanne." For a moment she thought she must be imagining the resemblance, but after she'd blinked her dark eyes, she knew as she looked again, that the bronze sculpture of the slight wiry naked figure was indeed Roxanne.

There was the pert face under long curling tresses of hair.

Deborah looked away, not because the thin pointed breasts upset her, but the slender arms jolted her; despite their muscular curves, shaped as triangles either side of her body, they looked so beautiful. Her strong tiny hands clasped her hips.

"And who might she be?" asked the policeman.

Deborah cleared her throat. "Well Grace always called her a niece, but she couldn't be because Grace was the only child in her family to survive the war, so I think she was some sort of cousin." She hesitated; she did not want to speak ill of the dead, but Roxanne had caused no end of trouble. The little minx had played up to Monty as well as Ned. Both her men had cried when Roxanne died.

Deborah's stomach churned. Her entire body shuddered at the memory of the ensuing crisis that engulfed her family. It was so unfair and so awful with her being a magistrate. She thought she'd never recover from the dire publicity that followed, but Ned was brilliant, so calm although he'd been so fond of Roxanne. Sometimes she thought Roxanne had broken his heart.

She mesmerised all the boys. Even Tarquin seemed to forget about Flick when she turned up, although Deborah had never realised that he'd been sufficiently infatuated with Roxanne to sculpt her. Everyone knew about the wooden figurehead of Flick, which Jules used to publicise his company, but Ned had never mentioned a model of Roxanne. *What a relief it had been when she was safely married to Jules — only it wasn't safely as it turned out.*

"Why do you think it was stowed in the television cabinet?" asked one of the boiler-suited men, breaking through her recollections. "It was very carefully wrapped up in a DVD box, as though it was meant to be hidden."

"I haven't a clue." Deborah turned away again. She needed to get back to her own home, to ring Ned. She had to speak to someone who'd understand how she felt.

She didn't usually ring him at work, but she could always contact him in an emergency. All the drive home she looked forward to hearing his soft voice.

"Why on earth did you go and see Grace," he asked, putting some dog's operation on hold to comfort his mother, "you know she always upsets you."

"I thought for once she could help me, over the bracelet."

"Oh no," groaned Ned, "you really should drop that Mum. It's only going to make you miserable. You've lived happily without it for ten years so why not just give it back to Rosie. She's not a thief, and after all she did bloody well buy it from someone or other."

"You don't think I should hang on to something special bought for me by your father."

"Why hang on to something that's only going to give you grief?" Ned whistled cheerfully. "There's no point in being sentimental."

"You're a fine one to talk," retorted his mother.

15. Impey receives a vulture

Impey looked up from the laptop she was working on in bed. At seven o'clock in the morning she did not expect to hear a fast car grind to a halt in the lane outside her cottage. She wandered to the window where she parted the curtains.

Hell there's Jules and he's coming to see me.

Her new employer was struggling to open the black wrought iron latch of her small wooden gate with one hand. He put down a large box he was carrying before he shut the gate carefully, as though Impey might have some animal which would escape, before he staggered up her garden path with the vast box again in his arms. A briefcase dangled from his wrist.

Impey flung on the jeans and tee shirt she'd worn yesterday which hung over her bedroom chair. Never mind that Jules, in his neatly creased grey trousers and smart but casual jacket looked as though he was going to work, she just wanted to have clothes on to greet him.

"Good morning," she said coolly as she opened the door.

"I'm terribly sorry to land on you so early, but I need your help. It's a bit of an emergency really." Jules turned half sideways with the box in his arms to wiggle into her tiny hallway. He put the box down carefully on the floor and dropped the briefcase on to her tiny hall table before he leant forward as though about to kiss her lightly on the cheek.

Impey drew back. Jules might look beautifully clean, but she was horribly aware she had not had time to wash or clean her teeth. "What can I do for you? Do you want a cup of tea or coffee?"

"Well...erm...if you're making something for yourself, whatever you have would be great." Leaving the box in the hall, he picked up his briefcase to follow her as she walked barefoot into her tiny kitchen.

"The thing is," he said, whilst she busied herself getting mugs out of her kitchen cupboard and spooning coffee into them, "I want to store something with you that might get damaged at my home. I hope that would be all right."

"Sure," said Impey casually whilst she switched on the kettle. She felt guilty that she'd done little to deserve Jules's retainer yet. She didn't like the idea of being more beholden to him, better if he owed her money. The box he'd brought wasn't that large, even if the way he handled it suggested whatever was inside it was fragile.

An ecstatic smile spread over Jules's broad face. His tufty blond hair seemed to stand up with pleasure as his eyebrows rose. "I'm so glad; I hoped you'd say that. You'll find Cally is an absolute pleasure to have with you."

Impey nearly dropped the kettle of boiling water she held. She tightened her grasp on the handle. The polished nails of her clenched fingers dug into the palm of her hand. She put the kettle back down on the work surface of her kitchen units. "You want me to look after your vulture?"

"Only for a while." Jules's cornflower blue eyes looked at her imploringly. "Here let me." He picked up the kettle and poured the boiling water into the mugs. "Cally's a darling bird; she'd be a great companion for you."

"I don't actually want a companion," complained Impey. She pointed at the fridge since Jules was evidently looking around for it to find the milk. "And since you'll obviously miss her dreadfully, why do you want me to keep her?"

Jules took the carton of skimmed milk out of the fridge. He looked at it with the distaste of a man who reckoned real men drank full cream milk, but he poured it into both mugs before asking whether she had any sugar.

Feeling at once relieved she had soft brown sugar to offer, yet at the same time resentful she should care whether her domesticity pleased him or not, she fetched it for him. Before she could suggest they went through to her sitting room, he perched on a stool, his feet resting on the bar across its legs, reminiscent of a bird of prey himself.

"Thanks" he said in a general way, shovelling a couple of spoonfuls into his mug. "I know you're going to enjoy this." He delved into the briefcase he'd dropped by his stool to pull out a large glossy paperback called "Birds of Prey" by Jemima Parry Jones. "This will help. Jemima P J is an absolute expert on hawks and falconry".

"But Cally's a vulture," protested Impey.

"Yes, but she's very tame, been born in captivity and all that."

"But I've got nowhere to keep her."

"Steve'll sort that out for you. He's standing by for you to ring him to arrange a time to come round, preferably this morning obviously. He'll knock up a cage and give you the basic training on how to hold her and other important things." Jules took a couple of sips of coffee. "I really needed this."

"Today's terribly inconvenient for me." Impey massaged her forehead with her fingers. She didn't want to have to stay in for anyone today: Wednesday was her day for golf. She widened her mouth into an expression which shared mock agony with a smile. "Don't you know it's ladies' day at the club?"

"You don't have to stay in for Steve; he's totally trustworthy. You can just leave a key under a flowerpot or the doormat with instructions as to where you want Cally's aviary to be, and he'll come round another time to teach you to handle her."

"But why can't Cally stay with you?"

Jules's face wrinkled into a frown. "I told you; I think she's in danger. It would be terribly easy for anyone who wanted to hurt me to get into my garden and do something awful to her. She's incredibly vulnerable at my house. It's terribly easy to poison vultures."

Impey wanted to say they should have strong stomachs feeding on carrion, but she knew Jules had a point. Asian vultures were in danger of dying out because they'd fed on cows treated with antibiotics which were toxic for the birds.

"Would someone really poison Cally to get at you?" Impey wrinkled her face up in doubt.

"I hope not, but I can't ignore the fact they might. I've had a few run-ins with people recently."

You can say that again.

"I'm afraid the idea of a wildlife golf course hasn't gone down too well at the club too," said Impey.

Jules's face wrinkled in surprise. "Are you sure of that? I've heard some people are charmed by the idea. Anyway, it's the way to rescue the place you know; the organic course is the way of the future." Perched on a high stool, his elbows on the kitchen units, with his broad hands clasped together, Jules rocked his arms backwards and forwards in determination.

"I'm not totally averse to the idea," said Impey, "only for a lot of people it's a complete no no, especially the better players. They want Bisley Heath to be a championship course so they like the fairways drained or watered as need be and they don't want stray animals roaming over the place; they certainly don't like crows digging up the course or animals' droppings on the fairway."

"But that's it," said Jules excitedly, "if only we had some hawks around, they'd keep the crows at bay. The reason we've got so many crows is because our natural hawk population has dwindled. They'd get the rabbits too."

"I thought you were expecting the odd wolf to do that," chuckled Impey.

"Certainly," Jules nodded eagerly, ignoring the irony in her tone, "but they'd be less acceptable than hawks, though wolves could actually function pretty well at Bisley Heath."

"How come?"

"They'd keep the deer population under control. In parts of Scotland where they've reintroduced the wolf, he's kept the deer at bay so the grass is a completely different shade of green." He glanced at his watch. "I'd love to tell you more, but I've got to go in a few minutes."

"Before you do," Impey fiddled with her coffee cup, "I've got to tell you that I'm not getting on very well with my enquiry about your figurehead. I never got to see Grace and Flick was not entirely helpful."

Jules slipped off his stool. "Please keep going. You've only just started, but things have already got worse. Goodness knows what's happened to Grace. Last time I saw her, she was absolutely fine, making a good recovery from her hip operation." He put his hand over her hand which lay on the kitchen units. "I'm really worried something awful has happened to her."

"You're not worried about Caesar though are you?" A picture of the teeth marks in Grace's leather handbag zipped into Impey's mind's eye. Why hadn't she thought of it before?

Caesar could have chewed up that bag. And the long coarse hairs she'd seen on the floor could have belonged to a wolf, rather than a dog. Maybe Jules had taken the wolf with him when he visited Grace with some, probably mistaken, idea the animal might comfort her.

"No, I wouldn't want him to be hurt of course, but he's very ancient now. It's amazing he's still alive, and Ned's a brilliant vet. He's got him through some sticky times health-wise. Steve looks after him brilliantly too when I'm not around. Anyway he's male. My instinctive fear is that women I care about are under threat."

"Because of you?"

"I'm afraid so. Grace is such a lovely person who's done so much for so many people, I can't understand why anyone should resent her, however successful she's been." Jules took his hand off Impey's, but his deep blue eyes locked on to hers.

"Not even your wives?"

Jules turned the palms of his hands outwards. "Possibly. I'm afraid they thought of her as a surplus mother-in-law, especially Tessa."

Impey knew he was referring to his third wife. "I'm going to see her next."

Jules's head dropped. "You'll like her," he said sadly, "everyone does at first, but then..." His voice trailed off.

"What happened with her?"

"She wanted to take command," he grinned, "like women often do when you get to know them too well."

Impey wanted to ask why on earth he'd married someone he didn't know properly, but guessed she'd pick that up from Tessa. She slipped off her stool to go with him to the front door.

"You'll get on with her though. She's a very interesting intuitive person, but unfortunately we didn't have much in common when it came to sharing our lives."

"How on earth did you meet her in the first place then?"

"After Roxanne died I went to her for bereavement counselling."

"Really," gasped Impey, surprised by his matter of fact tone.

He nodded. "I was so distraught about her death, scarcely able to function, that Grace suggested I went for counselling. Someone she knew recommended Tessa and so off I went. So did Ned. I think Grace herself had had a few sessions with her."

Why does it always come back to Grace? Impey opened the front door. "I hope she'll speak to me."

"She'll do that all right. Just don't let her get you bogged down with therapy." His eyes gripped her. "Promise me."

Impey shifted from one leg to the other awkwardly. "She must have done something for you for you to feel you wanted to marry her."

"Oh sure, I was crazy about her, felt my sanity depended on having her by my side. She's a pretty powerful personality you know, but in a quiet way." He hesitated to scrutinise Impey's face. "Ned saw the amber light before I did. I think he only had a couple of sessions with her. He said she was 'dangerous', which is a bit ridiculous."

Impey tried to hide her scepticism but knew she'd failed when Jules continued, "I know what you're thinking, that I must be a hell of a womaniser to marry four times, but I'm not. I've adored every woman I've been hitched too.

Tessa's the only one I've chosen to say good-bye to, but in the end my sanity depended on my getting rid of her, because she could never accept the fact that I didn't need any more of her counselling. She was the addict, not me."

"Physician heal thyself," nodded Impey.

"Precisely." Jules dropped his briefcase to put his arms loosely on to Impey's shoulders.

She felt the warmth of his lips against her cheek before they brushed briefly on to her mouth making her tingle before she drew back. "I'll do my best."

"I know you'll be wonderful with Cally." He stepped off her doorstep.

"Goodbye". She shut the door quickly.

"And hallo to you," she said to the plywood box that stood in the hall.

She knelt down beside it. Some slats had been cut out to make a barred window. Impey looked through them to see Cally, her head bent forward, was strutting crossly from one foot to the other.

"I'm sorry Cally. I didn't ask to have you to stay, but I'll do my best," said Impey wondering whether the bird had any appreciation of the human voice. She might have degrees in zoology, but she felt woefully ignorant of any practical handling of birds of prey.

Cally eyed her with a look which seemed to combine venom with suspicion. She shook her feathers then threw herself down on to the bottom of the box where she lay glaring up at Impey.

"There's no need to sulk," said Impey to the bird. Flick might have sneered at her for being employed by Jules to be Nancy Drew, Miss Marple and Inspector Morse rolled into one, but seeing a vulture in a box having a strop made her feel rather more like Alice in Wonderland.

16. Wednesday morning

It would be a Wednesday. Impey wondered whether she could follow Jules's suggestion and leave Cally's box outside the front door with a note for Steve saying he should put the birdhouse into the corner of her tiny garden opposite her little shed. There was no other obvious place for it to go.

Vexed she twiddled some strands of her hair, realising as she did that she had not brushed it yet this morning. Nor had she eaten breakfast. She went back into the kitchen where she dropped a couple of pieces of wholemeal bread into the toaster. On second thoughts she did not like the idea of Steve erecting an aviary in her garden without any supervision.

The more she thought about the arrival of Cally, the more irritated she became. She must have been half asleep to have agreed to Jules's ridiculous proposition, whatever he was paying her, or she owed him. She would have to find a way of moving her mortgage out of his clutches to stop any more absurd demands. She did not want another shack in her garden; she'd paid to have one taken away when she moved here.

Whilst she ate her toast and delicious homemade marmalade she'd bought from the Friday Women's Institute market, one of the benefits of living in the country, she glanced out of her kitchen window at the lawn bordered by shrubs. On the small stone terrace outside her kitchen window a couple of brown wrens pecked at crumbs on her bird table.

Cally's presence would frighten away all the little birds Impey enjoyed watching. To sit on her battered wooden garden chair on the rough paving stones outside her kitchen eating a piece of toast early in the morning whilst the songbirds chirped and warbled was such a joy.

166

When Steve turns up, I'll have to tell him to take Cally away again. I can't be jumped into accepting this, whatever the financial incentive.

First she would have to ring Rosie. Only last night when she'd finished babysitting for her, she'd confirmed their game of golf today. Rosie was full of excitement over the important things she'd got to tell her, but said she'd fill her in today on the golf course. They were due to play in a couple of hours.

The call to Rosie was even direr than Impey expected. Impey calling Rosie Roxy a couple of times did not help. She could not fathom why she should make such a slip, except that whenever she thought about Roxanne's grim story, the horror of it smothered her. She had not intended to admit to Rosie why she could not play, but her astute friend soon dragged it out of her. "Please don't tell me that you're ditching me for Jules Challenger."

"Well it's not exactly like that."

"No? You mean he hasn't made some urgent request you can't refuse?"

Impey sighed. "I want to refuse it that's why I'm staying in." She gave as low key an account of Cally's arrival as she could manage.

Rosie's reaction was predictable. "You do not want that bird out of the box, Impey. You must put it straight into the boot of your car, drive to club and leave it back on Jules's doorstep. Then you've only got to go next door to play with me. Leave a note on your door to say what you've done."

This Impey had to agree seemed an easier method of refusal.

"Anybody's allowed to have second thoughts," said Rosie. "Anyway, as I keep telling you, you should never have got tied up with that man."

"He's not the devil incarnate Rosie."

A sarcastic cough echoed down the line. "Plenty of people at the club think he is. Jack says there's a tremendous furore over what went on at the last committee meeting. He's sneaky Impey, trying to get control of the club by underhand means."

"I think he bought the club's debt quite honestly to help the club out."

"Do you? I'm not so sure. You know my bracelet that Deborah's pinched?"

"Yes," said Impey in a heartfelt tone.

"Jack's remembered where we bought it from, a second-hand jewellery shop in Woking. And you'll never guess who owned it."

Impey's heart sank: she could guess.

"Jules's mother, and that begs a question doesn't it. Where did she get my watch from?"

"I haven't a clue."

"Nor have I, but what I do know is that Deborah was heart-broken to lose it, just as I am and I can tell you what, it would do Jules good to lose something he was very attached to."

"That's a bit harsh." *So Jules was right.* Impey thought of Cally sitting in her hall.

"I don't think so, and there are plenty of people in the club who'd agree with me; they don't want the golf course turned into a zoo."

Impey's relief when the call ended changed to dismay as before she could pick up the bird box to put it into her car, there was a peal on her front doorbell.

Steve had arrived. With his casual blue short-sleeved check shirt hanging out side his beige chino trousers, he stood calmly on her doorstep a smile of greeting on his narrow face. His stance was so relaxed he might have been an old buddy coming to do some odd jobs as a favour.

"Didn't want to leave Cally too long in her travelling box," he said cheerfully in response to Impey's surprise at his prompt arrival. He explained that he'd been outside the house for a while. Through the kitchen window he'd seen her on the telephone and not wished to disturb her.

Impey glanced at her watch, which told her she must have been talking to Rosie for nearly three quarters of an hour. She'd tried so hard to mollify Rosie that she hadn't noticed the minutes slipping away.

Steve cut short her apology with a dismissive wave of his slim hand. "Never mind. I was able to use the time laying the foundations for the birdhouse."

Impey's jaw dropped. "But I don't want it. Anyway I thought I was meant to be ringing you to arrange a convenient time."

"I'm awfully sorry." Steve frowned. "I must have got the wrong impression from Jules, but he was, as usual, in a tearing hurry."

"What did he tell you?"

"That you had a frightfully important thing on today which you mustn't be late for so I was to come round to you immediately and get started – then you'd be comfortable going out and leaving me to it. Jules is very thoughtful that way."

"Oh!" huffed Impey, "this is very awkward – I didn't get a chance when Jules was here to consider having a bird of prey around, but it won't work. I love to hear songbirds and Cally will put them off coming into the garden."

Steve shook his head. "No she won't. They won't take any notice of her confined in a cage; they certainly don't at Jules's place. It's not as if she'll be eyeing them because she's far too well fed."

To Impey's alarm, he flipped open the lid of Cally's box.

Cally, who was now standing on a wooden bar in the box, fluffed up her feathers coquettishly, whilst Steve held out his arm to her. She half flew and half jumped on to his gloved wrist.

"See," said Steve, stroking her bald head. "She's a little darling, so tame."

Impey gulped. The bird did indeed appear to look at Steve affectionately, the way she held her head on one side to gaze into his hazel brown eyes.

"You hold her." With his free hand, he deftly undid the buckle of a canvas saddlebag which hung over his shoulder. He delved into it to produce a glove with gauntlets. "Jules thought this would probably be your size."

Impey took the glove thinking she did not wish to know which wife it might have belonged to –*not the tiny Roxanne anyway*. She slipped it on to her hand, feeling somewhat like Cinderella since the glove fitted her perfectly, though being handed a lump of red meat to hold in the other hand dented the picture.

"Now show her you want her," instructed Steve, "wave your arm a bit to the side.

To Impey's astonishment Cally jumped on to her arm. She plucked the meat out of her bare fingers almost in the same movement, but with such a deft peck that Impey saw the meat was gone before she realised she'd not felt the touch of Cally's beak.

"Such a big bird but she feels quite light," she exclaimed.

Cally turned her meagrely feathered head round to cast an appraising look at Impey with her large amber gold eyes. *Now do you like me?* She seemed to ask.

Impey gazed back at her, amazed at how quickly the bird had become an extension of her arm, another limb. The feel was magical.

"Listen," said Steve, "Jules wouldn't want Cally to be anywhere she wasn't wanted. He's got great instinct about people usually, but if he's wrong, I can take away those foundation blocks: they're only meant for a temporary cage anyway." He leant forward to stroke the soft brown feathers on Cally's wing gently. "And you wouldn't want to be somewhere you weren't wanted either."

"Oh its not like that," said Impey, suddenly realising she did not want to let go of Cally. "She is a lovely bird. It's just that the whole thing seemed a bit impractical, my having no experience of birds of prey."

"Oh you'll get it in no time. Jules sensed you'd be a natural. Leave me your house key and I'll set up a perch in your sitting room for when you want to have her with you watching TV in the evenings.

Impey gawped at him whilst the bird fluffed her feathers lightly as though this was the most normal suggestion.

The picture of herself and Cally spending harmonious evenings together began to seem less and less odd as Impey drove to the golf club, although she could not agree that the bird would not present problems. Already she was exceeding the speed limit to ensure she reached the club on time. She felt a mess too, because she'd had to change so quickly into golf clothes that she'd seized the a shirt and shorts with clashing blues.

She'd misjudged Steve. When she'd first met him at the Inn on the Beach, she'd assumed he was merely a gofer at Jules's beck and call. Now she realised how persuasive he was. He had a subtle chameleon knack of tuning in to every vagary she'd felt, enabling him to dispel any doubts she had.

Without him at hand, having Cally installed in her home looked very different, especially when Rosie greeted her at the club.

"Such a good thing you've dropped that bird off next door," she said when they changed their shoes in the cloakroom. "Whilst I was waiting for you people have been going on and on about Jules Challenger and what's going to be done about him and his ideas for the club."

"What do you mean?"

"Well the general idea was that if someone shot that bird he has, Jules might get the message that his ideas were not welcome at Bisley Heath."

"They were probably joking."

Rosie shook her head. "No. They're serious: they don't want our course mucked about and I don't blame them."

Outside the clubhouse as they pulled their trolleys full of clubs hurriedly across the edge of the car park to make their way to the first tee, Rosie nudged her. "Over there, the man with the round face, next the blue BMW, he's Adam Scrivenor."

"Yes, you pointed him out to me before."

"Did I tell you he'd taken Jack's place on the committee as treasurer?"

Impey nodded.

"Well I heard him mouthing off about Jules to the secretary. He said something about knowing Jules of old and that he wouldn't be easy to stop."

Impey didn't want to hear any more anti Jules talk. Golf was meant to be her relaxation, not work. She resolved not to admit to Rosie that she'd changed her mind about Cally; she was quite excited now about the prospect of learning to handle her. Good friend though she was, Rosie rarely visited her cottage: they met at her home or the club. She need not know about the bird.

Dapper in his business suit, the man in glasses across the car park, beside the BMW, did not look like the type to rush round with a shotgun shooting birds. It might be worth talking to him if he'd known Jules for a long time. Though he stood by his car, apparently ready to leave, he was in an earnest conversation with a large white-haired man now.

Whilst they waited by the first tee to start their game, another couple having taken their starting time, she watched the men across the car park. Could this neat respectable-looking man really be a threat to Jules? The chap Adam was talking to looked too aged to be ferocious, until he spotted her when he nudged Adam. They both looked across the car park to stare pointedly in her direction.

Impey turned away hurriedly. Beside her Rosie looked impatiently at the people in front of them, all obviously irritated Impey's late arrival had delayed the field. Impey tapped Rosie on the shoulder. "You didn't mention to anyone that I'd got Cally did you?"

Rosie looked blank.

"The bird,"

Rosie's shake of her head was contradicted by the blush which rose in her cheeks. "Well it doesn't matter does it, since you've taken it back?"

17. A session with a psychologist

Impey's fingers hovered over the telephone. She wondered how to approach Tessa. Prior to the demise of the News of the World, she might have masqueraded as a potential client, but that was taboo now. Anyway she guessed Tessa would be smart enough to seem through a fake patient.

She would have preferred not to have to mention Jules before she met Tessa face to face. The best way to get people to impart information was usually, Impey found, to start with some innocuous topic. That was how she'd been a successful door-stepper as a journalist. But you had to knock on the doors of people's houses at the right time. The problem with Tessa was going to be gauging that precise moment, since she worked both at a local health centre and from her home in Guildford. Her seeing clients at irregular hours meant it would be all too easy for Impey to turn up when Tessa had a visitor.

Eventually she rang Tessa on her ex-directory home number which Jules had given her. "We're on good terms," he'd said nonchalantly, "people with debts often want counselling so I lob them in Tessa's direction; I recommended our ex-treasurer who had his hands in the club till had some sessions with her. He pooh-poohed Impey's reaction that the Metcalfes would be appalled at his suggestion. "As a matter of fact they were very receptive and asked for her details."

Impey had pulled a face at the phone she held in her hand. *Odd Rosie never mentioned that to me.*

To Impey's further surprise, Tessa cut short her apologetic opening salvo, identifying herself as a journalist, involved in a story with which a psychologist like Tessa might be able to help. In a resigned tone, she agreed Impey should come and see her. She said she'd been expecting "something of this sort", which begged the question what exactly she was thinking would happen. Did she know about the mutilation of the figurehead?

Tessa lived in a three storey Victorian terraced house on the south side of Guildford. *Goodness, if this is funded by her marriage breakup with Jules, it's a good advertisement for the way he treats his ex-wives – she was only married to him for a couple of years.*

Impey followed her into a back room on the ground floor which was her consulting room, so chosen, Tessa explained, to avoid passers-by on the pavement seeing clients through the window.

Though sceptical about counselling, which she'd refused during the traumatic year she'd wrestled with her own divorce proceedings, Impey had to admit tacitly that the surroundings here were calming. Despite its position at the back of the building, Tessa's consulting place was a small elegant room with moulded skirting boards, whose shape was replicated round the edge of the ceiling, from which a glass chandelier with small tear drop shapes dangled. Gentle pastel paintings of flowers hung on the magnolia walls. Even the light brown carpet seemed soft under her feet.

If the room style might have been expected, Tessa's looks certainly were not. She was a tall plump woman with an oval shaped head, accentuated by her severe hairstyle. All her brown hair was scraped back off her face into a knot behind her head. The effect was compelling. Her face had a creamy smoothness but when she fixed her slightly protruding hazel brown eyes on Impey's, she felt as mesmerised as a rabbit caught by the glare of a wolf.

"Do sit down," invited Tessa. She pointed to a high-seated winged armchair. "That one's good if you've got a bad back."

"I don't actually," said Impey. Puzzled she wrinkled her face. "Do many of the people who you treat have back problems then?"

"Not necessarily, but bad backs often take a long time to heal which means sufferers tend to get depressed, so one problem feeds off another."

"I see." Impey sat down in a beige tub chair alongside a small light oak table only to stand up again quickly as she noticed lines flicker on Tessa's forehead. "Oh sorry. Is this your chair?"

Tessa waved a smooth hand in the air. "Doesn't matter. It's only when I'm in here working I sit there."

Impey looked at the five available chairs before she settled herself in an armchair, covered in a floral chintz, opposite the table. "Is it significant which chair your clients chose?"

"Not necessarily," repeated Tessa. "People can have all sorts of reasons for choosing a chair."

"Like?" asked Impey.

"An association is the most obvious, but it might not be at all a significant association."

"But you yourself obviously don't like the wing chair," guessed Impey.

Tessa's wide broad-lipped mouth stretched into a smile. "Yes, I have to admit I had a very irritating aunt who always wanted to sit on that sort of chair."

"That figures. It looks the sort of chair an important person would choose, or at least someone who wanted to be important."

"Do you think it wrong to want to matter then?" Tessa's voice reverted to a controlled neutral tone. She sat down in her tub arm chair facing Impey.

177

Ouch. I'm already getting into deep water here. "No, of course not." The thought that maybe she could show her sympathetic nature by revealing she had friends with problems prompted Impey to ask, "So which chair did Rosie Metcalfe choose then?"

The colour of Tessa's cheeks as well as the annoyance in her voice told Impey that Rosie had indeed visited the psychotherapist. "I hope you're not expecting me to discuss clients." Her hands fingered the shiny wooden edges to the arms of her chair.

"No, no, of course not. It's just that I have this friend who mentioned she might come and see you," lied Impey lamely.

"So what do you really want to see me about?"

""A project I've been asked to work on by Jules Challenger."

"Ah, I see." Her low soft voice dropped a tone. She raised her brown plucked eyebrows, "and how does Jules think I can help you with whatever this might be?"

"Because you understand him, I mean his situation, better than anyone; you could point me in the right direction." Impey stumbled on. "The thing is that the figurehead of Flick, his first wife, that's his masthead for all his office stationery and website as well as his boat, has been massacred."

"A good job too, I think I might say, since I'm not being required to be professional at the moment."

Impey stared at her in astonishment.

"That's not for quotation by the way. – I think you did mention you were a journalist."

"Oh absolutely. Jules has forbidden any publicity surrounding the subject, but why do you think something so damaging to Jules and his business is a good thing?"

"For a start it won't damage his business one jot. He's got his stationery set up and I don't think many clients need to visit the boat, if they ever did. The boat was always merely a show place for entertaining bigwigs."

Impey gulped, "Surely the figurehead meant something?"

"Yes twenty years ago, but not now. Jules needs to move on. His problem is that he can't and never has been able to. That's why you're here." Her voice sharpened slightly.

"Er...I think Jules is trying to move forward, but needs Flick's help. He seems a very loyal person. That's why he needs to know who chopped off her statue's arms."

Tessa's shoulders clenched as she shuddered. "Ugh. Did what happen?"

Impey nodded.

"So someone literally chopped off the arms?"

"Not as such I understand. Tarquin told me the arms were such an awful mess that he couldn't restore the model."

Tessa's smooth face creased as she laughed. "Don't say Jules has dug him up again?"

Impey nodded.

"You're saying that what was left of the arms was really chewed up?"

"Yes, so I understand."

Tessa frowned thoughtfully. "Then probably Caesar did it. He'd chew up anything."

"I suppose that's possible, but how would he have got hold of it? Jules said the sculpture, which he'd taken off the yacht to be varnished, was in his garage, which was open, but

Caesar would have been in the house or in his pen in the garden."

"So, someone could have gone into his pen. It's not locked or at least it never used to be."

"Surely they wouldn't dare?"

Tessa laughed again. "Anyone who knew Caesar, any of the handlers would go there without a second thought. Caesar's very much a pack animal; he responds to loads of people. Once when he got out a policeman brought him back to the house with a chain round his neck – he thought Caesar was a dog! No, my guess is that someone's got fed up with Jules hankering after what has been and decided to put an end to it."

"Was that why you and he broke up?" ventured Impey.

"More or less. Roxanne was more of a problem than Flick in those days, but frankly Jules could never put either of them behind him."

"You didn't find talking about his past helped him get it out of his system?"

"That may be all right on a couch in a consulting room, but it's pretty good hell in a marriage. I thought when he asked me to marry him that he really wanted to move forward, embark on a new life, but that wasn't to be."

Impey twiddled a strand of her hair. "So you think someone, possibly a woman in Jules's life, might resent Flick's influence on him so much she threw her effigy to the wolf?" A picture of Camilla Wilmot, the large lady who'd played in the four with Jules at the invitation, flashed into her mind. Might not the current lady captain resent another woman being as powerful, or even having more influence at the club? The more she thought about this, the more obvious it seemed

Tessa could be right; someone probably threw the figurehead into Caesar's pen.

Tessa nodded. "I certainly felt like doing it plenty of times myself, though I'd have preferred to have got rid of Roxanne's bronze."

Did you do it? Impey asked her mentally but said instead, "What was that?"

"Another of Tarquin's works. Jules worshipped it. He had it in the bedroom until I banished it to his study. Mandy managed to get rid of it completely, gave it to some gallery I believe."

"Mandy?" Impey questioned.

"His fourth wife; she's a friend of mine." Tessa's protruding eyes seemed to revolve round Impey's face.

Impey wanted to ask whether Mandy was also a client, but thought *perhaps not,* after Tessa's earlier remark about Rosie. *A compliment would work better.* "Jules says he was in a terrible state after Roxanne's death and that you got him through it."

"Functioning perhaps, but I'd question the 'through it'. Jules can't grow up. He wants to stay being Peter Pan with Wendy. If only he could find her. That's his current game I expect." She eyed Impey with her soft popping hazel eyes.

"He manages to run a company."

"The insolvency business is like a game, a massive game of bluff."

This seemed a novel concept to Impey, but she found Tessa was quite serious. Buying debts, the psychologist avowed, was a gamble with other people's fortunes, something you could only do if you found it fun and Jules loved it. "He adores bluffing. That's his life, bluff and double bluff; he can persuade anyone to do anything, until they get to know him.

Then they may say 'no'. Of course he can never accept it so he keeps trying again to get you on side."

Her shoulders back, she sat very upright in her tub chair as she explained how Jules bought debts for about thirty per cent of what the debtor owed. He would always take a detailed history of the debt which he studied carefully, especially the manifold excuses people made for being unable to service whatever loan they had. He or one of his henchmen would then visit the defaulter.

"Henchmen?" Impey had queried.

"That's what I call them," Tessa insisted, "they're always close friends, people like Adam Scrivenor, whom Jules has personally selected because he trusts them to take the wolf with them."

"That must be terrifying for someone insolvent."

"Of course it is, but it makes them think twice about making more excuses for non payment. Whoever goes, always explains how tame the wolf is, but naturally poor scared people don't believe that – they're just terribly relieved to be offered new terms for the money they owe, usually smaller sums payable over a longer term."

I can't believe it. It's sickening, cruel really. Impey bit back the exclamations. *She's his ex-wife; she's exaggerating.*

"So you see," Tessa leant out towards Impey, her head poked forward like a bird of prey eyeing a victim before swooping downwards, "there are probably plenty of people out there wanting to alarm Jules like he's frightened them."

"Why take it out on Flick's figurehead? She has nothing to do with the wolf."

"I know that. Taking Caesar to see clients was Roxanne's idea but no one knows or cares about that now. Flick's the face of the Griffon Trust, and a little bird told me

Jules wants to get back with her. So I'm not too surprised someone's tossed her sculpture to the wolf."

Belying her calm expression Impey could almost read in her face the unsaid repetition of her words, *I could have done it myself.* She wanted to ask about Mandy, wife number four, but Tessa clearly thought she'd said enough. She glanced at a large round clock with roman numerals on the wall, which she informed Impey was a present from Jules, before saying her time was up. Another client was expected.

She saw Impey to her front door which she opened for her. She held out her hand. In a surprisingly warm tone she said "Do come back again if there's anything more you want to know."

"Lots," replied Impey, "from what you've told me there seems to be unfinished business in the aftermath of Roxanne's death."

Tessa shrugged, "Possibly, but remember, I only came on the scene after the accident."

"But you talked to everybody, so you'd know a lot about it."

"Yes, but I'm not the best person to talk to about it because I made an awful," she now stressed the word, 'mistake'."

"What was that?"

"I thought she was murdered." With that she almost shoved Impey over the doorstep.

18. Tessa has an unwelcome visitor

Tessa slammed the door Impey had left open. *Such a silly woman,* she reflected as she wandered back to her consulting room. *Why did I bother to see her?*

She blamed her instinct. As she often told clients, "People trust their instinct to their detriment. Your instinct is the fount of old mistakes." She knew that to her cost. If she'd trusted her intellect she'd never have got involved with Jules, let alone marry him.

To warn that girl who'd come to see her would have been satisfying, although there was far less excuse for her to be seduced by Jules's charm. She must be in her mid-thirties at least, whereas Tessa had scarcely reached her late twenties when she entered Jules's orbit.

Newly qualified she was working for the National Health Service when the police approached her to do psychological profiles on the people involved in Roxanne's death. They wanted it done subtly so she was to be involved as a professional counsellor, since bereavement counselling for people caught up in sudden violent death situations was one of her specialities.

The police had taken Grace into their confidence, got her to suggest to everyone in her home at the time of Roxanne's death, that they should talk to Tessa. Apart from Grace, who'd adored Roxanne like a daughter, Jules was the most disturbed by the horrific event.

As she walked along her narrow hallway back to her consulting room, Tessa recalled with a shaft of happiness how good it had felt to help Jules. He had needed her so much. The skills she'd honed in so few years after finishing her training had helped him deal with the reality of his second wife's death. He'd been such a mess, unable to work because he would break down and cry in public.

People were impressed with the way she treated him. They said she'd cured him, but of course she hadn't: she'd simply got him back on to his old track, playing the same old game again. He didn't want to grow up any more than the silly girl who'd come to see her this afternoon.

You could tell that from her name. What sane woman would call herself "Impey", or allow others to? She was another child in adult's clothing. She probably played golf too. The game usually attracted people like that. Still at least it wasn't as dangerous as messing with wolves or chainsaws which Roxanne enjoyed.

Why didn't Impey see that someone would have thrown that stupid bit of carving to the wolf? Let the past devour history. Anyone fed up with Jules and his games would have done it.

She sank down into her favourite tub chair. Then she pushed herself up again. She needed a cup of tea to revive herself after the emotional upheaval of Impey's visit. She kept an electric kettle inside the antique armoire next her bookshelf. Making a hole in the back of it so she could plug the kettle into the wall behind had felt like sacrilege, but she didn't want to have anything electric on display in her room, or feel obliged to offer a drink to a client, although she kept a small fridge in the bottom of the armoire.

Whilst she fixed herself a cup of Rooibos tea, she reflected how odd it was Jules's old mates had returned to his fold. She'd thought they'd all gone their separate ways, which she'd tried tacitly to encourage. They were right to be angry with Jules for suggesting Roxanne did some tree felling for

Grace without someone qualified in horticulture alongside to help.

She ran over in her mind the event she'd avoided discussing with Impey. Why should she tell her about it anyway? It was not as though she'd been present at the time. It was not her fault everyone was so upset. She'd been there to help.

Ned was furious because the police had arrested him on suspicion of murder. Her profile might have tipped them in his direction, but his fingerprints on the chainsaw as well as Roxanne's body were supposedly damning, because no one could understand how anyone could chop off both arms by accident. He was only in custody a couple of days during which time forensic experts examining the tree came to the conclusion she had slipped whilst the chainsaw was balanced on a bough above her, on which she hung. The vibration had caused the saw to drop on to her arms, slicing them through.

Steve gave evidence that he'd seen Ned give Roxanne the kiss of life which had also exonerated him. He said he'd seen Ned switch off the buzzing saw before he flung it away in disgust, but it hadn't rung true to Tessa. Steve would say anything Grace wanted him say and Grace was too distraught by Roxanne's death to allow it to be anything but an accident.

Anyway, the question remained as to how Roxanne got hold of the chainsaw in the first place, since it was supposed to be locked in a shed. The only two men with keys were Steve and Adam. Both their mothers worked for Grace who also gave them work at weekends.

Tarquin wasn't involved, other than having done the dreaded sculpture of Roxanne. The memory of Jules suggesting he got Tarquin to sculpt her too made Tessa smile now. Good job she refused. Apparently the sculptor was quite offended. His career hadn't taken off at that stage. He needed the work, but that was his problem, not hers. Common sense told her the link with Tarquin had got to be broken. Thank goodness for that one sensible thought in her period of lustful madness.

She pursed her lips as she pictured Impey tottering on the edge of a ravine. *I ought to help her.* Tessa pulled open the hidden drawer beneath her table to take out a pad of paper and a biro. She occasionally suggested to clients, those who weren't obsessed with lists of course, that it can help you to think clearly if you jot down a few notes.

Strewth; she must be in a bad way if all she could do was to doodle hearts with arrows through them. She wrote the name Impey a couple of times, spelling it with a 'y' and an 'ie'. It was no use. She did a little drawing of Impey with her shoulder length hair. The moment she pictured her, she could see how things lay. The silly girl, was already a lost cause. She, Tessa, shouldn't even try to save her.

"Those who cannot remember the past are condemned to repeat it." She couldn't think who'd said it but that didn't make it any less true. Counsellors shouldn't try to save people. They had to save themselves. She'd failed with Mandy, Jules's fourth wife and if Impey wanted...She mustn't go there; she must not hear in her mind Impey's tone of voice when she uttered Jules's name.

She sipped her cup of soothing tea. Time to concentrate on herself.

A peal on the doorbell interrupted her thoughts. *How odd.* She didn't have a client; she'd invented one to get rid of Impey. *Probably it's a travelling salesman.* In case it was a troubled client calling, she got up to speak into the intercom, asking who was there.

A voice she recognised answered.

Oh God, it's him. "What do you want?"

"To talk to you."

"Why?"

"Something you should know," whistled down the intercom.

She sighed, got up and walked down the hall passage back to the front door.

The unreconstructed man was on her doorstep. "Hi." He smiled.

She knew that was dangerous. "You can't come in," she said as he tried to step into her house.

He put his foot in the doorway. His shoulder held the door open whilst he tried to push her backwards, his broad hands showing through the transparent close-fitting disposable gloves he wore.

"You can't come in," she repeated, putting her hand out to press the panic button on the wall.

"Here's fine," he hissed, knocking her arm away from the switch, before delving into his pocket. He pulled out a gun, which made her want to laugh since she could see it was merely a water pistol.

Her humour evaporated the moment he pulled the trigger. A fine spray of liquid hit her in the eye. Unintentionally she snuffed it up her nose.

She tried to scream, but her open mouth inhaled another dose of whatever chemical he fired at her. All she produced was a gurgle.

As her brain began to fuzz, her body shuddered. *Oh God. He's going to rape me.* She slumped against her hall wall. In an effort to plead with him she fixed her eyes up into his brown eyes. *Please,* she tried to ask, but she saw no sign of softness in his pale brown eyes. He had no empathy; he was a man without mercy. His mission was to kill her.

Her brain wearily tossed the idea around that maybe she was almost dead already. Rebellion rose inside her. She would not die without being avenged; she must do something, leave a message which would deceive this man. Against a descending torpor, she wriggled her back up the wall to pull herself upright before she staggered back to her consulting room. Her strength was draining away with every step, but she managed to reach it. With a strange feeling of triumph she flopped down into the winged armchair.

The man who followed her in watched her subside there.

That was convenient, since his work was only half done. He'd thought he'd have to put her somewhere like this to make her death look convincingly like suicide. Already there was a half-drunk cup of tea on the table beside the arm chair.

This really was his lucky day. A pad of paper with hearts pierced by arrows lay on a table near the winged chair. That would give the right impression too.

She even wore a full grey linen skirt which he could pull up easily. Luckily she had not changed her dress habits. He'd planned for that. Gently he rolled her body to one side in the chair. He threw up her skirt before pulling down her skimpy white knickers.

"Huh", he blew out the exclamation as he dragged them down her thighs. He could have guessed she'd wear something like this; after the divorce she probably wanted to revert to being a virgin. She got her kicks from hearing the gory details of other people's lives. Still no matter, the thought of killing her was excitement enough for him.

He left the knickers stretched out at her knees. No need to take them off altogether. He could manage without that.

She gave a slight groan as though she sensed what he was about to do, but the lump of her body simply sagged against the arm of the chair. Her head slumped on to her shoulder. She wasn't really aware of what was going to happen.

Pity she wasn't. He would have liked her to know he was the powerful one. Her days of toxic advice were over. Vulnerable girls like Mandy would be safe from her. He was in control now, not she with her self-righteous counselling.

His hands tingled on her soft skin. No he must not play with it, much as he liked bums. He reckoned he could tell what a woman was like from her bottom. This round white flabby one reminded him of a giant clam, that spongy undersea plant which trapped passing fish in its fronds.

Gently he prised apart her buttocks. He didn't want to leave a trace of what he was about to do. Any abrasion or bruise could be a give away, but with the small syringe he drew from his pocket, he could give her the enema without leaving a mark. Only thirty milligrams which he injected into her rectum would be enough to wipe the lady out.

The substance would be found in her bloodstream, or indeed in her hair samples in any autopsy, but if luck went his way, her body would not be found for at least twenty-four hours, possibly thirty-six since this was a Saturday afternoon. He had plenty of time to leave a trail of false clues as to her demise.

A cupboard, an old-fashioned armoire, stood against the wall with its door open. Inside was a kettle, a jar of coffee granules and some brands of different teas. He could leave the full packet of anti-depressants he'd brought with him in there, after he'd wiped her fingers on to the empty sachets he'd brought to throw into the waste-paper basket, except he couldn't see one. Ho hum, he'd have to leave the empty sachets in the armoire too.

He was pleased he'd used Ketamine, the party drug to knock her out. She might not be a regular taker, but she could have got it off the internet; she certainly needed it. She was a real bore at parties, sitting in a corner having an earnest heart to heart talk with someone pathetic enough to hang on her every word.

The morphine mixed with the Ketamine, might also be traceable, but he hadn't used enough to kill her. He prided himself it was a good choice, as he placed the packet of poppy seeds in the back of her cupboard on the wall. Good idea to make it look as though she'd hidden them. He'd taken the precaution of bringing a packet of bagels covered with poppy seeds as well; they could be left in the front of the cupboard. He doubted the coroner would pay too much attention to the minimum amount of morphine. It should be overshadowed by the amount of Temazepam found in her bloodstream. Even if her doctor maintained that he'd never prescribed it for her, it was widely available on the internet.

Another good thing about this killing was that he could leave the body where she died. Grace's little body was still in his chest freezer. Although he had padlocked it there was always a risk someone unexpected might break it open. To avert that danger he would have to dispose of her soon, although the ice would preserve her body and stop it giving off the stench of death.

He had an idea, a very good idea, of how to get rid of every trace of her, but it would take preparation. There was groundwork to be done before he could eliminate Grace entirely, but he would do it. His plan was foolproof. Grace could exist no more. Every smidgeon of her would vanish.

That way he'd get her completely out of his life. He'd felt he had to do this for a long time. Ever since the first day he'd met her, he'd felt she was like a bad little witch casting spells on all around her. The world would be a better place without her.

Tessa was no different, so bloody sanctimonious about doing good. She thought she knew how everyone felt. No, correction, she thought she knew how everyone ought to feel. She was a wrecker of lives, not a saviour, because she gained influence over people.

He should have killed her ages ago.

19 Dodger warns Impey

Someone was hammering on Impey's doorbell early in the morning again.

She leapt out of bed to fling on some clothes, wondering if Jules was going to pay her another early morning visit. He was supposed to be coming over some time to give her further lessons on how to look after Cally, but his visits had been fleeting. He had simply collected his bird to take her flying somewhere, then returned her later, staying for a cup of tea or coffee when he would ask Impey how she was progressing with the investigation.

During the weekend Steve had arrived to feed and exercise her.

When she'd looked out of her window on Saturday morning to see a pale gold Aston Martin DB5 parked at her garden gate, she'd assumed Jules must have arrived in a different car from his usual four by four. She could not imagine anyone else she knew would own the James Bond car. Steve's slight figure alighting from the car was a disappointment.

She was afraid her feelings were obvious since she'd been unable to stop herself exclaiming, "I wouldn't have expected you to drive that car." When Steve had replied that it was one of Jules's "cast-offs", she'd tried to be humorous. "Do you scoop up a lot of treasures then?"

Steve had nodded, then added with a wry grin, "Other than his women." He patted her on the shoulder. "Actually Jules really wanted to come today to show you Cally himself, but he'd promised his mother he'd play golf with her in some important competition. He said to be sure to tell you he'd rather be here with you."

That had assuaged the disappointment a little. Jules must feel something for her beyond just her being a useful employee. She felt a smidgeon of envy he should have parents alive. The memory of her own parents' death in a car crash five years ago hit her; she winced. The loss of two people who cared for her so much still hurt. In practical terms it meant she no longer had that backstop at weekends, somewhere to go when she had nothing else to do.

Yesterday Steve's visit filled that void. She was surprised how much she enjoyed it. Initially horrified by the height of the long pole inside aviary, which Steve had erected for Cally's perch, Impey found she enjoyed looking up at her. Until she'd seen a vulture so close, Impey had always thought of them as ugly birds. Now her view changed. The white down on Cally's head, the golden brown ruff round her neck and the different shades of her tawny feathers looked quite beautiful glistening in the sunniest corner of her tiny garden.

Once she'd discovered that Cally would not fly away over her head the moment she opened the door, she was less worried about the prospect of looking after her. Cally, Steve explained, was imprinted; born in captivity, she didn't understand she was a bird, but regarded humans as her parents. Many falconers, he confided to Impey, were very critical of this; they were appalled Jules had taught her a gimmick like picking up golf balls. His mouth twisted into a lop-sided grin when he spoke.

Impey felt she'd under-estimated him when she saw the relationship he'd established with the bird; she was astonished Cally trotted beside him while he walked. At a gesture of his hand, Cally stepped on to the weighing machine Steve brought with him. He explained he had to weigh her every time before she flew so he knew exactly how much food to give her. Too much and she would not bother to take any exercise, but too little meant she would not have the muscle strength to fly.

"Complicated," Impey had commented.

"Not really," he'd replied, "quite straightforward really."

Impey was amazed Cally hopped into her box to go out.

"She's quite used to it," said Steve. He wrinkled his face up apologetically. "Do you mind if we take your car?"

Impey looked at him surprised. "How do you know I've got room?"

Steve smiled. "Nothing gets past Jules. He noted you'd got a Jazz, perfect for a bird and a girl, the way those back seats fold up leaving a big well. Here's a spare pair of gloves for you to keep in your car." He waved some tattered leather gauntlets at her.

Impey grimaced. "Okay." She might as well work out how to put the bird box in her car for when she wanted to return her to Jules. They were only going to drive round the corner to Bisley Common.

Once out in the open Cally soared away into the sky, so high she was almost out of sight, Impey could hardly believe she would ever return. Then relief turned to delight as the bird swooped back down to them. The thrill she felt at the sight of Cally growing from a speck in the distance to a the size of a huge bird as she dived down from the greenery at the top of a vast oak tree to land beside them when Steve knelt down to give her the signal amazed Impey.

After they'd returned Cally to her aviary, they'd gone out for a pub lunch together. Though the vegetarian dish was a pasta which Impey did not particularly like, she chose it. The memory of the tray laden with pieces of raw chicken, rabbits and rats, which Steve asked her to put in her freezer for Cally, made her squirm at the thought of meat today.

Steve, choosing the most expensive steak on the menu, had no such qualms. He brushed away her offer to pay her share of the bill with a perfunctory gesture because Jules would think *nothing about our putting it on expenses.*

Impey was still reeling from the experience of Cally soaring high through the air to return to her as well as Steve. How did she spot that tiny bit of meat she held between her thumb and forefinger in those thick brown gloves? Did she now recognise Impey as a friend? She was staggered too at how familiar Steve was with the bird; she could hardly believe how fond they seemed of each other.

He was so concerned for Cally that Impey could not help asking whether he would not have preferred to look after the bird himself. Thinking back to the Aston Martin, she asked with a raised eyebrow, "Wouldn't you like to have taken her off Jules's hands yourself?"

Steve had replied in a similar ironic tone. "As I said before, I don't take over Jules's female possessions, be they birds or women; they're usually second-hand anyway."

"Not even the gorgeous Mandy?" asked Impey. Rosie had taken Impey to one of Mandy's sales, where Impey had picked up a couple of pairs of trousers. At the time she had not connected Mandy with Jules because she called herself Mandy Park.

"What makes you think a six foot blonde with an insatiable appetite for clothes would be interested in me?" quipped Steve.

"Strange attractions happen. What made her connect with Jules?"

"Business; they met through the course of his work."

"She owed money?"

"Big Time."

The way Steve's mouth twitched in a smile as he nodded made Impey ask, half joking, "She married him 'cos he'd paid off her debts?"

Steve did not deny it.

Impey was glad to be able to get him on to the subject of women. Here amongst the jovial Sunday lunchtime crowd in the White Hart, sitting one side of a dark wooden table opposite Steve, was a chance to plumb him for some more background information. She was hardly likely to find him much more relaxed. He'd drunk more than half the bottle of red wine they'd shared.

"You know," she remarked in a casual manner, "Tessa reckons Flick's sculpture could have been chewed up by Caesar."

"She was always a ready reckoner." Steve's face crinkled. "And she could have reckoned right. Those shoulders were well masticated."

"But Jules doesn't think the arms were chewed by Caesar does he?"

"He doesn't know any more than we do," said Steve, "if Tarquin had done his job properly, Jules would never have known there were no arms."

"Where did the original arms go to?"

At this Steve had merely shrugged and said "God only knows."

"But did you send the arms with the body to Tarquin."

Steve rolled his eyes. "I'm not sure even he could have made much use of chippings and sawdust."

"If you knew Caesar had chewed up the arms, why didn't you tell Jules?"

"We didn't know things would get out of hand? I didn't know when Jules said he wanted to meet you, or rather see a private detective, what it was about. Anyway, what does it matter?"

"Enough for Jules to employ me to find out who did it."

"Needle in a haystack," said Steve, "anybody with a grudge or without one, some intruder who saw the figurehead in the garage."

"I'm amazed you didn't have it under lock and key."

"Her, please," Steve picked up the wine bottle and poured the rest of the wine into his glass which he then slurped back. "Listen, that's not Jules's style. He likes to keep an open house so friends can pop in to see Caesar when they want."

"Pop in to see Caesar?"

"Sure. Wolves are pack animals. Jules thought for a long time about getting another wolf to be Caesar's mate, possibly a bitch, but he decided in the end he wasn't set up for it – and anyway Caesar had got too humanised."

Steve explained that Jules liked anyone who'd had close contact with Caesar to stay involved, to come and take him for a walk on the common. He was keen people should be educated about wolves, taught they were not the vicious predators damned by so many fables, but played an important part in nature.

"Visiting debtors is hardly part of nature," remarked Impey.

"Caesar's not hostile. He's meant to reassure clients that someone strong and creditable is in charge. Our clients love him." Steve laughed at her sceptical expression. "Even people who start by being terrified change. Look at Mandy: she's even used Caesar for a fashion shoot. He was in the centre pages of some flashy magazine with her modelling clothes." He grinned. "Not that she was wearing much, but that shows how safe she felt with Caesar. Funny thing is, though she used to moan about the mess he made, she often pops in to see him.

Names of others who visited the wolf included Ned the vet, Adam the club's new treasure who'd been a childhood friend of Jules's and Tarquin, whom Steve called Toby, the sculptor. So Tessa was right. Someone who didn't mind going into Caesar's pen could have given Flick's statue to Caesar. Maybe the loss of the arms was a simple coincidence. When Steve retrieved the sculpture from Caesar's pen, he sent it to Tarquin before Jules could see it looking so chewed, because it would obviously upset him. Annoyed though Jules was at the destruction of any forensic evidence for the vandalism, Steve acted in haste to spare him.

Jules himself was certainly impulsive, thumping on her door so early on a Monday morning. Well he was work, not part of her social life. All the same he'd have to wait whilst she put on a bit of makeup. After what Tessa told her, she wanted to preserve a bit of dignity, not be treated like a pawn on the chessboard, to be moved about at will.

Three minutes later, during which time the hammering on the door had continued, she opened it to find her visitor was Dodger.

She hardly knew whether to be glad or irritated at his appearance. The last time they had spoken their conversation had been, if not acrimonious, hardly friendly. Much as she liked him, she was irritated his failed conjuring trick at the club had caused so much trouble with Rosie. Yet now the alarm in his face told her he must have an urgent reason for calling. "Come in. I suppose it's not simply breakfast you're here for."

He rubbed his head with a couple of stubby fingers as he stepped over the threshold into her hall. "No, but something to eat would be good as I haven't had any food this morning yet."

"Okay," she led the way to the kitchen.

Following her, he said to her back, "The thing is I've got to warn you."

She looked over her shoulder as she opened the kitchen door, "Warn me?"

"Tessa's committed suicide."

Impey slumped against the units before quickly pulling herself upright again. "Tell me you are joking."

"No I'm not."

"How do you know this?" She asked suspiciously. *Your last bloody stunt really misfired but if this is a trick it's beyond the pale.*

"Because she was found dead in her consulting room by a couple of her friends."

"Okay, but that's nothing to do with me." Impey took a couple of strides across the floor to reach the breadbin. "Toast okay?"

"Actually I'd like bacon and eggs if you've got them, and I'm afraid it is to do with you. She killed herself on Saturday, after she'd seen you."

"That's ridiculous," said Impey, whilst she ferreted in the fridge for the eggs and bacon. "She was perfectly okay when I left. Actually she was expecting another client, and anyway," she repeated, "how do you know all this?"

"The girl friends she was meant to meet for a meal on Saturday night got worried about her when they couldn't contact her by Sunday night on her mobile so they went round to her house, and when they couldn't get any answer from her flat there, they called the people who rent the top floor."

"So she doesn't own the whole house then?"

"Christ no; she only has a flat in the building and the one consulting room downstairs."

"Anyway those guys were a bit worried because there was a bit of a smell in the building, so they broke into her consulting room and found her dead in there."

"I still don't see what it's got to do with me."

"They found a piece of paper with your name on it and pictures of hearts on it."

Impey cracked an egg hard on the side of the non-stick frying pan which she had coated lightly with oil and put it on top of her oven. "That's absurd. She wasn't a moonstruck teenager."

"Must have been underneath," said Dodger. "Anyway her friends obviously thought she was still hung up on Jules because they rang him and gave him hell last night."

"Why hasn't Jules rung me."

"He was nervous about compromising you in some way so he rang me; he says the police will obviously be round to see you because they're bound to have seen that incriminating piece of paper when they searched Tessa's place."

"This is ridiculous." Impey flung a couple of slices of bacon into the frying pan. "I can hardly be blamed for something she scribbled on a piece of paper." She flipped the bacon around with a fish slice. "I can't believe it. She seemed perfectly sane when I last saw her."

She plucked a loaf of brown bread out of a tall white enamel breadbin. The vision of Tessa sitting dead in her consulting room had taken away her appetite, but she thought she ought to eat something, especially if she was going to have to face a police enquiry today. Holding the loaf with one hand whilst she sawed a couple of thick slices with the other helped her feel in command of something.

"Thanks." Dodger picked up a fat slice and tossed it into the frying pan.

"That is so bad for you; all that cholesterol. You'll have an early death."

"I'd rather commit suicide this way." Dodger grimaced. "Sorry, bad taste."

"You haven't told me how she did kill herself?"

"They think she must have swallowed something because there was a cup of tea on the table by her chair."

"That can't be right. Her favourite chair isn't by the table," said Impey.

"Well I may have got that detail wrong, but what I was told was that they found her sitting flopped, or rather stiff, in a chair."

More he could not tell her. Nor could he give her the names of any of Tessa's friends who'd found her. Frustrated, all Impey could do was to wait for the police to call her.

20. Mandy talks to Flick

Flick wished she had not answered the phone. She'd scheduled a morning of tackling a stack of paperwork before an afternoon's play. On her antique pine desk were three scarcely begun proposals for interior designs of houses, work she was lucky to have in these lean times. She could not afford to delay preparing plans to give to clients, or they would simply find someone else who would work more speedily. Plenty of hungry folk were out there, needy enough to work all night if necessary to produce plans on time.

Even if she had all the time in the world, she would still not feel inclined to speak to the woman on the other end of the line. Fortunately when Mandy had wanted, or rather Jules had wanted her to join Bisley Heath, the club still had a long waiting list and there was no good reason for Flick to help her climb it.

The thought of two Mrs Challengers at Bisley Heath was anathema. She hadn't minded when she was first married, playing second fiddle to the gorgeous Faye Challenger, until the Challenger parents left under a cloud. The relief of acquiring another married name out-lived her second marriage by only a couple of years before that wretched man, also a club member, acquired wife number two, making it not so good to be first fiddle after all. Reverting to Flick Challenger then seemed a good idea. Her remote connection to the romantic but distant Jules was okay. His parents' misdemeanours were forgotten now they were ensconced at one of the grander clubs a few miles away.

Anyway Jules cherished his image of her. Their break-up hadn't been vicious, simply a natural course of events for two people scarcely out of their teens. Every Christmas he sent her a card with a personal note, along with her twice yearly dividend from his company. That showed his constancy towards her.

His mother, always bewailed their parting. From the start Faye had been a good friend to Flick, introducing her to golf. She'd somehow inveigled the beginner Flick into Bisley Heath in those days when the club had a long waiting list full of experienced players clamouring to join.

She should not have been surprised he turned to his mother for help with Mandy; or that Faye was able to charm her fourth daughter-in-law into her smart nearby club. Even in her late sixties, Faye, with the blonde curls, had a personality which opened doors.

Flick wanted to ask why Mandy wasn't crying down the phone line to her mother-in-law now. Until Mandy arrived on the scene Flick had remained close to Faye. She glanced at her mantelpiece over the marble fireplace. There were three beautiful Victorian figurines, a couple of shepherdesses and one of a man bearing water, which Faye had given her, pieces people had pawned but never reclaimed.

Until Jules married Mandy, Faye used to send her a Christmas present. After her son's engagement to both Roxanne and Tessa, Faye was on the phone to Flick bemoaning the forthcoming nuptials. Only when he paired up with Mandy did her attitude change. "Third time lucky" she'd cooed down the phone to Flick, forgetting Mandy was actually Jules's fourth wife, "such a lovely girl." Another time she'd called Mandy her "young confidante."

Irritating though it was, Flick supposed it was only natural Mandy would appeal to Faye because she was so feminine, she of the exotic apparel which caused comment wherever she went. A rumour one of the most superior clubs in Surrey once turned Mandy out of their lounge because her shorts were too short had irritated Flick's ears more than once. The glamour Faye liked in Flick, she found in Mandy. Yet whilst Jules had not cared a rap what Flick wore, he'd set up the Flag Stick, Flick's secret name for Mandy, in a career selling golf clothes.

"My idea," Faye told Flick when she'd invited her to an invitation meeting at her prestigious club. She'd then made it clear she hoped Flick would introduce Mandy to Bisley Heath to sell her garments.

No way José. "I'll do my best darling."

Happily Mandy, being a modern sort of girl, had not wanted to use the name Challenger. She'd established herself in her initial career as a model using the name Park, which she felt had a certain ring to it, so she'd kept it for her glamorous ladies' golf clothes which she insisted, were leisure wear.

Flick hated the way she pronounced the word *leisure.* The emphasis on the e-sound seemed to epitomise everything she hated about Mandy. She knew it was snobbish but she couldn't help it.

With the phone clamped to her ear, Flick pushed her leather chair away from the desk to stand up. She might as well move round the room tidying things up whilst Mandy was bleating on about Jules.

Flick dreaded bumping into Mandy. Once she'd had to avoid her stall pitched all too centrally at some charity event. On another occasion she'd arrived in the Bisley Heath lounge, to find her sitting right in the middle of the room. Fortunately there'd been enough empty chairs around the place for Flick to keep her distance from her. She was relieved when a year or so ago, she heard, surprisingly from Faye, that Jules and Mandy were splitting up.

"I blame that ghastly Tessa," Faye moaned, "Jules was mad to introduce them."

"Why did he do it?" Flick remembered asking.

"Because he wanted to help her."

Flick hadn't inquired further. She didn't want to know. Only when one of her grey permed-haired older chums at Mandy's club described Mandy as an *anorexic shopaholic* did Flick realise why he introduced one wife to another. Bringing business to Tessa the psychologist was probably part of the divorce settlement. Still who was she to object? Jules had introduced her to loads of people with large houses who wanted help with interior decoration.

Useful though that was, she had no desire to meet his subsequent wives. She certainly did not want their presence in her sitting room which was her haven, her own personal space with no relics of her own couple of marriages, apart from the ornaments Faye had given her.

This was the third call in one month from Mandy. Her relationship with Jules was finished. Why should she object to his making contact with Flick? Yet complain she had. She wasn't even a club member, yet she was furious at Cally's presence at the Ladies' Invitation event. How dare Jules bring that efff-ing bird out on a competition day? Didn't Flick realise it was a vulture sitting on his trolley?

Flick had tried to get her off the phone by being as charming as possible, saying truthfully, that actually she thought Cally was rather a darling bird. She'd certainly replenished Flick's supply of good class golf balls.

To which Mandy had replied, "I don't suppose you had her sitting watching television with you every evening when you were married to him."

I don't want to go there; I'm certainly not discussing my marriage with you. The pet owl Jules had in those days was the least of Flick's problems.

Today Mandy did not want to discuss at length, as previously, what she called Jules's batty ideas for a wildlife course, which Mandy said everybody objected to. What a cheek she had to try to insist Flick "did something about it". Now her voice sounded even more hysterical as she cried, "We're in danger."

Flick stopped walking towards the mantelpiece from which she wanted to remove some old cards. Out of date invitations make you look such a loser when people visit. "What on earth makes you think that?"

"Tessa's died."

For a moment Flick couldn't think whom Mandy was talking about; she'd never met Jules's third wife and knew nobody else called Tessa. "That's a pity," she said.

"It's awful," sobbed Mandy. "She was such a splendid person, a tower of strength and now she's gone."

"Not knowing her," said Flick, picking up the three old invitations from the mantelpiece to drop them into a woven cane wastepaper basket; natural materials are calming. "I'm afraid I'm not touched in quite the same way, sad though it is."

"But don't you see we're both involved, having been married to Jules. The man's obviously jinxed. That's two of his wives who've died."

"Listen," said Flick "it's nothing to do with me and I'm sorry I can't help you but I've got other things..."

Mandy evidently didn't want to know what else might interest Flick. "We're in danger, don't you see, because we're both still identified with him. You're his icon, the symbol of his company. You're his figurehead."

"Was," muttered Flick before she could stop herself. A chill sensation swept through her as she pictured her armless sculpture. She pinioned her own slender muscular arms to her body. Thankfully they were still intact.

"How can you say 'was'?"

"Someone had a go at that statue, that's all, cut off the arms I gather, but don't worry about it. It's obviously nothing to do with you or probably me. You never knew Roxanne and I only met her a couple of times."

"But there you are," cried Mandy, "you've been dragged into whatever's going on with Jules, like I have. Tessa wrote the name of a girl, Impey Dalrymple, who belongs to your golf club on a piece of paper in her dying breath."

"Listen you don't have to worry about her. She's perfectly harmless. I've seen her myself recently." *Now buzz off; I really must get on with things that matter.* No she couldn't say that; it was too harsh. "She's a sort of journalist who does ... sort of enquiries for people. I gather she's working for Jules."

"That's the whole thing – she's not only working for him; she's involved with him." Mandy's voice raised a pitch. "It wasn't only her name on the paper. There were hearts drawn on it too."

Flick's own heart gave a lurch. *Bloody double-dealing Jules hiding things.* She rearranged the delicate china pieces Faye had given her on the mantelpiece. Jules used to talk about his owls mantling when they hid their food with their wings. He told her the word "mantel" came from falconry; he was a bit of an intellectual in that way. She swallowed a lump of saliva in her throat. "I'm not going to speculate about the love life of someone I've never met. Who can guess what was in the mind of someone desperate enough to kill herself?"

"She never seemed desperate," Mandy wailed, "she was such a lovely person, always so supportive. I could ring her any time of the day or night for help; she was a true friend."

What a nightmare. That said something about Tessa's love life or lack of it. Flick's close friends knew better than to ring her in the middle of the night. She slumped down on to her Victorian chaise longue, conscious it was Faye's cast-off which she'd had re-upholstered in a wavy floral pattern right for that era, but which she now felt too fussy for her small sitting room.

Flick did not want clutter in her life. "Listen, I'm truly sorry I can't help you darling." The endearment slipped out. Another bad habit she'd caught off Faye which she had meant to drop. Still it gave her an idea. "Why not ring Faye. She thinks the world of you. I'm sure she'd want to help."

"Probably I will," gulped Mandy, "there's something I've got to tell her too, sort of scandal thing that happened at your club."

Flick jerked herself upright. At last Mandy had something to say which she ought to hear.

"It's all right, it's not about you."

"Anything that happens at the club concerns me now I'm on the main committee."

Mandy's snuffle echoed down the line. "I suppose that's right, 'specially since Jack Metcalfe used to be on the committee."

"You're not talking about that money Jules caught him taking."

"No, the watch-bracelet that's been stolen from Rosie Metcalfe."

That unfortunate incident. "What about it?"

"Rosie, she's one of my customers who's become a good friend, actually, says she's absolutely certain that she bought it from a jewellery shop that used to be in Woking which had closed down."

"So?"

"When she described the shop I knew exactly which one it was."

Now Flick groaned. She guessed what was coming.

"It was Faye's shop, the one you did up for her. She was forever going on about it being exactly your style."

Flick winced.

"I know Rosie's honest because she buys a lot from me, but I bet you anything that bracelet was pawned."

21. Shooting rabbits

Dan, the cook, slung his gun over his shoulder. "I reckon we've got enough for one day, or rather one night."

"Yeah, ten's a pretty good score," agreed Ross, his good mate on the ground staff, who looked after the course, "though fifteen's the record, and this may be our last chance to beat it."

Dan looked at his watch. It was ten-thirty but they might catch a drink at the pub if they hurried. Fun though it was, there would be other nights when they could come out to shoot rabbits. Anyway he had more than enough for his purposes. The freezer in the clubhouse kitchen was already half full of rabbits he'd skinned; that wasn't counting the ones he'd made into pies. The rest would go into pâtés and soups.

The rabbit pie business was the most lucrative of the sidelines he'd established since ex lady captain, Mrs Deborah Cordrey OBE, had got him the job of second chef at Bisley Heath. What a lucky coincidence it had been that she'd walked into the kitchen and found that bracelet hanging over the wine bottle the night of the ladies invitation. He'd been tempted to pinch it himself to flog on Ebay.

"Don't tell me we're not going to get on Bisley Heath's honours' boards for shooting the most rabbits." He quipped.

Ross flung open the driver's door of the ancient battered jeep. "The way things are going, any old person will be on the club's honours boards. The good players will all leave if they don't spend more on the ground's maintenance."

Dan walked round to the other side of the car. He climbed into the passenger seat. "There's not much chance of that now with the new man Scrivenor in charge, I hear. They say he's as mean as they come."

"Not him." Ross started the car's noisy engine. "It's Jules Challenger we're worried about. There'll be rabbit holes all over the fairways if he gets his way."

"You mean that nutter who spoke at the last party?" asked Dan.

"The man with the money," said Ross. "He's an animal nut who wants the course to go wild. It'll be 'Come on little bunnies; have a picnic and shit on the greens. Then dig as many holes as you like in the fairways, you dear little burrowing critters, and it won't be just rabbits, but foxes and badgers as well."

"The members will never put up with that," said Dan. "You don't hear them talking in the clubhouse like I do. They get very stroppy if the fairways are a mess. And they're very partial to rabbit pie. That's how dear old dame Debbie got me working for the club. I did a rabbit pie for some of the movers and shakers."

"You can forget about that now," Ross told him as the car bumped down a sandy path. "I'm fecking telling you, it's the foxes who'll be eating the rabbits."

"Can't have that. Our business would go down the drain. I've got a load of orders for pies after that last party at the club. You know" he chuckled, "one of the members accused me of having a deal with Brakes Brothers."

"What did you tell him?"

"The truth naturally; that my pies are made from organic free range rabbits. I've got a mate who knocks up invoices and so I've got a wad of paper with some posh west country butcher's name at the top."

"You might not get many more chances to use it."

"You mean we're not going to be allowed to shoot them any more."

"Not officially. Jules Challenger doesn't like guns. Like I said, he's got some idea that foxes and wolves will keep the deer population down too."

"Wolves!" gasped Dan. His eyes widened. "You're kidding."

"No I'm not mate. He's actually got a pet wolf; he even runs with it on the course in the early mornings. That's why we're going to have to be careful. If he sees us out shooting he'll cause a stink, like he did with Jack Metcalfe. He got rid of him."

"You mean he'll wreck my business because he's got a ruddy wolf?"

"That's about the size of it.

"I'll believe that when I see it." Dan peered out of the jeep's side window into the starry night. "Where does this fucking guy live?"

"Right there." Ross took his right hand off the steering wheel to point to a thicket with a finger. "He keeps the wolf in his garden the other side of those trees."

Dan reached down and pulled up the handbrake so the car lurched to a stop.

"What d'you do that for you berk?" shouted Ross.

"I wanna see it for myself." Dan opened the car door and jumped out. "Come on you can show me." He reached back into the car to pick up his gun. But I'm bloody well going to take this to defend myself if he gets rough."

Ross leant against the steering wheel. "You probably won't see him. I never have."

"Well now's your chance." Dan took a couple of steps towards the trees before turning round to beckon with his entire long arm back at Ross.

The green staff sat with his elbows resting on his knees, his chin cupped in his hands. "What do you hope to get out of this?"

"Know what we're dealing with. How do you know it's not some joke?" Dan peered into the trees. "I can't see any garden through here."

"It's no joke." Ross alighted from the car. He walked round to the back of the car to open the boot, out of which he picked up a lantern. He shook it into lighting up, then walked over to join Dan. "This way." He delved between some trees.

After a few minutes scrabbling, the men found a close boarded new wooden fence about six foot high. The other side of it rose the eight foot high wire netting of Caesar's compound.

Ross gesticulated with his stubby hand. "There you are mate. That's where the wolf lives, but there's nothing to see."

"If we got over that fence we could probably see it," said Dan.

"How?" asked Ross.

"Dead simple." Dan pointed to a nearby beech tree with a bough adjacent to the fence. "Up on that and you can drop over easily." He pulled his gun wide open to hand to Ross. "Take that for a moment would you?"

With both large hands Dan grasped the bough. He jumped, swinging his legs up horizontally until he could hook them over the branch; he rolled round it and sat up with his long legs dangling either side. Then he lowered himself awkwardly over the fence so that he stood between it and the pen. Standing on tip toe he could just see over the six foot fence to call to back Ross to hand him his gun. "Come on."

214

Ross held the gun's barrel up so that Dan could grasp the handle. He handed him the lantern. "Okay, but hold the light up as high as you can. I want to see what I'm doing."

In a couple of minutes, he too had climbed into the garden.

Dan swung the lantern backwards and forwards. "Can't see him," he said in disappointment.

"There!" Ross indicated a dark shape with the flat of his hand. "Over there."

Dan swung the lantern in the direction he pointed. "Oh my God," he squeaked. "I think you're right." In a thin piping voice he cried, "Come over here; come over here."

Amongst the shadows from the surrounding trees and piles of logs in the enclosure, the dark shape moved.

"For God's sake," said Ross. "Now you've seen him, let's go."

"Not properly; let's get him closer. I know a way." He dropped the lantern to fish in the pocket of his canvas jacket and pulled out one of the newly dead rabbits, his fur matted with blood. "This should tempt him." Dan waved the rabbit backwards and forwards. "Ah here he comes."

Ross stood transfixed as the black shape prowled forward, a lean four-legged ghost in the darkness, with two startling gold lights in its head. Then suddenly the apparition broke into a run. The wolf hurtled itself at the wire fence and leapt upwards hit the top of the fence and dropped back before crouching on his haunches to leap again. His body coiled back to spring once more up the wire fence.

To his horror, Ross now saw two paws pass over the top of the fence.

Above them in the air the wolf seemed to be flying. His back legs spread out behind his body whilst his front legs, the paws rolled up underneath them, were buckled under his haunches. Even in the dim light from the lantern, the fur on the wolf's underside shone with many different colours; red, gold, white and amber made up the grey. His head was clearly visible too; his ears were cocked and his mouth was so wide he could have been smiling.

Open-mouthed Ross stood dumbfounded; he gazed in awe at the magnificence of the wolf's out-stretched body until a shot jolted him.

Then there was another bang.

The wolf's hind-quarters dropped on to the top of the wire netting. His head hanging down, he was caught on the wire.

"That was a near one," said Dan. "Strewth. Glad I brought the gun."

"You nutter." Ross cursed him through clenched teeth. "What the hell have you done? "

"Not enough." Dan's face puckered. "Sod it; I thought I'd got him."

With an eerie noise between a howl and a snarl, as blood trickled from his under carriage, the wolf struggled to free himself . His golden eyes burnt with rage as, his forelegs a few feet away from the men's faces, Caesar's hind legs scrabbled against the wire netting.

Dan raised his gun to take aim again, but Ross threw his arms round his hips to pull him back. "Leave it. For God's sake let's get out of here." Ross grabbed the gun out of Dan's loosened grip. "Run for it."

Dan looked about helplessly. *Where?* Trapped as they were between the wolf's enclosure and the wooden fence, there was nowhere to go.

Ross bounded back to the tree which they'd used to climb into the garden. With one deft movement he threw the gun over the fence before he clasped the overhanging branch with both hands so that he could walk his feet up the fence to hook his legs over the branch. "Come on," he shouted back to Dan as he slithered back into the safety of the golf course.

There was a creaking noise as the heavier man attempted the same manoeuvre and a frightened cry of "Help!" Then, a couple of minutes later, the reassuring sound of cracking twigs and rustling leaves disturbed on the ground heralded the large cook's arrival.

Ross had already flung the gun into the Jeep. He sat in the driver's seat of the car with the front passenger door open.

Dan leapt in and slammed the door shut. "Bloody hell. That was a near one," he gasped, his large chest wheezing noisily as he breathed. "And you made me drop two rabbits."

"So what. You've got plenty." Ross pressed his foot down on the accelerator, making the car jerk as it plunged forward."

"Someone else will get those rabbits now," complained Dan.

Ross eyed the mirror. "Give the wolf a good supper when he gets back home."

"What do you mean?"

"Look behind you."

Dan turned round to see the wolf in the air again, only this time he was soaring over the fence between Jules's garden and the golf course.

22. Impey meets Mandy

On Monday afternoon Impey sat strumming Brahms waltzes at her ancient Steinway piano. It soothed her nerves. The beautiful upright oak piano with carved roses on the front was like a friend.

The loud chords she played helped relieve her feelings ,even if they could not guide her thoughts. She wished she could think of someone to turn to for advice, but the people closest to her, who understood the situation, would be unhelpful because they were too involved themselves. Dodger was working for Jules, whilst Rosie was understandably vehemently biased against him. In a phone call last night she'd said she believed the shop where she purchased the watch bracelet from belonged to Jules's mother, which added to her fury with the entire Challenger family.

Moving on to a more lyrical number Impey decided. *This is too much emotional strain.* She didn't mind being hostess to Cally, but she must abandon the investigation. It could not be her fault Tessa topped herself. *Ludicrous, absolutely ludicrous, I should be blamed because my name was scribbled on a piece of paper in Tessa's consulting room.*

People didn't commit suicide on the spur of the moment. Such a drastic step must be the result of issues which had preyed on Tessa's mind for ages, not the consequence of one short meeting in an afternoon. Besides, Tessa had seemed calm when they'd talked.

Impey could not say the same for Mandy Park, Jules's fourth wife. They'd had an agonising conversation earlier this morning, but then Impey had not realised Mandy was among the girlfriends who'd discovered Tessa's dead body or she would never have door-stepped her.

She recalled the whole ghastly interview with a shudder.

A dishevelled barefoot Mandy wearing a black designer jumpsuit came to the door of her modern mews house in Camberley. She didn't invite Impey into the house, but stood in the doorway talking.

Impey had debated with herself what to wear to visit someone renowned for her passion for clothes. Since writers in the fashion industry judged people by their clothes, she had picked out her snazziest white jeans which's she'd teamed with a pink stripy top. Unfortunately her impression on Mandy was unsympathetic.

"I don't know if you want to talk about this," Impey had said after introducing herself, "but Jules has asked me to see you for a chat about things."

"It was dreadful," Mandy wailed. "Tessa looked like waxwork. I couldn't believe she was dead so I touched her; I actually felt her dead body and it was all hard. Chloe, who was with me, screamed and screamed."

"Sudden death is always terribly hard to take in," agreed Impey. She remembered all too vividly her own horror after her parents death in a car crash five years ago.

"I can't; I simply can't talk to you. Not in the circumstances." Mandy's long slim body sagged whilst she propped herself against the open door.

"I really do feel for you; I don't want to hurt you in any way," said Impey.

"Did you know," shouted Mandy aggressively, "your name was written on a piece of paper by her dead body?"

Sensing they had an audience, Impey glanced round to see that a woman opposite with a short gold perky hairstyle had her head crooked in their direction. Though she leant on a spade dug into a neat flower bed, her body language suggested she was all too interested in their conversation. "I don't think my name could have meant anything significant."

"How can you say that? Your name must have been the last thing on her mind before she died."

"She'd probably simply been doodling; she hardly knew me."

"She was such an intuitive person," sobbed Mandy, "she'd have sensed what you were like."

"I was only seeing her, like I'm seeing you, to ask whether she had a clue how the arms of Flick's figurehead might have been lopped off."

"That was no accident," cried Mandy in a high pitched voice. "It was a warning to Jules."

"I don't think that's necessarily so," Impey tried to say calmly. "He's only investigating the possibility, because he's a debt collector. You know how people feel about bankers at the moment. He's concerned in case someone might be trying to upset him and undermine his work. As you were obviously close to him and understand his business, he thought I should talk to you."

"Well I wish he hadn't," she wailed. "Oh God. I knew it. I told Flick as much. We're all jinxed. I should never have got involved with him. Tessa appreciated that; she told me how manipulative he is. She was such a wonderful person. Didn't she help you?"

Impey wanted to say she did not need help, or not the help Tessa might provide, but she didn't want to curtail the conversation yet, despite the evident eavesdropping of the woman opposite. Mandy might yet provide her with something useful.

"Can you think of anyone else, who might have had the grudge you talk about, against Jules?"

"Jules is a very annoying person," said Mandy through clenched teeth. She'd obviously noticed another neighbour had come into her front garden to see what was going on in the doorway of number five. "He upsets plenty of people."

"Name one."

"One of my customers, Rosie Metcalfe for starters; she's a member of Bisley Heath too, like Flick. But there are loads of others. The wretched man's trying to turn the golf course into a wildlife park. Naturally no one likes it."

Impey had tried to explain that some people might be in favour of an organic wildlife course. She too had heard rumours about wild boars circulating round Surrey, but they must be untrue. Everything about the wildlife Jules wanted to introduce had got grossly exaggerated.

"It's not exaggerating to say he's got a pet vulture that flies around Bisley Heath, I can tell you, or that he has a pet wolf which wanders around the house. Do you really think members will want those creatures in the clubhouse? I didn't want them in my home."

Impey eyed the neat garden in front of Mandy's door. Around a manicured circle of grass, the surrounding flowerbeds were edged with semicircular tiles. Each bed was full of colour co-ordinated flowers, from blues through purple to pink, they all looked as though they were standing to attention. She could not see the back garden behind the house, but could only imagine it would be quite unsuitable for a wolf, however tame.

"Obviously you and Jules were not really compatible," said Impey, hoping to soothe her, "it's lucky he was able to introduce you to Tessa to help you."

"Jules won't be compatible with anyone," shouted Mandy. She stamped her foot on the doorstep. "Tessa would have told you that."

"Well, she was quite critical," admitted Impey, "but obviously she and Jules had different standards."

"Rubbish. Jules has only one standard; that's his own. I tried to please him far too much. Tessa made me see it was impossible. I need to be myself, not try to please someone else, be it my parents or a husband, especially if that husband is Jules. I shouldn't have to be thin or sell x number of clothes, or be the face of fashion to be a proper satisfactory person. I'm okay as me."

"How did Jules react to Tessa's advice to you?"

"He didn't like her influence over me, which was ridiculous because he suggested I went to see her in the first place, like he did you."

"No...erm I meant that's not quite right. Jules didn't want me to see Tessa for counselling," said Impey

"Why else would he suggest you saw her?"

Although Mandy seemed to have forgotten Impey's earlier explanation of her role in Jules's life, Impey did not deem it helpful to remind her of a possible grudge against him. She cleared her throat. "He's examining his life," she said, feeling her words sounded all too feeble.

Fortunately Mandy accepted this. "He certainly needs to do that. Tessa thinks," she gave a sob, "thought, I mean, that he's got a problem with dominance; he can't tolerate equality because he's got to be in charge."

"Probably goes with running a successful company."

"It's everybody, not only people who work for him, but everybody, but then everybody he knows ends up working for him. Adam said I would."

"You don't mean Adam Scrivenor, the Bisley Heath club treasurer, do you? How do you know him?"

Mandy rolled her eyes at Impey as if to ask how ignorant she could get. "I met him clubbing, long before I met Jules. We went out for a bit, but he was worried about getting serious because I owed so much money, so he introduced me to Jules and one thing led to another."

"How did Adam react?" asked Impey curiously.

"How do you think? He got pretty ratty, said Jules made a habit of taking other men's girls, that he'd gone off with a girlfriend of Ned's, but that was ages ago and Ned seemed pretty cool about it."

Mandy, it appeared, had something of a crush on Ned. Amongst tearful gulps, she gushed about him. "Isn't he just like Justin Bieber with a few years added?" Ned's visits to see Caesar were the only thing which made the wolf's presence bearable. "He didn't do that awful wrestling that Jules does to control Caesar. He just talks to him softly and strokes him."

She took a paper tissue out of her trouser pocket to wipe her nose. Then she gave a couple of sniffs. "I don't know why you're asking me all this stuff anyway. Please will you go away now?"

Impey had been glad to leave. Though they'd only talked for about ten minutes, she'd felt emotionally battered. Driving back home one or two tears strayed down her cheeks, as though Mandy's grief was catching.

Strumming at the piano relieved the tension.

I do not have to go on with this, she sang in her mind, *however short of money I am.. I don't owe him that much money. I'll just have to borrow it from someone else and pay him off. I'm happy to be Jules's friend, but I must butt out of this investigation.*

Her little silver mobile lay on top of the piano. She picked it up, but before she could press the key for Jules's number it flagged up the same digits as it rang. Shocked at the coincidence Impey stared at the little screen for a couple of seconds before she touched the green phone picture to answer. "Hi Jules."

"Hello Impey," he said.

Was it her imagination or did he also sound a bit tearful? No, she really didn't think she could bear it if he was going to throw a wobbly over Tessa's death too.

"I'm awfully sorry about Tessa," she said.

"Yes, well it's terribly tragic and I suppose I should get a grip on my own woes. She wouldn't think much of the way I feel now."

"Listen," said Impey, "if you don't mind, I'd rather not talk about Tessa any more this morning," she glanced at her watch to see it was now one thirty, "or rather, this afternoon. I think I should..."

"No. No." Jules interrupted. "I'm sorry you've had a terrible shock, for getting you drawn into something so horrible."

"It's not your fault," said Impey. She frowned at the carved roses on the front of the Steinway. *Tessa would say it was. So would Mandy.*

Jules echoed her thoughts. "Some people would say it was. But actually I was going to ask you something else, only maybe in the circumstances I shouldn't." His voice trailed off.

Could he really be tearful? She thought she heard him cry. *In for a penny; in for a pound.* "Ask away," she said.

"You're sure you don't mind. It's rather horrid."

224

"Not a bit." Now she was curious; she had to know what he had in mind.

"It's Caesar. He's been shot."

"How on earth did that happen?"

"I've no idea. I found him lying on the ground outside my garden, gasping with blood oozing from his belly. The thing is I'll have to take him straight to the vet, and I wondered if you'd come with me and hold my hand."

Pity stirred in Impey. She gulped. "What now?"

"Yes, if you're free. I'd really like you to be there. I need someone with me and I can't think of anyone better to ask. There's something about your presence that's very comforting. Steve said that too."

"Wouldn't you want him to be there, rather than me?"

Jules gave a melancholy chuckle. "He wouldn't be as good at holding my hand."

Impey's heart gave a lurch. *Oh come on.* She scolded herself. *This is ridiculous. You hardly know the guy.* "I'm not sure that I can be much of a help. I mean I don't know anything about nursing sick animals."

"It's me you'd be helping, not Caesar. I feel so lonely at the thought of losing him. He's really in a bad way."

23. At the Vet with Caesar

Impey was waiting at her gate with a mini rucksack by her feet when Jules arrived in his navy blue Land Rover to pick her up. She hopped into the front passenger seat alongside him whilst he kept the engine running. Before she'd shut the door, the car started to move.

"This is so good of you." Jules pressed his foot down on the accelerator making the car lurch. "Oh God, I hope that didn't hurt him. Can you see if he's all right?"

Impey glanced over her shoulder to see Caesar lying wrapped in a bloodstained brown check rug, secured by seat belts, on the leather back seat of the Land Rover. He lay so still she guessed he was either unconscious or already dead. "I don't think he felt it," she ventured to say.

"I don't know if that's bad or good," said Jules in a choked tone. He sniffed. Whilst he kept his left hand on the steering wheel, he fished in his pocket for a large navy blue spotted handkerchief to dab at his eye. "You probably think I'm bloody ridiculous being like this." He dropped the handkerchief on to his lap.

He did look slightly odd driving the Land Rover in his pale grey trousers striped with white, topped with a white shirt speckled with blood. His matching suit jacket hung on a hook between the windows on the side of the vehicle with a tie patterned with birds on it, wound round the coat hanger. He must have come straight back from work to find the wolf shot.

She was glad she'd managed to find time to change out of her white jeans into aged denims, since she imagined she might have to help carry the wolf into the veterinary surgery. "No, I understand. How did you get Caesar into the car."

"I used a wheelbarrow." Jules pursed his lips as he accelerated round a corner. "It was the only way. I had to curl his body up to staunch the bleeding whilst I moved him."

"How awful for you to find him in that state." Impey hesitated, wondering if she dared ask the obvious question. "You don't think someone from the golf club shot him do you?"

"Probably," answered Jules. "I found him on the golf course but I didn't have time to investigate because I was so desperate to get medical help. Once I'd rung Ned, I rang you. I haven't had time to get on to the police. All I could think of was trying to save my boy."

"If anyone can save him, I'm sure Ned will; I've heard he's a brilliant vet."

"Yes, for animals," agreed Jules, "but I wouldn't take Cally, or any other bird to him for that matter."

They reached Ned's surgery opposite the green in the little village of Pirbright near Bisley in less than ten minutes. His receptionist must have alerted him of their arrival because he was at the door before Impey reached it. She'd hopped out to save time while Jules parked the Land Rover in the car park to the side of the building.

Ned took a stretcher out to the car. Holding one end, he handed Jules the other. When he'd opened the car door, in a deft movement he unloosed both seat belts to roll the unconscious wolf onto the stretcher, which he and Jules bore carefully through a side door into the waiting area, where a grey-haired receptionist stood behind a high counter with leaflets stacked upon it.

As they passed in front of her to go into the surgery, Impey was awed by the tenderness with which the two men carried the slain wolf. This couldn't only be the memory of

Roxanne. She glanced at Caesar's face. His mouth was slightly open as though caught mid howl, but his expression was calm. This close she suddenly appreciated what a handsome animal he was, truly regal. Even the whitish grey fur on his long pointed nose suggested eminence in old age. In any pack he surely would have been the alpha male. No wonder Jules had to wrestle with him to show who was boss.

"Come in, if you like," Jules invited her over his shoulder, as he followed Ned through into his surgery.

Impey shook her head. "I'll wait out here, unless you need me." She did not want to witness a gory operation. She sat down on a wooden bench opposite the counter in the small area which served as a waiting room.

After what seemed ages, but Impey knew from a large round white rimmed clock on the wall, was exactly nine minutes, Jules opened the door to poke his head out in her direction. His face was blotchy. "Please would you come in?"

Impey walked into the surgery to find Caesar stretched out on a large white table. She scarcely noticed the cupboards or any of the posters which adorned the walls. Her eyes were riveted to the still body of the wolf.

"He's almost dead," said Ned softly, but his voice seemed to penetrate Caesar's brain because his ears twitched.

"Are you sure?" cried Jules. "He just moved, didn't you see him?"

"Sort of involuntary spasm," said Ned calmly. "Truly the kindest thing to do is to help him pass out peacefully. Sixteen's a great age, too old for him to make a good recovery from a shot like this." He turned round to step towards a white cupboard which hung on the wall. "I hope you're going to nail the bastard who did this."

"I don't know I'll be able to," said Jules dully, "unless someone comes forward and tells me they know who did it."

"You know he used a shot gun; you might even find a cartridge in your garden."

Ned put a needle into a tiny bottle of liquid which he drew up into a syringe. He tapped it with a finger to get rid of a bubble in the liquid. "Silly me. Force of habit. Doesn't matter if air gets into his vein now." He plunged the needle into the dog's chest. "He'll only have a few seconds more pain. Thiopental works wonderfully quickly. I'd like it if I had a terminal illness."

Impey put her arm round Jules. His body shook. "I'm so sorry," she said.

"Thanks. I'm sorry I'm so pathetic. I've never, I mean I once lost someone close to me and this brings it all back."

Impey saw a muscle in Ned's face twitch as he unhooked the lid of a plastic box into which he dropped the syringe.

"You'll feel a damn sight better when you catch the bastard who did this," said the vet. "I hope you're going to create a stink at the golf club."

"Well I don't know," faltered Jules.

"Oh come on," said Ned. "Surely it's got to be one of them. You said they were out for your blood."

"I thought they were after Cally, not Caesar, because she's been much more a presence on the course. So Impey's looking after her for me." He turned to give her a half smile.

"Is she?" Ned stared at Impey. "That's brave of you, having a killer bird at your home."

"I don't think she'd have shot Caesar," remarked Impey, in an unfortunate bid to lighten the atmosphere. The mixture of appalled but doleful expressions on the two men's faces told her the jest had fallen into the gutter.

"I'll have to tell the police of course," said Jules in a low tremulous voice.

"Of course you damn well will," said Ned, "and obviously I'll wait to cremate Caesar until their vet's had a chance to examine the wolf if he wants."

Impey felt Jules's body stiffen with horror. "You're not going to cremate Caesar."

"Well obviously we'll have to at some stage."

"I'm not having him burnt alive," said Jules, his wide mouth set into a firm line.

"Come on old boy," Ned said gently. "Caesar's dead, not alive, and we have to dispose of his body somehow."

"I want to bury him." Jules thumped his fist defiantly on the table where the dead wolf lay. "I know lots of people who have dead dogs in their gardens."

"It's not healthy," said the vet. "A wolf is a large animal. Even if you make a deep hole, other animals will try to dig him up. And don't forget there's an impact on the health of people living in your area. Your neighbours probably won't be happy about having a wolf buried near them. You have to think about pollution of water supplies and the land."

"Maybe I won't have him in my garden then, but I definitely want him buried, not cremated."

"I strongly advise against it."

"It's not your problem Ned, or your decision. He's my wolf."

Impey looked from one man to the other. Fury shone in both their eyes.

Ned glared at Jules whose fists were clenched as though he was about to punch the vet. His body was so taut she dropped her arm from him. He was too angry to notice. "I'm taking Caesar home."

Ned's mouth wrinkled in an effort to give a smile of sympathy. "Come on Jules, for goodness sake think. Where will you keep him? You can't have a rotting corpse in your house."

"Well where will you keep him?"

"In my mortuary until I can make disposal arrangements." Ned's head nodded grimly as he avoided using the word cremation.

"I'll make the disposal arrangements," said Jules loudly. He turned to Impey. "You're my witness." His blue eyes narrowed as he looked back at Ned. "And I'll sue you if you burn up my wolf."

"Okay, fine." Ned shrugged. "I'll keep Caesar in the mortuary until you let me know what you want to do. I'll give you all the help I can. If you're so desperate to bury Caesar you could try one of the Sustainability Centres. They might be able to help you, but it'll cost."

"I don't care," said Jules. "Wolves should be part of the earth when they die; it's their heritage."

Impey looked at Ned to see his reaction. Inadvertently she caught his eye. He winked at her.

"So be it." Ned stroked the dead wolf's head which twitched slightly at his touch. "I hope the police will try to catch whoever shot him, not just log it in a file."

"Might it not have been an accident?" queried Impey. "I mean there's an awful lot of shooting in Bisley with the ranges being there."

"It went in quite deep for a stray bullet," said Ned whilst he clamped Caesar's large jaws together. He turned to take a cloth from off the top of a dresser which stood against

231

the wall of the surgery and started to wipe blood off the table around dead wolf. "Whoever shot him meant to kill him in my opinion, and I you hope nail the bastard."

"I'll try," said Jules dully. He turned to face Impey. "Maybe you'll will help me."

"That would be good." Ned looked at her. "I wish you every success. Now, if you don't mind, I think you should leave Caesar with me."

"I can't believe Ned," said Jules as he drove Impey home. "I'd have thought he would hate the idea of not being able to visit Caesar's grave."

"He could still go if Caesar was cremated," said Impey, "I go to my parents' graves sometimes."

Jules made no response for a few minutes. Then he screwed up his face. "He's weird," he muttered, "always been a bit weird."

"What will you do?" asked Impey.

"We'll have to have a funeral," said Jules.

"For a wolf?" asked Impey before she could stop herself.

"Of course," replied Jules. "That's something I learnt from Tessa. It's part of the grieving process. Caesar's been a huge part of my life, plus the fact that he is or rather he was, the only legacy I've got of Roxanne."

Mandy I've maligned you. Impey winced. *I don't think I could have lived with all those memories of previous wives.*

"You will do it won't you?" Jules broke into her thoughts.

"What?"

"Come to Caesar's funeral."

"Of course, I thought you were going to say ..."

"That I want you to find our who shot Caesar? Of course, that as well."

24. Impey investigates on the golf course

Yet again as she drove to Bisley Heath next day, Impey cursed the Nikos family. If only she hadn't spent such ages on their memoirs she might have picked up other work which would not have left her obliged to work for Jules. She wished he were not so clever at flattery, or that she was stronger at resisting it. When she'd protested she knew nothing about guns or shooting, and was therefore a useless person to try to discover who'd shot Caesar, he'd insisted he had such faith in her investigative powers that she found herself agreeing to try.

Now she realised as she pulled the Jazz's handbrake up sharply, when she reached the club's practice ground, that she might prefer not to know who had shot Caesar. She was in *shoot the messenger* territory. If the offender was a Bisley Heath member she would not be popular in the club for identifying him or her, with Jules threatening dire revenge.

The two old men hitting balls on the practice ground looked quizzically in her direction as she alighted from her car dressed in her jeans and wearing trainers. It struck her as she reached back into the boot for her rucksack that one of them looked familiar. She glanced across at them. *Omigod; there's Uncle George.* When the other guy lifted his head she recognised him too as George's old army pal the General.

She might have guessed George would be around on the practice ground, if not on the course at two o'clock on a Wednesday afternoon, even if he was nearly eighty. Much as she loved George, he was the last person she wanted to see her there dressed in jeans. George was manic about keeping up traditional standards in every way.

She gave a half-hearted cursory wave of her hand in his direction, hoping he might not have recognised her but the vigorous sweep of his arm with which he returned her gesture suggested that was unlikely. Anyway he would have recognised her car. She hastened away, along the wide public footpath to the clump of trees on the boundary of the course at the edge of Jules's garden,

At first glance there seemed nothing to note when she pushed herself through the foliage to reach Jules's wooden fence. The only sign of the late Caesar's pen was the two or three feet of netting which rose above the fence, but at a casual glance, it might have surrounded a large tennis court. Jules had been so wrung out with grief when Caesar died that he could not remember where he found the wolf, though he knew it was on the course near his garden fence. He also said the bridle path which the ground staff used to cut through the copse was nearby.

This was not used much by riders on horseback, but players came along it when there was a competition where they had to start at different places on the course. The weather had been dry for the last week, so it would be difficult to find any significant tracks for her to identify footprints or even an usual vehicle.

Impey stared around at the undisturbed ground. Once out of his pen a wolf could easily have jumped this fence, but there should be signs of his impact on the earth. Somewhere there must be evidence of his death. She ran her fingers along the close boarded fence whilst she pushed her way along until she found a small clearing near the bridle path.

She did a high five against the fence. This had to be it. The path was a mere few yards away. Not only had sand from it sprayed out either side of the path, but the ground was heavily furrowed as though a vehicle with thick tyres had turned round in haste. Impey walked backwards and forwards between the path and the fence, unsure what she was looking for until she spotted them; there were some grey hairs, matted together with blood. Impey lifted her rucksack off her back, got out her tweezers and one of her plastic food bags. These hairs were definitely too long and grey for a fox, but they might belong to a dog.

Her excitement flagged as she tramped backwards and forwards over the clearing. She could find nothing else to suggest Caesar was shot here. She turned to go back to her car. This was, as she expected, a pointless excursion. There was nothing to find, unless someone had somehow managed to shoot the wolf over the fence from inside Jules's garden. She started to walk away, then turned back. Maybe she should walk round the perimeter of the garden from this side; she might have missed something. Anyway, she would like George and his pal the General, both former club presidents, to have finished on the practice ground before she returned. She started to wend her way between the trees which bordered the fence.

After a couple of minutes she reached another space where the ground staff had evidently been working. A branch of a beech tree which must have overhung Jules's garden had been sawn off. A pile of long logs, presumably from it, stood stacked up against Jules's fence. If she clambered up those logs she would be able to see over the fence into Jules's garden. She thought she might as well take a look.

Beneath her feet, the logs wobbled perilously, but she was able to steady herself by grabbing the top of the fence. From her perch she could see the pen clearly. She screwed up her eyes. About ten feet to her right, she thought she could see hair on the top of the netting. She scrutinised the spot.

There was definitely some disturbance on the ground there beside the pen. A small bundle of fur lay there too.

Impey took out her binoculars and trained them on to the fur. It was a dead rabbit, but there appeared to be dried blood on it's body. She looked around the lifeless creature noting there were definite footprints beside it.

With her stance on the logs, the fence was waist high. She hauled herself on to the top and dropped down to the other side. Delving into her rucksack again, she got out a clean polythene bag to pick up the rabbit which looked as though it had been shot. Impey examined the ground around. Here were definite marks where people had recently stood.

She looked again at the rabbit inside the transparent bag. Yes, she was sure it had been shot, but from where? And why had whoever shot it, not disposed of it elsewhere? Further examination of the surrounding ground revealed an empty yellow cartridge lying by the pen. She picked it up and dropped it into her rucksack.

For a moment she wondered whether this had contained the pellets which killed the rabbit, then she realised this was unlikely, if not impossible, since no one would have got so near a rabbit to shoot it. She turned to look at the pen more closely. Perhaps it was her imagination, but she thought she saw some of the wire was bent slightly outwards as though the wolf had hurled himself against it. Near this distension, about six foot from the ground, were more grey and white hairs caught where the wire criss-crossed. She reached up to pluck them off the fence. They felt coarse between her fingers, much more like a wolf's than a man's. But could they be Caesar's? Would he, an old wolf be able to leap that high?

Puzzling over the fragments she'd gathered, Impey made her way along the outside of the pen. Now she was inside Jules's garden, she might as well see round it. She thought she would have to go through the garden to the house and then down the drive to turn into the clubhouse drive, a long walk back to her car at the practice ground, because she did not see how she could scale the six foot border fence from this side. To her relief however, when she reached the corner of the pen, she noticed a small concealed door in the woodwork of the fence.

It was hard to push it open since there seemed to be stuff piled against it the other side, but eventually Impey was able to shift the door enough to create a sizable gap for her to squeeze through it. Finding herself standing in a heap of grass cuttings, twigs and other garden refuse, she felt relieved to be back on to the property of the golf club.

The glad sight of her car, when she reached the practice ground, was marred by the view of another car. Parked next her Jazz was George's ancient black Ford. He must have moved it there; he himself had changed his place from the far end of the practice ground to hit balls in the slot nearest car park area.

"Hi!" she called, although at the moment he was not someone she wanted to speak to. Her mind was too full of the investigation for Jules which, worse than being of no interest to George, would probably enrage him.

"Hello there," he picked up his golf bag, hoisted it over his shoulder and walked towards her. "What have you been doing?" His tone was level, but not angry.

"Oh nothing much." She tried to give an amiable non-committal smile as she opened her car door.

"Really?" A grin stretched over his large broad face. "What've you been collecting in your rucksack then? Wild flowers?" He dropped his bag on to the ground beside them.

"No of course not. You wouldn't be interested."

"Try me. I'm always interested in what you do." His hand rested on the door to the boot of his car.

She was about to refuse, jump into her car and make a dash away when it occurred to her that George's view on the contents of her rucksack might be useful. He knew about guns; he might know what sort of gun that cartridge came from or whether it would contain enough lead to kill a wolf. If by some horrible chance, it was fired from his gun, she guessed she might even know it from his expression. She undid the buckle of her rucksack, delved into it and felt for the cartridge but inadvertently pulled out the plastic bag with the dead rabbit in it.

"Heavens," laughed George. "I didn't think you were into catching rabbits."

"I'm not," said Impey. She put her rucksack on the ground and was about to drop the rabbit back into it when George put out his hand.

"Can I see that?"

Impey handed the bag to him.

He turned it over in his large hands. "Hm. Someone's not a very good shot. Not you I presume?"

"Of course not. What do you mean anyway?"

"Well he's caught it in the rear, by the back legs." With a large forefinger he pointed to the bloodstain on the rabbit's body. "Poor little varmit would have been in agony as it tried to drag itself away with paralysed back legs."

"So where would you shoot a rabbit?"

"In the head of course," said George as though it was the most obvious place. "That's where you shoot to kill. With smaller creatures, you usually don't want to ruin the flesh for eating, and with larger ones, like lions or bears, you don't want them coming to attack you back after you've shot them."

"So if you shot a wolf...?"

"Not that I would, since even though they're not protected any more, I don't happen to go on wolf hunts." George's brow knitted as he examined her face. "So that's what all this is about? Has someone shot that damn wolf?"

Impey nodded.

"And you think it's somehow connected with this rabbit."

"I don't know, but I think," she fished inside her rucksack again, "this could be the cartridge." She held out the yellow tube with a gold end to him.

He handed back the polythene bag with the rabbit in it and took the cartridge from her. With his large broad fingers he twisted it round to examine it. "Bit small for attacking a large animal," he commented, "more the sort of thing you'd use in an air rifle for small game." A smile crossed his big round ruddy face again. "Obviously not a big game hunter involved."

"I don't know about that," said Impey. "I think he got the wolf near his heart."

"By accident," said George. "I told you, if he'd been any sort of hunter, he'd have put the bullet into the beast's brain so he couldn't get up again, not his back."

"Oh no, the bullet went into his tummy," explained Impey.

"Now that is interesting." Her uncle examined the cartridge in his hand again. "Looks to me as if he shot in self-defence. The wolf wouldn't have rolled over to be hit in the stomach. He must have been leaping for his assailant to show his belly."

"Blimey. I never thought of that. Jules will be terribly upset when I tell him."

"What's all this to you Impey? You're not working for that idiot are you?"

"It's just a project," she replied evasively. "Anyway I don't think he's so dreadful. I like animals and there are an awful lot of people in Surrey like me who want to preserve our native wildlife here."

"Native's the word. I'm happy to support harmless little hedgehogs, and if that means using organic fertiliser so be it, but Jules is running around at night with a wolf and a vulture. No wonder people want to stop him." George rolled the cartridge between the palms of his hands before handing it back to Impey with a grimace.

"Actually I think an animal sanctuary is rather a lovely idea."

"Not on a golf course." George shook his head dismissively. "Hasn't it ever occurred to you what the golf club is Impey?" Before she could answer he continued, "It's somewhere you can come and be with true friends, people you can trust. That's enshrined in the spirit of the game."

"But they could still do that."

"Not with wild animals wandering over the course. The whole point of golf is that it's the most civilised game. You know what our boys do off duty in Afghanistan?"

Impey shook her head.

George moved his hands in front of his own large belly in the imitation a putt. "They play golf. They've made a makeshift golf course where they play."

"Heavens do the Afghans play as well."

"Could do – they're a very athletic lot. They'd find it a lot more fun than sneaking about in caves or planting bombs in the road."

"I don't think Jules would dispute that."

"He might not, but his animals would. We play our game to a set or rules. Wild animals obey the rules of the jungle, or maybe the heath if they're in England, but they certainly don't have any respect for people. They'll stamp around all over the place wrecking the work of the ground staff." He blew air out of his mouth with a judder. "Good God Impey, do you really want shit all over the fairways? Cows may look nice tethered in the distance, but you don't want dollops of dung all round your ball which you can't move because they're not a 'burrowing animal'".

Impey looked at him. "I suppose you do have a point."

"Of course I've got a point. What's more your animals would be endangered here. Sooner or later some pony would be hit by a golf ball and lose an eye and then there'd be hell to pay."

"I don't think Jules has got horses in mind."

"Wasn't a wolf enough to go by? He's crazy Impey and you're silly to have anything to do with him. And you'd better be damn wary who you accuse of shooting animals or you could make yourself damned unpopular." He threw his clubs into the boot of his aged Ford which rattled loudly when he banged it shut.

But I love the club. It's done so much for me since my divorce.. "I don't see why I should be hated for finding out who shot Caesar. Jules does have a right to know who shot his pet."

"True." George stepped round to the driver's door of his car. "Only he doesn't have a right to involve you, unless he owns you body and soul." He pulled open the rusty door of his car whilst he raised his tufted white eyebrows with the unasked question *Does he?*

"Certainly not," said Impey, "only the mortgage on my home."

"Plenty of other people here could sort that out for you. You could come and stay with Val and me, or shack up with your friend Dodger." He eyed her keenly. "Club members do help each other. Come on Impey. Where's your loyalty?" He knew he did not have to remind her of the way her mother's golfing friends had rallied round whist she was in hospital dying, washing her clothes and bringing her tempting appetising food in a desperate attempt to persuade her to eat.

"Jules has got a big stake in the club. He only wants it to succeed."

"And so it can in the proper way. We've got great members, a superb course and wonderful facilities now, not to mention our great catering staff." He eyed the rabbit inside Impey's polythene bag. "Our food's fabled all over the county especially..." His voice died away as he stepped into his car.

"The rabbit pie." Impey finished for him, but she didn't know whether he heard because of the noise his car starting.

25. Breakfast in the clubhouse

Why am I here? Flick sat in one of the new armchairs in the clubhouse sitting room. Through the non-reflective glass windows she'd insisted were a 'must' when she'd redesigned this room, she could see the sun was shining on the course. If she was going to take time out from work, it would be a great day to be out there on the grass feeling her body move with the light breeze that stirred the leaves on the oak tree by the side of the eighteenth.

Waiting for Jules to turn up and have breakfast with her was not such a good idea. She'd been silly to agree but he'd caught her half asleep at seven o'clock in the morning. Even so, she detected a note of hostility in his voice, but perhaps it was worry that made his normal light jovial tone sound chilly. He said he needed to speak to her so presumably he had something to ask her. She must not, she resolved, agree to whatever it was he might request her to do.

When he'd come back into her life, which was only last year though it seemed an eternity away, she'd been pleased. The club needed him; or at least it needed his money. The renovation of the clubhouse had zoomed out of the members' financial orbit. Every stage of the works had required more money than was estimated. Were it not a listed building, it would have been cheaper to knock the place down, much as that would have upset the older members. They were devastated that their club, which had celebrated its centenary fifteen years ago, was threatened with closure.

Jules had appeared at the right moment to say this wouldn't happen. When he'd made the announcement at the annual general meeting, standing in front of three hundred members gathered in the lounge, wearing his smart charcoal pinstriped suit over a plain golden yellow shirt which toned in with his golden hair, he'd looked great. He'd even worn a tie, admittedly with birds on it, but in her past with him, he'd often caused a stir by refusing to wear ties on formal occasions when it was customary. His new gravitas suited him, especially as he hadn't lost his sense of humour or his panache, that sense he could shock people just enough to get away with it.

Afterwards he'd cornered her, said she was the person who could help him most. He'd suggested she should try for the main committee herself. Until that moment, over a drink in the spike bar, she'd forgotten how attractive he could be when you had his total attention.

She was getting bored of David. They weren't tied together in any way, either legally or domestically. David had never suggested she should move into his house though it was easily big enough for both of them. He didn't say it, but they both knew there were too many complications, namely his children and her son. Besides, she would have to sort out the mess in his house, which she had the wit to know would not be greeted with enthusiasm by his family. She shuddered; she couldn't live with all that clutter.

Until Mandy's three phone calls, she'd thought Jules's life was relatively uncomplicated for a forty-two year old millionaire. He must have been batty to take on the club, but obviously he thought once again he'd manage the impossible. She should refuse to do anything to help him, but it was difficult when he'd baled her out in the past. There was only one time when it was a big bale out. That happened during his marriage to Tessa, light relief for him really. At least he couldn't be wanting condolences for his grief over her death. She grinned. Consolation from Tessa was needed *when he was married to her*. Thankfully his third wife never knew, according

245

to Jules, that he'd cancelled a debt of hers to a large aggressive fabrics company. Apparently she never took any interest in his business affairs anyway.

So what if they'd shared a night of passion in one of the best golf hotels in Norfolk. It was only a fling, merely a rather fun toss about in very luxurious surrounding. She didn't feel guilty. After all, she was not then yet hitched to her husband number two, even if Jules had reached his third wife.

Actually he owed her something since she'd suggested the debt collecting thing in the first place. She glanced at her watch. Jules had said meet at eight o'clock. It was now quarter past. What could be keeping him?

When she looked up she saw he was approaching her. Thank goodness he was wearing light gabardine trousers rather than jeans. His striped blue shirt had a collar and he'd even bothered to put on a tie. Perhaps he was going on to some work appointment since he also carried a rather shabby black plastic-looking briefcase.

"So sorry," he apologised, when he reached her. He bent over to greet her with the customary kisses on both cheeks. "The police called to see me."

Flick's jaw dropped. "What out of the blue?"

"Not completely unexpectedly though I thought they might turn up later in the day. I rang them yesterday." He put out his hand to grasp hers and pull her on to her feet. "Listen, why don't you come through to the dining room and then I'll explain."

"I don't know if anyone's in the kitchen yet," said Flick.

"Yes they are. I rang Matt to say we'd be eating here and he said it would be all right. He'll sort it with Dan."

Typical, thougt Flick, *he just arranges things like that to suit himself, regardless of staff rotas. Really don't want Dan upset; he's such a brilliant chef.*

"So what's the matter then?" she asked when they both had steaming plates of eggs and bacon in front of them on a table in the dining room. Though she'd have to go without lunch after a breakfast of this size, she might as well use the time profitably by consuming a meal, if she was losing valuable working hours.

Jules looked down at his plate. "Caesar," he muttered, "he's been shot. Well he's dead actually."

"You mean someone's killed him?"

Jules nodded.

"But that's awful." Flick shivered. Had she heard right? Did Jules say "shot"? "How come?" Mentally she asked apprehensively, *What's it got to do with me?*

Across the small table Jules beamed his blue eyes straight into hers. His voice was louder now with a note of accusation in it. "We think someone from the club hit him. I found him on the golf course."

"Must have been an accident." Flick hoped she wasn't blushing. Out of the corner of her eye, through the dining room window she could see Horace playing with Adam on the second hole. His words about shooting at the last committee meeting, which were echoed by others, rang in her ears. *But surely they were talking about killing the bird, not the wolf.*

"Couldn't have been." Jules's mouth turned down at the corners as he gave a vigorous shake of his head. "He was shot; the bullet went deep into his body."

"You really think someone aimed to kill Caesar?" asked Flick. She was relieved that Adam, who was looking in her direction from where he stood on the course, would be

247

unlikely to be able to identify her. Good thing she insisted on the extra expense putting in special glass through which diners could see out, but golfers could not see into the room.

"I do, and I'm sure the police will too."

"But why should anyone want to kill an old wolf?"

"That's what I was hoping you'd find out for me."

Flick pushed her plate away. She had nearly finished the egg and bacon, but now felt she could not touch the rest. "You can't drag me into this Jules. It's probably completely random, nothing to do with the club." She hesitated. "All sorts of people stray on to the course."

Jules's head was slightly on one side as he looked at her. His knife and fork lay on his plate, the tips meeting at one another to make the apex of a triangle which pointed at her.

"Surely this is the sort of thing you should get Impey Dalrymple to do. That's what you're employing her for."

"Well she's done some investigation for me," he admitted, his face reddening a little, "but she thinks it would be inappropriate for her to take it any further forward." He pursed his broad lips and frowned. "Actually she's being very difficult about it but I suppose it's understandable. You know she hasn't been a member here for very long."

"Oh come on Jules, she was a junior member for heavens sake." Flick picked up a piece of brown toast out of the pretty silver toast rack. She spread some butter on to it. She might as well make the most of this breakfast. Then she could miss lunch. Dan said the marmalade was homemade and it certainly looked delicious.

"That was a long time ago and in present terms she's pretty much a newcomer. I told her I thought she was being a bit wet about it, but when she said she thought you would be a much better bet to take it forward, your being on the committee as the social member, I had to agree with her."

So she said that did she? Clever bitch. "What on earth makes her think someone in the club shot Caesar?"

"She doesn't say that necessarily; she simply thinks something should be checked out in case it's relevant."

"What exactly?"

Jules bent down, unlatched his briefcase and fished out a transparent polythene bag which he held up over the table at eye level. Inside was the bloodstained body of a dead rabbit.

Flick dropped her piece of toast. "That is disgusting." She shuddered, "Take it away before I vomit – it's completely unhygienic here."

Jules looked offended. "No, it's not," he said, "it's well frozen. I've had it in my freezer for a couple of days."

"Than you'd jolly well better get rid of all the other contents," ordered Flick, brushing her hand in the air at the rabbit, but making sure she did not touch its body bag.

Jules dropped it down on the edge of the table. "The thing is, I want you to take it."

"Take it?" Flick repeated. "Are you mad? What on earth would I want a dead rabbit for."

"It's evidence; it was found in my garden and since no one would go into my place to shoot rabbits, I can only assume someone came in from the golf course."

"Carrying a rabbit to shoot your wolf?" *Sounds like a demented nursery rhyme.*

"Something like that."

"Well we can't possibly have a dead rabbit in the dining room," insisted Flick. "You'll have to take it outside now and put in the dustbin or something. I mean health and safety would have our guts for garters if they knew."

"I can't see the problem," said Jules, "a, it's frozen and b, surely people hang game for a while before they cook it anyway."

"Not in the dining room," said Flick firmly, wrinkling her nose, but she saw Jules's mouth clinch in an obstinate expression. "Please would you put it back where you got it from for the moment. That bag is revolting."

"Okay. Okay" His sulky voice was horribly reminiscent of the times they'd argued twenty years ago. "I'll find something better." Still holding the bag he pushed his chair back to stand up. He walked over towards the kitchen from where she heard him call out to the cook, "Dan could you get me something for this?"

In a couple of minutes he'd returned with something that resembled a sandwich tin which thankfully was not transparent and presumably had the rabbit inside it. Back at her side of the table he balanced it on the top of her capacious handbag. How unfortunate she happened to have brought a large one along today. Inevitably Jules commented that there would be plenty of room inside it for half a dozen rabbits.

How does he get away with this sort of thing every time?

She gritted her teeth and forced herself to smile. "Listen Jules dear, a dead rabbit's not much to go on. A fox could have dragged it under the fence. It might nothing to do with your wolf's death."

"But I'm sure this has." Jules bent down to delve into his briefcase again. When he straightened up he placed an empty little yellow tube with a gold metal end on the table.

"What's that?"

"A gun cartridge."

"So?"

"Impey found it alongside the rabbit just outside Caesar's pen."

Flick sighed. "I really don't know what you expect me to do about all this."

"Use your charm." Jules put his elbows on the table whilst he leant over it towards her with his hands clasped together; he shook them backwards and forwards in her direction. "Exert your position as social affairs manager on the committee. Get people talking. I know how resourceful you are; you'll find out something. Everyone wants to be your friend."

"I don't know that I want to behave like that, kind of snooping on our members."

"Do it for Bisley Heath."

"But darling, why it's so important to the club?"

Jules spread his mouth into a wistful smile, an expression she remembered from the past when he'd tried to cajole her into doing something she didn't want to do. "Well I don't know that I want to invest in a place where people are going round shooting animals. I'm not interested in that sort of behaviour."

"No, I quite understand what you mean darling; I'm sure everyone here appreciates that."

"I hope they do. And if they don't, it's time they did. Shooting defenceless animals is barbaric." He lifted his hands off the table and evidently caught sight of his watch as he did. "Heavens, is that the time. I'm afraid I must rush. – But do what you can. And keep in touch. I'll let you know when Caesar's funeral is." He stood up to go.

Strange he never mentioned Tessa's death, Flick reflected afterwards. What a mistake she'd made thinking he'd got more normal. He was more, rather than less eccentric, these days. She got rid of the rabbit – the friendly dustman took that away without any trouble. If he asked about it, she'd say the neighbour's cat had it, but what could she say about the funeral? Fancy asking her to go to a wolf's wake. "Show solidarity with me," he'd said. He seemed quite hurt when she said she didn't think she was "up for it".

She prayed she would not discover anyone in the club had anything to do with the wretched creature's demise when Jules was threatening to pull his plug out of the club and let it go to whatever financial wolves awaited it. People were already pointing an accusing finger at her for her perceived extravagance over doing up the clubhouse. Jules's money was a life line. Without his backing, the club could literally go down the drain. "I'm not prepared to support a club whose members shoot my animals. I want that person chucked out of Bisley Heath. I tell you Flick, either he or she goes or I do."

26. The Police call on Impey

Inevitably it was a fine sunny Wednesday, the ladies' club day, when the police arrived early in the morning to see Impey. Since they brought a liver and white Springer spaniel dog with them, she did not initially realise that the large burly man wearing a light grey jacket over an open-necked pale blue shirt with a non-descript abstract design, and the young woman in tight brown trousers were police officers.

The prospect of having to cancel golf with Rosie again, made Impey reluctant to let them into the cottage, but once they told her they were plain clothes detectives investigating a sudden violent death, she had to talk to them that morning. She let the pair, who'd introduced themselves as Nick and Paula, into her sitting room whilst she went into the kitchen, shutting the door firmly, in the hope the officers would not be able to hear what she was saying.

As she expected, Rosie was not pleased to be cancelled at such short notice. With children to collect from school, it was going to be difficult for her to go out with the sitter, the reserve player who waited until the end of the morning to play with anyone who'd lost her playing partner.

"The police," she echoed in disbelief when Impey explained it was rather hard to put off her surprise visitors. "What do they want so urgently with you?"

"Sudden violent death," repeated Impey, "that I appear to have got involved in. Apparently Jules Challenger's third wife committed suicide minutes after I'd seen her."

"There, I told you," complained Rosie impatiently, "nothing good would come of working for such a man. I've discovered that my watch-bracelet which Deborah is hoarding found its way into Jules's mother's shop. It's beginning to look very much like she's received stolen property."

"Good heavens. Are you sure?"

"Pretty much. I have it on good authority, his fourth wife Mandy actually. I tell you what: I'd be very interested if you started investigating that theft. After all, if only Ned had come to the invitation instead of Dodger, I'd still have my bracelet."

"Okay, I owe you one. I'll talk to Jules's mother and try to find out whether she's got any record or remembers where she got your bracelet."

Impey returned to the sitting room with a bowl of water for the dog to find the animal still on a lead snuffling around the furniture with Paula, the young female policewoman in tow, whilst Nick stood awkwardly in the middle of Impey's small room. Puzzled she was about to demand an explanation from Paula who, with her blonde pony tail swishing about as she watched the dog's nose, looked to be younger than herself, probably in her late twenties.

The words died in her throat. Rhythmically like a clock ticking in her mind, the realisation that the dog must be a sniffer dog,, was followed by the conclusion she was being investigated for possession of drugs.

She wanted to asked *what the hell are you doing*, but Impey crushed her indignation. It was pointless to ask them to produce search warrants when she had nothing to hide. She had not looked closely at the identification they'd showed her when she opened the door to them. Maybe they had already shown her a search warrant. Instead she asked with what she hoped was an innocent smile, "What are you looking for? I thought you wanted to talk about Tessa Challenger."

Paula jerked the liver and white dog to a standstill beside her. She smiled at Impey. "Yes that's why we're here."

Impey put the bowl of water down in front of the dog. "Is he allowed water, or will it get in the way of his investigations?"

"No, no, no, thank you very much," assented Paula, though it sounded as though she was refusing.

"I'm sure he'll be very grateful," added Nick with a dry chuckle.

Whilst the dog lapped away at the water, the police accepted Impey's invitation to sit down. Nick started the questioning by asking her how she had found Tessa Hope, which he reminded Impey, was the surname Tessa used, or rather had taken to using, instead of Challenger.

"She was fine," said Impey.

"Not depressed?"

"Not that I noticed, but I don't suppose a professional psychologist would necessarily show feelings like that to someone like me."

"Why were you seeing her?" the man asked. "Are you depressed?"

"No I wasn't seeing her professionally in that way."

"So why were you visiting her consulting rooms on a Saturday then?"

Impey tried to turn her grimace into a smile. She glanced around her room with her vast number of books stuffed higgledy-piggledy into her built-in white floor to ceiling shelves. Animals, music and best-selling romances would not have given the police a clue that she had morphed accidentally into an occasional private investigator. "I was doing a survey for someone."

She was pleased with that reply. All sorts of people were forever doing *surveys*.

"On what precisely," asked the policeman.

"Behaviour patterns," said Impey nonchalantly.

"Who is your employer?"

"The Griffon Trust."

"I see." The man's voice dropped as he lengthened the e of see with a knowing note. "You mean her ex-husband's company, the debt business?"

"Yes, Mr Challenger has or rather had enormous respect for Tessa's expertise in psychological matters."

This appeared to satisfy the policeman who changed tack with his next question. "Did you get the impression that she was still emotionally attached to Mr. Challenger."

"No, rather the reverse."

"You mean she hated him?" Nick's brown eyes scrutinised Impey's face. He had a lean strong face, *lantern jawed,* she thought irrelevantly, *like the hero of an old-fashioned romantic novel. My mother would have wanted me to marry a man like that.*

"No." Impey shook her head. "She was simply very professional and detached when she mentioned him."

"So can you explain this?" He delved into a small attaché case by the side of his armchair to pick out a sheet of paper. Leaning forward he was tall enough to thrust out a long arm to hand the paper to Impey. On it was her name written three times with some hearts and a few caricature flowers dotted around.

Impey stared at it sickened. She hoped she wasn't blushing, but it was embarrassing seeing her own name scrawled inside a red felt tip drawing of a heart that was about three inches high and the same across. "Obviously Tessa wasn't as balanced as she appeared."

"So it would seem," agreed the policeman.

"I suppose she took a massive dose of tranquilisers," said Impey. "She looked at the dog. "Or are you thinking, I mean have you found something else?"

"I can tell you," said the policeman, "since it will come out at the inquest anyway, that in the post-mortem, traces of other drugs were found in M/s Hope's body, in her hair samples to be precise."

"What were they?"

"Morphine."

Impey wanted to laugh, almost hysterically. In days gone by she might have snuffed the odd joint of cannabis, but heroin never. She'd left London for a wholesome country life, not to become a junkie. "You are joking; you think I might have supplied her with dope?"

"We don't know."

Impey stared at the dog. "You're welcome to take whatisname round my house, what there is of it, to search for any weed you like."

"I will take Flintoff around if you don't mind." The policewoman got up and walked to the door.

Impey got up to follow her, then sat down again; it would show greater confidence if she let Paula go alone. After all, she wasn't going to find anything. She smiled at the policeman. "Is there anything else you want to know about my visit to Tessa Hope?"

"Yes, we wondered whether she offered you a cup of tea or coffee whilst you were there."

Impey shook her head. "Really I was there for a very short time. Tessa couldn't help me very much."

"What with?"

"My questions."

"You don't have a copy of them, do you? I mean the questionnaire you use for your survey." There was an air of feigned innocence on the guy's long face whilst a smile played at the corner of his mouth.

"'Fraid not; it was a kind of preliminary excursion."

"With what in mind precisely?"

"The company's emblem," said Impey. "The Griffon Trust has a statue as it's masthead on the website, letter headings and its showpiece office. You may have seen it; Flick, Jules's first wife was the model for it."

"What about it?"

"It was vandalised; her arms chopped off and Jules wanted to know whether Tessa had any ideas about it." She hoped she was sounding impersonal and professional.

"I see." He nodded, showing a thick thatch of his liver brown curly hair streaked with grey.

She was relieved to see Paula reappear through the door of the sitting room with Flintoff. He was a diversion, the only one of the police force present who looked like a rank amateur. Paula and Nick might not be uniformed, but they were the real thing, proper police investigators who looked the part, amiable but not friendly like the brown and white spaniel. He'd slunk into the room with an apologetic expression, his head on one side, but lips curled up from his long white teeth almost as though he was smiling.

Impey could not restrain herself from walking over to him and patting him. "Good dog," she said, knowing from his body language that he could not have found anything significant.

He wagged his tail.

"It's always a worry that something completely innocuous like herbal tea in one's kitchen may contain traces of an illegal substance." Impey tried to inject jollity into her voice, as though she understood these situations.

Nick and Paula exchanged significant glances.

"Very true," said Nick. He frowned. "You are sure that M/s Hope didn't offer you any sustenance during your visit like a herbal tea or something to eat?"

"I've told you she didn't once. Why do you ask again? What might she have offered me?"

"A poppy seed bagel perhaps," said Paula with an offhand laugh, as though she might be making a joke.

"Good lord no." *Why on earth did she ask that?* A sudden vivid picture of the inside of Grace's kitchen cupboard came into her mind's eye. There was a packet of poppy seed bagels. "I haven't seen one since..."

"Since when?" asked Nick in all too innocent a tone.

"Nothing, a while ago."

"It would really help us if you could remember." Paula's blonde ponytail bobbed up and down as spoke. She smiled disarmingly as if to say *we're your friends.*

It was the wrong call she decided later. Why oh why did she let herself be drawn into any conversation about poppy seed bagels. She should never have been seduced by the listening skill of the police. They'd been so attentive, lapping up her words as eagerly as Flintoff's pink tongue had slurped up the water she'd given him.

She'd felt as though she was on a stage, compelled to go on speaking because she enchanted the audience. Her saying she was surprised Tessa should have bread in a cupboard in her consulting room when she must have a kitchen with a breadbin upstairs in her flat, absorbed them, even if they did not take written notes.

Something about their eager reaction to all her information frightened her. She wished she'd never mentioned her visit to Grace Deer's house. That made Nick's eyes brighten. *Was this before she disappeared?* He wanted to know. "I believe so; I don't know," she'd replied, trying to downplay the incident.

It obviously hadn't worked. When they left they thanked her for her help far too profusely. Nick wished her luck with her *survey,* but his look said something different, something more on the lines that they were rather further ahead with their investigation than Impey was with hers.

27. Deborah's charity morning

In the drizzling rain Deborah plucked a variety of roses from her garden. It was lucky she still had some blooms in late summer. She wanted to make her drawing room look especially pretty today for her coffee morning. The peach and white flowers were at exactly the right stage, sufficiently open without being overblown. Both varieties had a beautiful scent too.

She snipped off a dozen blooms, enough to fill the large cut glass vase she would put on the round pedestal stand mahogany table, which would be the centre piece in her drawing room where her guests gathered. They must, or at least one guest in particular, should feel her generosity. Her goodwill needed to be displayed. She did not want anyone to think she had been pushed into the decision she'd made.

In her small kitchen, which she would love to have extended, if only she and Monty could have afforded the building work, she trimmed the leaves off the bottom of the stems before crushing the ends with the secateurs turned on their side. That should help the roses last until her bridge dinner party at the weekend.

Today was an annual charity event which she held for Save the Children Fund. She'd persuaded Rosie to come because she'd suggested it would be such a good opportunity to give her watch-bracelet back in person in front of other people. The word would then get around that Rosie's possession of it was honest.

Ned had not been in favour of a public handover of the watch-bracelet, but was sufficiently relieved his mother was returning it, not to object too much to the way she did it. He'd told her in no uncertain terms that her taking it from the kitchen and then keeping it, *hanging on to it,* he called it, damaged her standing at the club.

Even if Rosie had stolen the watch-bracelet, he argued, Deborah could not prove it. All she could do was to make herself look silly. He also pointed out that he couldn't remember her ever wearing it. That was hardly surprising since it had been missing for ten or more years, she'd replied, but she had to admit to herself she'd rarely worn it. Monty hadn't wanted her to wear it when Grace was around, probably because he'd been on a business trip when he bought it.

Ned was right. She'd hardly looked at the watch-bracelet in the jewellery box which she had hidden in her bedroom since she'd taken it back, so why did she want it? She could remember Monty without it. Anyway Ned was more important to her now. He'd been so good flying back from his holiday to look after her when she'd had shingles. His views were what mattered. He said Rosie might go and see Faye Challenger to ask where she got it from, which would be unfortunate at the present time. With Tessa's death, and of course Caesar's, not to mention Grace's disappearance, Ned didn't think it was at all a good time to get muddled up in the Challengers' problems.

Naturally he didn't know Faye was coming today. She was hardly what Deborah might call a kindred spirit, but they went back a long way. They'd even played a bit of golf together when Faye first joined Bisley Heath, until Faye found her own set of friends to play with.

That was fine by Deborah. Not that there was anything wrong with Faye. Rather the reverse; she was so sweet Deborah found it irritating. With those golden curls and big blue eyes, both of which Jules was lucky enough to inherit, Faye was a natural sweetie-pie. Her rounded cheeks and pretty pink rosebud mouth reminded Deborah of the favourite doll she'd had as a child. The doll however had worn a modest dress whereas Faye always wore trousers which, in Deborah's opinion, were at least a shade, if not a couple of sizes, too tight since they revealed every voluptuous curve.

She wondered whether Faye's dress sense had changed over the last few years. This was the first time for about five years that Faye had accepted her invitation to the coffee morning. She wasn't in the same position as Deborah, obliged to attend anything at which Grace was bound to be present.

Grace, having been a "saved" child from the Nazis, was passionate about Save the Children Fund. She'd given a lot of money to the charity herself. Happily this one of her enthusiasms met with Deborah's. When Monty asked her to become involved with it, she'd been glad to help. She'd made it her charity when she was Lady Captain of Bisley Heath. Her annual coffee morning had followed on since.

She liked to hold the event in her garden, but it was too wet today. Somehow she would have to accommodate everyone indoors. Not that she was expecting as many people as usual. Without Monty, and now she was no longer on the bench or a town counsellor, her popularity had waned.

In the circumstances, she was surprised Faye wanted to show herself, but Deborah was glad she did. She might not especially like her, but the woman was an asset in any social gathering, even if she did talk slightly too loudly and coo *Darling* at people she hardly knew.

Deborah sighed as she plunged the roses into the cut glass vase she'd managed to pick up from the Oxfam shop. That coup, only spoiled some years ago when Faye, blue eyes goggling, had topped this modest revelation with the information that she'd bought the gorgeous trouser suit she wore from the Help the Aged charity shop.

Funny this year all five mothers were going to be here. None of them were girls she'd have expected to have as friends. In the past Deborah had resented their association, not liking the feeling she was as needy as these other women, so dependent in some way on Grace that they also allowed her to be an honorary godmother to their sons.

Thankfully Mary Hobbs, Tarquin the sculptor's mother, felt as she did about Faye, if not more so. Mary would be bound to arrive in a floral cotton skirt she'd made herself, looking reassuringly like the farmer's wife she was. She and Giles were a sensible couple. Amazing that they'd had such a way-out, if talented, child as Tarquin. Deborah sensed Mary was uncertain whether they should have accepted help from Grace with their son, but they had nearly been wiped out by foot and mouth outbreaks. Although they never discussed it, she once did confide in Deborah that she hadn't liked Grace encouraging their son to change his name, telling the ten year old that *Toby* might not suit a famous sculptor, with the result Tarquin had chosen a new name for himself from a fighter in his favourite comic.

Deborah felt a twinge of guilt as she placed the vase in the centre of the table on an handmade embroidered linen mat which she'd bought from Mary a couple of years ago. Whilst Tarquin, aka Toby, might have inherited his skill with his hands from his mother, neither Mary nor Giles were keen for their son to embark on a career in the art world. She, Deborah, had not been able to sympathise when they said plaintively that Toby was so good with animals he really should be a farmer; she'd cringed when Mary, who could never bring herself to say Tarquin, told her Toby enjoyed time with Caesar so much she hoped it might make him think again about farming or some other work with animals.

Yet when Jules walked off with Ned's girlfriend Roxanne, Mary Hobbs was the one other mother who provided solace. "I know how it feels to have your child hurt," she'd said. "I cried for Toby when Jules married Flick." Sometimes now Deborah regretted she had not tried to be more friendly with Mary. At least she could rely on her to turn up with an array of homemade stuff like jam, biscuits and cakes to be sold at the coffee morning.

Back in the kitchen Deborah placed the biscuits she'd bought from the women's institute market out on a large blue pottery plate, which should please Patsy Scrivenor, Adam's mother, since she'd chosen these plates as a company present for executives after some junket in Portugal. Poor woman had worked for Grace as some sort of secretarial dogsbody.

Patsy was a pleasant woman with a facial tick. Whether one side of her chin twitched periodically as a result of an abusive marriage or a genetic problem, Deborah forbore to ask. She wondered too whether Adam and his sister resented the demands Grace had made upon their mother. Monty sometimes suggested Patsy had a tough time, always having to do everything behind the scenes, because Grace did not want prestigious customers to see Patsy's face twitch.

As Deborah expected, Frankie, Steve's mother, was the first to arrive. She was always punctual in case there was something she could do to help. It was nice of her to continue the habit even now when she was no longer Grace's housekeeper, expected to turn her hand to helping any of Grace's friends at the wave of *Wonder woman's* wand.

Privately Deborah wondered whether Grace's patronage of Steve hadn't been counter-productive. He'd been a bright if rather timid little boy who, Ned told her, followed Jules around. Shame that habit seemed to have stuck.

Frankie's first words after they'd kissed each other on both cheeks in greeting were, "What would you like me to do to help?"

Stay on afterwards and clear up the house? If only she could ask that. In these recession days, Deborah could afford cleaning help only once a week. Prior to her promotion to housekeeper, Frankie had been Grace's cleaner, or rather *domestic help,* as she liked to be called, but whatever the name, her work was brilliant. It would never do to insult her.

Frankie was no longer the thin sad divorcée with straggly black hair scraped behind her head into a ponytail, but very much the lady these days. Her cropped tinted hair shone whilst with her slim slight figure she always looked elegant. Married to the builder who'd done up Grace's bungalow, with no need to go out to work herself, Frankie had somehow made friends with the most unlikely people. Deborah put it down to her flower arranging and cookery capabilities, practicalities which made her a very useful chum.

She tried to forget Monty never liked Frankie. He said she snooped. On what, Deborah was not sure, but Monty said it often enough for her not to be able to ignore it whenever she saw Frankie, even if they were on Mmm Mmm, kissing on both cheeks, terms now.

"Nothing dear," said Deborah as she led the way through to the drawing room. "I think we're pretty well ready. Several people have dropped things off already. They're all through there." She waved airily at the double patterned glass doors which separated her drawing room from the dining area where she had carefully displayed all the work for sale on her

266

dining room table, covered with a beautiful embroidered table cloth bought from Mary Hobbs.

Frankie gasped.

"What is it dear?" asked Deborah.

"That bracelet thing you're wearing. Grace had one just like it."

"Oh did she?"

"Yes, but it disappeared years ago. We turned the house upside down looking for it, but never found it."

"It seems they have a habit of doing that," said Deborah drily. A nasty suspicion formed in her mind which she brushed away. A couple of times when Monty was ill, then again when he was dying, Grace had sent Frankie over to give Deborah some help around the house. "Actually this one belongs to a young friend of mine, Rosie Metcalfe. I'm only wearing it to remind myself to give it back to her today."

So Ned was right; bless him. It was obviously sensible to give the bracelet back to Rosie. This bracelet surely couldn't have been the same one Grace lost, but the coincidence was sufficiently awkward for Deborah not to feel entirely comfortable wearing it.

Frankie coloured. Her shoulders hunched as she shrunk back slightly. "I'm sorry. I'm afraid I can't stop thinking about Grace at the moment, her having disappeared. It's so dreadful not knowing what's happened to her."

"I know," said Deborah. She tried to add brightly, "I keep thinking she'll simply turn up with some very good reason for not having used her bank account for three weeks."

Frankie bit her lip. "I didn't know that. That's dreadful. You mean she might be wandering around somewhere having lost her memory." She hesitated, but before Deborah could reply, continued, "no she couldn't be

267

going anywhere; she'd only just had that hip operation. She was in a wheelchair."

"I heard it from a friend," said Deborah. No point in saying that the friend she was at university with now happened to work in the home office, with responsibility for the police force. "I've been terribly concerned about Grace too."

She was relieved when her other guests began to arrive, some bearing gifts to be sold which had to be placed on the dining room table. Her conversation with Frankie could then resort to the practicalities of the occasion, such as making coffee or handing round the homemade biscuits Mary Hobbs had brought with her.

For a while Deborah was worried Rosie would not turn up, despite the promise of the bracelet's return. Eventually, an hour after everyone else had arrived, by which time some were leaving, Rosie appeared in the drawing room having pushed open the front door, which Deborah had left on the latch.

"How wonderful to see you dear," gushed Deborah, acutely aware Faye, a couple of people away on her left, should be able to hear her next words. She unlatched the bracelet to give it to Rosie. "I had to wear it to make sure I didn't forget," she said with a tinkling laugh.

"Thank you." Rosie, instantly buckled the watch-bracelet on to her own wrist. "It's nice to have it back."

Deborah thought her tone a little haughty in the circumstances. "I appreciate you feel you are the rightful owner. Even if it did belong to me, I know you would never have come by it dishonourably."

Rosie took a couple of steps to the side to tap Faye on the shoulder. "Excuse me Mrs Challenger, do you remember this watch?" She flourished her arm in the air.

Faye reddened, almost to the colour of the cherries patterned on her pristine white dress. She glanced at Deborah. "I don't think so. You must realise huge amounts of jewellery passed through our shop. I didn't even see every piece."

Why then, Deborah wanted to ask her, *are you looking so embarrassed?*

She did not get a chance.

Faye looked at her own watch. "My goodness, is that the time. I really must fly; I've got lunch date. Lovely party as always Debbie. Goodbye darling."

Deborah bristled. If there was one thing she hated, it was being called Debbie. Nonetheless she responded politely as they brushed each cheek in a simulated kiss. "Au revoir," she bade Faye coolly.

"I suppose I'll be seeing you again in a couple of days anyway," said Faye.

"Really?" Deborah frowned, trying to recall some golf or bridge do she was going to attend where Faye might be present.

"At the funeral?"

"No. No. I didn't know Tessa."

"Oh not Tessa," Faye gave a silvery laugh. "Caesar's funeral."

Deborah's stomach lurched. *Omigod I hope Ned doesn't expect me to go. No he'd hate me anywhere near something like that.* "I don't think so," she said drily.

28. Lunch with Deborah

Frankie did stay to help clear up, which meant everything seemed to arrive in the dish-washer as fast as the crockery leapt into the machine of its own volition in a Walt Disney film she'd seen as a child. She would, Deborah guessed, have stayed anyway without the invitation to a scrap lunch.

Mary and Patsy seemed delighted to be asked to stay on too. They both obviously wanted to talk about Grace's disappearance and the impact it was having on their boys.

Patsy, who still worked three days a week for the new owners of Grace's company, said they were all "extremely concerned". Though retired for over ten years, Grace had been in touch regularly with them by phone, email or even text. They felt her silence was extraordinary to the point of being sinister.

"How did Adam take it?" asked Mary, in between congratulating Deborah on the rabbit pâté they were eating. It was as delicious as usual. – So lucky Dan was happy to sell her any surplus he didn't need for club meals. Last winter he'd sold her some tubs of rabbit broth which had also been very useful for her small hen parties. Pity there was a rumour circulating that Adam, in his new treasury role, might put a stop to this way of using left-overs, when it was so useful for her and other female club members in the know.

Patsy looked embarrassed. Her chin wobbled. "I'm afraid he's not really concerned," she said awkwardly. "He hasn't been near Grace for years. At the moment he only mentions her in connection with Jules's plans for Bisley Heath, because he knows she helped fund the Griffon Trust."

"That must be difficult for you," said Deborah sympathetically.

"Awfully," sighed Patsy, neatly spreading a thin layer of rabbit pâté on a piece of brown toast. "Of course he's trying to be reasonable and understanding, because Adam's like that. Now he's married he's put that business of Jules going off with Mandy out of his mind, but he's absolutely furious with Jules for dividing the club and getting everyone so upset about his plans for this wildlife course."

Deborah nodded sympathetically; she murmured how much she understood Adam's feelings. She felt much the same herself.

"Thank goodness Toby," began Mary, "I mean Tarquin of course, doesn't play golf. I heard a bit about Jules's plans when Giles met him at market looking at wild boars, but I don't think he bought any. Giles told him he was being ridiculous."

"Like a lot of Jules's plans," agreed Deborah, "burying a wolf in his garden for instance. Ned says it's terribly unhygienic. And whoever heard of a wolf having a funeral?"

"Steven thinks it's a good idea," piped up Frankie, who liked to refer to her son by his full name. "He's helping Jules with all the arrangements as you might expect. After all, Jules has been very good to him." She looked at Deborah as if to say *but of course he's been good to Ned too.*

Deborah wanted to say all too many people, including her own son, spent an absurd amount of time and energy doing things for Jules, even if Ned did say he was only interested in looking after Caesar. She clenched her teeth to keep the words back. Instead she said coolly, "Jules is very lucky to have someone as bright and efficient as Steven to work for him."

"I expect Toby will go to the funeral," said Mary.

The other women stared at her in surprise.

"He loved that wolf," explained Mary. "He spent a lot of time with Caesar when he did that sculpture of him."

"Of course," said Frankie, "Steven told me about that. What happened to it?"

"I don't know," said Mary. "Actually Toby, Tarquin to you of course, is pretty keen to find it. Caesar was so tame he was able to get a fantastic likeness."

"Perhaps Grace had it. She had the one of Roxanne," said Deborah. "I was knocked out when I saw it; I knew immediately who'd made it."

"Oh he only did that one because he wanted to do the wolf," said Mary hastily. "He made a sort of bargain with Grace; he'd do Roxanne if he could do the wolf as well."

"What does he want it for, now his work is completely different?" asked Patsy.

"With all the cutbacks he's having to look for work that sells. Organisations, public or private aren't looking for abstract work to put in forecourts any more. They haven't got money to spend on art. Toby's got to start thinking about what ordinary private buyers like. If he could have that sculpture of Caesar, he could take a mould, reduce it and sell loads of replicas."

"That doesn't sound like the Tarquin I used to know," commented Deborah drily. She could have added *he would have been ashamed to touch anything so commercial.* She stood up to start clearing away the plates.

She was relieved Frankie did not follow her out to the kitchen to help. She did not want to discuss her feelings about Caesar's death. Steven, or rather Steve as he was now, might be happy working for Jules, but proximity to him was,

Deborah felt, not good for Ned. There were too many poignant memories. Caesar's demise might actually help him move on, but she couldn't spell that out to Frankie or the other two women.

She opened the dishwasher to load the plates into it before she opened the fridge to take out the little glass bowls on coloured pedestals with homemade strawberry mousse inside them. She had a very easy recipe she knocked up for occasions like these. There was a fifth helping which she'd made for Faye, in case she changed her mind about staying for lunch; she'd been known to do that before.

When she returned to the dining room, with the desserts carefully balanced on a tray, she heard Mary continuing with her explanation to the other women as to why Tarquin was returning to the sort of work he'd done as a child. He was a talented boy, but the fuss Grace made about it was over the top.

"Needs must," said Mary. "I'm quite pleased. I loved it when he made models I recognised. He's good with animals too. I'd love him to do more work like Nic Fiddian-Green who does beautiful sculptures of horses – the horse at Marble Arch is his work."

"Lots of people love horses," said Patsy, nodding earnestly, "but I'm not sure models of wolves would have the same appeal, as far as company sponsorship is concerned I mean."

"Toby could do any animal," said Mary defiantly. "He likes animals as much as Ned does." She smiled at Deborah as she put the puddings on to the table. "Remember when Ned used to come and help us on the farm in the holidays? I always thought he'd end up doing something with animals he loved them so much – sometimes I thought he preferred them to people."

Deborah pursed her lips in silent fury as she sat down. Mary had made stupid remarks like that about Ned before. She might think she understood Ned because he'd spent some time working for Giles, but she hadn't a clue what Ned was really like, any more than she understood why her own son enjoyed sculpting metal rods instead of making three dimensional replicas of animals.

Suddenly, for no good reason, the children's party game, "The Farmer wants a wife" sang her head, probably because she wanted so badly for Ned to find a soul mate. *If only he weren't so picky.* No. Unlike Tarquin, Ned's problem was loyalty; he had never got over losing Roxanne, whilst Tarquin, she'd heard, had a partner who was pregnant, having already discarded another older woman who'd had a child by him. Anyway Mary had a daughter with three children so she also had grandchildren, whilst Patsy's son Adam had recently married.

Though Patsy never admitted it, Ned told her Adam had been gutted when Jules married Mandy. She was such a town girl that Adam had never imagined she would appeal to Jules, or he would never have introduced them. He'd simply thought Jules might help her out, because she'd run up such enormous debts on credit cards for stores all over London.

Adam himself had expensive tastes, which was entirely Grace's fault. She paid for him to go to a particularly glossy public school, a bad choice according to Monty, who said it was for rich men's sons, but that probably appealed to Grace. She could swan around on open days amongst the soigné, being lady bountiful.

274

Deborah gestured at the little pots of strawberry mousse. "Do help yourselves. It's made with fromage frais so it's not too fattening." It was time they stopped talking about their grown up children. They were perilously near discussing the mess Tarquin had made of Flick's sculpture, about which Mary seemed oblivious. Must be nice to be that placid. Yet surely Giles would have mentioned it? Even without Monty to tell her club gossip, she knew jokes about Flick's new resemblance to the Venus de Milo were being bandied amongst the men.

Tarquin had been a bully as a child, but Ned could stand up to him; he wouldn't stand for any nonsense.

"I think Adam would love to have a model of Caesar," twittered Patsy. "He was very fond of the wolf, though it terrified me and of course Grace never wanted it near her."

Frankie nodded in agreement. "Yes, but you know it's very odd. Grace must have had Caesar in her house because when I was cleaning up the last time, when I got worried because she'd disappeared, I found coarse grey hairs in her sitting room that must have been a dog's if not a wolf's."

"I hope you informed the police," said Deborah.

Frankie looked embarrassed. "Well I didn't really think it was my business..."

29. A Wake for a wolf

Impey unloaded Cally from her car.

"We did such a lot as a threesome". Jules's insistence he wanted his bird to come to the wolf's funeral had sounded bizarre, until Impey remembered Rosie's description of Jack meeting Jules jogging with Caesar, accompanied by Cally soaring overhead.

Rosie's words came back to her, "He was on his hands and knees when the bird swooped down on him." She pictured Jack frantically looking for his car key in the dark, after his misguided borrowing from the club's safe. *Of course; it was the signal. You kneel when you want Cally to land on you. She wasn't on the attack.* Cally supposed she was meant to drop down to Jack because he was on his knees.

Impey would explain that to Rosie. Their friendship had blossomed again, now Rosie had re-possessed her bracelet. "Deborah was so sweet about it and obviously I gave a big donation to her charity to show my appreciation." Apparently they'd agreed it was probably a good thing Faye didn't know, or remember, who'd provided her with the jewellery to sell. So now, Rosie told Impey, there was no need for her to talk to Faye.

Nonetheless Impey's journalist's antenna was still flashing. She wanted to know how that bracelet had changed rightful owners. Today could provide a chance to find out. She walked through the open door in the fence into Jules's wild garden. Prior to his arrival, it might have been well tended. Remnants of flowerbeds surrounded a sloping lawn, but the flowers in them were mingled with weeds. Most of their edges were messy.

Jules had chosen the smartest bit of his garden for the ceremony. Around a circular arrangement of rose beds with a grey stone sundial at the centre a large clump of mourners, were gathered. Amongst them would be Faye. Jules had told her his mother was coming, which Impey found rather odd, not so much that Faye would be present, but that Jules found so natural she'd be there. She recognised her instantly. Faye was far the best dressed, or, in her elegant black long-sleeved shirt dress, the most formally dressed person there. Her golden tresses were so beautifully curled, she looked as though she might have been to the hairdressers that morning.

"Come on," Impey said to Cally who waddled alongside her over the unkempt grass to join the group.

"Hi there." A deep well known voice of an unseen person greeted her.

Startled, she jumped, making Cally lurch to one side.

Dodger emerged from behind a tree in an outfit of beige trousers teamed with a greenish brown shirt that looked almost like scrubs. "I thought you'd turn up." He shook his head. "Bloody ridiculous the whole thing."

"So why are you here?" She asked in a whisper as the three of them moved forwards to where the group gathered.

"Duty, whaddidyer think?"

"I thought you were a friend of Jules and would be here in sympathy."

"Give me a break." Dodger punched her lightly on the arm. "No I'm here as a muscle man in case things get rough, but I'm not meant to be making myself too obvious."

"Hadn't you better go back and hide behind that beech tree again?"

"No, being your escort will do fine." Dodger grinned. He moved smartly to the other side of Impey away from Cally whose neck was stretched out with her head poked forward as though she was about to peck him. "Provided you keep that bird at bay. What on earth made you bring her? I thought you were meant to be keeping her out of here as part of Jules's persecution complex." He mouthed the words into her ear so the people gathered in the crowd around them could not hear.

"He wanted her here," Impey whispered back, "she's a big part of his life."

"Absolutely mad, bringing a vulture to a funeral." Dodger's mouth was at her ear again. "She'll want to eat the carcass."

"She can't," said Impey. "Caesar will be inside a coffin so she won't even know he's dead or there's a body. Vultures don't have a sense of smell; they work things out by sight."

Dodger looked down at Cally standing patiently by Impey. "Well she won't be seeing much with all these heads in the way."

As though she'd heard and understood his words, Cally gave a sudden spring forward. She flapped her vast white wings with such force that Impey staggered against Dodger. With a quick turn to the side and a couple of hops forward she was airborne. Within seconds she had flown to perch on the bough of another large tree, a vantage point from which she would be able to view the proceedings around the sundial without difficulty.

"Look, look, there's Cally," said someone.

"I thought she was being minded elsewhere," said another person.

"Shh. Shh.." said a third. "They're starting."

Impey wondered whether she should try to retrieve her. Through a gap in the crowd she could see Steve and Jules beside a willow wicker casket. They both glanced up at the tree as though they sensed Cally's presence, so presumably one of them would call her if they were afraid the bird would fly away. She raised her arm to try to attract their attention in case Jules wanted her to do something, but he was preoccupied, talking to a man with a guitar who started to strum on his instrument.

On the tree, Cally moved from one foot to the other almost as though she knew the tune.

Maybe Jules and Steve haven't seen her. Impey gave Dodger an apologetic look. She patted his arm. "I'd better go and see if I'm needed."

"Good luck," he said.

She wove her way forward between people shushing each other because Jules was waving his arms for silence so that he could speak. "Please would you all join in singing," he asked. "I'd like to begin with an old-fashioned song that I'm sure everyone knows which fits the moment."

Impey cringed. Here at the front, everyone would be able to see her. She did not want to join in and felt ridiculously self-conscious. It would be much more fun to worm her way back to Dodger making sardonic remarks, but that was not possible. Jules had seen her. His face lit up into a smile of welcome as the guitarist began to play "A four-legged friend."

To Impey's surprise she found herself singing lustily with everyone else, "A four-legged, friend, a four-legged friend, he'll never let you down. He's honest and faithful right up to the end; that wonderful one, two, three, four-legged friend." At the end of each verse, the guitarist gave the congregation the words of the next verse to sing with the refrain sung again at the end.

However sad he might be, Jules was in his element as master of ceremonies. Dressed in smart jeans and an open neck shirt patterned with birds, he produced a small battery microphone to address his audience on the importance of wolves in the ecosystem. Caesar, he explained, had come into his life by accident. Through the death of his second wife, he had been left "holding the baby", but this had brought him into another world of wildlife. He had come to understand how vital these creatures were to the sustenance of human life because they were intimately linked to the food chain.

On a personal note he had learnt how intelligent a creature the wolf was, as well as what a wonderful companion this precursor of the dog could be. His voice wavered with emotion as he bent over the willow coffin.

With a flourish of her wings, Cally interrupted the scene, swooping down to the ground beside him.

He gave her a beatific smile before his expression turned to horror as she started to peck at the coffin.

From somewhere behind him, Ned jumped forward. "For God sake stop it. There's a body in there."

"It's all right," shouted Jules above the appalled gasps of the crowd. "She doesn't know this box is a coffin." He started to whistle the first few bars of Mozart's clarinet concerto, which was her signature tune.

Cally turned round. With her head on one said she gave him a look as if to say *Come on. Tell me what's going on in here.*

"Stop her; stop her," screamed Ned, "she'll tear the body open." He stood a couple of feet away from Cally with the palms of his hands and his fingers curved as though he was ready to leap forward and strangle the vulture.

Jules knelt down. He started whistling again.

With a half-hearted swirl of her wings, Cally turned to him. She hopped on to his outstretched arm. Slowly Jules managed to rise on to his feet with the huge bird on his ungloved arm.

Everyone except Ned started to clap their hands. He bowed his head muttering something which Impey couldn't hear. Only natural he should feel emotional. He too had nurtured the wolf for sixteen years.

Jules turned to Impey. "Here, take her."

Tentatively Impey held out her gloved arm. She didn't like holding Cally on her arm for long because she was so heavy, but reckoned she could manage for a short while.

Jules delved into his pocket to draw out some sheets of paper. "And now I would like you to hear a couple of poems. The first one *[1] is particularly appropriate."

To Impey's amazement, after all her hostility to Jules's pets, Mandy, dressed in a short slinky black sleeveless dress with her hair tied back in a large shiny black ribbon, stepped forward, a large sheet of paper in her long slender hands. In a loud sing-song tone she recited a poem called "His last howl".

"The last howl
That sounded
Was from the wolf's heart
Forever to echo
In his pack's ears
Forever to remain
In their hearts
For a heartless hunter

---

[1] By Codi Rogers copyright the poet but taken from the Wolf Song of Alaska website

Rose his gun that day
And his victim was
This wolf his pack
Sings about every day
The man took his body away
The pack howls
As one
In sorrow
In pain
They shall forever
Remember the wolf
That fell that
One fateful winter day."

When Mandy's voice had drifted away, an eerie silence fell over the crowd. Everyone bowed their heads as though in prayer. Behind her, Impey heard sobs. She glanced over her shoulder to see a couple of fashionably dressed girls wipe their eyes.

Even Cally, gripping Impey's arm, seemed to feel the tension as Jules said in an emotional tone "Thank you Mandy." With his hand on her shoulder he said, "Thank you all for sharing my feelings, for being part of Caesar's pack."

At this suggestion there was an embarrassed shuffling of feet whilst Jules announced he would now read "Four-feet" by Rudyard Kipling.

"I have done mostly what most men do
And pushed it out of my mind
But I can't forget, if I wanted to,
Four-feet trotting behind.

Day after day, the whole day through.
Wherever my road inclined
Four-feet said, 'I am coming with you!'
And trotted along behind.

Now I must go by some other road,
Which I shall never find
Somewhere that does not carry the sound
Of Four-feet trotting behind.

By the time he had finished reciting the poem with it's rhythmic repetition of the "Four feet trotting behind" and ended with having to find "some other road that did not carry the sound", there were even more sobs. Jules paused for a couple of minutes to let his words sink in before he read his final wolf poem prayer.

Only Dodger seemed unperturbed as he watched the mourners.

"I'll take him," Steve's voice broke into Impey's thoughts. He held out his arm for Cally to hop on to it. "I'll put her in to the aviary, whilst you're at the wake."

Impey was not sure she wanted to stay, but at least Dodger was there. She also recognised Tarquin, with a gasp, since he'd cut his long black hair. Otherwise, amongst the fifty or so people she joined, gathered in the sitting room, there were very few people she recognised.

Unlike the study, this room was beautifully decorated in cream with attractive furnishings, making Impey wonder whether Faye had a hand in the design. Then, noting the odd touch of fuchsia pink, she remembered that Flick was an interior decorator. This had to be her work.

"Not your greatest hour as a falconer," teased Dodger, waving the bottle of Champagne, which presumably he was meant to be circulating round the room to pour into guests' glasses. He refilled her glass for the third time. "Better drink up whilst you can. Still don't worry if you get the sack. I'll take you out for fish and chips tonight."

He was still making jokes about her ineptitude when Jules hurried up to her as soon as he entered the room. She had, he insisted, nothing to reproach herself about. He had wanted Cally at the ceremony and Ned was making a ridiculous fuss, but that was only to be expected because he'd been so involved with Caesar's life and he wasn't a bird man, though Jules hoped he might become so one day.

"Now," said Jules, "I really want you to meet my mother." He put his hand on her shoulder and swivelled her round. "Come this way. She's over here."

Impey turned her head back to signal to Dodger that she would see him later, but he scowled back, obviously angry she had acquiesced with their acting employer. *It's hardly my fault, you introduced him to me.* Impey gritted her teeth with irritation as Jules led her over to meet his glamorous mother.

After a few minutes aimless conversation, Impey managed to bring up the subject of the Chaika watch bracelet, but first she ascertained that Faye had kept meticulous records of all her purchases of jewellery.

You've caught me there. Impey saw the unsaid words in the colouring of Faye's pink cheeks. She claimed she had no recollection of it, even when she'd seen it again at Deborah's lunch party.

Before Impey could ask more, there was a loud peal on the door bell.

Faye excused herself. She was acting as hostess too, she said.

When she came back into the room, there were two burly men with her, one of whom Impey recognised as Nick, the detective who'd visited her to ask about her involvement with Tessa.

"They want to see you," Faye said incredulously to Jules. "They're police," she whispered.

"Sorry to interrupt Sir," said one of the men, "but we urgently need a sample of hair from your deceased wolf."

"Of course," agreed Jules. "I'd like you to find the bastard who shot him."

"We'd certainly like to help you," said the larger policeman politely, but Impey noticed he cast a look at Nick, raising a smooth brown eyebrow, in a way which contradicted Jules's assumption the detectives' mission was to search for Ceasar's assailant.

Jules gazed round the room. He beckoned to Ned. "I'd like my vet to come and take the sample for you."

"We'd actually like you to come as well to identify your pet," said Nick.

"Yes, yes, fine," said Jules.

"I'll stay here," said Ned, who'd strolled over to join then, "and look after your mum." In his hand he too held a bottle of Champagne which he poured into Impey's glass, filling it to the brim before she could cover it with her hand.

She was too absorbed at the sight of Faye tottering on her high heels in anger. Jules's mother looked as though she would have liked to bop the detectives with the black framed handbag which was swaying under her shaking clenched fist.

"I can't believe it," she said, as soon as the detectives, accompanied by Jules, had left the room. "They're not looking for the person who shot Caesar. When they showed me their police cards on the doorstep, the name they gave me was Grace."

"Well they're bound to be looking for her," said Ned calmly in his breathy voice. My mother said they were searching Grace's house when she went to see her."

"But they can't think Caesar's got anything to do with Grace," cried Faye. "She would never have anything to do with the wolf, even when Roxanne was alive; Jules always made sure Caesar was shut up out of the way if Grace was around."

"Maybe the hairs will eliminate Caesar from their enquiries." Impey tried to be consoling. "You see when I went to interview Grace there were some hairs around which could have been wolf's hairs and I found a handbag with some tooth marks in it, though they could have been a dog's." Her voice drifted off lamely.

She sipped some of her Champagne. Goodness, this tasted much stronger than the last bottle, although it had the same label.

"Too bad you didn't meet Grace." Ned refilled her glass. "She was such a character, she'd have made a wonderful interview for you."

"She would indeed have," agreed Faye.

"I did try to see her." Impey looked from one to the other. They both seemed to stiffen. Maybe she'd better change the subject. "Such a good thing," she remarked gaily, "Rosie Metcalfe has the Chaika watch back. I gather you both had a hand in that."

Another complicit flash of eyes swept between Ned and Faye.

286

Impey felt unnerved. There was an undercurrent she could not understand, but it made her feel uncomfortable; she must find a way out of this investigation. Perhaps Jules would sack her, since she was so incompetent.

Rather the reverse; he seemed intent on becoming more, rather than less involved with her. "Stay for a while," he begged her, when half an hour later, she came to the top of a short queue of people waiting to say good-bye to their host.

"I really think it would be better if I went," she pulled back a little as he clasped her slim out-stretched hand with both of his broad sturdy ones.

"Do stay," Jules pleaded. "I need someone close to me when they come from the Crematorium to take Caesar's body away – and of course afterwards."

"It's rather awkward," said Impey. "You see I've said I'll go out with Dodger."

"Oh don't worry about him." Jules squeezed her hand. He leant forward to give her a lingering kiss on her cheek. "I'll sort him out," he whispered in her ear.

30.   A Romantic Evening

A black Volvo estate arrived to pick up the willow coffin at exactly six o'clock as instructed, Steve told Impey who happened to be standing next him then. "We wanted a feeling of evening drawing in when we said good-bye." He put the word around the twenty or so remaining guests left in the room that Jules wanted them all in the drive to sing a parting song.

As they filed through the front door, Jules handed them each a song sheet with the words for Celine Dion's "Cry". He fondled Impey's shoulder when he gave her one. "Hang on," he whispered before he disappeared elsewhere.

A few paces away from her stood the guitarist but he was busy getting his instrument ready to strum whilst he muttered that he felt like a medieval troubadour.

To the sound of the singing he led, Jules, accompanied by Ned, Steve and a couple of men in black, presumably from the cremation company, went down the garden to collect the willow coffin. They returned with slow dignified steps bearing the coffin on their shoulders.

Surprising how heavy that box looks. Impey watched the men struggle to slide the coffin off their shoulders to a level which enabled them to shove it into the vehicle. Presumably with relief, one of the men slammed the tailgate pre-empting the moving end of the song. Whilst the car pulled away, drowning their final words, some of the guests were crying.

"Can't think why he had to chose our song," wept Mandy. She seemed not notice Impey nearby, who herself found a tear trickle down her face. She guessed she would have loved Caesar if she'd met him more than a couple of times; she'd adored the black Labrador dogs her family had kept when she was a child. Their deaths had been traumatic, but her parents had not believed in the healing power of ceremonies like this. "No weeping, wailing and gnashing of teeth," her father would have said. Now she questioned whether he was right. An outpouring of grief must be doing something for Jules or he would not have arranged this party.

"He needs people around him," confided Faye to her in the kitchen half an hour later whilst Impey helped her wash up the glasses which the caterers, who'd provided the canapés, would not be taking away. "Caesar's been a big part of his life for a long time now."

"I suppose so," mumbled Impey on automatic pilot. All the other guests seemed to have left, leaving her, the mug, who'd offered to help clear up. Where was Dodger who said he'd take her out to supper? No sign either of Mandy or any of the other tearful girls who'd fawned round Jules earlier. Their departure must be due to the continued presence of Faye. She still managed to look so immaculate, even stuck in to the most mundane jobs in the kitchen. Her yellow rubber gloves augmented rather than detracted from her golden curls.

The intimacy of working together, drying the ornamental glasses which Faye stood on the draining board, stirred Impey to mention the bracelet again. In a casual tone she asked, "You know Jules did some debt collecting for you – he wasn't involved with that Chaika watch was he?"

Faye shook her head. "Oh no, that was Ned." Long teeth suddenly appeared over her fleshy bottom lip as her chin dropped.

"Ned," exclaimed Impey. "How was he involved?"

"Oh ignore that; I shouldn't have said it." Faye's narrow body wiggled in denial.

"So it was Ned who pawned the watch?" said Impey.

"I haven't said that," said Faye briskly as she braced her shoulders.

No, but you implied it.

Faye picked a silver tray out of a cupboard beneath the kitchen units. She placed some of the glasses which Impey had dried on to it. "Why don't you take these through to Jules; he's in the sitting room."

Jules was unperturbed by the same question. Preoccupied by stacking his glasses into their allotted places in an antique corner cupboard, he answered nonchalantly, "I don't know the thing people have been going on about, but Ned might have pawned something with Mum." He kept hold of a couple of wine glasses which he put on a small carved oak sideboard.

"Why would he do that?" Impey sipped the white wine Jules had poured for her. She already felt so light-headed from the amount she'd drunk that she knew she'd have to take a taxi home unless Dodger reappeared. Since he seemed to have gone home without her, she might as well drink with Jules. He was insistent she should try this bottle of wine because Ned had brought it. He'd said with a laugh that it must be good because Ned pinched it from his deceased father's cellar. The late Monty was a connoisseur of fine wine.

She was relieved to lounge in a soft chair after the tension of trying to look after Cally amongst a crowd, most of whom were strangers to her, although it upset her to see the vulture perched on a bar on top of a Steinway grand piano.

"Monty was a bit of a gambler, one of those smart guys who have to keep up appearances, so he got Ned to take the odd bit of stuff to Mum and Dad to sell."

"Without his mother knowing presumably?"

"Possibly." Jules shrugged. "Deborah was always frightfully busy with being a magistrate as well as her golf."

"Doesn't sound like a full time job to me." Impey hoped she didn't sound churlish, but surely magistrates didn't sit that often?

"She did masses of good works as well, raising money for charity and the like; she was a local councillor too."

"So did Ned spend a lot of time with you as a child then?"

"No, he used to go round to Tarquin's, or rather Toby, as he was called in those days."

"Wouldn't have thought they'd have had much in common."

"They didn't, but Ned was mad about animals and Tarquin's parents had a farm. Don't think Deborah's very keen on animals though; seem to remember she's allergic to them."

Impey frowned. *It's still strange her son should pawn one of her treasured possessions.*

"I wonder what Jack paid your mum for the watch. How much did she usually make on those deals?"

Jules wide mouth dropped open revealing white teeth. He got up from the sofa where he was sitting, to walk over to her. Bending down he ruffled her hair with his hand. "That is a very cheeky," he grinned down at her, "or I might say a very intimate question."

Impey shrank back in the chair. "Personal perhaps." She had a sudden picture of Tessa's face when she talked about 'bluff' being the way Jules made money. Had that applied to his mother? Impey knew nothing about the pawn business, but she assumed there must be a large gap between the amount given to the person pawning the jewellery and the money taken from a purchaser. "I'm sorry if I offended you."

Jules straightened up; he laughed. "No offence taken. Fact is I've no idea what Mum's margins were."

Not sure I believe you. Even in her befuddled state it seemed strange Jules would not understand the details of his parents' business. Still, there was no point in saying that. It didn't seem to matter any more. Jules was being so lovely to her. Instead she asked, "Was Monty, Ned's father, a bit of a rogue?"

Jules stroked her hair again, but this time she didn't resist. She felt strangely tingly. Normally any mention of a womaniser upset her because her own ex-husband had given her such an unhappy time, but the way Jules spoke made Monty sound light and harmless, "Depends what you mean by rogue. Monty was a lot more popular with women than poor old Ned, not that Ned was interested in any girl 'til Roxy came along." He sighed. "But don't let's go there." He paced across the room to a cabinet and opened its glass door. "I'll put on some music for Cally."

Impey blinked at him. "For Cally?"

He nodded. "Yes, she's very musical."

"Hm, I see." Impey tried to focus her eyes on Cally. She wanted to say that whatever her other lovely qualities, this particular bird's voice was so ugly that she could not envisage musicality in any vulture.

Jules must have picked up her feelings from the expression on her face. "You'll see she likes Mozart." He plucked a disc out of its case to push it into a slot in his silver player.

Despite strange ethereal feelings floating through her, Impey recognised the twenty-first piano concerto. *Elvira*

292

Madigan theme tune coming soon; who could fail to be seduced by that?"
She'd vowed to spend a year without a man in her life when
she left her husband, but that date had passed. With this
enticing music flooding through her, the right moment had
arrived. She was ready for love.

Jules was an attractive fun guy who liked her enough
to want her with him at his most vulnerable. He'd lost his
kindred spirit, a creature who was more a companion to him
than a pet. *There can't be much wrong with someone who loves animals.*
Some great author said that. She couldn't think at that moment
who, but no matter. It must be true. That's what counted.

"Do you like it?" Jules stepped back towards her.

"Yes," Impey frowned, uncertain. In the background
she could hear a strange rhythmic thudding. Could there be
something wrong with the disc, or was this an odd recording?

"Cally's amazing isn't she?" said Jules, presumably
interpreting her bemusement.

Impey looked across at the piano to see the bird
hopping from one foot to the other. "Is she dancing?"

"Yeah. That's I call it. She's got rhythm." Jules did a
little gyration with his hips. "Think we should join her?"

Impey was not sure what sort of action this first
movement dictated, but she rose to her feet. "Why not?"

Jules reached out to pick up the remote control from
an occasional table. He fast-forwarded to the Andante before
he clasped Impey round the waist.

Will Cally be jealous, she suddenly wondered. Instead
she asked, "Did you have Caesar and Cally with you all the
time?" *Does she go upstairs? Do you have her in your bedroom? No.*
Mandy would have said; she'd never have tolerated that.

"Pretty much whenever I could, which was far from always," he replied, rocking backwards and forwards with her in time to the music.

She relaxed in his arms, letting the sounds waft over her. "You should trust me," he murmured, his lips brushing her ear. "I'm a one girl man." Feeling light-headed, she let him swirl her round the room to the soft tones.

Why not be happy? How good it is to be with someone who cares about me. He hugged her so tightly now she fancied she felt his heart beat. *Steady as a rock. He's been so unlucky in love, but that could change, with the right person, someone less way out than his previous women. He's right: four's not so many for a man over forty.*

He released her gradually as the Andante drifted to a close, so that he could reach for the wine bottle which he picked up.

She felt herself sway as she waved her hand in the air to refuse another drink, but he walked across the room to refill her glass. "I think I'd better stop there; I'll never be able to drive home." She staggered against a chair. "I mean," she heard her words slur, "I'll not be able to ring for a taxi."

"Why bother?" He brought her glass over to where she stood. "There's plenty of room here for you to stay over." He spoke as casually as the owner of a bed and breakfast might inform a passer-by he had vacant beds on offer.

"I think I'd better not." The words tumbled out. She would not be eager. If Jules wanted her to stay with him, it was up to him to make her feel wanted, someone precious, not just an available body.

He must have sensed her feelings; he put his arm round her. He nuzzled his face in her hair. "I'd be honoured if you stayed," he murmured. His hand slipped inside her shirt to stroke her bosom. The buttons popped apart and Jules slipped the shirt off her shoulders. Her head swimming, Impey bent down to retrieve the shirt which had fallen to the floor, but as she did she felt the ping of her bra hook undo. She was not sure how the skimpy white lace object came off her body but she saw Jules toss it on to a nearby chair.

"Let's dance again," he said when she reached out to retrieve the underwear. Before she could put it on, he'd grasped her with one arm whilst he flicked the remote control at his music machine with the hand at the end of his other arm. More seductive notes came from the player.

"Okay," she staggered against him, listening to him croon softly to a sensuous jazz tune. She didn't need her top. It was very warm summer evening. Jules had taken his shirt off too and it felt good to feel his naked chest clasped against hers. She didn't have to make any effort to dance. Her man was guiding her, letting her body sway against his. Maybe she should take off her trousers. Picked to look respectable for the wake, they were wrong for this sort of dancing. "One minute." She stepped away from him whilst she undid her belt, pulled down the zip and slipped out of them before she snuggled up to him again.

A short low rattle disturbed the music, a sound that was out of tune and sync with the dreamy rhythm which danced with her thoughts. The noise penetrated the haze in Impey's brain. Someone was rapping on a nearby window. She looked up to see Dodger's angry eyes staring through the pane at her.

"Omigod you've come back." She heard the slurred words drift out of her mouth. Her brain no longer seemed under her control. Everything around her shook into different shapes, an unwanted kaleidoscope making odd patterns with shiny little coloured pieces.

"I'll deal with him." Jules's words echoed in Impey's mind. Hadn't he said something like this before?

With his right arm still attached to Impey, Jules used his left hand to unlatch the window. He pulled it open. With his head turned to face Dodger, he called affably, "Listen old fellow, I'll pay you la..."

"You fucking tosser." Dodger's arm shot through the window and caught Jules on the nose. "You promised you wouldn't make a move on her if I introduced you."

Am I her? Impey felt Jules withdraw his arms from her. Amongst the flashing lights which danced around her, she saw a bright red stream gush on Jules's face. He pulled something white out of his trouser pocket to dab his bloody nose.

Dodger vaulted through the open casement window. One of his hands pushed Impey aside, making her stumble into a chintz covered armchair; his other grabbed Jules. He pinned him against the wall. "You bastard; you've got her bloody well stoned."

"No!" Jules shouted. His knee came up to hit his assailant in the groin, but Dodger anticipated his move. With a jerk of his own leg he tripped Jules on to the floor.

Impey staggered to her feet. "Stop, stop," she cried. She tottered forward to clutch Dodger's back.

He turned his head. "You all right?" He asked gruffly.

"Yeah fine," she stammered, noting to her horror, Jules jump to his feet and manage to land a kick in Dodger's groin.

With anguished howl Dodger doubled up. He looked about to crash to the floor, but instead it was Jules, caught by the calves of his legs, who was flung face downwards on to the cream Wilton carpet.

Dodger had one foot on his back when Faye charged into the room with a bucket of water. *She must have been mopping the kitchen floor.* A bizarre cartoon of Faye on her hands and knees spread over Impey's mind as a couple of gallons of mucky water sloshed over the three of them. *This water's filthy.*

"I've called the police," screamed Faye shrilly. Her face contorted as she glared at Impey. "It's all your fault, you dirty little slut. I'll make sure the police get you for it."

31. The Captain calls an urgent meeting

Adam and his wife Polly sat opposite Flick in the Bisley Heath lounge. They were going to stay for lunch, but she'd agreed to meet up with them, plus whoever else from the committee could make it, for a pre-prandial drink. Matthew, the club Captain had rung at ten o'clock this morning to say he would like to see as many of the committee as possible at midday, even if it was a bank holiday Monday. There was something urgent he wanted to discuss.

Since David her on-off boyfriend was away this weekend and her son Ben was on a play date, today was a good opportunity for her to meet committee people. The presence of Polly was a nuisance. Although she was a promising golfer, she was too new in Adam's life to understand any club politics they might have to deal with, but that unfortunately did not stop her talking knowledgeably about everything.

"It's going to be okay", said Adam reassuringly. He poured the Chardonnay he'd bought, at Polly's request, into three tall glasses.

Flick, who normally only drank Chardonnay under protest, demurely picked up her glass to sip the wine. "I'm glad to hear it. What makes you so sure?" She wondered what "everything" was. Matthew had sounded extremely worried when they'd spoken earlier.

"The wolf gone to be cremated. There's no question of his being buried on the golf course, or even in the garden next door."

"What about the ashes?" asked Polly, the eyebrows on her pretty round face raising and her blue eyes widening. "We

298

don't know what's going to happen to them. He might sprinkle them on the course."

Flick tried not to glare at her. Unpleasant expressions give you wrinkles. All the same she hated this parvenu criticising Jules, even if he was her ex-husband who'd let her beautiful statue be mauled by his pet wolf. "We don't have to worry about a few ashes that'll blow away. It's a body being dug up by foxes or polluting our watering system that's the main problem, or worse still, some sort of shrine." She turned her face to Adam's. "You know how sentimental Jules is."

Adam gave a dry ironic laugh. "Yes, I gather yesterday's wake was a monument to that."

"Did you go?" asked Flick in surprise.

He shook his head. "No, but my mother did. She said she was crying at the end. It made her think about Grace and what might have happened to her. Luckily Ned was there. He was a tower of strength, apparently."

"Really?" Flick had never regarded Ned as having great social skills. Her memory of him was of a rather awkward youth, wonderful though he might be with animals. "What did he do?"

"Chatted up the old ladies. They, my mother and the like, were rather upset by the arrival of the police."

"Police," exclaimed Flick, alarmed, "what were they doing there?"

"Came to collect a few wolf hairs, I gather, before Caesar's body finally disappeared."

Flick leant forward in her chair, her slim hands clasped together whilst she digested this bizarre information. It did not sound good. She undid her hands to grip the arms of the tub chair in which she sat. Her vibes were usually right, but she did not want to admit this to Adam, who might be sceptical. He was too darn pleased with himself these days.

When she first met him, she'd been surprised to learn he'd been at a glossy public school because he was so shy and lacking in confidence, although by that stage he was at Oxford University. He was a different man today, in his early forties. In his deep red shirt with a silver tie, which had some sort of significant crest on it, he looked every inch the suave city accountant he'd become.

She was glad when Matthew strode into the room followed by Mark and Andy, but her relief soon dissolved. After some obviously forced smiles of greeting with no kisses involved, the men's faces hardened into grim expressions. Her apprehension increased when Matthew said they should go upstairs to talk, as he did not want their conversation floating around the lounge. All three men refused to take a drink up to the conference room.

Once everyone had sat down at one end of the large oak table, all eyes trained on Matthew's sober face, he spoke. "Jules Challenger has been arrested."

Amongst the gasps, Flick heard her own shuddering breath loudest. "That's ridiculous; Jules is above the law."

"I'm afraid that's what he may have thought," agreed Matthew drily.

Since her words were not what she intended to say, Flick was not surprised the others laughed. "I mean," she said, "Jules wouldn't have done anything wrong. He's not like that; what I meant was he'd always stay the right side of the law."

"I'd like to believe that too," said Matthew, "but apparently the evidence is against him,"

Flick glanced round at the three other men. The expressions on their faces, Adam's round one, Mark's triangular one and Andy's long craggy Scottish one, told her they were all in the know. "What's he supposed to have done?" she asked, carefully expunging any flirtatious note from her voice. This was not the way to deal with men in this sombre mood.

Mark, the solicitor answered. "He's been arrested in conjunction with the disappearance of Grace Deer, but there are other charges too I understand."

"This is too ridiculous." Flick couldn't keep anger out of her voice. "Jules had no good reason to get rid of Grace. He was her great protégé, for goodness sake."

Matthew, sitting at the top end of the table, raised his large hands and opened them, palms forward, like a priest about to give a blessing. "Ours is not to reason why, but work out how we as Bisley Heath club should react to this happening to a prominent member."

"Nor to forget the fact he's a major creditor," said Andy, rolling the r in creditor.

"We have to stick up for him, for goodness sake. I might be divorced from him, but I know he's a good person basically. We were far too young when we got married; that's all." Flick glared round at the others. "Surely supporting our members is part of what belonging to a club's about."

"Of course we should be loyal to our members." Matthew rested his muscular arms on the table. The rolled back sleeves of his blue casual shirt showed the light sandy hairs on his freckled arms matching the colour of thick wavy hair on his head. "But fidelity goes two ways. At Bisley Heath we expect our members to behave in a way that does not bring the club into disrepute."

"Or the game of golf," added Andy. "Golf is absolutely not the game of gangsters. Canna not ye imagine how we'd be looked at with a mobster in our midst. No other club would want to play us."

"For heaven's sake," protested Flick, wishing she'd worn something lighter than a long sleeved shirt and trousers. The hot midday sun blazed through the window, accentuating the heat she felt with her anger at the pomposity of the men around her. "I don't believe anything's been proved against Jules. You're condemning him without hearing his side of the story."

Adam, who sat next her, patted her on the shoulder. "We're not condemning him yet, but we've got to be prepared for the worst."

Flick shook his hand off. "Why not hope for the best and fight his corner. We were happy to take his money for the club, for goodness sake. We need him."

"You haven't let Mark explain everything," said Adam calmly. He turned his head towards Mark on the other side, who looked at Matthew.

"Go ahead," said the Captain, "what's said in this room is not to be recorded. It is entirely between ourselves; I think we all understand that."

The lean-faced lawyer's thin mouth turned down at the corners. "My information is that drugs were found in his home."

"No," roared Flick, surprising herself at her bellow. "He's always been dead against drugs."

"Maybe when you and I knew him well," said Adam gently, "but that was years ago. He might have got...," he hesitated, "more sophisticated tastes since?"

"I don't believe it," cried Flick. Why could these men not see this was completely out of character for Jules? She'd agree, he had his faults. He could be horribly single-minded, but she wanted to say his horribleness was clean. He was never druggy.

"When he was arrested on Saturday evening, drugs were found in his house," said Mark. "There was a woman there with him who was completely stoned from the rave they'd had that afternoon."

Adam's body stiffened in the upright light oak dining chair. "Actually it was a perfectly respectable gathering. My mother was there. It must have been after she and the other ordinary guests left that Jules got the girl high."

Flick gaped at him. She noticed Polly drop her arm down beside her chair to squeeze his hand. A pang went through her. Jules was meant to be coming back to her, or at least yearning for her whilst she decided whether or not her waning relationship with David should be binned. The idea of his plying some bint with drugs to shack up with her for a one night stand in his house revolted her. It couldn't be right. Mark was making a mistake. Jealously was at the root of these ghastly false accusations. With his over-hanging nose and jutting out chin, not to mention his squinty eyes, women wouldn't be queuing up to spend the night with Mark unless they were stoned.

"Some women throw themselves at Jules because he's rich. Or he could have taken pity on someone and offered to put her up for the night." During their brief marriage, to Flick's annoyance, Jules had often invited guests to stay the night when they had drunk too much to drive home.

"After a drug orgy in his house?" Polly said sceptically.

Why the hell was she in the room? This might not be a formal committee meeting, but it concerned private matters of which only the cognoscenti should be informed.

Please would you leave the room. The words formed in Flick's throat, but she managed not to say them. She was in a minority, probably of one, here; she was not going to do herself any good alienating Adam who, with his past association, should be the most sympathetic person in the room. Far better to try to explain what Jules was really like.

"You don't understand," she said. "Jules wasn't giving a party on Saturday night." She gestured at Adam. "You know as well as I do that he held a wake."

"We can check that out with the undertakers I suppose," nodded Mark sardonically.

"That wouldn't exactly be appropriate," said Flick. "The wake was for Caesar, his pet wolf; he adored that creature."

"Begad," guffawed Andy. Even his sarcastic laugh somehow sounded Scottish. "That's the best ruse I've heard for a long time."

"It was genuine," cried Flick angrily. "He was obsessed with that wolf; he was kind of a boyfriend."

"Now you're making him sound r-r-really kinky." Andy rolled his eyes with his r of really.

Matthew raised his arm holding out the flat of his hand again. "This isn't helpful. We've got to be very careful about any remarks we make about Jules Challenger, in case we sound as though we're responding to his allegations that someone on our course, possibly a member, shot the wolf. And yes, you are right Flick: there definitely was a service of sorts to honour the life of the wolf. I'm told it was a moving ceremony, but that does not alter the damaging facts. On Saturday night the police found traces of drugs in Jules's house when they were called to sort out a disturbance. Oddly enough they were called by his mother."

"Faye," gasped Flick, "but she'd never report her own child for anything."

"Jules was being beaten up, that's why," explained Mark.

"Never," said Flick, "Jules is incredibly fit and strong."

"Not when faced with our club champion," said Mark. An ironic grin spread over his lean face.

"Dodger?" *My foursomes partner? This gets worse and worse.* Flick felt herself sweat. She hoped visible damp patches were not spreading under her arms on her cream silk shirt.

"He's our other problem," said Matthew with a roll of his eyes. "Mrs Challenger called the police when an intruder, who turns out to be our club champion, would you believe it, broke into the house, and assaulted Jules."

"But why would Dodger attack Jules?"

"Apparently he was seducing another one of our members by plying her with some unsavoury substance. The whole situation beggars belief for a club like Bisley Heath," said Matthew.

"Well I can't believe it," said Flick. She revolved her head back and forth from Matthew to Mark. "Where does all this information come from, may I ask?"

Matthew gestured at Mark. "We're lucky Mark has some contacts in the police force."

"Surely they shouldn't have told him something like that?" said Flick fiercely.

"For the sake of the club we're lucky he was told." Matthew glanced around at the walls of the room.

Dignified by ornate gold frames, large oil painted portraits of the club's greatest captains and champions hung there. Mathew's golf record matched any of theirs. He'd once played as an amateur in the Open besides performing regularly in prestigious events like the annual Halford Hewitt at Deal. With his rugged rectangular face, Malcolm would look fine amongst these people who'd contributed so much to the game as well as the club's heritage. Provided Bisley Heath survived, he could expect his own picture to be displayed alongside these other great players, which included knighted captains of industry and military heroes.

Flick had had all the portraits cleaned, restored and a couple reframed. Ghastly to think of them all being stacked against the warehouse wall of some saleroom waiting to be auctioned if Jules pulled the plug on Bisley Heath. "Well what are you going to do about all this?" she demanded.

Malcolm bit his fleshy bottom lip. "That's what we're here to discuss. Our reputation would suffer terribly if we ignored the behaviour of prominent members. Our constitution forbids the membership of felons.

"Well shouldn't we start with wretched girl who stirred up all this trouble?" asked Flick. "Don't tell me she's another prominent member. I can tell you for an absolute certainty she's not in our Hicks team. None of our girls who play in county matches are remotely interested in taking dope. They're far too keen on their game. – I hate to say this, but can't we get rid of her first?"

An appalled silence greeted this suggestion.

Flick cast a quick glance round the room. "I'm sorry; it's only that Dodger and Jules are so crucial to this club in different ways, I thought..."

"We could make a scapegoat of someone else," said Matthew drily. "No we can't. Anyway, we mustn't be panicked into doing anything rash. It's important to remember no one's actually been charged with anything yet. That's right isn't it Mark?"

"It's an odd situation." The solicitor pursed his thin lips. "Dodger and the girl were taken into custody on Saturday evening, but they were released later, pending charges being made. Heaven knows what they told the police because early this morning, in a dawn raid, they arrested Jules for murder."

"Murder?" Flick gulped. A dizzy clammy sensation swept over her making her feel faint. She clasped the sides of her chair.

"Listen," said Malcolm in a firm voice. "We must know what allegations have been made against Jules and what exactly is going on. One of the men had better tackle Dodger, but I'd like you Flick," he directed his blue eyes straight into hers, "to go and see Impey Dalrymple. Talk to her woman to woman and find out exactly what the position is."

32. Impey goes to a cremation

Impey sat curled up in the foetal position on the sofa in her sitting room. Thunderous rain beat down on the window outside. It added to the depression which sat like a load on her head. She'd clasped her arms round her head to try to dull her headache, since she was determined not to take even an aspirin today. Nothing could take away the awful flush of embarrassment she felt. How could she have been so daft on Saturday night?

She didn't care too much what Jules thought about her, but the prospect that the world and his brother might know she'd been so high on a drug she'd been hauled off to a police station was torturous. How could she not have realised her drink was spiked? She wished she knew how it had happened, but the police were too canny to divulge any information they had; she didn't even know whether any other guests had taken the drug.

The details of Saturday night were a blur to her now on Tuesday morning. The glorious memory of the night spent with Dodger, who'd somehow recovered his car from Jules's place to rescue her from the police station and drive her home were obliterated by her worry about his situation now. When Impey had denied he was an intruder and said he would have had not intention of stealing anything, the police asked why he'd entered through a window. They'd looked exceedingly sceptical when Impey insisted Jules had opened the window for him. Was she sure it wasn't her who let him in as an accomplice? He was certainly likely to be charged for assault, if not grievous bodily harm.

Once she had managed to persuade the male police officer that it was a complete surprise, though a relief, that

Dodger had appeared, she had been led her off to be questioned by a female police officer. Initially she'd been pleased the tall long dark-haired policewoman was so sympathetic, but soon she became worried when the officer asked if she often took "ravers' smack". Impey cringed at the memory of her confidence when she was asked to give a blood sample, only to be told later it revealed the presence of illegal drugs in her body. Her allegation that her drink must have been spiked, and denial of a relationship with Jules, led the policewoman to ask whether Impey thought she had been a potential victim of a date rape. At the time she'd felt so dozy, she'd initially said she didn't know, which the policewoman took to be a "yes".

Even though it was a bank holiday, the police produced a female lawyer to talk to her. She pressed Impey to make charges against Jules, because "Men should not get away with this sort of thing."

Impey agreed men should not be allowed to vandalise women, but once she suggested that was not the case with Jules, she seemed to be admitting she'd happily taken drugs he provided. Her story sounded even lamer when she insisted she neither wished to embark on an affair with Jules or have a one night stand.

When the policewoman bade her good-bye, thankfully without any charge, she said in a wise tone, "I think you've had a lucky escape."

Impey had thought she meant from spending a night in a prison cell, but policewoman's further comment chilled her. "When we pick up someone like Challenger, it's amazing how many other women's bodies surface" clearly implied she imagined Impey's own body could have subsequently have been unearthed in some cellar. "Or maybe Miss Deer won't surface at all," she added grimly, "seeing's he'd got that vulture."

Impey had held back from telling her she was talking nonsense. Cally had far too good a diet of wholesome dead rabbits and suchlike to want eat a dead old lady. She poked her head out to look at Cally sitting on her piano in her sitting room. The bird was her solace. She had her head on one side as though she knew exactly how Impey was feeling.

Steve had not wanted her to fetch Cally. He said he'd rather look after her himself, because he was so angry with Impey, whom he held responsible for Jules's arrest. He seemed to believe the accusations levelled at Jules must have emanated from her. The only reason he allowed her to collect the bird was on the off chance there might be someone out to harm her to get at Jules, who had also managed to text him that he wanted Impey to continue looking after Cally.

She hoped Jules would be released today, since it was now over twenty-four hours since his arrest on Monday morning. His presence was needed to halt the stories spreading round the club. Though she had not been near Bisley Heath, she knew rumours abounded.

Rosie was on the phone oozing sympathy. Ever since Jack's first meeting with him, she'd been suspicious of Jules. Surely Impey remembered her warnings about the man. If only Impey had hooked up safely with Ned on the Turkish holiday, all this trouble might have been averted.

Hooked up with Ned. Hooked up with Ned. The phrase reverberated in Impey's mind. She had a vivid picture of his pouring Champagne into her glass but to her consternation it was replaced by a vision of Dodger doing the same. And Dodger was annoyed when Jules whisked her off. But Ned? Why should he bother to spike her drink?

The door bell rang. Could she be bothered to go and see who was there? No, far better to pretend she was out. She couldn't believe she was going to want to see whoever was there. It wouldn't be Dodger. When he'd kissed her good-bye he'd told her he would have to try to see a solicitor today.

The bell rang instantly again. *Omigod, they've guessed I'm at home. It's probably Jules who's been released.*

She supposed she ought at least to go and see, although at the moment she did not want to speak to Jules. Both the police and the on-duty solicitor had advised her strongly against communication with him. She realised they reckoned she might have been duped, not employed as an investigator but an accomplice. Much as she fought against the idea, she could see the logic in it.

How she wished she could think of someone with whom she could discuss things. Her brain ticked through her friends at the club. No; they were all far too involved with the club's fraught situation over Jules for that to be helpful. Nor did she want to relay her news to any of her journalist friends. The thought of her plight leaking out further made her feel even sicker. She did not want even the tiniest mention of herself coupled with Jules in any newspaper.

Reluctantly she swung her feet off the sofa on to the floor, pulled herself into a standing position to walk to the front door, where she opened the flap over the peep hole to peer through it.

I must be still be high; I'm seeing things.

Flick, wearing a golf wetsuit, stood shivering in the rain on the doorstep.

Impey pulled the door open. "You'd better come in." She knew she sounded ungracious, but Jules's first wife was almost the last person she wanted to see.

311

"Thanks." Flick stepped into her hall looking uncharacteristically awkward. She massaged a small pink clutch bag in her hand. "I had to come and see you. How are you?"

"Well sort of okay in the circumstances, I suppose." Impey answered cautiously. Her mind whirled round. What could Flick want? For once she looked less than beautiful, even rather bedraggled after tramping up the path to Impey's cottage in pouring rain. When she took off her navy blue rain hat, her flattened golden streaked hair stuck to the to the side of her head.

Impey held out her hand. "Would you like me to take your jacket? If I hang it up for a couple of minutes in the kitchen, it might dry off a bit." She thought she'd better make the offer although she doubted Flick would want to stay a moment longer than necessary.

Flick followed her into the small kitchen where she slipped off the sodden garment and her waterproof over-trousers. She held out the dripping clothes to Impey, who instantly felt embarrassed because she didn't have a utility room with a tumble drier for them. Instead, in the corner of her kitchen, beside her fridge, she kept a folded-up old-fashioned clothes horse.

With her spare hand, she pulled it out to assemble it. Then she dragged it in front of her electric oven. Draping the garments over the horse, she asked, "Are these things okay in front of direct heat? It's the only way I can dry them quickly."

"Thanks." Flick nodded. "They'll be okay there for a short time."

Impey switched on the oven and opened its door.

There was an awkward moment's silence before Flick purred, "You've obviously been through a frightful ordeal. I

312

just wondered if there was anything we in the club should be doing to help you."

"The answer's no," said Impey, "I don't want to hurt Jules or Bisley Heath. I don't know what people are saying about me or Jules but the whole thing is bloody," *hell I nearly said efffing,* "embarrassing."

"I see." Flick hovered on one leg with the other leg rubbing the back of it. "Erm, do you know how Jules is?" she asked a little more warmly.

"No, but I believe they'll have to let him go tomorrow, at the latest, unless they're going to charge him with something." She couldn't bear to say the word *murder.*

There was a pause before Flick said, "So you haven't heard from him?"

No thank God. Anyway what's it got to do with you?

"Only a text message."

"So he's okay then?" Genuine anxiety sounded in her voice.

"I don't know. He simply asked if I would go to Caesar's cremation this afternoon, but I'm not sure I want to go to something grisly like that by myself."

"Oh do. Jules wouldn't ask anyone to go somewhere like that without a good reason." She paused again to glance at her clutch-bag. "No I can't get out of it at this stage, but I'd come with you if only there wasn't an important Hicks match this afternoon."

Impey studied her face. She really meant it. Bizarre though it might seem, she felt here was a friend. *I am a wimp; one pathetic mistake and I'm ready to throw in every sponge in the house.* She picked Flick's rain jacket off the dryer. "I'm afraid it's still a bit wet, but if I'm going to be at the Crematorium by midday, I'd better get ready then."

"You're sure there's nothing I can do," asked Flick again. "Tell you what, I'll call back after the match and see how you are if you want."

To her own surprise Impey found herself saying, "Actually that would be great."

Half an hour later she was on the road driving to the Respect Pet Crematorium in Frensham. She could not imagine why Jules should be so keen for her to witness the final burning of his beloved wolf. After all, he could pick up the casket of ashes himself any time, provided the police didn't keep him in custody. Anyway, why not ask Steve or someone more involved with Caesar to do this last service?

She was surprised to find Damian Horne who ran Respect expected her. When she rang the bell of the small converted farmhouse, the tall thin man with a long face greeted her. "You must be Impey Dalrymple?"

She shook his proffered hand. "Yes, I've come to see the end of Caesar, Mr Challenger's pet wolf."

"You're just in time," said Damian. "He's next in line. Come this way."

He led the way along a passage through the building to what looked like a primitive utility room tacked on the back of a kitchen. Inside the unlined brick shed-like construction were two vast dusky dark green ovens which looked like huge old-fashioned central heating boilers.

Caesar, who had obviously been removed from the wicker casket, lay stiff and glassy-eyed in an open basket by the side of the first oven. Even dead he was a fine looking animal.

"This is Eddie," said Damian, gesturing at a thickset man in a navy boiler suit, with grey dust in his black hair, standing by the oven.

"Hi Eddie," said Impey nodding at him.

"Hi," he returned her greeting. "Please would you stand back as I'm about to open the oven door and it's very hot. I don't want you to get burnt."

Impey hopped out of the way. The room itself was warm enough for her to realise the oven must be exceedingly hot. As soon as he'd opened the door, she felt the blast of heat from the flames that licked the back charcoal coloured wall of the oven.

She watched Eddie pick up a large tray from the side of the room, on to which he carefully loaded Caesar. He then heaved the tray on to a metal trolley which he wheeled in front of the oven.

"God bless you Caesar," he said as he slid the wolf's body into the oven.

"You needn't wait here, if you would rather sit in the waiting room," offered Damian. "You've seen that we cremate animals individually so if you'd like to come back when Eddie says he's finished, we can find somewhere more comfortable for you."

Impey hesitated. She did not want to stand in this hot room for however long it might take for Caesar to burn, but she felt it was important to see her task through. Maybe she'd spent too much time with Dodger being a magician, but if there was any point in being here at all, her instinct told her to stay by the oven. She shook her head. "Thanks but I'll stay."

"I'll leave you then," said Damian.

After what felt like much longer the ten minutes which had expired, Eddie opened the oven. "Not too many bones."

"Surely they've been burnt," said Impey. She stared at the smouldering remains at the bottom of the oven.

Eddie shook his head. "No the bones don't burn." He gestured at a machine which looked like an old-fashioned mangle at the side of the room. "We have to grind them up in that. They're the pet's real remains that we put in caskets to give people who want to keep what's left after cremation."

He picked up a fork-like instrument and started to rake the rubble which lay on the oven floor. "Crikey," he said, "odd bones for a dog."

"Caesar was a wolf," corrected Impey.

"Yes, but you'd expect the bones to be much like a dog's wouldn't you?"

Impey nodded.

"Take a look at this then." He pointed at something with his fork. "What does that remind you of?"

Impey gulped. What she saw looked remarkably like the skeletal remains of a small human hand.

"Oh well, I suppose a wolf will eat anything," said Eddie cheerfully, raking the hand-like pieces on to a shovel.

"So what's that then? Has something come off the inside of the oven." She pointed to a long piece of metal with a knob on it.

Eddie stared at it. "Looks like a hip replacement to me. That metal won't burn either." He reached for a pair of large tongs on a shelf high on the brick wall. "Mind yourself. I'll get it out. We can recycle them you know."

"But surely that one's too big for an animal?" queried Impey. "It looks more like a size that would fit a person."

"Yeah," agreed Eddie casually. "Never seen one that big myself actually."

"You wouldn't let me take it away with me would you?" asked Impey. "I mean I am the representative of the

316

wolf's owner and he's not available to make a decision about the recycling at the moment."

"Sure," said Eddie. "You'll want to wait 'til it cools of course, and I'll have to clear it with Damian first, but I can't see why not. Only normally the owners don't worry about keeping their animal's hip or elbow replacements themselves. What they want are the genuine ground up bones of their animals, like those pieces of skull." He pointed to some bits of bone which were recognisably parts of Caesar's head.

"Yes, well I think Mr Challenger might be sentimental about this hip replacement," said Impey, a horrible sick suspicion forming in her mind.

33. A fight in Impey's garden

The large metal spike with the ball on top lay alongside her computer whilst Impey studied hip replacements on the internet. In action herself, she felt much more cheerful. The rain had stopped too, leaving an apologetic rainbow. The sun was shining through the window as though to congratulate her on what she was now achieving.

At last she was in a position to justify working for Jules. Her research was going to save him, to prove she was right to take this job after all. She had done it; after an half an hour's strenuous googling on the internet, she had identified the metal shape with its knob on the top as an artificial hip for use in humans.

This hip joint must have belonged to a person. It was much too large for a pet such as a dog, or even a wolf. She sighed. This was not going to solve the problem. There must be thousands of men and women in Surrey with hip replacements. If she went to the police and they went to question Eddie, he would admit he had let her take the hip replacement from Caesar's remains, but she would still have to prove that joint belonged to Grace.

She picked up the joint to examine it again. Her initial thought that she should not tamper with evidence had deterred her from any attempt to clean it. The metal spike with its knobbly end was thickly speckled with dust and ash. Maybe if she washed that off she would find something to identify it. She needed some mark to tie it to a human owner. There was a chance – no it was more than a chance – a probability, even in her mind, a certainty, this piece of metal belonged to Grace Deer. With the joint in her hand, she pushed her chair back to get up and walk through to the kitchen.

She went over to her sink where she turned on both taps to fill her pink washing-up bowl in the stainless steel sink with warm water. Into the bowl she plunged the joint. Then she picked up an oblong green sponge, with a dark green scouring edge on one side, to clean it; she squirted a drop of her creamy "gentle to hands" washing-up liquid on to the sponge before she dabbed gingerly at the joint.

For a moment of two as she worked the sponge over the smooth surface of the metal, she felt she was engaged in a ridiculous enterprise, splashing around in the sink with a piece of metal retrieved from a dead wolf. Then she turned the sponge over to use its dark green abrasive side. Suddenly, to her horror, the piece of metal came apart in her hands. In her right hand she held a cup, whilst in her left, she held the rest of the joint.

Then she heaved a sigh of relief. *That's all right.* She looked at the fastenings on the edge of the cup. *It's obviously meant to come off.* Carefully she placed it on the draining board beside the sink whilst she scrubbed the gunge off the rest of the metal. At last it began to resemble the pictures she'd seen on the internet.

How had it got into Caesar?

Someone must have put it into the animal, probably the same someone who also must have taken out some of Caesar's body to make room for it. Eddie's casual remark came back to her. "Not a lot of bones for a wolf." Bile rose up from her stomach. She pictured the bones she'd seen in the Crematorium's oven. How like a human hand some of those bones had been.

She grimaced as her suspicions took shape. Organs from a human body had been planted into Caesar. She did not have to ask herself why. It was horribly obvious. Someone

319

who'd been killed had to disappear. His or her dead body needed to be hidden somewhere it could be disposed of without trace. What better place than inside an animal destined to be burnt in a crematorium?

Her musings were interrupted by a ring on her doorbell. This was not a moment she wanted to speak to anyone, but she supposed she'd better go. Jules might be there, let out of prison or wherever he'd been kept by the police.

She wiped her hands on a tea towel lying on the work surface near the sink. *Not very hygienic when you think where that metal's been. Still can't worry about that now.* A further impatient sounding long ring made her hurry down her short hallway. Her hand on the latch, she hesitated to turn the silver handle. Did she really want to see Jules after what had happened on Saturday?

For the second time that day she squinted through the peephole on her door. Twiddling back the covering flap she bent her head to peer through the tiny lookout. There in her little porch stood Ned, scowling.

A shaft of fear stabbed her. *Ned.* Of course she should have known all along. He had stored Caesar's body in a chest freezer for a week. What or rather who else did he keep there?

Perhaps thinking the bell was not working, he rapped on the door with the knocker.

Raising herself up, Impey shuddered. Despite the warmth of the day she felt cold. The terrible realisation hit her that Ned was the only person with access to the wolf's body and the operational skill to dispose of part of Grace's body inside it. He was the one who would have taken Caesar to see Grace, let the wolf chew up her handbag. A feeling of shame waved over her; she shouldn't have needed Faye to tell her Jules would never take Caesar near Grace.

The picture of Ned's agitated face when he was putting the wolf down swam into her mind. He must have planned this whole operation before then or he would not have been so worried by Jules's initial wish to bury Caesar's body in his garden. Then there was his opposition to the Respect Crematorium where animals were individually cremated. Yes, he must have had Grace's disposal all perfectly planned.

A vision of his horror at the sight of Cally pecking at Caesar's casket during the funeral assailed her. It seemed another era, but it was only a couple of days ago that Ned kept re-filling her glass at the wake. For the first time ever she'd found him charming, dispelling any earlier suspicions she'd had. She should have guessed he was responsible for the mess she was in, especially when Jules produced that second bottle saying Ned had given it to him. No wonder she was blotto that night.

But no longer. She would not let him in. Despite the sight of her car in the drive he could not know for certain she was inside the house. Anyway, if he did not go away soon, she would ring the police. She bent down to look through the peephole again. She sighed with relief. He was walking slowly back up her garden path to his four by four parked outside her gate.

She had time to finish the job.

Back in the kitchen, she picked the joint out of the sink and rubbed it dry with a cloth which lay on the work surface beside her. It was so clean now, it gleamed in the post rain sunlight. She ran her finger tips over the clean smooth metal. There was nothing to see here.

Disappointed she picked up the cup which lay on the draining board to examine that. Suddenly there they were, on the rim, a string of numbers with the letters BN. More important, there was also a trade mark. Inside the letter C were printed the words Charing Orthopaedics. Here was something she could use. She picked up the three pieces of metal and walked back to her sitting room to sit down beside her computer again. "Charing Orthopaedics", she repeated the name to herself whilst she tapped the letters into her search engine.

Up came the firm's website with diagrams of various artificial joints, some of which she had already seen in her previous searches. She clicked on to "Contact us" to find a number to ring the company. Once someone from the switchboard answered, she asked for their public relations department. Since she was a journalist she felt it was easier to suggest she was researching joints for an article than to admit she was acting as a private detective, a role for which she felt she had zero credibility. Anyway it was true to say she wanted to discover whether joints could be traced. So what, she asked, did the number BN 467 mean?

To her chagrin the pleasant marketing manager, to whom her call had been diverted, said it was a "Batch number".

Disappointment surged through Impey. A batch number meant more than one person. "How many people are there in a batch?" she asked.

The reply was "A dozen".

"Is there any way one could find out who was fitted with a particular hip joint?"

"Through the surgeon," replied Charing Orthopaedics' marketing manager casually.

Impey wanted to groan. Any doctor would be bound by medical ethics to keep a patient's details confidential. "So who might batch 467 have gone to?" she asked as nonchalantly as she could.

"Obviously I can't tell you which surgeon, but I could probably look up the hospital if that's any help."

"That would be great," said Impey eagerly.

"But I'd have to ring you back."

I hope you will. "Thank you so much," she gushed.

Stymied she put the phone down. What could she do now? She balled her fist and thumped her desk in frustration before the obvious next move struck her. She must find out the hospital where Grace had her hip replaced.

She got up to look for the Yellow Pages where all the local hospitals might be listed. Her hand was on the directory when a crashing noise from the kitchen made her start. Really she was ridiculously jumpy at the moment. It was probably just a saucepan falling off the wall. The hooks she'd screwed in weren't secure. She had not been able to afford to do anything to the kitchen when she had moved here, or she would have plastered the walls so that she didn't have to keep messing around filling holes.

At the moment she needed to concentrate on other things. No, she didn't need the Yellow Pages; somewhere on her phone she had stored the number of the woman she'd met at Grace's house. She picked it up whilst she racked her brain for the name. *Sally,* she was sure it was *Sally Something.* She started to sift through the contacts on her mobile.

Ah Sally Markham. That has to be it. I don't know anyone else called that.

The voice that answered Impey's call was familiar, but sounded guarded when Impey began her spiel, "I don't know if you remember me, but we met at Grace Deer's house."

"Did we?"

"Yes, I'm the journalist who was going to interview her." She hoped Sally hadn't subsequently realised she'd broken into Grace's house.

"Yes." Sally's tone was even more defensive. She was not eager to chat, but eventually Impey managed to worm out of her the name "Wellington", the exclusive private clinic where Grace had been for her hip replacement.

One step forward, two steps back. A further search on the internet showed Impey there were eight orthopaedic surgeons specialising in the lower limbs who operated at the Wellington. She was wondering which one to start with, whether perhaps one might be a member of Bisley Heath whom someone might know, when her phone rang.

She clicked it on, irritated at the unfamiliar cheerful voice at the other end speaking as if he were her new best friend, "Hi there". But the Charing Orthopaedics marketing manager's next words lifted her out of the slough. "Batch 467 went to the Wellington Clinic."

It was enough. If not complete proof, she'd found the crucial link to it. She had something tangible to give the police.

With the three pieces of metal in her hands, she walked back to the kitchen.

"Eureka. I've got you Ned," she said as she opened the door. Then she shouted it out loud as she walked into the room.

"What have you got on me?" asked an oily voice.

A tall black-haired man stood in the middle of her kitchen.

"Oh hello Ned." Her voice came out squeakily.

How long have you been here? No it can't be you. I must still be under the influence of drink or drugs. This is just a nightmare. His right arm is even scratched and bloody.

"Hi," he said, taking a step towards her.

"What do you want?" she asked, although it was obvious. He must have been in touch with the crematorium, asking for the hip joint and been told she'd taken it.

How the hell had he got in? She knew her front door was locked and she hadn't opened the back door out of the kitchen since she'd left the house to go out to the cremation. The key was still in the lock. She looked over the room. The window was open, but it was also broken.

In the second she realised he'd smashed his fist through the window to open the latch. That noise she'd heard was him, breaking into her kitchen.

How long had he been here in her house? In a flash she realised that wasn't important. All that mattered was the cup of the hip replacement with the number. Behind Ned was the vast, gaping hole in her kitchen window. With a deft throw she flung first the spike, then the knob of the hip joint through the window.

"Go and fetch it," she cried, slipping the cup, with the all important details engraved on it, into her trouser pocket.

Ned gaped at her. He turned round to look at hip joint which lay on the uneven wet grass of Impey's untidy garden, twenty yards in front of her back door.

"I'll deal with you first," he hissed, advancing towards her.

She dodged sideways and seized an oven glove off the floor. Then she grabbed the still erect clothes horse to use as a buffer between them. A moment later, whilst Ned stumbled over the clothes horse, she vaulted out of the kitchen window.

He was not far behind her as she ran up the garden pulling the oven glove on to her hand. When he bent down to pick up the hip joint, she opened the aviary to let Cally hop on to her wrist.

The sight of Cally perched on her flowery oven-gloved right hand made him laugh. "Novel falconer's equipment," he jeered, delving into his trouser pocket.

Now it was Impey's turn to give a hysterical giggle. In Ned's hand was a small dull red plastic water pistol. Her momentary relief that this was a mere toy evaporated as the knowledge it must contain some noxious substance dawned on her. But he was thirty yards away, he would have to come nearer to spray her or Cally. Though she could feel Cally's talons agonisingly on her wrist through the glove's material, she jerked her right arm upwards for the bird's flight straight towards Ned.

"Get," she shouted, her fingers outstretched from her flat left palm, pointing towards the gun.

For a moment Impey thought all was lost. Cally simply soared into the air. Whilst she gazed upwards after the disappeared bird, Ned advanced towards her without a glance upwards. "Bad luck old thing," he sneered.

"If only you meant it," said Impey, trying to be brave. Maybe she could play for time, keep him talking. Wasn't that what one was supposed to do in these situations?

"It's the sort of thing Jules would say, isn't it? I thought it would comfort you."

"You've got what you came for so you might as well go away," said Impey, "after all there isn't any proof it isn't a wolf's hip joint is there?"

"Except that Jules knows I didn't put one in," said Ned, "and whereas the assistant at the Crematorium could have mistaken what he saw, backed up by you, it's a different story. And of course there's always the handbag which you informed me you had so kindly removed from the scene of Jules's criminal activities at Grace's house. Still, that might be better left in your cottage Could be something for the police to find after your suicide."

Omigod, he's going to kill me like he killed Tessa. He really did kill her too. Cally where are you. You could at least die with me. She looked up to see a speck far above in the sky. No use in calling her, she was too far away, but there was something else she could do.

She knelt down, head forward. This would avoid the first spray, but would Cally take the signal? "Please don't hurt me," she pleaded. Though it stuck it her throat she was going to force out some words like, "I'll try and help you."

Before she could speak she heard the whoosh of Cally's wings as she swooped. When Impey looked up, she saw the vulture descend on to Ned's outstretched right arm.

He gave a cry of pain as her talons sunk into his bare flesh and another as her vast curved beak pecked at the gun, but he still clutched it.

Impey jumped up, fearful Cally would bate and fall off Ned's dropped arm, which was obviously what he intended. She could not fly off his arm at that angle.

Instead she hopped off, on to the ground, but before he could lift his damaged arm, she'd lunged forward and pecked his leg.

"Ouch," he cried as he kicked out at her, catching her outstretched wing as she rose into the air. With his bleeding arm, again he pointed the gun at Impey, but she ducked as he pulled the trigger. Falling to her knees, she grabbed him round his calves, tackling him, pulling him to ground whilst she willed Cally to come back.

In seconds he was on his feet, still clutching the gun as he tried to prise her arms away from her face which she'd buried in her chest.

"That damn bird," he cried as Cally descended again, but this time she landed on his bent over back and was pecking at his shoulders.

Impey felt his grasp of her loosen. She glanced up to see him drop the water pistol as he tried to shake Cally off his back. Grabbing it, she rolled out of his reach to stand up. She pointed it at his face and pulled the trigger. "Have some of your own medicine," she shouted.

At first she thought it had done no good. With the bird still on his back, he lunged for her hand. "Won't affect me," he shouted. "It's only water."

She hesitated, but only for a second, before she stepped forward and shot again, aiming at his mouth and nose, then his eyes. Relief flooded through her, then fear when he staggered backwards, rubbing his eyes with his blood stained hands. What had she done? She'd acted in self-defence, but had she killed him?

Confused emotions jostled inside her as she ran past him to her garden gate singing the Mozart clarinet concerto. Surely Cally must follow her? But what should she do now. The only way back into her house was through the kitchen window and if Ned was only stunned as she hoped, he might recover enough to attack her again.

She ran up the flag-stoned path alongside her end of terraced house with Cally hopping along behind her. Desolation hit her when she rounded the corner of her cottage to stand by her front door. She'd chosen this place for its peaceful rural setting, but now she cursed it. There was little casual traffic down this lane.

Suddenly there was the blest noise of a car's engine. In the distance she saw a smart silver Golf approaching. She put up her hand to flag it down, but it was slowing down anyway.

A couple of moments later it stopped outside her house. Out stepped Flick.

"What's going on now?" she asked.

"Ned," screamed Impey. "Look there he is." She pointed to the tall black-haired man staggering round the corner of her house. "What shall we do?"

Flick opened the passenger door of her car. "Get in," she commanded.

"But what about Cally?" asked Impey.

"She'll look after herself," said Flick, giving Impey a push.

Impey toppled into the car whilst Flick nipped round to the driver's side and slammed the door shut. As she drove away, Impey stared into the left side wing mirror with apprehension.

Her stomach knotted when she saw Ned lunge like a drunken madman at the bird on the pavement. She cried with horror when he appeared to kick her, but perhaps he missed. A moment later she caught sight of the vulture high in the sky soaring away above the car.

Impey waved frantically at the flying bird.

"Do you think she'll follow us?" Flick asked sceptically.

"No," said Impey. She frowned. "By the way, where are we going?"

"To the police station of course." Flick told her.

34. Deborah visits a prison

Deborah looked at her son. Despite everything he looked so normal, the same boy she'd given birth to, known all his life and loved. He was wearing clean lightweight beige trousers with a soft casual piquet shirt, clothes he could have worn for a morning's golf. Maybe things would have been different if she'd succeeded in making him play more, become involved in the game; perhaps he wouldn't have become so lawless. She'd really tried, but he'd always been a rebel. From an early age he'd told her he hated rules.

She'd struggled hard to make him realise you simply had to obey rules to get on in life and it had been worthwhile. He had eventually settled down at school and done well enough to go to university. Despite the intense competition, he'd managed to become a vet.

How proud of him she'd been. She hoped he understood that. Despite what everyone said, she thought the evidence against him sounded flimsy. However impoverished she was, she would help him financially. Even if she had to sell her house, she would do it to help Ned. They'd get the very best lawyers they could find. From her work as a magistrate, she knew the right people.

It was outrageous they were confined here in this square blank walled room with a uniformed policeman looking on. There wasn't much light from the high window either, nothing to lighten the pain which seared her chest. She had never felt so over-wrought before, even when Monty died.

To comfort him, and herself, she would like to have rushed round to the other side of the table where they sat and hugged her son, only he'd have been embarrassed. It would

331

be inappropriate too. Anyway, they had business to discuss and she wouldn't be allowed to stay here for long.

"Who are we going to get to defend you darling?" she asked.

Ned gave her a lop-sided smile which made her heart lurch. "It's under control Mum," he said calmly. "You don't have to do anything."

"But who have you got?" she persisted. "It's really important you have the right person, someone who believes in you. Believe me, I've seen it in court. You can't have someone cynical in a case like this, however bright he may be."

"Mother, it's okay; don't involve yourself."

"You know anything to do with Grace will mean you'll be attacked by the toughest barristers."

"Yeah, well, she's not exactly in a position to commission anyone herself." Her son, smirked.

"Listen," she said crossly, "I may not have liked Grace that much, but you must show respect Ned. She deserves that." She didn't want to speak like this in front of the watching, and presumably listening policeman, but it must be said. The boy must accept he was being accused of two murders. Obviously he hadn't done them, but it would look and sound terrible if he was flippant in court.

"No she doesn't. Face it Mum, she doesn't deserve anything from us. She was carrying on with Dad for years. She bought him like she bought anyone she fancied."

"No, no," cried Deborah, even more acutely aware of the policeman standing by, "it wasn't like that."

"It certainly was. Why do you think I gave that stupid watch-bracelet thing to Faye to flog?"

"My Chaika watch, your father bought for me? You did that?"

"Face it Mum," repeated Ned. "It wasn't for you. He bought it for Grace, well with her money, or at least out of money she paid him, but it's the thought that counts," he cackled, "that's why I had to get rid of it. He couldn't possibly have her think he'd bought another one for you."

"No. No. It wasn't like that. He brought it home for me from his Russian trip."

"With her," emphasised Ned, "they, with their matching suitcases, shared room, a bed in the same room if you must hear the gory details. Dad drooled all over her, but he couldn't help himself. You were a saint to put up with him."

The warmth in his voice when he finished speaking lifted her heart. It was natural for boys to hate their fathers, or rather be jealous. Monty was such a beautiful man whilst Ned, though nice-looking was ordinary, plain but appealing rather like her really. She could look good when she made the effort, spent enough money on her looks.

"I loved your father Ned, but he was just one of those men whom women adore and throw themselves at. He wasn't really lecherous." She wriggled in her chair. A picture of a Valentine card she'd once found in Monty's desk came into her mind. She wouldn't mention it. Her marriage had been happy. That's what Ned had got to believe. She couldn't have him saying these things.

"You'd think differently if you'd got married," she said. "Sometimes one has to ignore things that don't mean anything when you've got a profound relationship with someone."

"Ha Ha," Ned gave his cynical laugh. "I don't think any modern day therapist would agree with that, or not the ones I've met."

"You mean Tessa," said Deborah, "well that was awful what she said about you."

"She accused me of killing the woman I loved," said Ned. "That was worse than awful."

"Well thankfully we now know the poor woman was unstable and suffering from depression," said Deborah. "She was not a rational detached person."

"So obviously she committed suicide," laughed Ned.

"It's not funny," said Deborah annoyed. If Ned carried on like this he would condemn himself in court. He didn't seem to appreciate the seriousness of being charged with murder. She would have to make him see how bad it all was. "Her death is as ghastly as Roxanne's."

A terrible expression came over her son's face. His eyes blazed as he thumped the wooden table between them with his fist. His lips trembled as violently as they had when he was a tiny child in a rage before she'd managed to find a speech therapist to cure, well almost cure, his stuttering lisp.

"No," he eventually managed to spit at her. "Roxy died in pain, terrible pain. Tessa wouldn't have felt a thing."

Deborah gazed at her son. Numb with horror she felt the truth hit her. *You did it.* She turned to look at the policeman. Had he taken in what Ned admitted?

The policeman averted his face. His expression was blank, as though he was bored.

Deborah rose out of her chair. She took a couple of steps towards him. "Please," she asked in her most commanding magisterial voice, "would you leave me to have some private time with my son."

"Well I'm afraid he is considered a danger to himself and others," said the policeman awkwardly.

"I'm his mother and a magistrate," said Deborah in her commanding voice. "He will be safe with me and I will be safe with him." She gestured at the reinforced glass window at the top of the door to the room. "You could watch through that and you may take my handbag if you fear I am going to provide him with drugs." Her voice, which she'd tried to keep authoritative, faltered. She heard herself sob.

"That's all right," said the policeman, "I'll leave you to it, for a few moments, that's all." He walked to the door and let himself out.

Deborah walked round the table to where Ned sat, and pulled herself up so she was sitting next him. "Did you hate Tessa?" she asked in a whisper.

Ned crossed his arms on the table beside her. "She told the police I murdered the woman I loved. I was banged up for three days before they realised that actually I tried to save Roxanne's life."

"Someone must have told them she'd been your girlfriend. I suppose they thought you resented her marriage to Jules."

"Of course I hated her marrying him, but not as much as I hated Grace when she made me break up with Roxanne."

"How very interfering of her."

"Well I could hardly marry my own sister could I? Not with the mess I've seen breeders make over mating pedigree dogs."

"Oh God," gasped Deborah. Her stomach retched. She clasped the flat of her hand over her mouth.

"Watching Roxy die was the most terrible experience of my life, but it was great for Tessa, and okay for Jules, of course. They waltzed off into the sunset together."

What a good thing that was. Tessa got them out of our hair.
Deborah dropped her hand from her mouth. She must have courage to support Ned. Monty couldn't have wanted Roxanne or he would have asked for her help, as he did over everything else. Maybe he didn't even know about her existence. "If only you could have found another woman, everything might have been different." She stroked her son's sleek dark hair.

He shook her hand off his head. "I didn't want another woman, not after Roxanne, but I wasn't allowed to keep anything. Jules got Caesar."

Deborah shuddered again. "He's caused an awful row at the club over that wolf, what with accusing all and sundry of shooting Caesar and then threatening to bury him on the course." She looked into her son's murky brown eyes. Her voice faltered as she asked, "You didn't shoot... I mean you'd never kill an animal like that would you?"

"Kill Caesar? You are joking I hope. When have you ever known me use a gun?" Ned glared at her. Tears glistened in his brown eyes. He wiped his face with his sleeve just as he had when he was a small boy. "My life's work has been keeping Caesar alive. He was all I had left of Roxanne."

Deborah wriggled in her chair. She should never have asked him that. Ned had always hated guns. To Monty's fury he had hurled a toy rifle his father gave him for Christmas across the room lisping, "Don't likth gunths."

She swallowed as tears pricked her own eyes remembering how angry Monty got when Ned cried as a child. His sensitivities caused terrible rows between them. Monty was so irritable when their son, in Monty's words, "turned on the taps". She would never let him spank Ned, which now was thankfully against the law, to "give him something to cry for".

Ned glared at her. "I can't believe you've asked that. You know how I abhor shooting."

"You did like using your water pistol when you were a child."

She was relieved to see Ned grin at the memory. "Yeah well a water pistol often comes in useful when you can't use a spray can, but to shoot an animal like someone shot Caesar is crime." Ned's eyes narrowed. "I'd like to kill the bastard who did it."

"I hope the court will take into consideration your extreme affection for Caesar," nodded Deborah. "You will tell your lawyer how much you loved the wolf and how upset you were by the cruel way he was killed."

"You want me to say I was unhinged, that's why I stuffed Grace's body inside him?" Ned put his head on one side as he spoke in a mock coy voice. "Well I wasn't." He hissed. "I did it because it felt like the final retribution. I didn't mean to kill her, but once I had, I was glad. – I got revenge for the misery she put you through. And me. You know what, I felt really happy cutting ..."

Deborah recoiled from him. She put her hands over her ears; she could not bear to hear her son speak like this. The sweet lisp he'd had as a child had become a ghastly hiss. "Don't tell me."

"That most of her went into a horse. There were a few bits left over that I kept in the freezer to stuff into the next large animal that had to be put down and when Caesar arrived it seemed right to fill him with the rest of her, a kind of poetic justice. Silly of me to forget her metal joint wouldn't burn."

Deborah's hands dropped from her ears to cover her mouth. She gagged; she thought she was going to vomit. This wasn't, couldn't be her son talking. He was a vet. Everyone knows they are good caring people. Vets don't go about murdering women and cutting them up, but he had said it was an accident. She must cling on to that.

A faraway look came into her son's eyes. "You know, well you don't know, but wolves are very intuitive. They're pack animals. They like to be part of a gang. I'm sure if we could have discussed it, he'd have said, 'count me in'."

Deborah smiled sadly at her son. He did have feelings, only they were mad ones. He needed help, professional help. He wasn't a bad person; he just thought and felt wrong. "Do you really think you did what Roxanne wanted?"

"She'd have wanted someone who loved her to have her statue," said Ned sulkily, "but Grace kept that, for no good reason. Roxy was closer to Caesar than she was to Grace, even Tarquin saw that and sculpted them together. That's why I took Caesar to see her for the last time."

Deborah shivered at the memory of seeing the bronze in Grace's empty house. "I know you don't like my saying it, but I wish you could have moved on, found someone else. It's such a pity you didn't like her, but you might have got it together with Impey Dalrymple; she's perhaps a bit gauche, but a nice girl underneath. By the way what were you doing in her garden?"

"Just wanted to talk about Caesar. I couldn't get to the cremation, but she did." His mouth twisted into a strange grin. "She got completely hysterical, sprayed muck in my face, and started accusing me of all sorts of things. Then Flick turned up and that really put the lid on it." He patted her hand. "Anyway, there's no point in regretting anything about her. Impey Dalrymple is next on Jules's list for his harem."

"I think I heard someone suggest that."

"Take it from me; they're a pair of rutting goats."

35. Matters of the heart

Impey sat opposite Jules in the Golden Cockerel in Fleet. The Chinese restaurant was his choice. It belonged to a new business contact. To her relief he thought it unlikely to be patronised by any other member of Bisley Heath.

"This is a nice place," she said, alarmed her tone sounded horribly like a nonagenarian lady at the golf club when she saw the shiny new coffee machine.

The sight of Jules across the white clothed table, with a discreet bandage on his nose to cover the splint holding it straight. upset her. Shadowy dark yellow patches, relics of the bruises inflicted by Dodger, were also visible on the left side of his face. In her younger days she'd fantasised about men fighting over her, but now it had happened she was charged with guilt.

Ned was in prison, awaiting trial. Much to his mother's chagrin, he had been refused bail. More evidence, Impey understood, was mounting against him. Searches of his veterinary premises revealed tiny traces of Grace's DNA. There was less to tie him to Tessa, except for the ketamine she'd inhaled which the pathologists found during her post mortem. Although it is a known "party" drug, Ned kept it in his surgery, he said to quieten aggressive dogs when they needed treatment. The police found tiny drops of the same drug in the water pistol which Impey gave to them.

"I'm glad you like it," said Jules. His broad-lipped mouth spread into a smile. "I owe you so much." He beckoned to a waiter who bustled over with the wine list.

Jules flipped open the crimson leather folder. He turned to the last page. "Champagne. We'll have Bollinger."

"Okay." Impey smiled. Despite the tragedy of deaths, they could celebrate the end of the job. A cheque from the Nikos family arrived in the post this morning. She would tell him once the cork had popped out of the bottle and the bubbles were frothing in their glasses, that she need no longer work for him.

His face fell when she spoke.

"Is this about Dodger?" He asked. "until he arrived that night, I really thought we were getting on so well together."

"I suppose so, but of course I was absolutely off my head." She pulled a face at him, "I can't even begin to remember what I said."

"What a shame. You were so lovely; you really helped me through a terribly difficult time."

"I thought I'd caused you a lot of trouble when Dodger come in like that."

"That was my fault. I should have sorted the situation out, but don't worry it won't happen again. He knows I'll have his guts for garters if he comes near you again."

"But won't you do that anyway – in court I mean?"

"Good God no." Jules shook his head. "What would I gain from that? Dodger already owes me money. I don't want to have to lend him more to pay some fine. No, I'm certainly not pressing charges."

"That's really noble of you," said Impey, impressed. She looked at the spread of food around them which Jules had ordered. This was more of a banquet than a mere thank-you meal.

"I'm glad you feel like that." Jules's face reddened. "It's mainly because of you that I'm holding back on Dodger. I owe you so much and I would hate to put you through the torment of a court hearing and see you attacked by some aggressive barrister."

Impey wanted to protest that she could defend herself, but at the same time she hated the thought of Dodger being charged with assault, imprisoned or given a fine he had not the money to pay. He would never accept a penny from her. *How ironic it is that in the wild Dodger would have beaten Jules. Only here in the civilised world would he be in command.*

"I'd like to protect you," continued Jules eagerly, "make sure you're all right."

"I'm fine. I can look after myself you know."

"No man is an island," quoted Jules. "All creatures need other like-minded ones they can bond with. We all need to belong to a pack. That's what I realised from the poem I got Mandy to read at the wake. I failed Caesar because I tried to make him part of a pack that didn't want him. Wolves belong in the wild where they can be supported by their own kind. They do look after each other you know."

He did not have to say that he liked to look after people. His wide mouth broke into that smile across his oval face which had enraptured her when she first met him. "Have something to eat. They do this awfully well." He pushed the plate of crispy aromatic duck towards her.

"No thanks." She helped herself to some aubergine flavoured with fish and a bean curd casserole.

"You're not a vegetarian?" He asked anxiously.

"Oh no," she laughed. "I'm just not terribly keen on duck, but I do like to see them flying free as well."

"That's a relief. I was really hoping we might spend more time together." He gazed at her with his forget-me-not blue eyes; his but his voice took on a husky tone. "I have dreams; I want you to be part of them."

342

"That's a bit Freudian," Impey giggled. The passion in his voice alarmed her. "What dreams?" She avoided adding *could I share.*

"Creating a wildlife place where animals really can run wild. There's a tract of woodland for sale in Devon I've got my eye on. There are already ponies on Dartmoor and I think people there would be more in tune with me. You'd be a great person to run a wild animal sanctuary."

Impey wrinkled her forehead whilst she pondered the idea. Though she had come round to having Cally in her sitting room sometimes, she was glad Jules had taken his vulture back home; she did not have to worry about putting down newspapers in case the bird made a mess somewhere. She had found looking after her a tough responsibility. The idea of tying up looking after wild creatures with business administration did not appeal. Tessa's words came back to her. "Jules's business is all about bluff." That was how he'd got her to work for him in the first place. Although he'd never threatened her, she'd feared she would loose her home if she didn't do what he wanted.

"I'm not sure I'm cut out to work at business administration," she said. That was the best, least hurtful way of putting it.

"No it wouldn't be like that. This would be a charitable enterprise, a place you could put your heart and soul into like the UK Wolf Conservation Trust in Berkshire. It would be about supporting animals in the wild where they should be, not at the mercy, or worse the sport of people." Passion shone in his blue eyes. He began to speak faster. "This is what I should be doing, not messing around on the golf course. I've found my way forward, how I can make a difference by helping the earth. You could be part of that."

"I'm afraid," said Impey, after a pause whilst she sucked air through her teeth, "my heart's in Surrey."

"Surrey?" He looked at her in astonishment.

"My family and friends are here. It's where my emotional bonds are."

"You could bond with me. Together we'd make new friends. Tessa always told me I should make a new life and I could do that with you," said Jules, "I want you to be in my life, with me all the time. Sometime in the future I'd like you to marry me. Everything was going so well after the wake. I thought..."

"My drink was spiked," said Impey. "I'm afraid I really don't remember much."

Jules looked hurt. "We had a great time and I could make you feel good without any help from..." Jules's voice trailed off, "if only you'd let me."

Impey gulped down some aubergine before she blurted out, "The royal precedent isn't a very good one."

"But it's a wonderful one; William and Kate are one of the world's most beautiful happy couples, if not the most blissful."

"I wasn't thinking of them." Impey twiddled her fork in the bean casserole. How could she tell him Henry V111 was on her mind? *Divorced, beheaded, died, divorced, beheaded, survived.* Before she could stop herself she blurted out, "On the Tudor principle, I think I'd rather be wife number six."

Jules looked aghast, but grinned gallantly. "May I hold you to that? I expect I could fit someone else in first." He joked.

She too believed in a future for animals in the wild. Fighting against the creeping urbanisation that destroyed wildlife habitats was one of her causes too. "I can always help you with turning Bisley Heath into a more organic golf course as far as small animals are concerned," she offered brightly. "I'm involved as a volunteer with wildlife projects in Surrey."

"It's a bit late for that." He shrugged his shoulders.

"What do you mean?"

"I've sold my stake. The deal's going through now, at this moment."

Impey gasped. "Why have you done that?"

"It's not what the members want," he said resignedly. "More to the point, I don't want them."

"But I thought you were going to fight for your beliefs?" she protested, suddenly worried for the future of the club. "You said a lot of people thought it was a charming idea, having the course truly organic. Okay they may have had the odd concern about wild pigs on the greens, but that was always a bit absurd."

"Yes, but shooting my wolf wasn't. That was real vandalism."

"I thought no one knew who did it, that there was no proof it was anyone connected with the club?" She could have added she hoped it might remain an unsolved mystery.

"No proof," agreed Jules, "but instinctive knowledge. You provided me with the answer. That's why I like having you working for me. You may not always know exactly what you're doing, but your methods are sound."

That's a backhanded compliment. "What did I do?"

"You found the rabbit."

"I'm glad it helped, but how?"

"I happened to show it to Dan in the kitchen by chance, and he was completely nonplussed. That was the moment I knew he'd killed it. The look of horror on his face told me he'd done it. I didn't understand why, until I spoke to

345

Adam. He's done a forensic job on the club's accounts and he's found Dan's running a rabbit pie business on the side."

"What? From rabbits he shoots at Bisley Heath?"

"So we assume."

"What are you going to do? Tell the management to sack him?"

Jules gave her a sad, wistful grin. "I'd hand him over to the police if I could prove he'd definitely killed Caesar, but that wouldn't bring my boy back as well as causing a massive upset because somehow Caesar got on to the golf course." He dropped his knife to thump the table with his fist. "They say Caesar must have been attacking someone to have been hit in the belly, but he never would. He never ever had; he had no need to hurt anyone because he'd always been well fed."

"Don't you think it would be best if everyone knew what really happened?"

Jules shook his head. He picked up his knife again to cut into the crispy duck. "Sure I do and the truth will out. Someone will know and someone will tell, but I won't be here to suffer the horror of hearing it talked about."

"You're leaving?"

He nodded. "I don't want to be part of the place where my wolf was killed. For fourteen years he was my best mate. He even helped the business."

"So you really did take him with you to frighten debtors into paying up?"

"Caesar never scared anyone." The garlic from the sauce covering the sautéed mange tout wafted across the table on his breath in his indignation. "He was the friendliest creature. You should know that; you met him. He relaxed clients. When he jumped out of his pen, he probably only wanted to play with Dan; he'd have thought it was a game."

346

Impey played with her fork in the bean and cashew nut casserole on her plate. "He must have been frightened to shoot Caesar.

"Maybe he was; I can't worry about it now I've sold my stake in the club."

"You mean you haven't told whoever's buying it?"

Jules stabbed another piece of duck with his knife. "You don't exactly advertise the award winning chef is cooking the books when you sell a stake in a business. It's up to the buyer to examine the accounts, but she should know what she's doing. Her parents made a fortune running restaurants." He waved his hands in the air as though signalling he was absolving himself. "Maybe she won't care what animals Dan throws into his stews."

Impey gasped. "That's so callous."

"Not at all. I don't say it will be like that. Judging from this place Suzi Chang is pretty keen that everything is as classy and up-market as members of Bisley Heath would expect." He grinned. "She's a pretty good player too; she's got a lower handicap than yours."

Ouch. Well I suppose I deserve that. Impey looked round at the red and gold decor with the cockerel motive splashed about in a rather brighter style than anyone would associate with a golf club like Bisley Heath. "So she owns this."

Jules nodded. "That's why we're having a free meal here."

Impey gulped. "That's nice," she managed to say. "I'm really sorry you're leaving. It would have been lovely to have had ponies ranging on Bisley Heath."

"Well that dream is over, as far as I'm concerned. My money's going into wildlife places where animals like wolves can roam free in packs of their own choice." He grinned at Impey. "Humans will only visit on sufferance."

She felt her mouth twitch in a wistful smile. The more she pictured large wild animals roaming the Surrey heath, the more the idea appealed to her. – If only it were not so unsympathetic to the practice of golf. The joy people had from playing the game on the land they tended was what mattered. Golf was the ultimately civilised game. Friendships and even marriages were founded on the golf course. "I understand; it would never work. A golf course is..." She stopped short noticing Jules frown at the warmth in her voice. He would never accept what she was going to say next. *A golf club is a human sanctuary.*

Acknowledgements

My greatest thanks must go to Tsa Palmer the director and inaugurator of The Wolf Conservation Trust at Beenham in Berkshire. When I first met Tsa at a West Heath School reunion the idea of writing a novel with a wolf character was germinating. The days I spent at Beenham watching these magnificent animals, walking with the ambassador wolves and talking to the volunteers who work there have changed my perception of wolves. I have huge admiration for the work the trust does supporting wolf projects all over the world as well as educating people like me to understand the value of these animals.

The behaviour of Caesar is not taken from any particular animal at the trust and like any other true pet, he has his own idiosyncrasies. My concept of a wolf in captivity has been influenced by Professor Mark Rowlands immensely enjoyable true tale, "The philosopher and the wolf".

My gratitude also goes to the Wolf Song of Alaska website on which poems about wolves are published. This site is run entirely by volunteers for the sake of wolves and the poets who write about them. It is moving to feel the unconditional love that so many talented writers feel for wolves. On this website I found Codi Rodgers poem "The Last Howl" which so fitted the wake in my story; I am indebted to her for her permission to use her words.

Cally, the vulture, the other captive creature, is also fictional. I know of no vulture which picks up golf balls, although I am reliably informed by the Hawk Conservancy Trust that it is possible to target train vultures. I am also hugely impressed by the work done at the Hawk Sanctuary at Andover where I spent a most enjoyable day learning about handling birds of prey. Mike Riley, a bird handler at the sanctuary, who once trained a vulture called Micawber, has been a source of inspiration as well as information. It must be stressed however that responsible bird lovers and handlers prefer to see birds in the wild and would repatriate them wherever possible. Gimmicks like picking up golf balls are not encouraged.

Throughout writing Crisis in a Surrey Harem I have come to respect more and more all those people involved in animal care in death as well as life. Kevin Spurgeon of the Dignity Pet Crematorium gave up his valuable time to show me round his Dignity Pet Crematorium at Hook in Hampshire. His dedication to his work was a revelation.

I am also indebted to Ethane Ashling-Perry and her daughter Jo both of whom I met on a trip to Rumania in search of wolves. Jo's husband Martin Reber, who is a vet, gave me a couple of crucial ideas for this story and information about veterinary practice. If I have anything wrong, it is my fault rather than his. However fact is usually, I find, invariably stranger than fiction.

Once again I must thank my husband Rupert and Johnathan Krish who both read the first draft of Crisis in a Surrey Harem. Bee Wood subsequently read a later proof. All have made invaluable criticisms and suggestions. I am also delighted with the cover by Zoe Pirret who enters my imaginary world with such enthusiasm.

Thank you all from the bottom of my heart.

Lucy Abelson

Born in Brundall in Norfolk, Lucy Abelson grew up in Kent where her father ran a small tutorial establishment and her mother practised as a doctor. Since they met playing mixed foursomes at the Wildernesse club, golf there played a big part in family life.

Lucy herself always wanted to write fiction. She spent much of her time after school in the children's corner of the Sevenoaks bookshop. Although she devoured fiction, she managed to win a general knowledge competition set by the bookshop which led to a prize-giving ceremony by Noel Streatfield. On hearing the ten year old wanted to be "a writer like you" when she grew up, the great author responded, to hoots of laughter from the assembled grown-ups, with the remark, "This little girl wants to steal my job."

Undeterred, Lucy started contributing to magazines such as "Young Elizabethan" during her senior school days at West Heath. Her journalistic career began on Honey magazine, but she also wrote for many other magazines before progressing to newspapers. For 17 years she was on the staff of the Sunday Express as a feature writer and columnist.

Lucy gave up her job in journalism to look after her third daughter who is handicapped. She is married with two other daughters and six grandchildren.

"Crisis in a Surrey Harem" is her third novel featuring Impey, the reluctant sleuth.